P9-DES-331

THE

# MAN IN LITERATURE

PROGRAM

Other titles in the
MAN IN LITERATURE program include:

---

THE HUMAN CONDITION
Literature Written in the English Language (casebound)

---

AMERICAN MODELS
A Collection of Modern Stories (paperback)

---

MARQUEE
Ten Plays by American and British Playwrights (paperback)

---

Other books in preparation

---

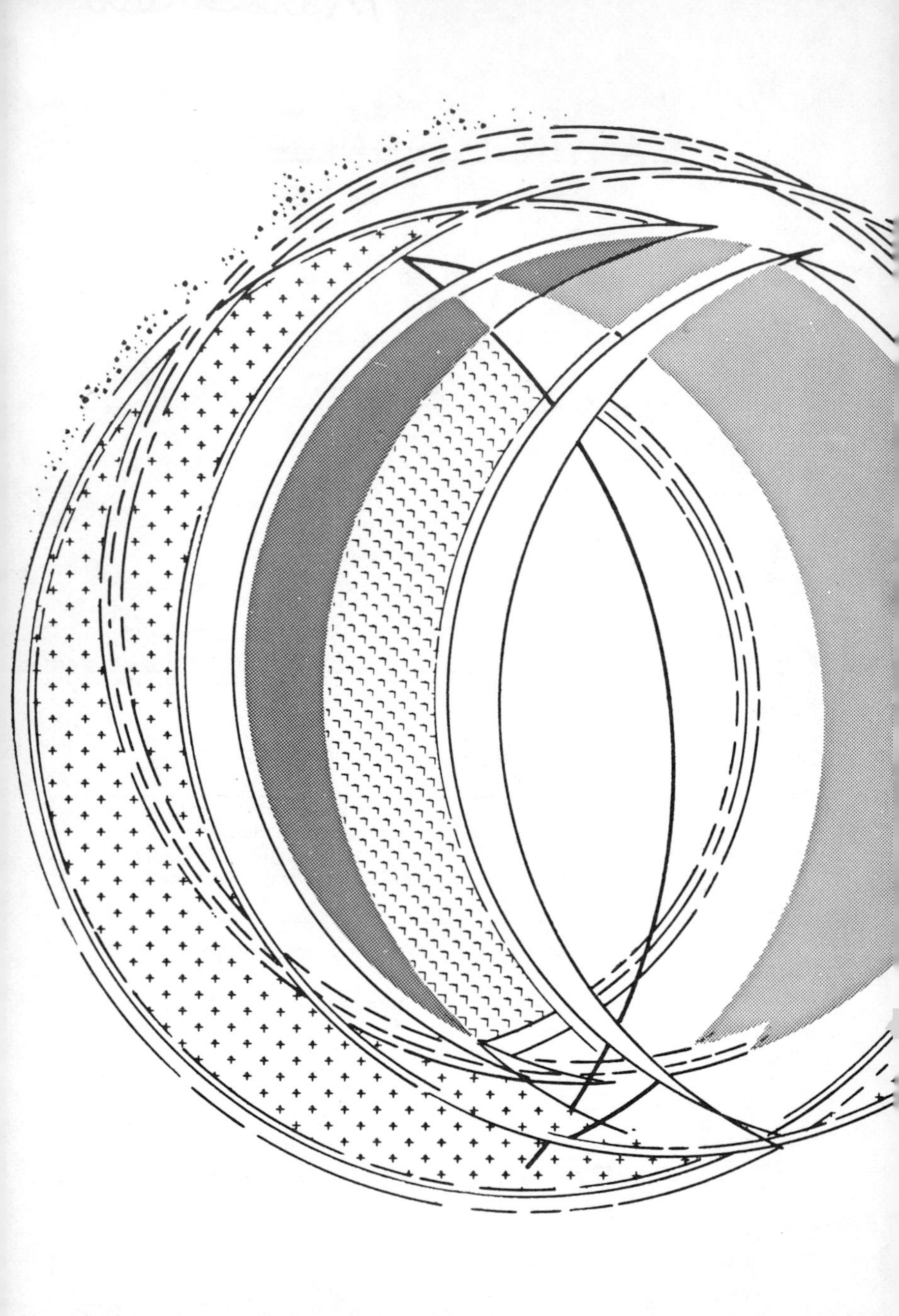

## A COLLECTION OF MODERN STORIES

JAMES E. MILLER, JR.

Professor of English, University of Chicago. Fulbright Lecturer in Naples and Rome, 1958-59, and in Kyoto, Japan, 1968. Author of *Quests Surd and Absurd: Essays in American Literature; Word, Self, Reality: The Rhetoric of Imagination;* and other works.

ROBERT HAYDEN

Professor of English, University of Michigan. Recipient of the Hopwood Award, the Grand Prix de la Poesie of the First World Festival of Negro Arts, Dakar, and the Russell Loines Award. Author of *A Ballad of Remembrance, Selected Poems,* and *Words in the Mourning Time.*

ROBERT O'NEAL

Professor of Humanities, San Antonio College. Formerly Chairman and Professor of English, San Antonio College. Author of *Teachers' Guide to World Literature for the High School, NCTE,* and *English for You.*

SCOTT, FORESMAN AND COMPANY

EDITORIAL DIRECTION

Leo B. Kneer

DEVELOPMENT

Margaret Rausch

WITH

Ghia Brenner
Fitzgerald Higgins
Bonnie Kepplinger
Eduardo Schoua
Ellen Wettersten

DESIGN

Robert Amft

ISBN: 0-673-03415-1

Copyright © 1973 Scott, Foresman and Company,
Glenview, Illinois.
Philippines Copyright 1973 Scott, Foresman and
Company. All Rights Reserved.
Printed in the United States of America.

Regional offices of Scott, Foresman and Company are
located in Dallas, Texas; Glenview, Illinois; Oakland, New Jersey;
Palo Alto, California; Tucker, Georgia; and Brighton, England.

To ascertain the tastes, the abilities, and the preferences of those for whom this book is intended, the following individuals read the many short stories submitted to them, judged their appropriateness and interest, and solicited the reactions of young people. The authors and editors of *British Motifs* wish to express their appreciation for this valuable assistance.

Mary Anne Bowen
JACKSON, MISSISSIPPI

Venita Bridger
SPRINGFIELD, MISSOURI

Michael G. Callahan
SAN MATEO, CALIFORNIA

Sister Eugene Fox, S.C.
BAY CITY, MICHIGAN

Barbara Goldsmith
OAK PARK, MICHIGAN

William A. McCleery
BEREA, OHIO

Robert P. Romano
WILMINGTON, MASSACHUSETTS

Cover: "Blue Moon" by Constance Howard, from INSPIRATION FOR EMBROIDERY by Constance Howard, Courtesy of B.T. Batsford, London

Graphics: Bronwyn Moore

# CONTENTS

# Kingsley Amis

## INTERESTING THINGS

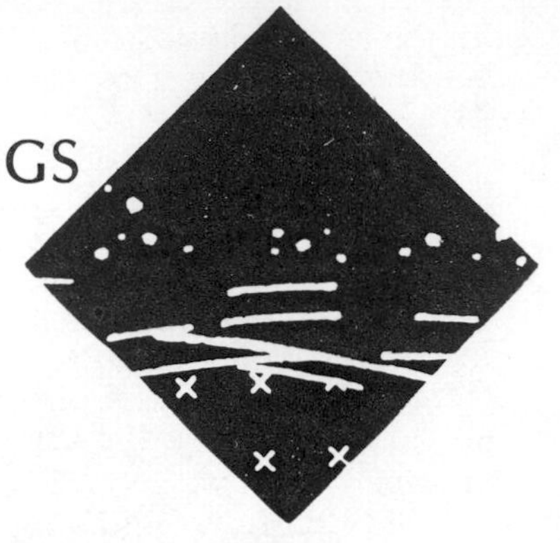

Gloria Davies crossed the road towards the Odeon on legs that weaved a little, as if she was tipsy or rickety. She wasn't either really; it was just the high-heeled shoes, worn for the first time specially for today. The new hoop earrings swayed from her lobes, hitting her rhythmically on the jaws as she walked. No. They were wrong. They had looked fine in her bedroom mirror, but they were wrong, somehow. She whipped them off and stuffed them into her handbag. Perhaps there'd be a chance to try them again later, when it was the evening. They might easily make all the difference then.

She stopped thinking about the earrings when she found she couldn't see Mr. Huws-Evans anywhere in the crowd of people waiting for their friends on the steps of the Odeon. She knew at once then that he hadn't really meant it. After all, what could an Inspector of Taxes (Assessment Section) see in an eighteen-year-old comptometer operator? How stuck-up she'd been, congratulating herself on being the first girl in the office Mr. Huws-Evans had ever asked out.

---

Copyright, 1956, by Kingsley Amis. Reprinted from his volume, MY ENEMY'S ENEMY, by permission of Harcourt Brace Jovanovich, Inc. and A.D. Peters and Company.

Just then a tall man who'd been standing close by took off his beige mackintosh hat[1] with a drill-like movement, keeping his elbow close to his chest. It was Mr. Huws-Evans.

"Hallo, Gloria," he said. He watched her for a bit, a smile showing round the curly stem of the pipe he was biting. Then he added: "Didn't you recognise me, Gloria?"

"Sorry, Mr. Huws-Evans, I sort of just didn't see you." The hat and the pipe had put her off completely, and she was further confused by being called Gloria twice already.

He nodded, accepting her apology and explanation. He put his hat on again with a ducking gesture, then removed his pipe. "Shall we go in? Don't want to miss the News."

While Mr. Huws-Evans bought two two-and-fourpennies Gloria noticed he was carrying a string bag full of packets of potato crisps.[2] She wondered why he was doing that.

It was very dark inside the cinema itself, and Mr. Huws-Evans had to click his fingers for a long time, and tremendously loudly, before an usherette came. The Odeon was often full on a Saturday when the football team was playing away, and Gloria and Mr. Huws-Evans couldn't help pushing past a lot of people to get to their seats. A good deal of loud sighing, crackling of sweet packets and uncoiling of embraces marked their progress. At last they were settled in full view of the screen, on which the Duke of Edinburgh was playing polo. Mr. Huws-Evans asked Gloria loudly whether she could see all right, and when she whispered that she could he offered her a chocolate. "They're rather good," he said.

Almost nothing happened while the films were shown. The main feature was on first. As soon as Gloria could tell that it was old-fashioned she was afraid she wouldn't enjoy it. Nobody did anything in it, they just talked. Some of the talking made Mr. Huws-Evans laugh for a long time at a

---

1. *mackintosh hat,* a waterproof hat. 2. *string bag . . . potato crisps,* a bag formed by a mesh of string, containing packages of potato chips.

time, and once or twice he nudged Gloria. When he did this she laughed too, because it was up to her to be polite and not spoil his pleasure. The film ended with a lot of fuss about a Gladstone bag and people falling into each other's arms in a daft, put-on way.[3]

Gloria kept wondering if Mr. Huws-Evans was going to put his arm round her. She'd never yet gone to the pictures in male company without at least this happening, and usually quite a lot more being tried on, but somehow Mr. Huws-Evans didn't seem the man for any of that. He was older than her usual escorts, to start with, and to go on with there was something about that mackintosh hat and that string bag which made it hard to think of him putting his arm round anyone, except perhaps his mother. Once she caught sight of his hand dangling over the arm of the seat towards her, and she moved her own hand carefully so that he could take hold of it easily if he wanted to, but he didn't. He leaned rather closer to her to light her cigarettes than he strictly needed to, and that was all.

After a pair of tin gates had been shown opening in a slow and dignified way, there was about half an hour of advertisements while everybody whistled the tunes that were playing. The cereals and the detergents came up, then a fairly long and thorough episode about razor blades. During it Mr. Huws-Evans suddenly said: "It's a damned scandal, that business."

"What's that, then?"

"Well, all this business about the modern shave. All these damned gadgets and things. It's just a way of trying to get you to use a new blade every day, that's all."

"Oh, I get you. You mean because the——"

"Mind you, with the kind of blade some of these firms turn out you've got to use a new blade. I grant them that." He laughed briefly. "If you don't want to skin yourself

---

3. *a Gladstone bag . . . put-on way.* Evidently the movie is a filmed version of Oscar Wilde's comedy *The Importance of Being Earnest.*

getting the beard off, that is. And of course they don't give a damn how much they spend on publicity. It's all off tax. Doesn't really cost them a bean."

Gloria was going to say "How's that, then?" but Mr. Huws-Evans's manner, that of one with a comprehensive explanation on instant call, warned her not to. She said instead: "No, of course it doesn't."

He looked at her with mingled scepticism and wistfulness, and ended the conversation by saying violently: "Some of these firms."

While the lights went down again, Gloria thought about this brief exchange. It was just the kind of talk older men went in for, the sort of thing her father discussed with his butties when they called to take him down to the pub, things to do with the government and pensions and jobs and the Russians, things that fellows who went dancing never mentioned. She saw, on the other hand, that that kind of talk wasn't only tied up in some way with getting old, it also had to do with having money and a car, with speaking properly and with being important. So a girl would show herself up for a lump with no conversation and bad manners if she gave away to an older man the fact that uninteresting things didn't interest her. Next time Mr. Huws-Evans got on to them she must do better.

The second film promised to be full of interesting things. There were some lovely dresses, the star looked just like another star Gloria had often wished she looked like, and there was a scene in a kind of flash night club with dim lights, men in tail coats and a modern band. The star was wearing a terrific evening dress with sequins and had a white fur round her shoulders. A man with a smashing profile sitting at the bar turned and saw her. Her eyes met his for a long moment. Gloria swallowed and leant forward in her seat.

Mr. Huws-Evans nudged Gloria and said: "Don't think much of this, do you? What about some tea?"

"Oh, we haven't got to go yet, have we?"

"Well, we don't want to sit all through this, do we?"

Gloria recollected herself. "No, right you are, then."

They moved effortfully back along the row, taking longer this time because some of the embraces were slower in uncoiling. In the foyer, Gloria said: "Well, thank you very much, Mr. Huws-Evans, I enjoyed the film ever so much," but he wasn't listening; he was looking wildly about as if he'd just found himself in a ladies' cloakroom, and beginning to say: "The crisps. I've left them inside."

"Never mind, don't you worry, it won't take a minute fetching them. I don't mind waiting at all."

He stared out at her from under the mackintosh hat, which he'd pulled down for some reason so that it hid his eyebrows. "I shan't be able to remember the seat. You come too, Gloria. Please."

After a lot more finger clicking inside they found the row. In the beam of the usherette's torch Gloria saw that their seats were already occupied. Even more slowly than before, Mr. Huws-Evans began shuffling sidelong away from her; there was some disturbance. Gloria, waiting in the aisle, turned and looked at the screen. The man with the profile was dancing with the star now and all the other people had gone back to their tables and were watching them. Gloria watched them too, and had forgotten where she was when a moderate uproar slowly broke out and slowly moved towards her. It was Mr. Huws-Evans with the crisps, which were rustling and crunching like mad. Men's voices were denouncing him, some of them loudly and one of the loud ones using words Gloria didn't like, in fact one word was the word she called "that word." Her cheeks went hot. Mr. Huws-Evans was saying things like "Very sorry, old boy" and "Hurts me as much as it hurts you," and every so often he laughed cheerily. Everywhere people were calling "Ssshh." Gloria couldn't think of anything to do to help.

A long time later they were outside again. It was clear at once that the rain had stopped holding off hours ago. Mr.

Huws-Evans took her arm and said they'd better run for it, and that was what they did. They ran a long way for it, and fast too, so that the high heels were doing some terrible slipping and skidding. Opposite Woolworth's Gloria nearly did the splits, but Mr. Huws-Evans prevented that, and was just as effective when she started a kind of sliding football tackle towards a lady in bifocal glasses carrying a little boy. That was just outside Bevan & Bevan's, and Gloria didn't mind it much because she'd guessed by now that they were going to Dalessio's, a fairly flash Italian restaurant frequented by the car-owning classes—unless, of course, they were making for Cwmbwrla or Portardulais on foot.

There was a queue in Dalessio's and Gloria panted out the news that she was going to the cloakroom, where there was another, but shorter, queue. While she waited her turn she felt her hair, which must have been looking dreadful, and wondered about her face, to which she'd applied some of the new liquid make-up everyone was talking about. She was glad to find, in due time, that she hadn't been looking too bad. Touching up with the liquid stuff didn't quite provide the amazing matt finish the advertisements described, in fact she wondered if she didn't look a bit like one of the waxworks she'd seen that time in Cardiff, but there was no time to redo it and it must surely wear off a little after a bit. She gazed longingly at the earrings in her bag, and at the new mascara kit, but these must certainly wait. Taking a last peep at herself, she reflected gratefully, as her father had often exhorted her to do, that she was very lucky to be quite pretty and have all that naturally curly naturally blonde hair.

Mr. Huws-Evans had a table for two when she joined him. He took the bag of crisps off her chair and laid them reverently at his side. Gloria thought he seemed very attached to them. What did he want them for, and so many of them too? It was a puzzle. Perhaps he guessed her curiosity, because he said: "They're for the party. They said I was to get them."

"Oh, I see. Who'll be there? At the party? You did tell me when you asked me, but I'm afraid I've forgotten."

"Not many people you'll know, I'm afraid. There'll be Mr. Pugh, of course, from Allowances, and his wife, and Miss Harry from Repayments, and my brother—you've met him, haven't you?—and my dentist and his, er, and his friend, and two or three of my brother's friends. About a dozen altogether."

"It sounds lovely," Gloria said. A little tremor of excitement ran through her; then she remembered about poise. She arranged herself at the table like one of the models who showed off jewellery on TV, and purposely took a long while deciding what to have when the waitress came, though she'd known ever since passing Bevan & Bevan's that she was going to have mixed grill, with French fried potatoes. She was soon so lost in thoughts of the party and in enjoying eating that it was like a voice in a dream when Mr. Huws-Evans said:

"Of course, the real difficulties come when we have to decide whether something's income or capital."

Gloria looked up, trying not to seem startled. "Oh yes."

"For instance," Mr. Huws-Evans went on, drawing a long fishbone from his mouth, "take the case of a man who buys a house, lives in it for a bit and then sells it. Any profit he might make wouldn't be assessable. It's capital, not income."

"So he wouldn't have to pay tax on it, is that right?"

"Now for goodness' sake don't go and get that mixed up with the tax on the property itself, the Schedule A tax."

"Oh yes, I've heard of that. There were some figures I——"

"That still has to be paid." He leaned forward in an emphatic way. "Unless the man is exempt, of course."

"Oh yes."

"Now it'd be much easier, as you can imagine, to catch him on the sale of several houses. But even then we'd need to show that there was a trade. If the chap simply buys them as investments, just to get the rents, well then you couldn't catch him if he sold out later at a profit. There'd be no trade, you see."

"No." Gloria swallowed a mushroom stalk whole. "No trade."

"That's right." He nodded and seemed pleased, then changed his tone to nonchalant indulgence. "Mind you, even the profit on an isolated transaction could be an income profit. There was the case of three chaps who bought some South African brandy, had it shipped over here and blended with French brandy, and sold it at a profit. But the court still said there was a trade. They'd set up a selling organisation."

"Ah, I get it."

"You'll be perfectly all right just so long as you remember that income tax is a tax on income."

Gloria felt a little dashed when Mr. Huws-Evans found nothing to add to his last maxim. She hadn't spoken up enough and shown she was taking an interest. He couldn't just go on talking, with nobody helping to make it a proper conversation. And yet—what could she have said? It was so hard to think of things.

Mr. Huws-Evans launched off again soon and she cheered up. He questioned her about herself and her parents and friends and what she did in the evenings. He watched her with his big brown eyes and tended to raise his eyebrows slowly when she got near the end of each bit she said. Then, before asking his next question, he'd let his eyes go vacant, and drop his jaw without opening his mouth at all, and nod slightly, as if each reply of hers was tying up, rather disturbingly, with some fantastic theory about her he'd originally made up for fun: that she was a Communist spy, say, or a goblin in human form. During all this he dismantled, cleaned, reassembled, filled and lit his pipe, finally tamping down the tobacco with his thumb and burning himself slightly.

At last it was time to go. In the street Gloria said: "Well, thank you very much, Mr. Huws-Evans, I enjoyed the food ever so much," but he wasn't listening; he was rubbing his chin hard with some of his fingers, and beginning to say: "Shave. Got to have a shave before the party. That blade this morning."

They boarded a bus and went a long way on it. Mr. Huws-Evans explained, quoting figures, that a taxi wasn't worthwhile and that he personally was damned if he was going to lay out all that cash on a car simply to make a splash and impress a few snobs. He paid the conductor with coins from a leather purse that did up with two poppers. This purse, Gloria thought, was somehow rather like the mackintosh hat and the string bag with the crisps. After doing up the purse and putting it safely away Mr. Huws-Evans said that his digs, where the shave was going to happen, were quite near Mr. Pugh's house, which was where the party was going to happen. He added that this would give them just nice time.

They got off the bus and walked for a few minutes. The rain had stopped and the sun was out. Gloria cheered up again, and didn't notice at first when Mr. Huws-Evans suddenly stopped in the middle of the pavement. He was looking about in rather the same way as he'd done in the foyer of the Odeon. He said: "Funny. I could have sworn."

"What's the matter, then?"

"Can't seem to remember the right house. Ridiculous of me, isn't it? Just can't seem to remember at all."

"Not your digs it isn't, where you can't remember, is it?"

"Well yes, my digs. This is it. No, there's no TV aerial."

"Never mind, what's the number?"

"That's the silly part. I don't know the number."

"Oh, but you must. How ever do you manage with letters and things? Come on, you must know. Try and think, now."

"No good. I've never known it."

"What?"

"Well, you see, the landlady's got one of those stamp things to stamp the address at the top of the notepaper and

I always use that. And then when I get a letter I just see it's for me and that's all I bother about, see?" He said most of this over his shoulder in the intervals of trying to see through some lace curtains. Then he shook his head and walked on, only to bend forward slightly with hands on knees, like a swimmer waiting for the starting pistol, and stare at a photograph of a terrier which someone had arranged, thoughtfully turned outward, on a window sill. "The number's got a three in it, I do know that," he said then. "At least I think so."

"How do you manage as a rule?"

"I know the house, you see."

Mr. Huws-Evans now entered a front garden and put his eye to a gap in the curtains. Quite soon a man in shirt-sleeves holding a newspaper twitched the curtain aside and stood looking at him. He was a big man with hair growing up round the base of his neck, and you could guess that he worked at some job where strength was important. Mr. Huws-Evans came out of the garden, latching its gate behind him. "I don't think that's the one," he said.

"Come on, why not just knock somewhere and ask?"

"Can't do that. They'd think I was barmy."

Eventually Mr. Huws-Evans recognised his house by its bright red door. "Eighty-seven," he murmured, studying the number as he went in. "I must remember that."

Gloria sat in the sitting room, which had more books in it than she'd ever seen in a private house before, and looked at the book Mr. Huws-Evans had dropped into her lap before going up to have his shave. It was called *Income Taxes in the Commonwealth,* and he'd said it would probably interest her.

She found it didn't do that and had gone to see if there were any interesting books in the bookcase when the door opened and an old lady looked in. She and Gloria stared at each other for about half a minute, and Gloria's cheeks felt hot again. The old lady's top lip had vertical furrows and there was something distrustful about her. She gave a few grunts with a puff of breath at the beginning of each one, and went out. Gloria didn't like to touch the bookcase now and told herself that the party would make everything worthwhile.

When Mr. Huws-Evans came back he had a big red patch on his neck. "These razor blade firms," he said bitterly, but made no objection when Gloria asked if she could go and wash her hands. He even came to the foot of the stairs to show her the right door.

The liquid make-up looked fine, the mascara went on like distemper on a wall and the earrings were just right now. She only hoped her white blouse and rust cocktail-length skirt, the only clothes she had that were at all evening, were evening enough. When she came out the old lady was there, about thirty inches away. This time she gave more puffing grunts than before and started giving them sooner. She was still giving them when Gloria went downstairs. But then Mr. Huws-Evans, as soon as he saw her, jumped up and said: "You look absolutely stunning, Gloria," so that part was worthwhile.

After they'd left, what Gloria had been half-expecting all along happened, though not in the way she'd half-expected. It now appeared that they were much too early, and Mr. Huws-Evans took her into a park for a sit-down. Before long he said: "You know, Gloria, it means a lot to me, you coming out with me today."

This was hard to answer, so she just nodded.

"I think you're the prettiest girl I've ever been out with."

"Well, thank you very much, Mr. Huws-Evans."

"Won't you call me Waldo? I wish you would."

"Oh no, I don't think I could, really."

"Why not?"

"I . . . I don't think I know you well enough."

He stared at her with the large brown eyes she'd often admired in the office, but which she now thought looked soft. Sadly, he said: "If only you knew what I feel about you, Gloria, and how much you mean to me. Funny, isn't it?

I couldn't have guessed what you were going to do to me, make me feel, I mean, when I first saw you." He lurched suddenly towards her, but drew back at the last minute. "If only you could feel for me just a tiny bit of what I feel for you, you've no idea what it would mean to me."

An approach of this kind was new to Gloria and it flustered her. If, instead of all this daft talk, Mr. Huws-Evans had tried to kiss her, she'd probably have let him, even in this park place; she could have handled that. But all he'd done was make her feel foolish and awkward. Abruptly, she stood up. "I think we ought to be going."

"Oh, not yet. Please. Please don't be offended."

"I'm not offended, honest."

He got up too and stood in front of her. "I'd give anything in the world to think that you didn't think too hardly of me. I feel such a worm."

"Now you're not to talk so silly."

When it was much too late, Mr. Huws-Evans did try to kiss her, saying as he did so: "Oh, my darling."

Gloria side-stepped him. "I'm not your darling," she said decisively.

After that neither spoke until they arrived at the house where the party was. Mr. Huws-Evans's daft talk, Gloria thought, was to be expected from the owner of that mackintosh hat—which he still wore.

When Mr. Huws-Evans's brother caught sight of her their eyes met for a long moment. It was because of him—she'd seen him once or twice when he called in at the office—that she'd accepted Mr. Huws-Evans's invitation. Originally she'd intended just to look at him across the room while she let Mr. Huws-Evans talk to her, but after what had happened she left Mr. Huws-Evans to unpack his crisps and put them in bowls while the brother (it was funny to think that he was Mr. Huws-Evans too, in a way) took her across the room, sat her on a sofa and started talking about interesting things. ◆

# Elizabeth Bowen

# THE CAT JUMPS

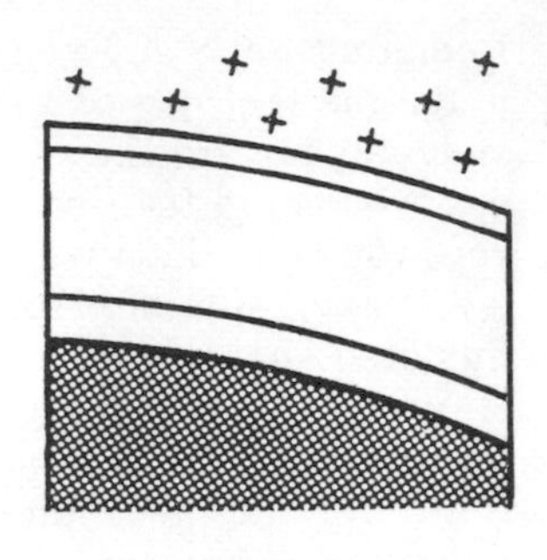

After the Bentley murder, Rose Hill stood empty two years. Lawns mounted to meadows; white paint peeled from the balconies; the sun, looking more constantly, less fearfully in than sightseers' eyes through the naked windows, bleached the floral wallpapers. The week after the execution Harold Bentley's legatees had placed the house on the books of the principal agents, London and local. But though sunny, up-to-date, and convenient, though so delightfully situate over the Thames valley (above flood level), within easy reach of a golf course, Rose Hill, while frequently viewed, remained unpurchased. Dreadful associations apart, the privacy of the place had been violated; with its terraced garden, lily pond, and pergola cheerfully rose-encrusted, the public had been made too familiar. On the domestic scene too many eyes had burnt the impress of their horror. Moreover, that pearly bathroom, that bedroom with wide outlook over a loop of the Thames . . . "The Rose Hill Horror": headlines flashed up at the very sound of the name. "Oh, *no,* dear!" many wives had exclaimed, drawing their husbands hurriedly from the gate. "Come away!"

---

"The Cat Jumps" from LOOK AT ALL THOSE ROSES, (British title: THE CAT JUMPS AND OTHER STORIES) by Elizabeth Bowen. Copyright 1941 and renewed 1969 by Elizabeth Bowen. Reprinted by permission of Alfred A. Knopf, Inc. and Jonathan Cape Ltd.

they had urged, crumpling the agent's order to view as though the house were advancing upon them. And husbands came away—with a backward glance at the garage. Funny to think a chap who was hanged had kept his car there.

The Harold Wrights, however, were not deterred. They had light, bright, shadowless, thoroughly disinfected minds. They believed that they disbelieved in most things but were unprejudiced; they enjoyed frank discussions. They dreaded nothing but inhibitions: they had no inhibitions. They were pious agnostics, earnest for social reform; they explained everything to their children, and were annoyed to find their children could not sleep at nights because they thought there was a complex under the bed. They knew all crime to be pathological, and read their murders only in scientific books. They had vitaglass[1] put into all their windows. No family, in fact, could have been more unlike the mistaken Harold Bentleys.

Rose Hill, from the first glance, suited the Wrights admirably. They were in search of a cheerful weekend house with a nice atmosphere, where their friends could join them for frank discussions, and their own and their friends' children "run wild" during the summer months. Harold Wright, who had a good head, got the agent to knock six hundred off the quoted price of the house. "That unfortunate affair," he murmured. Jocelyn commended his inspiration. Otherwise, they did not give the Bentleys another thought.

The Wrights had the floral wallpapers all stripped off and the walls cream-washed; they removed some disagreeably thick pink shades from the electricity and had the paint renewed inside and out. (The front of the house was bracketed over with balconies, like an overmantel.) Their bedroom mantelpiece, stained by the late Mrs. Bentley's cosmetics, had to be scrubbed with chemicals. Also, they

---

1. *vitaglass,* a type of glass that does not obstruct ultraviolet rays.

had removed from the rock garden Mrs. Bentley's little dog's memorial tablet, with a quotation on it from *Indian Love Lyrics.* Jocelyn Wright, looking into the unfortunate bath—*the* bath, so square and opulent, with its surround of nacreous tiles—said, laughing lightly, she supposed anyone *else* would have had that bath changed. "Not that that would be possible," she added; "the bath's built in. . . . I've always wanted a built-in bath."

Harold and Jocelyn turned from the bath to look down at the cheerful river shimmering under a spring haze. All the way down the slope cherry-trees were in blossom. Life should be simplified for the Wrights; they were fortunate in their mentality.

After an experimentary weekend, without guests or children, only one thing troubled them: a resolute stuffiness, upstairs and down—due, presumably, to the house's having been so long shut up—a smell of unsavoury habitation, of rich cigarette-smoke stale in the folds of unaired curtains, of scent spilled on unbrushed carpets; an alcoholic smell—persistent in their perhaps too sensitive nostrils after days of airing, doors and windows open, in rooms drenched thoroughly with sun and wind. They told each other it came from the parquet; they didn't like it, somehow. They had the parquet taken up—at great expense —and put down plain oak floors.

In their practical way, the Wrights now set out to expel, live out, live down, almost (had the word had place in their vocabulary) to "lay" the Bentleys. Deferred by trouble over the parquet, their occupation of Rose Hill (which should have dated from mid-April) did not begin till the end of May. Throughout a week, Jocelyn had motored from town daily, so that the final installation of themselves and the children was able to coincide with their first weekend party—they asked down five of their friends to warm the house.

That first Friday, everything was auspicious; afternoon sky blue as the garden irises; later, a full moon pendent over the river; a night so warm that, after midnight, their enlightened friends, in pyjamas, could run on the blanched lawns in a state of high though rational excitement. Jane, Jacob, and Janet, their admirably spaced-out children, kept awake by the moonlight, hailed their elders out of the nursery skylight. Jocelyn waved to them: they never had been repressed.

The girl Muriel Barker was found looking up the terraces at the house a shade doubtfully. "You know," she said, "I do rather wonder they don't feel . . . *sometimes* . . . you know what I mean?"

"No," replied her companion, a young scientist.

Muriel sighed. "No one would mind if it had been just a short sharp shooting. But it was so . . . prolonged. It went on all over the house. Do you remember?" she said timidly.

"No," replied Mr. Cartaret. "It didn't interest me."

"Oh, nor me either!" agreed Muriel quickly, but added: "How he must have hated her . . . "

The scientist, sleepy, yawned frankly and referred her to Krafft-Ebing.[2] But Muriel went to bed with *Alice in Wonderland;* she went to sleep with the lights on. She was not, as Jocelyn realised later, the sort of girl to have asked at all.

Next morning was overcast; in the afternoon it rained, suddenly and heavily—interrupting, for some, tennis, for others, a pleasant discussion, in a punt, on marriage under the Soviet. Defeated, they all rushed in. Jocelyn went round from room to room, shutting tightly the rain-lashed casements along the front of the house. These continued to rattle; the balconies creaked. An early dusk set in; an oppressive, almost visible moisture, up from the darkening river, pressed on the panes like a presence and slid through the house. The party gathered in the library, round an expansive but thinly burning fire. Harold circulated photographs of modern architecture; they discussed these ten-

---

2. *Krafft-Ebing.* Richard von Krafft-Ebing (1840–1902) was a German physician and neurologist, and author of *Psychopathia Sexualis* (1886).

dencies. Then Mrs. Monkhouse, sniffing, exclaimed: "Who uses 'Trèfle Incarnat'?"

"Now, *who* ever would——" her hostess began scornfully. Then from the hall came a howl, a scuffle, a thin shriek. They sat too still; in the dusky library Mr. Cartaret laughed out loud. Harold Wright, indignantly throwing open the door, revealed Jane and Jacob rolling at the foot of the stairs, biting each other, their faces dark with uninhibited passion. Bumping alternate heads against the foot of the banisters, they shrieked in concert.

"Extraordinary," said Harold; "they've never done that before. They have always understood each other so well."

"I wouldn't do that," advised Jocelyn, raising her voice slightly; "you'll hurt your teeth. Other teeth won't grow at once, you know."

"You should let them find that out for themselves," disapproved Edward Cartaret, taking up the *New Statesman*. Harold, in perplexity, shut the door on his children, who soon stunned each other to silence.

Meanwhile, Sara and Talbot Monkhouse, Muriel Barker and Theodora Smith, had drawn together over the fire in a tight little knot. Their voices twanged with excitement. By that shock, just now, something seemed to have been released. Even Cartaret gave them half his attention. They were discussing *crime passionnel*.

"Of course, if that's what they really *want* to discuss . . . " thought Jocelyn. But it did seem unfortunate. Partly from an innocent desire to annoy her visitors, partly because the room felt awful—you would have thought fifty people had been there for a week—she went across and opened one of the windows, admitting a pounce of damp wind. They all turned, startled, to hear rain crash on the lead of an upstairs balcony. Muriel's voice was left in forlorn solo: "Dragged herself . . . whining 'Harold' . . . "

Harold Wright looked remarkably conscious. Jocelyn said brightly, "Whatever *are* you talking about?" But, unfortunately, Harold, on almost the same breath, suggested:

"Let's leave that family alone, shall we?" Their friends all felt they might not be asked again. Though they did feel, plaintively, that they had been being natural. However, they disowned Muriel, who, getting up abruptly, said she thought she'd like to go for a walk in the rain before dinner. Nobody accompanied her.

Later, overtaking Mrs. Monkhouse on the stairs, Muriel confided: absolutely, she could not stand Edward Cartaret. She could hardly bear to be in the room with him. He seemed so . . . cruel. Cold-blooded? No, she meant cruel. Sara Monkhouse, going into Jocelyn's room for a chat (at her entrance Jocelyn started violently), told Jocelyn that Muriel could not stand Edward, could hardly bear to be in a room with him. "Pity," said Jocelyn. "I had thought they might do for each other." Jocelyn and Sara agreed that Muriel was unrealised: what she ought to have was a baby. But when Sara, dressing, told Talbot Monkhouse that Muriel could not stand Edward, and Talbot said Muriel was unrealised, Sara was furious. The Monkhouses, who never did quarrel, quarrelled bitterly, and were late for dinner. They would have been later if the meal itself had not been delayed by an outburst of sex-antagonism between the nice Jacksons, a couple imported from London to run the house. Mrs. Jackson, putting everything in the oven, had locked herself into her room.

"Curious," said Harold; "the Jacksons' relations to each other always seemed so modern. They have the most intelligent discussions."

Theodora said she had been re-reading Shakespeare—this brought them point-blank up against *Othello*.[3] Harold, with Titanic force, wrenched round the conversation to relativity: about this no one seemed to have anything to say but Edward Cartaret. And Muriel, who by

---

3. *Othello*, a tragedy by William Shakespeare in which the protagonist Othello, wrongfully believing that his wife Desdemona has been unfaithful to him, strangles her, and discovering his error, kills himself.

some mischance had again been placed beside him, sat deathly, turning down her dark-rimmed eyes. In fact, on the intelligent sharp-featured faces all round the table something—perhaps simply a clearness—seemed to be lacking, as though these were wax faces for one fatal instant exposed to a furnace. Voices came out from some dark interiority; in each conversational interchange a mutual vote of no confidence was implicit. You would have said that each personality had been attacked by some kind of decomposition.

"No moon to-night," complained Sara Monkhouse. Never mind, they would have a cosy evening; they would play paper games, Jocelyn promised.

"If you can see," said Harold. "Something seems to be going wrong with the light."

Did Harold think so? They had all noticed the light seemed to be losing quality, as though a film, smoke-like, were creeping over the bulbs. The light, thinning, darkening, seemed to contract round each lamp into a blurred aura. They had noticed, but, each with a proper dread of his own subjectivity, had not spoken.

"Funny stuff," Harold said, "electricity."

Mr. Cartaret could not agree with him.

Though it was late, though they yawned and would not play paper games, they were reluctant to go to bed. You would have supposed a delightful evening. Jocelyn was not gratified.

The library stools, rugs, and divans were strewn with Krafft-Ebing, Freud, Forel, Weiniger, and the heterosexual volume of Havelock Ellis.[4] (Harold had thought it right to install his reference library; his friends hated to discuss without basis.) The volumes were pressed open with paper knives and small pieces of modern statuary; stooping from

---

4. *Freud . . . Havelock Ellis,* scientists whose work dealt with the psychology of sex.

one to another, purposeful as a bee, Edward Cartaret read extracts aloud to Harold, to Talbot Monkhouse, and to Theodora Smith, who stitched *gros point* with resolution. At the far end of the library, under a sallow drip from a group of electric candles, Mrs. Monkhouse and Miss Barker shared an ottoman, spines pressed rigid against the wall. Tensely one spoke, one listened.

"And these," thought Jocelyn, leaning back with her eyes shut between the two groups, "are the friends I liked to have in my life. Pellucid, sane . . . "

It was remarkable how much Muriel knew. Sara, very much shocked, edged up till their thighs touched. You would have thought the Harold Bentleys had been Muriel's relatives. Surely, Sara attempted, in one's large, bright world one did not think of these things? Practically, they did not exist! Surely Muriel should not . . . But Muriel looked at her strangely.

"Did you know," she said, "that one of Mrs. Bentley's hands was found in the library?"

Sara, smiling a little awkwardly, licked her lip. "Oh," she said.

"But the fingers were in the dining room. He began there."

"Why isn't he in Broadmoor?"[5]

"That defence failed. He didn't really subscribe to it. He said having done what he wanted was worth anything."

"Oh!"

"Yes, he was nearly lynched. . . . She dragged herself upstairs. She couldn't lock any doors—naturally. One maid—her maid—got shut into the house with them: he'd sent all the others away. For a long time everything seemed so quiet: the maid crept out and saw Harold Bentley sitting half way upstairs, finishing a cigarette. All the lights were full on. He nodded to her and dropped the cigarette through the banisters. Then she saw the . . . the state of the hall.

---

5. *Broadmoor,* an asylum for criminal lunatics in Berkshire, England.

He went upstairs after Mrs. Bentley, saying: 'Lucinda!' He looked into room after room, whistling; then he said *'Here we are,'* and shut a door after him.

"The maid fainted. When she came to, it was still going on, upstairs. . . . Harold Bentley had locked all the garden doors; there were locks even on the French windows. The maid couldn't get out. Everything she touched was . . . sticky. At last she broke a pane and got through. As she ran down the garden—the lights were on all over the house—she saw Harold Bentley moving about in the bathroom. She fell right over the edge of a terrace and one of the tradesmen picked her up next day.

"Doesn't it seem odd, Sara, to think of Jocelyn in that bath?"

Finishing her recital, Muriel turned on Sara an ecstatic and brooding look that made her almost beautiful. Sara fumbled with a cigarette; match after match failed her. "Muriel, *you* ought to see a specialist."

Muriel held out her hand for a cigarette. "He put her heart in her hatbox. He said it belonged in there."

"You had no right to come here. It was most unfair on Jocelyn. Most . . . indelicate."

Muriel, to whom the word was, properly, unfamiliar, eyed incredulously Sara's lips.

"How dared you come?"

"I thought I might like it. I thought I ought to fulfil myself. I'd never had any experience of these things."

*"Muriel . . . "*

"Besides, I wanted to meet Edward Cartaret. Several people said we were made for each other. Now, of course, I shall never marry. Look what comes of it. . . . I must say, Sara, I wouldn't be you or Jocelyn. Shut up all night with a man all alone—I don't know how you dare sleep. I've arranged to sleep with Theodora, and we shall barricade the door. I noticed something about Edward Cartaret the moment I arrived: a kind of insane glitter. He is utterly pathological. He's got instruments in his room, in that black bag. Yes, I looked. Did you notice the way he went on and on about cutting up that cat, and the way Talbot and Harold listened?"

Sara, looking furtively round the room, saw Mr. Cartaret making passes over the head of Theodora Smith with a paper knife. Both appeared to laugh heartily, but in silence.

"Here we are," said Harold, showing his teeth, smiling.

He stood over Muriel with a syphon in one hand, glass in the other.

At this point Jocelyn, rising, said she, for one, intended to go to bed.

Jocelyn's bedroom curtains swelled a little over the noisy window. The room was stuffy and—insupportable, so that she did not know where to turn. The house, fingered outwardly by the wind that dragged unceasingly past the walls, was, within, a solid silence: silence heavy as flesh. Jocelyn dropped her wrap to the floor, then watched how its feathered edges crept a little. A draught came in, under her bathroom door.

Jocelyn turned away in despair and hostility from the strained, pale woman looking at her from her oblong glass. She said aloud, "There *is* no fear"; then, within herself, heard this taken up: "But the death fear, that one is not there to relate! If the spirit, dismembered in agony, dies before the body! If the spirit, in the whole knowledge of its dissolution, drags from chamber to chamber, drops from plane to plane of awareness (as from knife to knife down an oubliette), shedding, receiving agony! Till, long afterwards, death, with its little pain, is established in the indifferent body." There was no comfort: death (now at every turn and instant claiming her) was, in its every possible manifestation, violent death: ultimately, she was to be given up to terror.

Undressing, shocked by the iteration of her reflected movements, she flung a towel over the glass. With what desperate eyes of appeal, at Sara's door, she and Sara had looked at each other, clung with their looks—and parted.

She could have sworn she heard Sara's bolt slide softly to. But what then, subsequently, of Talbot? And what—she eyed her own bolt, so bright (and, for the late Mrs. Bentley, so ineffective)—what of Harold?

"It's atavistic!"[6] she said aloud, in the dark-lit room, and, kicking her slippers away, got into bed. She took *Erewhon*[7] from the rack, but lay rigid, listening. As though snatched by a movement, the towel slipped from the mirror beyond her bed-end. She faced the two eyes of an animal in extremity, eyes black, mindless. The clock struck two: she had been waiting an hour.

On the floor, her feathered wrap shivered again all over. She heard the other door of the bathroom very stealthily open, then shut. Harold moved in softly, heavily, knocked against the side of the bath, and stood still. He was quietly whistling.

"Why didn't I understand? He must always have hated me. It's to-night he's been waiting for. . . . *He wanted this house.* His look, as we went upstairs . . . "

She shrieked: "Harold!"

Harold, so softly whistling, remained behind the imperturbable door, remained quite still. . . . "He's *listening* for me . . . " One pinpoint of hope at the tunnel-end: to get to Sara, to Theodora, to Muriel. Unmasked, incautious, with a long tearing sound of displaced air, Jocelyn leapt from the bed to the door.

But her door had been locked from the outside.

With a strange rueful smile, like an actress, Jocelyn, skirting the foot of the two beds, approached the door of the bathroom. "At least I have still . . . my feet." For some time the heavy body of Mrs. Bentley, tenacious of life, had been dragging itself from room to room. *"Harold!"* she said to the silence, face close to the door.

---

6. *atavistic,* primitive, particularly in the case of the reversion of a higher to a lower type. 7. *Erewhon,* a satirical novel (1872) by Samuel Butler describing a utopian society.

The door opened on Harold, looking more dreadfully at her than she had imagined. With a quick, vague movement he roused himself from his meditation. Therein he had assumed the entire burden of Harold Bentley. Forces he did not know of assembling darkly, he had faced for untold ages the imperturbable door to his wife's room. She would be there, densely, smotheringly there. She lay like a great cat, always, over the mouth of his life.

The Harolds, superimposed on each other, stood searching the bedroom strangely. Taking a step forward, shutting the door behind him:

"Here we are," said Harold.

Jocelyn went down heavily. Harold watched.

Harold Wright was appalled. Jocelyn had fainted: Jocelyn never had fainted before. He shook, he fanned, he applied restoratives. His perplexed thoughts fled to Sara—oh, Sara certainly. "Hi!" he cried, "Sara!" and successively fled from each to each of the locked doors. There was no way out.

Across the passage a door throbbed to the maniac drumming of Sara Monkhouse. She had been locked in. For Talbot, agonised with solicitude, it was equally impossible to emerge from his dressing room. Further down the passage, Edward Cartaret, interested by this nocturnal manifestation, wrenched and rattled his door handle in vain.

Muriel, on her silent way through the house to Theodora's bedroom, had turned all the keys on the outside, impartially. She did not know which door might be Edward Cartaret's. Muriel was a woman who took no chances. ◆

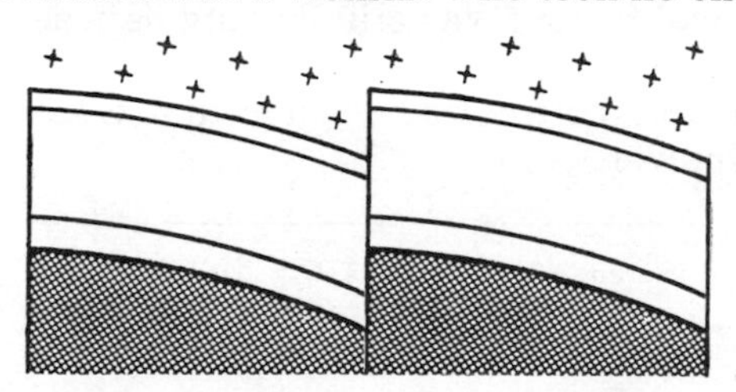

# Morley Callaghan

## IT MUST BE DIFFERENT

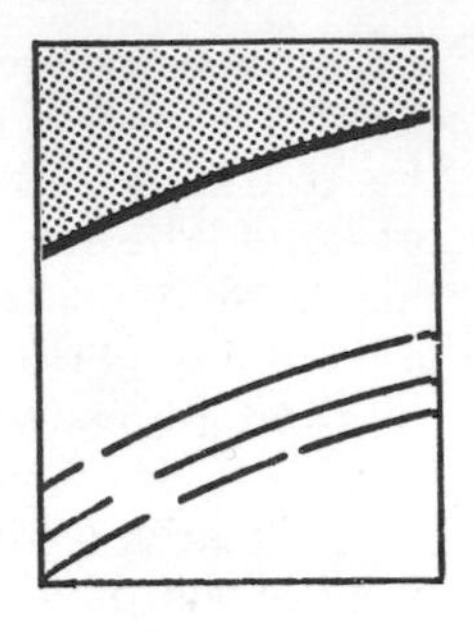

SYLVIA WEEKS AND MAX PORTER had known each other five months, but she never took him home to her place till that autumn evening when they had walked in the streets after the show, and the rain had begun to fall.

It had started when Max began suddenly to tell her that there was a real chance for him to get along in the radio business, and then her heart had begun to beat unevenly, for she became aware that he was getting ready to talk about wanting to marry her. He was so simple and honest about it, that she became humble and shy, and they walked along silently, both anxious about what was to be said; and then the rain began to fall in large heavy drops. Ducking their heads, they ran along the street hand in hand and stood breathless on the stoop outside her place, watching the wet pavement shining under the street light.

Sylvia could not bear to let him go as he had gone on other nights; it was as though they had looked for each other for months, and had now met suddenly face to face. That magical feeling was still flowing between them, and she couldn't bear to let him go until all the necessary words had been said, or the things done that would hold them together forever.

---

"It Must Be Different" from NOW THAT APRIL'S HERE AND OTHER STORIES by Morley Callaghan. Copyright 1936 by Morley Callaghan reprinted by permission of The Harold Matson Company, Inc.

"Come on in for a little while, Max," she said.
"Are you sure it'll be all right?"
"I think they'll be in bed," she said.
They laughed a little while Sylvia fumbled in her purse for her latchkey; then they tried to go in quietly. When they were in the hall, they heard some one coughing in the living room. Sylvia whispered uneasily: "I thought they'd be in bed."
"Maybe I'd better not come in," he said.
"Come on, anyway," she said.
In the living room Sylvia's mother, a large woman with a face that had been quite pretty once, but which was now soft and heavy, was standing with an alarm clock in her hand. She was on her way to bed, and she had been urging her husband, who still sat in an armchair in his shirt-sleeves and suspenders reading the paper, to go along with her, so he wouldn't disturb her later on. When Sylvia came in with Max following shyly, the mother was flustered and began to tidy her gray hair with her hand. "We were on our way to bed. We were just waiting for you, Sylvia," she said reproachfully.
"We wanted to walk after the show, Mother; but it rained. This is Max, Mother," Sylvia said.
"Oh, hello, Max. We've heard about you."
"If it's too late, I won't stay, Mrs. Weeks."
"So you're Max, eh," the father said, getting up. He was a furniture-maker who worked hard all day, and who usually hurried out of the room when a visitor came in in the evening; but now he stood there staring at Max as if he had been wondering about him a long time.
And Mrs. Weeks, looking at Sylvia, said: "You must have been having a good time, dear. You look happy and kind of excited."
"I'm not excited. I was just hurrying in the rain," Sylvia said.
"I guess it's just the rain and the hurrying that makes your eyes shine," the mother said; but the free ecstatic

eagerness she saw in her daughter's face worried her, and her glance was troubled as she tried to make her husband notice that Sylvia's face glowed with some secret delight that had come out of being with this boy, who was a stranger and might not be trustworthy. Sylvia and Max were standing underneath the light, and Sylvia with her flushed cheeks and her dark head seemed more marvelously eager than ever before. It was easy for them to feel the restlessness and the glowing warmth in her, and the love she had been giving; and then the mother and father, looking at Max, who seemed very boyish with his rain-wet hair shining under the light, smiled a little, not wanting to be hostile, yet feeling sure that Sylvia and this boy had touched some new intimacy that night.

In a coaxing, worried voice Mrs. Weeks said: "Now don't stay up late, Sylvia darling, will you?" Again her husband's eyes met hers in that thoughtful, uneasy way; then they said pleasantly: "Good night, Max. We're glad to meet you. Good night, Sylvia." And then they went to bed.

When they had gone, Max said: "They certainly made that pretty clear, didn't they?"

"Made what clear?"

"That they wouldn't trust me alone with my grandmother."

"They didn't say anything at all, Max."

"Didn't you see how they stared at me? I'll bet they're listening now."

"Is that why you're whispering?"

"Sure. They expect us to whisper, don't they?"

They sat down on the couch, but they both felt that if they caressed each other, or became gentle and tender, they were only making a beginning at something that was expected of them by the mother and father going to bed in the next room. So they were awkward and uneasy with each other. They felt like strangers. When he put his arm on her shoulder, it lay there heavy, and they were silent, listening to the rain falling outside.

Then there was a sound in the hall, the sound of shuffling slippers, and when they looked up quickly, they saw a bit of the mother's dressing gown sweeping past the door. Then the slippers were still. In a little while there was a worried, hesitant shuffling; then they came back again past the door.

"Did you want something, Mother?" Sylvia called.

"No, nothing," the mother said, looking in. She tried to smile, but she was a little ashamed, and she would not look directly at Sylvia. "I couldn't get to sleep," she said.

"Aren't you feeling well?"

"I lie awake, you know. I hear every sound in here. I might just as well be in the room with you, I guess." And then with that half-ashamed droop of her head, she shuffled away again.

"Is she policing us?" Max asked irritably.

"I think she's just not feeling well," Sylvia said.

They both sat stiffly, listening, though she wanted to put her cheek down on Max's shoulder. In a little while they heard the murmur of voices in the bedroom; and Sylvia knew that her father and mother were lying awake worrying about her. Out of their own memories, out of everything that had happened to them, they felt sure they knew what would be happening to her. The murmuring voices rose a little; the sounds were short and sharp as the mother and father wrangled and worried and felt helpless. And Sylvia, trying hard to recover those moments she had thought so beautiful hurrying along the street with Max, knew that it was no use, and that they were gone, and she felt miserable.

"I think I'll get out," Max whispered.

"Please don't go now," she coaxed. "It's the first night we've felt like this. Please stay."

She wanted to soothe the hate and contempt out of him by rubbing her fingers through his hair; yet she only sat beside him stiffly, waiting, while the house grew silent, for warmth and eagerness to come again. It was so silent she thought she could hear the beating of his heart. She was ashamed to whisper. Max kept stirring uneasily, wanting to go.

Then they were startled by the father's voice calling roughly: "Sylvia!"

"What is it?" she said.

"What's keeping you there? Why are you so quiet? What are you doing?"

"Nothing."

"It's getting late," he called.

She knew her father must have tried hard to stop himself calling out like that; yet she felt so humiliated she could not look at Max.

"I'm getting out quick," Max said.

"All right. But it's nothing; he's just worrying," she pleaded.

"They've been lying in bed all the time listening."

"They're very fond of me," she said. "They'd do it, no matter who it was."

But hating the house and her people, he snapped at her: "Why don't they put a padlock on you?"

Then she felt that the feeling that had been so good between them, that she had tried to bring into the house and bring into her own life, could not last here, that his voice would never grow shy and hesitant as he fumbled for a few words here, that this was really what she was accustomed to, and it was not good. She began to cry softly. "Don't be sore, Max," she said.

"I'm not sore at you."

"They felt pretty sure they know how it goes; that's all," she pleaded with him. "They think it'll have to go with me the way it went with them."

"That's pretty plain."

"I don't think either one of them want to see me get married. Nothing ever happened the right way for them. I can remember ever since I was a kid."

"Remember what?"

"They never felt sure of each other. They parted once, and even now when they get mad, they're suspicious of each other and wouldn't trust each other around the block. But that was years ago, really," she said, holding him tight by the arm, and pleading that he understand the life in her home was not loose and unhappy. "They're both very fond of me," she said apologetically. "They've had a tough time all their lives. We've been pretty poor, and—well—they worry about me; that's all."

Her eyes looked so scared that Max was afraid to question her, and they stood together thinking of the mother and father lying awake in the bedroom.

"I guess they feel that way about people, out of what's happened to them, eh?" he said.

"That's it."

"Their life doesn't have to be your life, does it?"

"It certainly doesn't," she said, and she was full of relief, for she knew by his face that the things she had blurted out hadn't disturbed him at all.

"I wrote my people about you," he said. "They want to see you. I sent them a snapshot."

"That was a very bad one; I look terrible in it."

"Can you get your holidays in August, Sylvia?"

"I think so. I'll ask a long time ahead."

"We'll go to the country and see my folks. I swear you'll like them," he said.

That moment at the door was the one fine free moment they had had since coming in, and it did not seem to belong to anything that had happened in the house that night. While they held each other, whispering, "Good-by, good-by," they were sure they would always be gentle and faithful, and their life together would be good. Then they laughed softly, knowing they were sharing the same secret contempt for the wisdom of her people.

Without waiting to hear the sound of his footfalls outside, she rushed resolutely to her mother's bedroom and turned on the light, and called sharply: "Mother."

But her mother and father, who were lying with their heads together on the pillow, did not stir, and Sylvia said savagely: "Wake up—do you hear? I was never so ashamed in my life."

One of her father's thin arms hung loose over the side of the bed, the wrinkled hand drooping from the wrist, and his shoulders were half uncovered. Her mother was breathing irregularly with her mouth open a little, as though her dreams too were troubled. They looked very tired, and Sylvia wavered.

Then her father stirred, and his blue eyes opened and blinked, and he mumbled sleepily:

"Is that you, Sylvia?"

"Yes," she said.

"All right. Turn out the light," he said, and he closed his eyes.

Yet she still stood there, muttering hesitantly to herself: "It's just that I don't want to get to feel the way you do about people."

Then she grew frightened, for the two faces on the pillow now seemed like the faces of two tired people who had worked hard all their lives, and had grown old together; and her own life had been simply a part of theirs, a part of whatever had happened to them. Still watching the two faces, she began to long with all her soul that her own love and her hope would be strong enough to resist the things that had happened to them. "It'll be different with me and Max. It must be different," she muttered.

But as she heard only their irregular breathing, her fright grew. The whole of her life ahead seemed to become uncertain, and her happiness with Max so terribly insecure. ◆

# Roald Dahl

## THE WAY UP TO HEAVEN

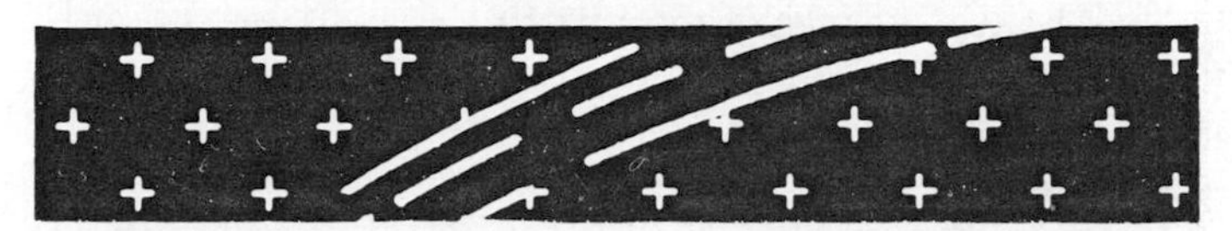

ALL HER LIFE, Mrs. Foster had had an almost pathological fear of missing a train, a plane, a boat, or even a theatre curtain. In other respects, she was not a particularly nervous woman, but the mere thought of being late on occasions like these would throw her into such a state of nerves that she would begin to twitch. It was nothing much—just a tiny vellicating muscle in the corner of the left eye, like a secret wink—but the annoying thing was that it refused to disappear until an hour or so after the train or plane or whatever it was had been safely caught.

It is really extraordinary how in certain people a simple apprehension about a thing like catching a train can grow into a serious obsession. At least half an hour before it was time to leave the house for the station, Mrs. Foster would step out of the elevator all ready to go, with hat and coat and gloves, and then, being quite unable to sit down, she would flutter and fidget about from room to room until her husband, who must have been well aware of her state, finally emerged from his privacy and suggested in a cool dry voice that perhaps they had better get going now, had they not?

Mr. Foster may possibly have had a right to be irritated by this foolishness of his wife's, but he could have had no

Copyright 1954 by Roald Dahl. Reprinted from KISS, KISS, by Roald Dahl, by permission of Alfred A. Knopf, Inc. and Michael Joseph Limited. Originally appeared in *The New Yorker*.

excuse for increasing her misery by keeping her waiting unnecessarily. Mind you, it is by no means certain that this is what he did, yet whenever they were to go somewhere, his timing was so accurate—just a minute or two late, you understand—and his manner so bland that it was hard to believe he wasn't purposely inflicting a nasty private little torture of his own on the unhappy lady. And one thing he must have known—that she would never dare to call out and tell him to hurry. He had disciplined her too well for that. He must also have known that if he was prepared to wait even beyond the last moment of safety, he could drive her nearly into hysterics. On one or two special occasions in the later years of their married life, it seemed almost as though he had *wanted* to miss the train simply in order to intensify the poor woman's suffering.

Assuming (though one cannot be sure) that the husband was guilty, what made his attitude doubly unreasonable was the fact that, with the exception of this one small irrepressible foible, Mrs. Foster was and always had been a good and loving wife. For over thirty years, she had served him loyally and well. There was no doubt about this. Even she, a very modest woman, was aware of it, and although she had for years refused to let herself believe that Mr. Foster would ever consciously torment her, there had been times recently when she had caught herself beginning to wonder.

Mr. Eugene Foster, who was nearly seventy years old, lived with his wife in a large six-story house on East Sixty-second Street, and they had four servants. It was a gloomy place, and few people came to visit them. But on this particular morning in January, the house had come alive and there was a great deal of bustling about. One maid was distributing bundles of dust sheets to every room, while another was draping them over the furniture. The butler was bringing down suitcases and putting them in the hall. The cook kept popping up from the kitchen to have a word with the butler, and Mrs. Foster herself, in an old-fashioned fur coat and with a black hat on the top of her head, was flying from room to room and pretending to supervise these operations. Actually, she was thinking of nothing at all except that she was going to miss her plane if her husband didn't come out of his study soon and get ready.

"What time is it, Walker?" she said to the butler as she passed him.

"It's ten minutes past nine, madam."

"And has the car come?"

"Yes, madam, it's waiting. I'm just going to put the luggage in now."

"It takes an hour to get to Idlewild,"[1] she said. "My plane leaves at eleven. I have to be there half an hour beforehand for the formalities. I shall be late. I just *know* I'm going to be late."

"I think you have plenty of time, madam," the butler said kindly. "I warned Mr. Foster that you must leave at nine-fifteen. There's still another five minutes."

"Yes, Walker, I know, I know. But get the luggage in quickly, will you please?"

She began walking up and down the hall, and whenever the butler came by, she asked him the time. This, she kept telling herself, was the *one* plane she must not miss. It had taken months to persuade her husband to allow her to go. If she missed it, he might easily decide that she should cancel the whole thing. And the trouble was that he insisted on coming to the airport to see her off.

"Dear God," she said aloud, "I'm going to miss it. I know, I know, I *know* I'm going to miss it." The little muscle beside the left eye was twitching madly now. The eyes themselves were very close to tears.

"What time is it, Walker?"

"It's eighteen minutes past, madam."

---

1. *Idlewild*, New York City's major airport, now called John F. Kennedy International Airport.

"Now I really *will* miss it!" she cried. "Oh, I wish he would come!"

This was an important journey for Mrs. Foster. She was going all alone to Paris to visit her daughter, her only child, who was married to a Frenchman. Mrs. Foster didn't care much for the Frenchman, but she was fond of her daughter, and more than that, she had developed a great yearning to set eyes on her three grandchildren. She knew them only from the many photographs that she had received and that she kept putting up all over the house. They were beautiful, these children. She doted on them, and each time a new picture arrived, she would carry it away and sit with it for a long time, staring at it lovingly and searching the small faces for signs of that old satisfying blood likeness that meant so much. And now, lately, she had come more and more to feel that she did not really wish to live out her days in a place where she could not be near these children, and have them visit her, and take them for walks, and buy them presents, and watch them grow. She knew, of course, that it was wrong and in a way disloyal to have thoughts like these while her husband was still alive. She knew also that although he was no longer active in his many enterprises, he would never consent to leave New York and live in Paris. It was a miracle that he had ever agreed to let her fly over there alone for six weeks to visit them. But, oh, how she wished she could live there always, and be close to them!

"Walker, what time is it?"

"Twenty-two minutes past, madam."

As he spoke, a door opened and Mr. Foster came into the hall. He stood for a moment, looking intently at his wife, and she looked back at him—at this diminutive but still quite dapper old man with the huge bearded face that bore such an astonishing resemblance to those old photographs of Andrew Carnegie.[2]

---

2. *Andrew Carnegie* (1835–1919), an American steel manufacturer.

"Well," he said, "I suppose perhaps we'd better get going fairly soon if you want to catch that plane."

"Yes, dear—*yes!* Everything's ready. The car's waiting."

"That's good," he said. With his head over to one side, he was watching her closely. He had a peculiar way of cocking the head and then moving it in a series of small, rapid jerks. Because of this and because he was clasping his hands up high in front of him, near the chest, he was somehow like a squirrel standing there—a quick clever old squirrel from the Park.

"Here's Walker with your coat, dear. Put it on."

"I'll be with you in a moment," he said. "I'm just going to wash my hands."

She waited for him, and the tall butler stood beside her, holding the coat and the hat.

"Walker, will I miss it?"

"No, madam," the butler said. "I think you'll make it all right."

Then Mr. Foster appeared again, and the butler helped him on with his coat. Mrs. Foster hurried outside and got into the hired Cadillac. Her husband came after her, but he walked down the steps of the house slowly, pausing halfway to observe the sky and to sniff the cold morning air.

"It looks a bit foggy," he said as he sat down beside her in the car. "And it's always worse out there at the airport. I shouldn't be surprised if the flight's cancelled already."

"Don't say that, dear—*please.*"

They didn't speak again until the car had crossed over the river to Long Island.

"I arranged everything with the servants," Mr. Foster said. "They're all going off today. I gave them half pay for six weeks and told Walker I'd send him a telegram when we wanted them back."

"Yes," she said. "He told me."

"I'll move into the club tonight. It'll be a nice change staying at the club."

"Yes dear. I'll write to you."

"I'll call in at the house occasionally to see that everything's all right and to pick up the mail."

"But don't you really think Walker should stay there all the time to look after things?" she asked meekly.

"Nonsense. It's quite unnecessary. And anyway, I'd have to pay him full wages."

"Oh yes," she said. "Of course."

"What's more, you never know what people get up to when they're left alone in a house," Mr. Foster announced, and with that he took out a cigar and, after snipping off the end with a silver cutter, lit it with a gold lighter.

She sat still in the car with her hands clasped together tight under the rug.

"Will you write to me?" she asked.

"I'll see," he said. "But I doubt it. You know I don't hold with letter writing unless there's something specific to say."

"Yes, dear, I know. So don't you bother."

They drove on, along Queens Boulevard, and as they approached the flat marshland on which Idlewild is built, the fog began to thicken and the car had to slow down.

"Oh dear!" cried Mrs. Foster. "I'm *sure* I'm going to miss it now! What time is it?"

"Stop fussing," the old man said. "It doesn't matter anyway. It's bound to be cancelled now. They never fly in this sort of weather. I don't know why you bothered to come out."

She couldn't be sure, but it seemed to her that there was suddenly a new note in his voice, and she turned to look at him. It was difficult to observe any change in his expression under all that hair. The mouth was what counted. She wished, as she had so often before, that she could see the mouth clearly. The eyes never showed anything except when he was in a rage.

"Of course," he went on, "if by any chance it *does* go, then I agree with you—you'll be certain to miss it now. Why don't you resign yourself to that?"

She turned away and peered through the window at the fog. It seemed to be getting thicker as they went along, and now she could only just make out the edge of the road and the margin of grassland beyond it. She knew that her husband was still looking at her. She glanced back at him again, and this time she noticed with a kind of horror that he was staring intently at the little place in the corner of her left eye where she could feel the muscle twitching.

"Won't you?" he said.

"Won't I what?"

"Be sure to miss it now if it goes. We can't drive fast in this muck."

He didn't speak to her any more after that. The car crawled on and on. The driver had a yellow lamp directed onto the edge of the road, and this helped him to keep going. Other lights, some white and some yellow, kept coming out of the fog toward them, and there was an especially bright one that followed close behind them all the time.

Suddenly, the driver stopped the car.

"There!" Mr. Foster cried. "We're stuck. I knew it."

"No, sir," the driver said, turning round. "We made it. This is the airport."

Without a word, Mrs. Foster jumped out and hurried through the main entrance into the building. There was a mass of people inside, mostly disconsolate passengers standing around the ticket counters. She pushed her way through and spoke to the clerk.

"Yes," he said. "Your flight is temporarily postponed. But please don't go away. We're expecting this weather to clear any moment."

She went back to her husband who was still sitting in the car and told him the news. "But don't you wait, dear," she said. "There's no sense in that."

"I won't," he answered. "So long as the driver can get me back. Can you get me back, driver?"

"I think so," the man said.

"Is the luggage out?"
"Yes, sir."
"Good-bye, dear," Mrs. Foster said, leaning into the car and giving her husband a small kiss on the coarse grey fur of his cheek.
"Good-bye," he answered. "Have a good trip."
The car drove off, and Mrs. Foster was left alone.
The rest of the day was a sort of nightmare for her. She sat for hour after hour on a bench, as close to the airline counter as possible, and every thirty minutes or so she would get up and ask the clerk if the situation had changed. She always received the same reply—that she must continue to wait, because the fog might blow away at any moment. It wasn't until after six in the evening that the loudspeakers finally announced that the flight had been postponed until eleven o'clock the next morning.
Mrs. Foster didn't quite know what to do when she heard this news. She stayed sitting on her bench for at least another half hour, wondering, in a tired, hazy sort of way, where she might go to spend the night. She hated to leave the airport. She didn't wish to see her husband. She was terrified that in one way or another he would eventually manage to prevent her from getting to France. She would have liked to remain just where she was, sitting on the bench the whole night through. That would be the safest. But she was already exhausted, and it didn't take her long to realize that this was a ridiculous thing for an elderly lady to do. So in the end she went to a phone and called the house.
Her husband, who was on the point of leaving for the club, answered it himself. She told him the news, and asked whether the servants were still there.
"They've all gone," he said.
"In that case, dear, I'll just get myself a room somewhere for the night. And don't you bother yourself about it at all."
"That would be foolish," he said. "You've got a large house here at your disposal. Use it."

"But, dear, it's *empty*."

"Then I'll stay with you myself."

"There's no food in the house. There's nothing."

"Then eat before you come in. Don't be so stupid, woman. Everything you do, you seem to want to make a fuss about it."

"Yes," she said. "I'm sorry. I'll get myself a sandwich here, and then I'll come on in."

Outside the fog had cleared a little, but it was still a long, slow drive in the taxi, and she didn't arrive back at the house on Sixty-second Street until fairly late.

Her husband emerged from his study when he heard her coming in. "Well," he said, standing by the study door, "how was Paris?"

"We leave at eleven in the morning," she answered. "It's definite."

"You mean if the fog clears."

"It's clearing now. There's a wind coming up."

"You look tired," he said. "You must have had an anxious day."

"It wasn't very comfortable. I think I'll go straight to bed."

"I've ordered a car for the morning," he said. "Nine o'clock."

"Oh, thank you, dear. And I certainly hope you're not going to bother to come all the way out again to see me off."

"No," he said slowly. "I don't think I will. But there's no reason why you shouldn't drop me at the club on your way."

She looked at him, and at that moment he seemed to be standing a long way off from her, beyond some borderline. He was suddenly so small and far away that she couldn't be sure what he was doing, or what he was thinking, or even what he was.

"The club is downtown," she said. "It isn't on the way to the airport."

"But you'll have plenty of time, my dear. Don't you want to drop me at the club?"

"Oh, yes—of course."

"That's good. Then I'll see you in the morning at nine."

She went up to her bedroom on the third floor, and she was so exhausted from her day that she fell asleep soon after she lay down.

Next morning, Mrs. Foster was up early, and by eight-thirty she was downstairs and ready to leave.

Shortly after nine, her husband appeared. "Did you make any coffee?" he asked.

"No, dear. I thought you'd get a nice breakfast at the club. The car is here. It's been waiting. I'm all ready to go."

They were standing in the hall—they always seemed to be meeting in the hall nowadays—she with her hat and coat and purse, he in a curiously cut Edwardian jacket with high lapels.

"Your luggage?"

"It's at the airport."

"Ah yes," he said. "Of course. And if you're going to take me to the club first, I suppose we'd better get going fairly soon, hadn't we?"

"Yes!" she cried. "Oh, yes—*please!*"

"I'm just going to get a few cigars. I'll be right with you. You get in the car."

She turned and went out to where the chauffeur was standing, and he opened the car door for her as she approached.

"What time is it?" she asked him.

"About nine-fifteen."

Mr. Foster came out five minutes later, and watching him as he walked slowly down the steps, she noticed that his legs were like goat's legs in those narrow stovepipe trousers that he wore. As on the day before, he paused halfway down to sniff the air and to examine the sky. The weather was still not quite clear, but there was a wisp of sun coming through the mist.

"Perhaps you'll be lucky this time," he said as he settled himself beside her in the car.

"Hurry, please," she said to the chauffeur. "Don't bother about the rug. I'll arrange the rug. Please get going. I'm late."

The man went back to his seat behind the wheel and started the engine.

"*Just* a moment!" Mr. Foster said suddenly. "Hold it a moment, chauffeur, will you?"

"What is it, dear?" She saw him searching the pockets of his overcoat.

"I had a little present I wanted you to take to Ellen," he said. "Now, where on earth is it? I'm sure I had it in my hand as I came down."

"I never saw you carrying anything. What sort of present?"

"A little box wrapped up in white paper. I forgot to give it to you yesterday. I don't want to forget it today."

"A little box!" Mrs. Foster cried. "I never saw any little box!" She began hunting frantically in the back of the car.

Her husband continued searching through the pockets of his coat. Then he unbuttoned the coat and felt around in his jacket. "Confound it," he said, "I must've left it in my bedroom. I won't be a moment."

"Oh, *please!*" she cried. "We haven't got time! *Please* leave it! You can mail it. It's only one of those silly combs anyway. You're always giving her combs."

"And what's wrong with combs, may I ask?" he said, furious that she should have forgotten herself for once.

"Nothing, dear, I'm sure. But . . . "

"Stay here!" he commanded. "I'm going to get it."

"Be quick, dear! Oh, *please* be quick!"

She sat still, waiting and waiting.

"Chauffeur, what time is it?"

The man had a wristwatch, which he consulted. "I make it nearly nine-thirty."

"Can we get to the airport in an hour?"

"Just about."

At this point, Mrs. Foster suddenly spotted a corner of

something white, wedged down in the crack of the seat on the side where her husband had been sitting. She reached over and pulled out a small paper-wrapped box, and at the same time she couldn't help noticing that it was wedged down firm and deep, as though with the help of a pushing hand.

"Here it is!" she cried. "I've found it! Oh dear, and now he'll be up there forever searching for it! Chauffeur, quickly—run in and call him down, will you please?"

The chauffeur, a man with a small rebellious Irish mouth, didn't care very much for any of this, but he climbed out of the car and went up the steps to the front door of the house. Then he turned and came back. "Door's locked," he announced. "You got a key?"

"Yes—wait a minute." She began hunting madly in her purse. The little face was screwed up tight with anxiety, the lips pushed outward like a spout.

"Here it is! No—I'll go myself. It'll be quicker. I know where he'll be."

She hurried out of the car and up the steps to the front door, holding the key in one hand. She slid the key into the keyhole and was about to turn it—and then she stopped. Her head came up, and she stood there absolutely motionless, her whole body arrested right in the middle of all this hurry to turn the key and get into the house, and she waited—five, six, seven, eight, nine, ten seconds, she waited. The way she was standing there, with her head in the air and the body so tense, it seemed as though she were listening for the repetition of some sound that she had heard a moment before from a place far away inside the house.

Yes—quite obviously she was listening. Her whole attitude was a *listening* one. She appeared actually to be moving one of her ears closer and closer to the door. Now it was right up against the door, and for still another few seconds she remained in that position, head up, ear to door, hand on key, about to enter but not entering, trying instead, or so it seemed, to hear and to analyze these sounds that were coming faintly from this place deep within the house.

Then, all at once, she sprang to life again. She withdrew the key from the door and came running back down the steps.

"It's too late!" she cried to the chauffeur. "I can't wait for him, I simply can't. I'll miss the plane. Hurry now, driver, hurry! To the airport!"

The chauffeur, had he been watching her closely, might have noticed that her face had turned absolutely white and that the whole expression had suddenly altered. There was no longer that rather soft and silly look. A peculiar hardness had settled itself upon the features. The little mouth, usually so flabby, was now tight and thin, the eyes were bright, and the voice, when she spoke, carried a new note of authority.

"Hurry, driver, hurry!"

"Isn't your husband travelling with you?" the man asked, astonished.

"Certainly not! I was only going to drop him at the club. It won't matter. He'll understand. He'll get a cab. Don't sit there talking, man. *Get going!* I've got a plane to catch for Paris!"

With Mrs. Foster urging him from the back seat, the man drove fast all the way, and she caught her plane with a few minutes to spare. Soon she was high up over the Atlantic, reclining comfortably in her airplane chair, listening to the hum of the motors, heading for Paris at last. The new mood was still with her. She felt remarkably strong and, in a queer sort of way, wonderful. She was a trifle breathless with it all, but this was more from pure astonishment at what she had done than anything else, and as the plane flew farther and farther away from New York and East Sixty-second Street, a great sense of calmness began to settle upon her. By the time she reached Paris, she was just as strong and cool and calm as she could wish.

She met her grandchildren, and they were even more

beautiful in the flesh than in their photographs. They were like angels, she told herself, so beautiful they were. And every day she took them for walks, and fed them cakes, and bought them presents, and told them charming stories.

Once a week, on Tuesdays, she wrote a letter to her husband—a nice, chatty letter—full of news and gossip, which always ended with the words "Now be sure to take your meals regularly, dear, although this is something I'm afraid you may not be doing when I'm not with you."

When the six weeks were up, everybody was sad that she had to return to America, to her husband. Everybody, that is, except her. Surprisingly, she didn't seem to mind as much as one might have expected, and when she kissed them all good-bye, there was something in her manner and in the things she said that appeared to hint at the possibility of a return in the not too distant future.

However, like the faithful wife she was, she did not overstay her time. Exactly six weeks after she had arrived, she sent a cable to her husband and caught the plane back to New York.

Arriving at Idlewild, Mrs. Foster was interested to observe that there was no car to meet her. It is possible that she might even have been a little amused. But she was extremely calm and did not overtip the porter who helped her into a taxi with her baggage.

New York was colder than Paris, and there were lumps of dirty snow lying in the gutters of the streets. The taxi drew up before the house on Sixty-second Street, and Mrs. Foster persuaded the driver to carry her two large cases to the top of the steps. Then she paid him off and rang the bell. She waited, but there was no answer. Just to make sure, she rang again, and she could hear it tinkling shrilly far away in the pantry, at the back of the house. But still no one came.

So she took out her own key and opened the door herself.

The first thing she saw as she entered was a great pile of mail lying on the floor where it had fallen after being slipped through the letter hole. The place was dark and cold. A dust sheet was still draped over the grandfather clock. In spite of the cold, the atmosphere was peculiarly oppressive, and there was a faint but curious odor in the air that she had never smelled before.

She walked quickly across the hall and disappeared for a moment around the corner to the left, at the back. There was something deliberate and purposeful about this action; she had the air of a woman who is off to investigate a rumor or to confirm a suspicion. And when she returned a few seconds later, there was a little glimmer of satisfaction on her face.

She paused in the center of the hall, as though wondering what to do next. Then, suddenly, she turned and went across into her husband's study. On the desk she found his address book, and after hunting through it for a while she picked up the phone and dialled a number.

"Hello," she said. "Listen—this is Nine East Sixty-second Street . . . Yes, that's right. Could you send someone round as soon as possible, do you think? Yes, it seems to be stuck between thc second and third floors. At least, that's where the indicator's pointing . . . Right away? Oh, that's very kind of you. You see, my legs aren't any too good for walking up a lot of stairs. Thank you so much. Good-bye."

She replaced the receiver and sat there at her husband's desk, patiently waiting for the man who would be coming soon to repair the elevator. ◆

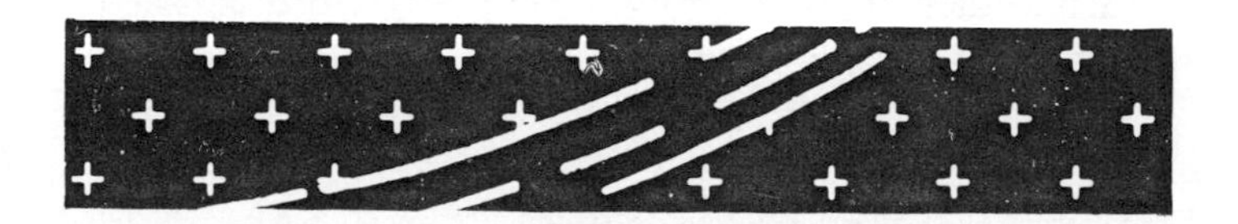

## Rhys Davies

# THE DILEMMA OF CATHERINE FUCHSIAS

PUFFED UP BY HIS SUCCESS as a ship chandler[1] in the port forty miles away, where he had gone from the village of Banog when the new town was rising to its heyday as the commercial capital of Wales, Lewis had retired to the old place heavy with gold and fat. With him was the bitter English wife he had married for her money, and he built the pink-washed villa overlooking Banog's pretty trout stream. And later he had set up a secret association with an unmarried woman of forty who was usually called Catherine Fuchsias, this affair—she receiving him most Sunday evenings after chapel in her outlying cottage—eluding public notice for two years. Until on one of those evenings, Lewis, who for some weeks had been complaining of a "feeling of fullness," expired in her arms on the bed.

In every village there is a Jezebel[2] or the makings of one, though sometimes these descend virtuous to their graves because of lack of opportunity or courage, fear of gossip or ostracism. Lewis the Chandler was Catherine Fuchsias' first real lover, so that for her to lose him like that not only

---

"The Dilemma of Catherine Fuchsias" from BOY WITH A TRUMPET by Rhys Davies. Reprinted by permission of Curtis Brown Ltd.

1. *ship chandler,* a dealer in supplies for ships. 2. *Jezebel,* the evil wife of Ahab, king of Israel. The name is applied to any bold and immoral woman.

dreadfully shocked her but, it will be agreed, placed her in a serious dilemma. She was not a born bad lot and, as a girl, she had been left in the lurch by a sweetheart who had gone prospecting to Australia and never fulfilled his promise to call her there. Thereafter she had kept house for her father, a farm worker, until he had followed her mother into the burial ground surrounding Horeb chapel, which she cleaned for five shillings a week; in addition she had a job three days a week in the little wool factory a mile beyond Banog. It was in Horeb chapel during service that Lewis first studied her and admired her egg-brown face, thick haunches and air of abundant health. Her cottage stood concealed on a bushy slope outside the village, and she had a great liking for fuchsias, which grew wonderfully in the rich lap of the cottage.

When her paramour died on her bed she at first refused to believe it, so pertinacious and active was he and so unlike her idea of a man of sixty-four. Nevertheless, she ran howling downstairs. There she madly poked the fire, flung the night cloth over the canary's cage, ran into the kitchen and swilled a plate or two in a bowl, straightened a mat, and tidied her hair. In the mirror *there* was her face, Miss Catherine Bowen's face, looking no different, a solid unharmed fact with its brown speckles. The autumn dusk beginning to arrive at the window was quiet and natural as the chirp of the bird winging past the pane. For a moment she listened to the grandfather clock ticking away the silence. Then, with a bustling haste, she filled the kettle, lit the oil cooker, took an apple tart out of a zinc safe,[3] looked at it, and put it back. She stood still again. And groaned.

She crept halfway up the stairs and called: "Mr. Lewis . . . Mr. Lewis, here I am! Just put the kettle on. Time's going, boy. Come down straight away . . . Mr. Lewis!" She raised her voice. "Lewis, stir yourself, boy. Come on now!" Only the clock replied. She sat on the stairs and groaned.

---

3. *zinc safe,* a galvanized chest for the preservation of food.

"Lewis," she whimpered, "there's a trick you are playing on me! Don't you come here again. I am offended . . . Yes, offended I am. I'll go for a walk, that's what I'll do. And don't you be here when I'm back." She tramped noisily down the stairs, unlocked the front door, and slammed it behind her.

Bats were flying round the cottage. The sunflowers were hanging their half-asleep heads, and the old deep well among the luxuriant chrysanthemum bushes at the bottom of the garden, on which her eye rested for a dazed but speculative minute, stood in secret blue shadow. But she hurried out of the garden by the side gate where a path led into a coppice of dwarf trees and bushes. "I'll go and pick mushrooms in Banner's fields, that's what I'll do," she assured herself. "Gone he'll be by the time I'm back." But she did not descend the slope to the farm's fields. She scrambled into a ring of bushes and hid herself there on a patch of damp grass. One eye remained open in palpitating awareness; the other was half-closed, as if she was in profound thought.

A bad shock can work wonders with a person's sensibility. Buried talents can be whisked up into activity, a primitive cunning reign again in its shady empire of old instincts. Or such a shock can create—women especially being given to escape into this—a fantasy of bellicose truth, a performance of the imagination that has nothing to do with hypocrisy but is the terrified soul backing away from reality. Catherine sprang up and hurried back to her whitewashed cottage. Already in the long dusky vale and the distant village a few lights shone out. She shot into the cottage and ran upstairs.

"Well, Mr. Lewis," she exclaimed loudly, "better you are after your rest?" She went close to the bed and peered down at the stout dusky figure lying on the patchwork quilt. "Well now, I am not liking the look of you at all," she addressed it, half-scoldingly. "What have you taken your jacket off for? Hot you were? Dear me, quite bad you look. Best for me to fetch your wife and the doctor. But you mustn't lie there with your coat off or a cold you will catch." Volubly tut-tutting, she lit a candle and set about the task. Already, in the hour that had elapsed, he had begun to stiffen somewhat. She perspired and groaned, alternately blenching and going red. He was heavily cumbersome as a big sack of turnips: she was obliged to prop up his back with a small chair wedged against the bedstead. Luckily he had removed only his jacket, but (since of late he had got stouter) this, which was of chapel-black vicuña, fitted tight as the skin of a bladder of lard. Downstairs, the grandfather clock ticked loud and hurried.

Finally, buttoned up complete, he rested tidy, and she staggered back sweating. To lay out her father she had got the assistance of the blacksmith's wife.

For a minute she stood in contemplation of her work, then ran downstairs to fetch up his hat, umbrella, and hymnbook. She dropped the umbrella beside the bed, placed the hat on the bedside table, and laid the hymnbook on the quilt as though it had fallen from his hand. And all the time she uttered clamorous remarks of distress at his condition—"Oh, Mr. Lewis, you didn't ought to have taken a walk, unwell like you are. Climbing! Lucky I saw you leaning over my gate. Dropped dead in the road you might have, and stayed there all night and got bitten by the stoats! You rest quiet now, and I won't be long." At another thought she placed a glass of water by the bedside. Then, giving her own person a quick look-over, she put on a raincoat and a flowered hat, blew out the candle, and hastened from the cottage. It was past nine o'clock and quite dark, and she never rode her bicycle in the dark.

Half an hour later she banged at the costly oaken door of the pink villa, calling excitedly: "Mrs. Lewis, Mrs. Lewis, come to your husband!" Milly Jones, the servant, opened the door and Catherine violently pushed her inside. "Where's Mrs. Lewis? Let me see her quick." But Mrs. Lewis was already standing, stiff as a poker, in the hall.

"Catherine Fuchsias it is!" exclaimed Milly Jones, who was a native of Banog. "Why, what's the matter with you?"

Catherine seemed to totter. "Come to your husband, Mrs. Lewis, crying out for you he is! Oh dear," she groaned, "run all the way I have, fast as a hare." She gulped, sat on a chair, and panted: "Put your hat on quick, Mrs. Lewis, and tell Milly Jones to go to Dr. Watkins."

Mrs. Lewis, who had the English reserve, never attended chapel, and also unlikably minded her own business, stared hard. "My husband has met with an accident?" she asked, precise and cold.

"Wandering outside my gate I found him just now!" cried Catherine. "Fetching water from my well I was, and saw him swaying about and staring at me white as cheese. 'Oh, Mr. Lewis,' I said, 'what is the matter with you, ill you are? Not your way home from chapel is this!' . . . 'Let me rest in your cottage for a minute,' he said to me, 'and give me a glass of water, my heart is jumping like a toad.' . . . So I helped him in and he began to grunt awful, and I said: 'Best to go and lie down on my poor father's bed, Mr. Lewis, and I will run at once and tell Mrs. Lewis to fetch Dr. Watkins.' . . . Bring the doctor to him quick, Mrs. Lewis! Frightened me he has and no one to leave with him, me watering my chrysanthemums and just going to lock up for the night and seeing a man hanging sick over my gate——" She panted and dabbed her face.

Milly Jones was already holding a coat for her mistress, who frowned impatiently as Catherine went on babbling of the fright she had sustained. Never a talkative person, the Englishwoman only said, abrupt: "Take me to your house. . . . Milly, go for the doctor and tell him what you've just heard." And she did not say very much as she stalked along beside Catherine, who still poured out a repeating wealth of words.

Arrived at the dark cottage, Catherine bawled comfortingly on the stairs: "Come now, Mr. Lewis, here we are. Not long I've been, have I?"

"You ought to have left a light for him," remarked Mrs. Lewis on the landing.

"What if he had tumbled and set the bed on fire!" said Catherine indignantly. In the heavily silent room she struck a match and lit the candle. "Oh!" she shrieked.

Mrs. Lewis stood staring through her glasses. And then, in a strangely fallen voice, said: "John! . . . John!" Catherine covered her face with her hands, crying in dramatic woe. "Hush, *woman* . . . hush," said Mrs. Lewis sternly.

Catherine moved her hands from her face and glared. *Woman,* indeed! In her own house! When she had been so kind! But all she said was: "Well, Mrs. Lewis, enough it is to upset anyone with a soft heart when a stranger dies in her house. . . . *Why,"* she began insidiously, "was he wandering in the lanes all by himself in his bad state? Poor man, why is it he didn't go home after chapel? Wandering lost outside my gate like a lonely orphan child!"

Mrs. Lewis, as though she were examining someone applying for a place in her villa kitchen, gave her a long, glimmering look. "Here is the doctor," she said.

"Yes indeed," Catherine exclaimed, "and I am hoping he can take Mr. Lewis away with him in his motor." The glance she directed at the corpse was now charged with hostility. "He is a visitor that has taken advantage of my poor little cottage." And was there a hint of malice in her manner as she swung her hips past Mrs. Lewis, went to the landing, and called down the stairs: "Come up, Dr. Watkins. But behind time you are."

Having verified the death and listened to Catherine's profuse particulars of how she had found him at the gate and strained herself helping him up the stairs, Dr. Watkins, who was of local birth and a cheerful man, said: "Well, well, only this evening it was I saw him singing full strength in chapel, his chest out like a robin's. Pity he never would be a patient of mine. 'You mind that heart of yours, John Lewis,' I told him once, free of charge, 'and don't you smoke, drink, or sing.' Angina he had, sure as a tree got knots."

"He liked to sing at the top of his voice," agreed Mrs. Lewis. She took up the hymnbook from the quilt, turned quickly to Catherine, and demanded: "Did he take this with him to the bed, ill as he was?"

"No!" Catherine's voice rang. With Dr. Watkins present, the familiar local boy, she looked even more powerful. "After I had helped him there and he laid a minute and went a better colour, I said: 'Now, Mr. Lewis, you read a hymn or two while I run off; strength they will give you.' "

"But you put the candle out!" pounced Mrs. Lewis. "It must have been getting quite dark by then."

"There," Catherine pointed a dramatic finger, "is the box of matches, with the glass of water I gave him." She stood aggressive, while Dr. Watkins's ears moved. "Candles can be lit."

"This," proceeded Mrs. Lewis, her eyes gazing around and resting in turn on a petticoat hanging on a peg and the women's articles on the dressing table, "*this* was your father's room?"

"Yes," Catherine said, defiant; "where he died and laid till they took him to Horeb. But when the warm weather comes, in here I move from the back; cooler it is and the view in summer same as on the post cards that the visitors buy, except for the old Trout Bridge. . . . What are you so inquisitive about?" She began to bridle. "Tidy it is here, and no dust. You would like to look under the bed? In the chest?"

Mrs. Lewis, cold of face, turned to the doctor. "Could you say how long my husband has been dead?"

He made show of moving the corpse's eyelids, pinching a cheek, swinging an arm. "A good two hours or more," he said with downright assurance.

"Then," said Mrs. Lewis, "he must have been dead when he walked up those stairs! It takes only half an hour to reach my house from here." She turned stern to Catherine:

"You said you came running to me as soon as you helped him up here to your father's room."

"A law of the land there is!" Catherine's voice rang. "Slander and malice is this, and jealous spite!" She took on renewed power and, like an actress towering and swelling into rage, looked twice her size. "See," she cried to Dr. Watkins, "how it is that kind acts are rewarded, and nipped by a serpent is the hand of charity stretched out to lay the dying stranger on a bed! Better if I had let him fall dead outside my gate like a workhouse tramp and turned my back on him to water my Michaelmas daisies. Forty years I have lived in Banog, girl and woman, and not a stain small as a farthing on my character." With her two hands she pushed up her inflated breasts as though they hurt her. "Take out of my house," she sang in crescendo, "my poor dead visitor that can't rise up and tell the holy truth for me. No husband, father, or brother have I to fight for my name. Take him!"

"Not possible tonight," said Dr. Watkins, bewildered but appreciative of Catherine's tirade. "Late and a Sunday it is, and the undertaker many miles away."

"The lady by there," said Catherine, pointing a quivering finger, "can hire the farm cart of Peter the Watercress, if he can't go in your motor."

"I," said Mrs. Lewis, "have no intention of allowing my husband to remain in this house tonight." The tone in which she pronounced "this house" demolished the abode to an evil shambles.

"Oh, oh," wailed Catherine, beginning again, and moving to the bedside. "John Lewis!" she called to the corpse, "John Lewis, rise up and tell the truth! Swim back across Jordan for a short minute and make dumb the bitter tongue that you married! Miss Catherine Bowen, that took you innocent into her little clean cottage, is calling to you, and——"

Dr. Watkins, who had twice taken up his bag and laid it down again, interfered decisively at last, for he had been called out by Milly Jones just as he was sitting down to some slices of cold duck. "Hush now," he said to both women, a man and stern, "hush now. Show respect for the passed away. . . . A cart and horse you would like hired?" he asked Mrs. Lewis. "I will drive you to Llewellyn's farm and ask them to oblige you."

"And oblige me too!" Catherine had the last word, swinging her hips out of the room.

The corpse, though not much liked owing to its bragging when alive, was of local origin, and Llewellyn the farmer agreed readily enough to disturb his stallion, light candles in the cart lanterns, and collect two village men to help carry the heavy man down Catherine Fuchsias' stairs. Already the village itself had been willingly disturbed out of its Sabbath night quiet, for Milly Jones, after calling at the doctor's, was not going to deprive her own people of the high news that rich Mr. Lewis had mysteriously been taken ill in Catherine's cottage. So when the farm cart stopped to collect the two men, news of the death was half-expected. Everybody was left agog and expectant of the new week being a full one. What had Mr. Lewis been doing wandering round Catherine's cottage up there after chapel? Strange it was. Married men didn't go for walks and airings after chapel.

On Monday morning, before the dew was off her flowers, Catherine's acquaintance, Mrs. Morgans, who lived next door to the Post Office, bustled into the cottage. "Catherine, dear," she exclaimed, peering at her hard. "What is this, a man dying on your bed!"

"My father's bed," corrected Catherine. And at once her body began to swell. "Oh, Jinny Morgans, my place in Heaven I have earned. I have strained myself," she moaned, placing her hands round her lower middle, "helping him up my stairs after I found him whining like an old dog outside my gate. A crick I have got in my side too. So stout he was, and crying to lay down on a bed. I thought he had eaten a toadstool for a mushroom in the dark."

"What was he doing, walking about up here whatever?" Mrs. Morgans breathed.

"Once before I saw him going by when I was in my garden. He stopped to make compliments about my fuchsias—— Oh," she groaned, clasping her stomach, "the strain is cutting me shocking."

"Your fuchsias——" egged on Mrs. Morgans.

"Very big they hung this year. And he said to me, 'When I was a boy I used to come round here to look for tadpoles in the ponds.' Ah!" she groaned again.

"Tadpoles." Mrs. Morgans nodded, still staring fixed and full on her friend, and sitting tense with every pore open. As is well known, women hearken to words but rely more on the secret information obtained by the sense that has no language.

Catherine, recognizing that an ambassador had arrived, made a sudden dive into the middle of the matter, her hands flying away from her stomach and waving threatening. And again she went twice her size and beat her breast. "That jealous Mrs. Lewis," she shouted, "came here and went smelling round the room nasty as a cat. This and that she hinted, with Dr. Watkins there for witness! A law of slander there is," she shot a baleful glance at her visitor, "and let one more word be said against my character and I will go off straight to Vaughan Solicitor and get a letter of warning sent."

"Ha!" said Mrs. Morgans, suddenly relaxing her great intentness. "Ha!" Her tone, like her nod, was obscure of meaning, and on the whole she seemed to be reserving judgment.

Indeed, what real proof was there of unhealthy proceedings having been transacted in Catherine's cottage? Mrs. Morgans went back to the village with her report and that day everybody sat on it in cautious meditation. In Catherine's advantage was the general dislike of proud Mrs. Lewis, but, on the other hand, a Jezebel, for the common good and the protection of men, must not be allowed to flourish unpunished. All day in the Post Office, in the Glyndwr Arms that evening, and in every cottage and farmhouse, the matter was observed from several loquacious angles.

On Wednesday afternoon Mr. Maldwyn Davies, B.A., the minister of Horeb, climbed to the cottage, and was received by his member and chapel cleaner with a vigorous flurry of welcome. Needlessly dusting a chair, scurrying for a cushion, shouting to the canary, that at the minister's entrance began to chirp and swing his perch madly, to be quiet, Catherine fussily settled him before running to put the kettle on. In the kitchen she remembered her condition and returned slow and clasping herself. "Ah," she moaned, "my pain has come back! Suffering chronic I've been, off and on, since Sunday night. So heavy was poor Mr. Lewis to take up my stairs. But what was I to be doing with a member of Horeb whining outside my gate for a bed? Shut my door on him as if he was a scamp or a member of the Church of England?"

"Strange," said Mr. Davies, his concertina neck, that could give forth such sweet music in the pulpit, closing down into his collar, "strange that he climbed up here so far, feeling unwell." He stared at the canary as if the bird held the explanation.

"Delirious and lighted up he was!" she cried. "And no wonder. Did he want to go to his cold home after the sermon and singing in chapel? No! Two times and more I have seen him wandering round here looking full up with thoughts. One time he stopped at my gate and had praises for my dahlias, for I was watering them. 'Oh, Mr. Lewis,' I said to him, 'what are you doing walking up here?' and he said, 'I am thinking over the grand sermon Mr. Davies gave us just now, and I would climb big mountains if mountains there were!' Angry with myself I am now that I didn't ask him in for a cup of tea, so lonely he was looking. 'Miss Bowen,' he said to me, 'when I was a boy I used to come rabbiting up here.' "

"Your dahlias," remarked Mr. Davies, still meditatively gazing at the canary, "are prize ones, and the rabbits a pest."

"Oh," groaned Catherine, placing her hands round her lower middle, "grumbling I am not, but there's a payment I am having for my kindness last Sunday! . . . Hush," she bawled threatening to the canary, "hush, or no more seed today."

Mr. Davies, oddly, seemed unable to say much. Perhaps he, too, was trying to sniff the truth out of the air. But he looked serious. The reputation of two of his flock was in jeopardy, two who had been nourished by his sermons, and it was unfortunate that one of them lay beyond examination.

"Your kettle is boiling over," he reminded her, since in her exalted state she seemed unable to hear such things.

She darted with a shriek into the kitchen, and when she came back with a loaded tray, which she had no difficulty in carrying, she asked: "When are you burying him?"

"Thursday, two o'clock. It is a public funeral. . . . You will go to it?" he asked delicately.

This time she replied sharp and rebuking: "What, indeed, *me?* Me that got to stay at home because of my strain and can only eat custards? Flat on my back in bed I ought to be this minute. . . . Besides," she said, beginning to bridle again, "Mrs. Lewis, the *lady,* is a nasty!" She paused to take a long breath and to hand him a buttered muffin.

"Her people are not our people," he conceded, and pursed his lips.

Fluffing herself up important, and not eating anything herself, Catherine declared: "Soon as I am well I am off to Vaughan Solicitor, to have advice." Black passion began to scald her voice; she pointed a trembling finger ceilingwards. "Up there she stood in the room of my respected father, with Dr. Watkins for witness, and her own poor husband not gone cold and his eyes on us shiny as buttons, and her spiteful tongue made remarks. Hints and sarcastic! Nearly dropped dead I did myself. . . . The hand stretched out in charity was bitten by a viper!" She began to swell still more. "Forty years I have lived in Banog, clean as a whistle, and left an orphan to do battle alone. Swear I would before the King of England and all the judges of the world that Mr. John Lewis was unwell when he went on the bed up there! Swear I would that my inside was strained by his weight. A heathen gypsy would have taken him into her caravan! Comfort I gave him in his last hour. The glass of water by the bed, and a stitch in my side racing to fetch his wife, that came here stringy and black-natured as a bunch of dry old seaweed and made evil remarks for thanks. . . . Oh!" she clasped her breasts as if they would explode, "if justice there is, all the true tongues of Banog must rise against her and drive the bad-speaking stranger away from us over the old bridge. Our honest village is to be made nasty as a sty, is it? No!"

Not for nothing had she sat all these years in close attention to Mr. Davies' famous sermons, which drew persons from remote farms even in winter. And, as she rocked on her thick haunches and her voice passed from the throbbing of harps to the roll of drums, Mr. Davies sat at last in admiration, the rare admiration that one artist gives to another. She spoke with such passion that, when she stopped, her below-the-waist pains came back and, rubbing her hands on the affected parts, she moaned in anguish, rolling up her big moist eyes.

"There now," he said, a compassionate and relenting note in his voice, "there now, take comfort." And as he pronounced: "There must be no scandal in Banog!" she knew her battle was won.

"Put your hands by here," she cried, "and you will feel the aches and cricks jumping from my strain."

But Mr. Davies, a fastidious look hesitating for a moment across his face, accepted her word. He took a slice of apple tart and ate it, nodding in meditation. A woman fighting to preserve the virtue of what, it is said, is the most priceless treasure of her sex, is a woman to be admired and respected. Especially if she is a Banog one. And it was natural that he was unwilling to accept that two of his members could have forgotten themselves so scandalously. Nevertheless, as Catherine coiled herself down from her exalted though aching state and at last sipped a little strong tea, he coughed and remarked: "It is said that nearly every Sunday night for two years or more Mr. Lewis never arrived home from chapel till ten o'clock, and no trace is there of his occupation in these hours. 'A walk,' he used to tell in his home, 'a Sunday-night walk I take to think over the sermon.' That is what the servant Milly Jones has told in Banog, and also that in strong doubt was Mrs. Lewis concerning those walks in winter and summer."

"Then a policeman she ought to have set spying behind him!" said Catherine, blowing on a fresh cup of tea with wonderful assurance. "Oh, a shame it is that the dead man can't rise up and speak. Oh, wicked it is that a dead man not buried yet is turned into a goat." Calm now, and the more impressive for it, she added: "Proofs they must bring out, strict proofs. Let Milly Jones go babbling more, and *two* letters from Vaughan Solicitor I will have sent."

"Come now," said Mr. Davies hastily, "come now, the name of Banog must not be bandied about outside and talked of in market. Come now, the matter must be put away. Wind blows and wind goes." He rose, gave a kind nod to the canary, and left her.

He would speak the decisive word to silence offensive tongues. But, as a protest, she still stayed retreated in the cottage; serve them right in the village that she withheld sight of herself from the inquisitive eyes down there. On Friday morning the milkman told her that Mr. Lewis had had a tidy-sized funeral the previous day. She was relieved to hear he was safely in the earth, which was the home of forgetfulness and which, in due course, turned even the most disagreeable things sweet. After the milkman had gone she mixed herself a cake of festival richness, and so victorious did she feel that she decided to put an end to her haughty exile on Sunday evening and go to chapel as usual; dropping yet another egg in the bowl, she saw herself arriving at the last minute and marching to her pew in the front with head held high in rescued virtue.

On Saturday morning the postman, arriving late at her out-of-the-way cottage, threw a letter inside her door. A quarter of an hour later, agitated of face, she flew from the cottage on her bicycle. The village saw her speeding through without a look from her bent-over head. She shot past the Post Office, Horeb chapel, the inn, the row of cottages where the nobodies lived, past the house of Wmffre, the triple-crowned bard whose lays of local lore deserved to be better known, past the houses of Mr. Davies, B.A., and Mrs. Williams Flannel, who had spoken on the radio about flannel-weaving, past the cottage of Evans the Harpist and Chicago Jenkins, who had been in jail in that place, and, ringing her bell furious, spun in greased haste over the crossroads where, in easier times, they hanged men for sheep stealing. She got out on to the main road without molestation.

"Judging," remarked Mrs. Harpist Evans in the Post Office, "by the way her legs were going on that bike the strain in her inside has repaired quite well."

It was nine miles to the market town where Vaughan the solicitor had his office, which on Saturday closed at midday. She stamped up the stairs, burst into an outer room, and demanded of a frightened youth that Mr. Vaughan attend to her at once. So distraught was she that the youth skedaddled behind a partition of frosted glass, came back, and took her into the privacy where Mr. Vaughan, who was thin as a wasp and had a black hat on his head, hissed: "What are you wanting? Closing time it is." Catherine, heaving and choking, threw down the letter on his desk and, after looking at it, he said, flat: "Well, you can't have it yet. Not till after probate. You go back home and sit quiet for a few weeks." Accustomed to the hysteria of legatees, and indeed of nonlegatees, he turned his back on her and put a bunch of keys in his pocket.

She panted and perspired. And, pushing down her breasts, she drew out her voice, such as it was—"Oh, Mr. Vaughan," she whimpered, "it is not the money I want. Come I have to ask you to let this little business be shut up close as a grave." A poor misused woman in mortal distress, she wiped sweat and tears off her healthy country-red cheeks.

"What are you meaning?" He whisked about impatient, for at twelve five, in the bar-parlour of the Blue Boar, he always met the manager of the bank for conference over people's private business.

She hung her head ashamed-looking as she moaned: "A little favourite of Mr. Lewis I was, me always giving him flowers and vegetables and what-not free of charge. But bad tongues there are in Banog, and they will move quick if news of this money will go about."

"Well," he said, flat again, "too late you are. There is Mrs. Lewis herself knowing about your legacy since Thursday evening, and——"

Catherine burst out: "But *she* will keep quiet for sure! She won't be wanting it talked that her husband went and left me three hundred pounds, no indeed! For *I* can say things that poor Mr. Lewis told me, such a nasty she was! It is of Horeb chapel I am worrying—for you not to tell Mr. Davies our minister or anyone else that I have been left this money." She peeped up at him humble.

"Well," he said, even flatter than before and, as was only proper, not sympathetic, "too late you are again. Same time that I wrote to you I sent a letter to Mr. Davies that the chapel is left money for a new organ and Miss Catherine Bowen the cleaner left a legacy too: the letter is with him this morning. In the codicil dealing with you, Mr. Lewis said it was a legacy because your cleaning wage was so small and you a good worker."

The excuse would have served nice but for that unlucky

death on her bed. She groaned aloud. And as she collapsed on the solicitor's hard chair she cried out in anguish, entreating aid of him in this disaster. Pay him well she would if he preserved her good name, pounds and pounds.

"A miracle," he said, "I cannot perform."

Truth, when it is important, is not mocked for long, even in a solicitor's office. The legatee went down the stairs with the gait of one whipped sore. She cycled back to her cottage as though using only one leg, and, to avoid the village, she took a circuitous way, pushing the cycle up stony paths. At the cottage, after sitting in a trance for a while, she walked whimpering to the well among the chrysanthemums, removed the cover, and sat on the edge in further trance. An hour passed, for her thoughts hung like lead. She went into the dark night of the soul. But she couldn't bring herself to urge her body into the round black hole which pierced the earth so deep.

Then, on the horizon of the dark night, shone a ray of bright light. For the first time since the postman's arrival the solid untrimmed fact struck her that three hundred pounds of good money was hers. She could go to Aberystwyth and set up in partnership with her friend Sally Thomas who, already working there as a cook, wanted to start lodgings for the college students. The legacy, surprising because Mr. Lewis had always been prudent of pocket—and she had approved of this respect for cash, believing, with him, that the best things in life are Free—the legacy would take her into a new life. She rose from the well. And in the cottage, shaking herself finally out of her black dream, she decided that Mr. Lewis had left her the money as a smack to his wife the nasty one.

No one came to see her. She did not go to chapel on the Sunday. Three days later she received a letter from Mr. Davies, B.A., inviting her to call at his house. She knew what it meant. The minister had sat with his deacons in special conclave on her matter, and he was going to tell her that she was to be cast out from membership of Horeb. She wrote declining the invitation and said she was soon to leave Banog to live at the seaside in quiet; she wrote to Sally Thomas at the same time. But she had to go down to the Post Office for stamps.

She entered the shop with, at first, the mien of an heiress. Two women members of Horeb were inside, and Lizzie Postmistress was slicing bacon. Catherine stood waiting at the Post Office counter in the corner. No one greeted her or took notice, but one of the customers slipped out and in a few minutes returned with three more women. All of them turned their backs on Catherine. They talked brisk and loud, while Catherine waited drawn up. Lizzie Postmistress sang: "Fancy Lewis the Chandler leaving money for a new organ for Horeb!"

"The deacons," declared the wife of Peter the Watercress, "ought to say 'No' to it."

"Yes, indeed," nodded the cobbler's wife; "every time it is played members will be reminded."

"Well," said single Jane the Dressmaker, who had a tape measure round her neck, "not the fault of the organ will that be."

They clustered before the bacon-cutting postmistress. On a tin of biscuits, listening complacent, sat a cat. The postmistress stopped slicing, waved her long knife, and cried: "Never would I use such an organ—no, not even with gloves on; and *I* for one won't like singing hymns to it."

"A full members' meeting about *all* the business there ought to be! Deacons are men. Men go walking to look at dahlias and fuchsias——"

"And," dared the cobbler's wife, "drop dead at sight of a prize dahlia."

Catherine rapped on the counter and shouted: "Stamps!"

The postmistress craned her head over the others and exclaimed: "Why now, there's Catherine Fuchsias! . . . Your inside is better from the strain?" she enquired. The others turned and stared in unison.

"Stamps!" said Catherine, who under the united scrutiny suddenly took on a meek demeanour.

"Where for?" asked the postmistress, coming over to the Post Office corner, and snatching up the two letters Catherine had laid on the counter. "Ho, one to Mr. Davies, B.A., and one to Aberystwyth!"

"I am going to live in Aberystwyth," said Catherine grandly.

"Retiring you are on your means?" asked Jane the Dressmaker.

"Plenty of college professors and well-offs in Aberystwyth!" commented Peter's wife.

"Well," frowned the postmistress, as if in doubt about her right to sell stamps to such a person, "I don't know indeed. . . . What you wasting a stamp on this one for," she rapped out, "with Mr. Davies living just up the road? Too much money you've got?"

"Ten shillings," complained unmarried Jane the Dressmaker, "I get for making up a dress, working honest on it for three days or more. Never will *I* retire to Aberystwyth and sit on the front winking at the sea."

"What you going there so quick for?" asked the cobbler's wife, her eyes travelling sharp from Catherine's face to below and resting there suspicious.

"Two stamps." The postmistress flung them down grudgingly at last, and took up Catherine's coin as if she was picking up a rotten mouse by the tail. "Wishing I am you'd buy your stamps somewhere else."

Catherine, after licking and sticking them, seemed to regain strength as she walked to the door, remarking haughtily: "There's wicked jealousy when a person is left money! Jealous you are not in my shoes, now *and* before."

But, rightly, the postmistress had the last word: "A cousin I have in Aberystwyth. Wife of a busy minister that is knowing everybody there. A letter *I* must write to Aberystwyth too." ◆

# E. M. Forster

## THE CELESTIAL OMNIBUS

THE BOY WHO RESIDED at Agathox Lodge, 28, Buckingham Park Road, Surbiton, had often been puzzled by the old signpost that stood almost opposite. He asked his mother about it, and she replied that it was a joke, and not a very nice one, which had been made many years back by some naughty young men, and that the police ought to remove it. For there were two strange things about this signpost: firstly, it pointed up a blank alley, and, secondly it had painted on it, in faded characters, the words, "To Heaven."

"What kind of young men were they?" he asked.

"I think your father told me that one of them wrote verses, and was expelled from the University and came to grief in other ways. Still, it was a long time ago. You must ask your father about it. He will say the same as I do, that it was put up as a joke."

"So it doesn't mean anything at all?"

She sent him upstairs to put on his best things, for the Bonses were coming to tea, and he was to hand the cakestand.

It struck him, as he wrenched on his tightening trousers, that he might do worse than ask Mr. Bons about the signpost. His father, though very kind, always laughed at

---

"The Celestial Omnibus" from THE COLLECTED TALES OF E. M. FORSTER. Published 1947 by Alfred A. Knopf, Inc. Reprinted by permission of Alfred A. Knopf, Inc. and Sidgwick & Jackson Ltd.

him—shrieked with laughter whenever he or any other child asked a question or spoke. But Mr. Bons was serious as well as kind. He had a beautiful house and lent one books; he was a churchwarden, and a candidate for the County Council; he had donated to the Free Library enormously, he presided over the Literary Society, and had Members of Parliament to stop with him—in short, he was probably the wisest person alive.

Yet even Mr. Bons could only say that the signpost was a joke—the joke of a person named Shelley.

"Of course!" cried the mother; "I told you so, dear. That was the name."

"Had you never heard of Shelley?" asked Mr. Bons.

"No," said the boy, and hung his head.

"But is there no Shelley in the house?"

"Why, yes!" exclaimed the lady, in much agitation. "Dear Mr. Bons, we aren't such Philistines[1] as that. Two at the least. One a wedding present, and the other, smaller print, in one of the spare rooms."

"I believe we have seven Shelleys," said Mr. Bons, with a slow smile. Then he brushed the cake crumbs off his stomach, and together with his daughter, rose to go.

The boy, obeying a wink from his mother, saw them all the way to the garden gate, and when they had gone he did not at once return to the house, but gazed for a little up and down Buckingham Park Road.

His parents lived at the right end of it. After No. 39 the quality of the houses dropped very suddenly, and 64 had not even a separate servants' entrance. But at the present moment the whole road looked rather pretty, for the sun had just set in splendor, and the inequalities of rent were drowned in a saffron afterglow. Small birds twittered, and the breadwinners' train shrieked musically down through

---

1. *Philistines.* The Victorian critic Matthew Arnold used the term *Philistines* to describe people lacking culture.

the cutting—that wonderful cutting which has drawn to itself the whole beauty out of Surbiton, and clad itself, like any Alpine valley, with the glory of the fir and the silver birch and the primrose. It was this cutting that had first stirred desires within the boy—desires for something just a little different, he knew not what, desires that would return whenever things were sunlit, as they were this evening, running up and down inside him, up and down, up and down, till he would feel quite unusual all over, and as likely as not would want to cry. This evening he was even sillier, and he slipped across the road towards the signpost and began to run up the blank alley.

The alley runs between high walls—the walls of the gardens of "Ivanhoe" and "Belle Vista"[2] respectively. It smells a little all the way, and is scarcely twenty yards long, including the turn at the end. So not unnaturally the boy soon came to a standstill. "I'd like to kick that Shelley," he exclaimed, and glanced idly at a piece of paper which was pasted on the wall. Rather an odd piece of paper, and he read it carefully before he turned back. This is what he read:

S. and C. R. C. C.
*Alteration in Service*

Owing to lack of patronage the Company are regretfully compelled to suspend the hourly service, and to retain only the

*Sunrise and Sunset Omnibuses,*

which will run as usual. It is to be hoped that the public will patronize an arrangement which is intended for their convenience. As an extra inducement, the Company will, for the first time, now issue

*Return tickets!*

---

2. *"Ivanhoe" and "Belle Vista."* Houses are often given names in England.

*(available one day only), which may be obtained of the driver. Passengers are again reminded that* no tickets are issued at the other end, *and that no complaints in this connection will receive consideration from the Company. Nor will the Company be responsible for any negligence or stupidity on the part of Passengers, nor for Hailstorms, Lightning, Loss of Tickets, nor for any Act of God.*

§ *For the Direction.*

Now he had never seen this notice before, nor could he imagine where the omnibus went to. S. of course was for "Surbiton," and R. C. C. meant "Road Car Company." But what was the meaning of the other C.? "Coombe and Malden," perhaps, or possibly "City." Yet it could not hope to compete with the South-Western. The whole thing, the boy reflected, was run on hopelessly unbusinesslike lines. Why not tickets from the other end? And what an hour to start! Then he realized that unless the notice was a hoax, an omnibus must have been starting just as he was wishing the Bonses good-by. He peered at the ground through the gathering dusk, and there he saw what might or might not be the marks of wheels. Yet nothing had come out of the alley. And he had never seen an omnibus at any time in the Buckingham Park Road. No: it must be a hoax, like the signposts, like the fairy tales, like the dreams upon which he would wake suddenly in the night. And with a sigh he stepped from the alley—right into the arms of his father.

Oh, how his father laughed! "Poor, poor Popsey!" he cried. "Diddums! Diddums! Diddums think he'd walky-palky up to Evvink!" And his mother, also convulsed with laughter, appeared on the steps of Agathox Lodge. "Don't, Bob!" she gasped. "Don't be so naughty! Oh, you'll kill me! Oh, leave the boy alone!"

But all that evening the joke was kept up. The father implored to be taken too. Was it a very tiring walk? Need one wipe one's shoes on the doormat? And the boy went to bed feeling faint and sore, and thankful for only one thing—that he had not said a word about the omnibus. It was a hoax, yet through his dreams it grew more and more real, and the streets of Surbiton, through which he saw it driving, seemed instead to become hoaxes and shadows. And very early in the morning he woke with a cry, for he had had a glimpse of its destination.

He struck a match, and its light fell not only on his watch but also on his calendar, so that he knew it to be half an hour to sunrise. It was pitch dark, for the fog had come down from London in the night, and all Surbiton was wrapped in its embrace. Yet he sprang out and dressed himself, for he was determined to settle once for all which was real, the omnibus or the streets. "I shall be a fool one way or the other," he thought, "until I know." Soon he was shivering in the road under the gas lamp that guarded the entrance to the alley.

To enter the alley itself required some courage. Not only was it horribly dark, but he now realized that it was an impossible terminus for an omnibus. If it had not been for a policeman, whom he heard approaching through the fog, he would never have made the attempt. The next moment he had made the attempt and failed. Nothing. Nothing but a blank alley and a very silly boy gaping at its dirty floor. It *was* a hoax. "I'll tell papa and mamma," he decided. "I deserve it. I deserve that they should know. I am too silly to be alive." And he went back to the gate of Agathox Lodge.

There he remembered that his watch was fast. The sun was not risen; it would not rise for two minutes. "Give the bus every chance," he thought cynically, and returned into the alley.

But the omnibus was there.

It had two horses, whose sides were still smoking from their journey, and its two great lamps shone through the fog against the alley's walls, changing their cobwebs and moss into tissues of fairyland. The driver was huddled up in a cape. He faced the blank wall, and how he had managed to drive in so neatly and so silently was one of the many things that the boy never discovered. Nor could he imagine how ever he would drive out.

"Please," his voice quavered through the foul brown air, "Please, is that an omnibus?"

"Omnibus est,"[3] said the driver, without turning around. There was a moment's silence. The policeman passed, coughing, by the entrance of the alley. The boy crouched in the shadow, for he did not want to be found out. He was pretty sure, too, that it was a Pirate; nothing else, he reasoned, would go from such odd places and at such odd hours.

"About when do you start?" He tried to sound nonchalant.

"At sunrise."

"How far do you go?"

"The whole way."

"And can I have a return ticket which will bring me all the way back?"

"You can."

"Do you know, I half think I'll come." The driver made no answer. The sun must have risen, for he unhitched the brake. And scarcely had the boy jumped in before the omnibus was off.

How? Did it turn? There was no room. Did it go forward? There was a blank wall. Yet it was moving—moving at a stately pace through the fog, which had turned from brown to yellow. The thought of warm bed and warmer breakfast made the boy feel faint. He wished he had not come. His parents would not have approved. He would have gone back to them if the weather had not made it impossible. The solitude was terrible; he was the only passenger. And

---

3. *"Omnibus est."* The driver answers the boy's question with a play on the English and Latin meanings of the word *omnibus.* Using the English meaning, *omnibus est* would mean "It is an omnibus." The original Latin meaning is "It is for everybody."

the omnibus, though well built, was cold and somewhat musty. He drew his coat round him, and in so doing chanced to feel his pocket. It was empty. He had forgotten his purse.

"Stop!" he shouted. "Stop!" And then, being of a polite disposition, he glanced up at the painted notice-board so that he might call the driver by name. "Mr. Browne! stop; O, do please stop!"

Mr. Browne did not stop, but he opened a little window and looked in at the boy. His face was a surprise, so kind it was and modest.

"Mr. Browne, I've left my purse behind. I've not got a penny. I can't pay for the ticket. Will you take my watch, please? I am in the most awful hole."

"Tickets on this line," said the driver, "whether single or return, can be purchased by coinage from no terrene mint. And a chronometer, though it had solaced the vigils of Charlemagne, or measured the slumbers of Laura,[4] can acquire by no mutation the double-cake that charms the fangless Cerberus of Heaven!"[5] So saying, he handed in the necessary ticket, and, while the boy said "Thank you," continued: "Titular pretensions, I know it well, are vanity. Yet they merit no censure when uttered on a laughing lip, and in an homonymous world are in some sort useful, since they do serve to distinguish one Jack from his fellow. Remember me, therefore, as Sir Thomas Browne."[6]

"Are you a *Sir?* Oh, sorry!" He had heard of these

---

4. *Charlemagne . . . Laura.* Charlemagne (742–814), king of the Franks and first of the Holy Roman Emperors, is one of those great national heroes, like Arthur of Britain, who are not dead, but only sleep, awaiting their countries' need. Laura was a French lady celebrated in the sonnets of the great fourteenth-century Italian poet, Petrarch. 5. *double-cake . . . Cerberus of Heaven.* In Roman mythology Cerberus was the three-headed dog that guarded the gates to the abode of the dead. When Aeneas made his trip to this land, according to Virgil's *Aeneid,* Cerberus was lulled to sleep with a cake seasoned with poppies and honey. 6. *Sir Thomas Browne,* a seventeenth-century physician, famous as one of the great English prose stylists.

gentlemen drivers. "It *is* good of you about the ticket. But if you go on at this rate, however does your bus pay?"

"It does not pay. It was not intended to pay. Many are the faults of my equipage; it is compounded too curiously of foreign woods; its cushions tickle erudition rather than promote repose; and my horses are nourished not on the evergreen pastures of the moment, but on the dried bents and clovers of latinity. But that it pays!—that error at all events was never intended and never attained."

"Sorry again," said the boy rather hopelessly. Sir Thomas looked sad, fearing that, even for a moment, he had been the cause of sadness. He invited the boy to come up and sit beside him on the box, and together they journeyed on through the fog, which was now changing from yellow to white. There were no houses by the road; so it must be either Putney Heath or Wimbledon Common.[7]

"Have you been a driver always?"

"I was a physician once."

"But why did you stop? Weren't you good?"

"As a healer of bodies I had scant success, and several score of my patients preceded me. But as a healer of the spirit I have succeeded beyond my hopes and my deserts. For though my draughts were not better nor subtler than those of other men, yet, by reason of the cunning goblets wherein I offered them, the queasy soul was ofttimes tempted to sip and be refreshed."

"The queasy soul," he murmured; "if the sun sets with trees in front of it, and you suddenly come strange all over, is that a queasy soul?"

"Have you felt that?"

"Why yes."

After a pause he told the boy a little, a very little, about the journey's end. But they did not chatter much, for the boy, when he liked a person, would as soon sit silent in his

---

7. *Putney Heath or Wimbledon Common,* large open areas between Surbiton and London.

company as speak, and this, he discovered, was also the mind of Sir Thomas Browne and of many others with whom he was to be acquainted. He heard, however, about the young man Shelley, who was now quite a famous person, with a carriage of his own, and about some of the other drivers who are in the service of the Company. Meanwhile the light grew stronger, though the fog did not disperse. It was now more like mist than fog, and at times would travel quickly across them, as if it was part of a cloud. They had been ascending, too, in a most puzzling way; for over two hours the horses had been pulling against the collar, and even if it were Richmond Hill[8] they ought to have been at the top long ago. Perhaps it was Epsom, or even the North Downs[9]; yet the air seemed keener than that which blows on either. And as to the name of their destination, Sir Thomas Browne was silent.

Crash!

"Thunder, by Jove!" said the boy, "and not so far off either. Listen to the echoes! It's more like mountains."

He thought, not very vividly, of his father and mother. He saw them sitting down to sausages and listening to the storm. He saw his own empty place. Then there would be questions, alarms, theories, jokes, consolations. They would expect him back at lunch. To lunch he would not come, nor to tea, but he would be in for dinner, and so his day's truancy would be over. If he had had his purse he would have bought them presents—not that he should have known what to get them.

Crash!

The peal and the lightning came together. The cloud quivered as if it were alive, and torn streamers of mist rushed past. "Are you afraid?" asked Sir Thomas Browne.

"What is there to be afraid of? Is it much farther?"

The horses of the omnibus stopped just as a ball of fire

---

**8.** *Richmond Hill,* a hill in a large park near London. **9.** *Epsom . . . the North Downs,* tracts of open land several miles south of London.

burst up and exploded with a ringing noise that was deafening but clear, like the noise of a blacksmith's forge. All the cloud was shattered.

"Oh, listen, Sir Thomas Browne! No, I mean look; we shall get a view at last. No, I mean listen; that sounds like a rainbow!"

The noise had died into the faintest murmur, beneath which another murmur grew, spreading stealthily, steadily, in a curve that widened but did not vary. And in widening curves a rainbow[10] was spreading from the horses' feet into the dissolving mists.

"But how beautiful! What colors! Where will it stop? It is more like the rainbows you can tread on. More like dreams."

The color and the sound grew together. The rainbow spanned an enormous gulf. Clouds rushed under it and were pierced by it, and still it grew, reaching forward, conquering the darkness, until it touched something that seemed more solid than a cloud.

The boy stood up. "What is that out there?" he called. "What does it rest on, out at that other end?"

In the morning sunshine a precipice shone forth beyond the gulf. A precipice—or was it a castle? The horses moved. They set their feet upon the rainbow.

"Oh, look!" the boy shouted. "Oh, listen! Those caves—or are they gateways? Oh, look between those cliffs at those ledges. I see people! I see trees!"

"Look also below," whispered Sir Thomas. "Neglect not the diviner Acheron."[11]

The boy looked below, past the flames of the rainbow that licked against their wheels. The gulf also had cleared, and in its depths there flowed an everlasting river. One sunbeam entered and struck a green pool, and as they passed

---

**10.** *a rainbow,* Bifrost, the rainbow bridge that connected Midgard, the world of man and Asgard, the world of the gods, in Norse mythology.
**11.** *Acheron,* one of the rivers of the underworld, in classical mythology.

over he saw three maidens rise to the surface of the pool, singing, and playing with something that glistened like a ring.[12]

"You down in the water——" he called.

They answered, "You up on the bridge——" There was a burst of music. "You up on the bridge, good luck to you. Truth in the depth, truth on the height."

"You down in the water, what are you doing?"

Sir Thomas Browne replied: "They sport in the mancipiary possession of their gold"; and the omnibus arrived.

The boy was in disgrace. He sat locked up in the nursery of Agathox Lodge, learning poetry for a punishment. His father had said, "My boy! I can pardon anything but untruthfulness," and had caned him, saying at each stroke. "There is *no* omnibus, *no* driver, *no* bridge, *no* mountain; you are a *truant,* a *guttersnipe,* a *liar."* His father could be very stern at times. His mother had begged him to say he was sorry. But he could not say that. It was the greatest day of his life, in spite of the caning and the poetry at the end of it.

He had returned punctually at sunset—driven not by Sir Thomas Browne, but by a maiden lady who was full of quiet fun.[13] They had talked of omnibuses and also of barouche landaus. How far away her gentle voice seemed now! Yet it was scarcely three hours since he had left her up the alley.

His mother called through the door. "Dear, you are to come down and to bring your poetry with you."

He came down, and found that Mr. Bons was in the smoking room with his father. It had been a dinner party.

---

12. *three maidens . . . a ring.* The Rhine Maidens were three water nymphs that guarded a treasure, the Rheingold, in Norse mythology. Part of the treasure was an enchanted ring, the Ring of the Nibelung. 13. *a maiden lady . . . quiet fun,* Jane Austen (1775–1817), an English novelist, whose works depict the society of the Regency period.

"Here is the great traveler!" said his father grimly. "Here is the young gentleman who drives in an omnibus over rainbows, while young ladies sing to him." Pleased with his wit, he laughed.

"After all," said Mr. Bons, smiling, "there is something a little like it in Wagner.[14] It is odd how, in quite illiterate minds, you will find glimmers of Artistic Truth. The case interests me. Let me plead for the culprit. We have all romanced in our time, haven't we?"

"Hear how kind Mr. Bons is," said his mother, while his father said, "Very well. Let him say his poem, and that will do. He is going away to my sister on Tuesday, and *she* will cure him of this alley-slopering."[15] (Laughter.) "Say your poem."

The boy began. " 'Standing aloof in giant ignorance.' "

His father laughed again—roared. "One for you, my son! 'Standing aloof in giant ignorance!' I never knew these poets talked sense. Just describes you. Here, Bons, you go in for poetry. Put him through it, will you, while I fetch up the whisky?"

"Yes, give me the Keats," said Mr. Bons. "Let him say his Keats to me."

So for a few moments the wise man and the ignorant boy were left alone in the smoking room.

" 'Standing aloof in giant ignorance, of thee I dream and of the Cyclades, as one who sits ashore and longs perchance to visit——' "[16]

"Quite right. To visit what?"

" 'To visit dolphin coral in deep seas,' " said the boy, and burst into tears.

"Come, come! why do you cry?"

---

14. *Wagner.* Richard Wagner (1813-1883) was a great German operatic composer, deeply interested in German nationalism, Germanic myths, and art. His major work is a vast cycle of four operas called *Der Ring des Nibelungen* ("The Ring of the Nibelung"), which is based on a group of Norse myths. 15. *alley-slopering.* Used in the colloquial sense, the verb *slope* means "to amble." 16. *"Standing aloof . . . to visit——,"* lines from Keats' sonnet "To Homer."

"Because—because all these words that only rhymed before, now that I've come back they're me."

Mr. Bons laid the Keats down. The case was more interesting than he had expected. *"You?"* he exclaimed. "This sonnet, *you?"*

"Yes—and look further on: 'Aye, on the shores of darkness there is light, and precipices show untrodden green.' It *is* so, sir. All these things are true."

"I never doubted it," said Mr. Bons, with closed eyes.

"You—then you believe me? You believe in the omnibus and the driver and the storm and that return ticket I got for nothing and——"

"Tut, tut! No more of your yarns, my boy. I meant that I never doubted the essential truth of poetry. Some day, when you have read more, you will understand what I mean."

"But Mr. Bons, it *is* so. There *is* light upon the shores of darkness. I have seen it coming. Light and a wind."

"Nonsense," said Mr. Bons.

"If I had stopped! They tempted me. They told me to give up my ticket—for you cannot come back if you lose your ticket. They called from the river for it, and indeed I was tempted, for I have never been so happy as among those precipices. But I thought of my mother and father, and that I must fetch them. Yet they will not come, though the road starts opposite our house. It has all happened as the people up there warned me, and Mr. Bons has disbelieved me like every one else. I have been caned. I shall never see that mountain again."

"What's that about me?" said Mr. Bons, sitting up in his chair very suddenly.

"I told them about you, and how clever you were, and how many books you had, and they said, 'Mr. Bons will certainly disbelieve you.' "

"Stuff and nonsense, my young friend. You grow impertinent. I—well—I will settle the matter. Not a word to your father. I will cure you. Tomorrow evening I will myself call here to take you for a walk, and at sunset we will go up this alley opposite and hunt for your omnibus, you silly little boy."

His face grew serious, for the boy was not disconcerted, but leapt about the room singing, "Joy! joy! I told them you would believe me. We will drive together over the rainbow. I told them that you would come." After all, could there be anything in the story! Wagner? Keats? Shelley? Sir Thomas Browne? Certainly the case was interesting.

And on the morrow evening, though it was pouring with rain, Mr. Bons did not omit to call at Agathox Lodge.

The boy was ready, bubbling with excitement, and skipping about in a way that vexed the President of the Literary Society. They took a turn down Buckingham Park Road, and then—having seen that no one was watching them—slipped up the alley. Naturally enough (for the sun was setting) they ran straight against the omnibus.

"Good heavens!" exclaimed Mr. Bons. "Good gracious heavens!"

It was not the omnibus in which the boy had driven first, nor yet that in which he had returned. There were three horses—black, gray, and white, the gray being the finest. The driver, who turned round at the mention of goodness and of heaven, was a sallow man with terrifying jaws and sunken eyes. Mr. Bons, on seeing him, gave a cry as if of recognition, and began to tremble violently.

The boy jumped in.

"Is it possible?" cried Mr. Bons. "Is the impossible possible?"

"Sir; come in, sir. It is such a fine omnibus. Oh, here is his name—Dan some one."

Mr. Bons sprang in too. A blast of wind immediately slammed the omnibus door, and the shock jerked down all the omnibus blinds, which were very weak on their springs.

"Dan . . . show me. Good gracious heavens! we're moving."

"Hooray!" said the boy.

Mr. Bons became flustered. He had not intended to be kidnapped. He could not find the door handle, nor push up the blinds. The omnibus was quite dark, and by the time he had struck a match, night had come on outside also. They were moving rapidly.

"A strange, a memorable adventure," he said, surveying the interior of the omnibus, which was large, roomy, and constructed with extreme regularity, every part exactly answering to every other part. Over the door (the handle of which was outside) was written, *Lasciate ogni baldanza voi che entrate*—at least, that was what was written, but Mr. Bons said that it was Lashy arty something, and that *baldanza* was a mistake for *speranza*.[17] His voice sounded as it he was in church. Meanwhile, the boy called to the cadaverous driver for two return tickets. They were handed in without a word. Mr. Bons covered his face with his hand and again trembled. "Do you know who that is!" he whispered, when the little window had shut upon them. "It is the impossible."

"Well, I don't like him as much as Sir Thomas Browne, though I shouldn't be surprised if he had even more in him."

"More in him?" He stamped irritably. "By accident you have made the greatest discovery of the century, and all you can say is that there is more in this man. Do you remember those vellum books in my library, stamped with red lilies? This—sit still, I bring you stupendous news!—*this is the man who wrote them.*"

The boy sat quite still. "I wonder if we shall see Mrs. Gamp?" he asked, after a civil pause.

"Mrs.——?"

---

17. *Lasciate . . . speranza.* This famous quotation identifies the driver ("Dan some one") as Dante, author of the *Divine Comedy*. In that poem the inscription, using the word *speranza* ("hope"), appears over the gates of Hell and means, "Abandon all hope, you who enter here." Mr. Bons quite naturally misses the point of the substituted word *baldanza,* which means "arrogance."

"Mrs. Gamp and Mrs. Harris.[18] I like Mrs. Harris. I came upon them quite suddenly. Mrs. Gamp's bandboxes have moved over the rainbow so badly. All the bottoms have fallen out, and two of the pippins off her bedstead tumbled into the stream."

"Out there sits the man who wrote my vellum books!" thundered Mr. Bons, "and you talk to me of Dickens and of Mrs. Gamp?"

"I know Mrs. Gamp so well," he apologized. "I could not help being glad to see her. I recognized her voice. She was telling Mrs. Harris about Mrs. Prig."

"Did you spend the whole day in her elevating company?"

"Oh, no. I raced. I met a man who took me out beyond to a race course. You run, and there are dolphins out at sea."

"Indeed. Do you remember the man's name?"

"Achilles. No; he was later. Tom Jones."[19]

Mr. Bons sighed heavily. "Well, my lad, you have made a miserable mess of it. Think of a cultured person with your opportunities! A cultured person would have known all these characters and known what to have said to each. He would not have wasted his time with a Mrs. Gamp or a Tom Jones. The creations of Homer, of Shakespeare, and of Him who drives us now, would alone have contented him. He would not have raced. He would have asked intelligent questions."

"But, Mr. Bons," said the boy humbly, "you will be a cultured person. I told them so."

"True, true, and I beg you not to disgrace me when we arrive. No gossiping. No running. Keep close to my side, and never speak to these Immortals unless they speak to

---

**18.** *Mrs. Gamp and Mrs. Harris,* coarse but delightful low-life characters in Dickens' novel *Martin Chuzzlewit.* **19.** *Achilles . . . Tom Jones.* Achilles was the greatest of the Greek warriors Homer wrote of in the *Iliad.* Tom Jones is the adventurous and likable hero of the novel of that name by Henry Fielding (1707–1754).

you. Yes, and give me the return tickets. You will be losing them."

The boy surrendered the tickets, but felt a little sore. After all, he had found the way to this place. It was hard first to be disbelieved and then to be lectured. Meanwhile, the rain had stopped, and moonlight crept into the omnibus through the cracks in the blinds.

"But how is there to be a rainbow?" cried the boy.

"You distract me," snapped Mr. Bons. "I wish to meditate on beauty. I wish to goodness I was with a reverent and sympathetic person."

The lad bit his lip. He made a hundred good resolutions. He would imitate Mr. Bons all the visit. He would not laugh, or run, or sing, or do any of the vulgar things that must have disgusted his new friends last time. He would be very careful to pronounce their names properly, and to remember who knew whom. Achilles did not know Tom Jones—at least, so Mr. Bons said. The Duchess of Malfi[20] was older than Mrs. Gamp—at least, so Mr. Bons said. He would be self-conscious, reticent, and prim. He would never say he liked any one. Yet, when the blind flew up at a chance touch of his head, all these good resolutions went to the winds, for the omnibus had reached the summit of a moonlit hill, and there was the chasm, and there, across it, stood the old precipices, dreaming, with their feet in the everlasting river. He exclaimed, "The mountain! Listen to the new tune in the water! Look at the campfires in the ravines," and Mr. Bons, after a hasty glance, retorted, "Water? Campfires? Ridiculous rubbish. Hold your tongue. There is nothing at all."

Yet, under his eyes, a rainbow formed, compounded not of sunlight and storm, but of moonlight and the spray of the river. The three horses put their feet upon it. He thought it

---

**20.** *Duchess of Malfi,* the heroine of the tragedy of the same name by John Webster (1580?–1625?).

the finest rainbow he had seen, but did not dare to say so, since Mr. Bons said that nothing was there. He leant out—the window had opened—and sang the tune that rose from the sleeping waters.

"The prelude to *Rheingold?*" said Mr. Bons suddenly. "Who taught you these *leitmotifs?*"[21] He, too, looked out of the window. Then he behaved very oddly. He gave a choking cry, and fell back on the omnibus floor. He writhed and kicked. His face was green.

"Does the bridge make you dizzy?" the boy asked.

"Dizzy!" gasped Mr. Bons. "I want to go back. Tell the driver." But the driver shook his head.

"We are nearly there," said the boy. "They are asleep. Shall I call? They will be so pleased to see you, for I have prepared them."

Mr. Bons moaned. They moved over the lunar rainbow, which ever and ever broke away behind their wheels. How still the night was! Who would be sentry at the Gate?

"I am coming," he shouted, again forgetting the hundred resolutions. "I am returning—I, the boy."

"The boy is returning," cried a voice to other voices, who repeated, "The boy is returning."

"I am bringing Mr. Bons with me."

Silence.

"I should have said Mr. Bons is bringing me with him."

Profound silence.

"Who stands sentry?"

"Achilles."

And on the rocky causeway, close to the springing of the rainbow bridge, he saw a young man who carried a wonderful shield.[22]

---

**21.** *Rheingold . . . leitmotifs. Das Rheingold* is the first opera of Wagner's *Ring* cycle. The *leitmotif,* a device which characterizes Wagner's music, is a passage which is used throughout a selection to represent a single character or idea. **22.** *a wonderful shield.* A long passage in the *Iliad* describes the elaborate sculpturing on Achilles' shield.

"Mr. Bons, it is Achilles, armed."

"I want to go back," said Mr. Bons.

The last fragment of the rainbow melted, the wheels sang upon the living rock, the door of the omnibus burst open. Out leapt the boy—he could not resist—and sprang to meet the warrior, who, stooping suddenly, caught him on his shield.

"Achilles!" he cried, "let me get down, for I am ignorant and vulgar, and I must wait for that Mr. Bons of whom I told you yesterday."

But Achilles raised him aloft. He crouched on the wonderful shield, on heroes and burning cities, on vineyards graven in gold, on every dear passion, every joy, on the entire image of the Mountain that he had discovered, encircled, like it, with an everlasting stream. "No, no," he protested, "I am not worthy. It is Mr. Bons who must be up here."

But Mr. Bons was whimpering, and Achilles trumpeted and cried, "Stand upright upon my shield!"

"Sir, I did not mean to stand! Something made me stand. Sir, why do you delay? Here is only the great Achilles, whom you know."

Mr. Bons screamed, "I see no one. I see nothing. I want to go back." Then he cried to the driver, "Save me! Let me stop in your chariot. I have honored you. I have quoted you. I have bound you in vellum. Take me back to my world."

The driver replied, "I am the means and not the end. I am the food and not the life. Stand by yourself, as that boy has stood. I cannot save you. For poetry is a spirit; and they that would worship it must worship in spirit and in truth."

Mr. Bons—he could not resist—crawled out of the beautiful omnibus. His face appeared, gaping horribly. His hands followed, one gripping the step, the other beating the air. Now his shoulders emerged, his chest, his stomach. With a shriek of "I see London," he fell—fell against the hard, moonlit rock, fell into it as if it were water, fell through it, vanished, and was seen by the boy no more.

"Where have you fallen to, Mr. Bons? Here is a procession arriving to honor you with music and torches. Here come the men and women whose names you know. The mountain is awake, the river is awake, over the race course the sea is awaking those dolphins, and it is all for you. They want you——"

There was the touch of fresh leaves on his forehead. Some one had crowned him.

## ΤΕΛΟΣ[23]

From the *Kingston Gazette, Surbiton Times,* and *Raynes Park Observer.*

The body of Mr. Septimus Bons has been found in a shockingly mutilated condition in the vicinity of the Bermondsey gasworks. The deceased's pockets contained a sovereign purse, a silver cigar case, a bijou pronouncing dictionary, and a couple of omnibus tickets. The unfortunate gentleman had apparently been hurled from a considerable height. Foul play is suspected, and a thorough investigation is pending by the authorities. ◆

---

**23.** *TELOS,* "The End." [*Greek*]

# Mavis Gallant

## APRIL FISH

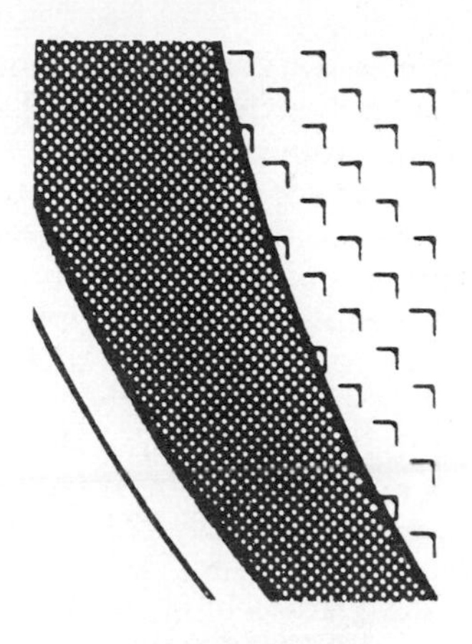

BECAUSE I was born on the first day of April, I was given April as a Christian name. Here in Switzerland they make Avril of it, which sounds more like a sort of medicine than a month of spring. "Take a good dose of Avril," I can imagine Dr. Ehrmann saying, to each of the children. Today was the start of the fifty-first April. I woke up early and sipped my tea, careful not to disturb the dogs sleeping on the foot of the bed on their own Red Cross blanket. I still have nightmares, but the kind of terror has changed. In the hanging dream I am no longer the victim. Someone else is hanged. Last night, in one harrowing dream, one of my own adopted children drowned, there, outside the window, in the Lake of Geneva. I rushed about on the grass, among the swans. I felt dew on my bare feet; the hem of my velvet dressing gown was dark with it. I saw very plainly the children's toys: the miniature tank Igor has always wanted, and something red—a bucket and spade, perhaps. My hair came loose and tumbled down my back. I can still feel

---

"April Fish" by Mavis Gallant from THE NEW YORKER, (February 10, 1968). Copyright © 1968 by The New Yorker Magazine, Inc. Reprinted by permission of the author.

the warmth and the comfort of it. It was auburn, leaf-colored, as it used to be. I think I saved Igor; the memory is hazy. I seemed very competent and sure of my success. As I sat in bed, summing up my progress in life as measured by dreams, trying not to be affected by the sight of the rain streaming in rivulets from the roof (I was not depressed by the rain, but by the thought that I could rely on no one, *no one,* to get up on the roof and clear out the weeds and grass that have taken root and are choking the gutter), the children trooped in. They are home for Easter, all three—Igor, with his small thief's eyes, and Robert, the mulatto, who will not say "*Maman*"[1] in public because it makes him shy, and Ulrich, whose father was a famous jurist and his mother a brilliant, beautiful girl but who will never be anything but dull and Swiss. There they were, at the foot of the bed, all left behind by careless parents, dropped like loose buttons and picked up by a woman they call *Maman.*

"*Bon anniversaire,*"[2] said Igor, looking, already, like any postal clerk in Moscow, and the two others muttered it in a ragged way, like a response in church. They had brought me a present, an April fish, but not made of chocolate. It was the glass fish from Venice everyone buys, about twenty inches long, transparent and green—the green of geranium leaves, with chalky white stripes running from head to tail. These children have lived in my house since infancy, but their taste is part of their skin and hearts and fingernails. The nightmare I ought to be having is a projection into the future, a vision of the girls they will marry and the houses they will have—the glass coffee tables and the Venetian-glass fish on top of the television, unless that space has already been taken up with a lump of polished olive root.

Igor advanced and put the fish down very carefully on the table beside me, and, as he could think of nothing else, began again, "*Bon anniversaire, Maman.*" They had noth-

---

1. *Maman,* mother. [*French*] 2. *Bon anniversaire,* happy birthday. [*French*]

ing to tell me. Their feet scuffled and scratched on the floor—the rug, soiled by the dogs, was away being cleaned.

"What are you going to do today?" I said.

"Play," said Robert, after a silence.

A morning concert struck up on the radio next to me, and I looked for something—an appreciation, a reaction to the music—in their eyes, but they had already begun pushing each other and laughing, and I knew that the music would soon be overlaid by a second chorus, from me, "Don't touch. Don't tease the dogs," all of it negative and as bad for them as for me. I turned down the music and said, "Come and see the birthday present that came in the mail this morning. It is a present from my brother, who is your uncle." I slipped on my reading glasses and spread the precious letter on the counterpane. "It is an original letter written by Dr. Sigmund Freud.[3] He was a famous doctor, and that is his handwriting. Now I shall teach you how to judge from the evidence of letters. The writing paper is ugly and cheap—you all see that, do you?—which means that he was a miser, or poor, or lacked aesthetic feeling, or did not lend importance to worldly matters. The long pointed loops mean a strong sense of spiritual values, and the slope of the lines means a pessimistic nature. The margin widens at the bottom of the page, like the manuscript of Keats, 'Ode to a Nightingale.' You remember that I showed you a photograph of it? Who remembers? Ulrich? Good for Ulrich. It means that Dr. Freud was the same kind of person as Keats. Keats was a poet, but he died. Dr. Freud is also dead. I am sorry to say that the signature denotes conceit. But he was a great man, quite right to be sure of himself."

---

3. *Dr. Sigmund Freud* (1856–1939), Austrian psychiatrist, founder of psychoanalysis. He first used hypnosis to study the unconscious, then later changed to free association, a method of analysis in which the patient is encouraged to say anything that comes into his mind. Freud believed that dreams reveal the unconscious, and considered *The Interpretation of Dreams* (1900) his greatest book.

"What does the letter say?" said Igor, finally.

"It is not a letter written to me. It is an old letter—see the date? It was sent about thirty years before any of you was born. It was written probably to a colleague—look, I am pointing. To another doctor. Perhaps it is an opinion about a patient."

"Can't you read what it says?" said Igor.

I tried to think of a constructive answer, for "I can't read German" was too vague. "Someday you, and Robert, and even Ulrich will read German, and then you will read the letter, and we shall all know what Dr. Freud said to his colleague. I would learn German," I went on, "if I had more time."

As proof of how little time I have, three things took place all at once: my solicitor, who only rings up with bad news, called from Lausanne, Maria-Gabriella came in to remove the breakfast tray, and the dogs woke up and began to bark. Excessive noise seems to affect my vision; I saw the room as blurry and one-dimensional. I waved to Maria-Gabriella—discreetly, for I should never want the children to feel *de trop*[4] or rejected—and she immediately understood and led them away from me. The dogs stopped barking, all but poor blind old Sarah, who went on calling dismally into a dark private room in which she hears a burglar. Meanwhile, Maître Gossart was telling me, from Lausanne, that I was not to have one of the Vietnam children. None of them could be adopted; when their burns have healed, they are all to be returned to Vietnam. That was the condition of their coming. He went on telling it in such a roundabout way that I cut him off with "Then I am not to have one of the burned children?" and as he still rambled I said, "But I want a little girl!" I said, "Look here, I want one of the Vietnam babies and I want a girl." The rain was coming down harder than ever. I said, "Maître, this is a filthy, rotten, bloody country, and if it weren't for

---

4. *de trop,* superfluous. [*French*]

the income tax I'd pack up and leave. Because of the income tax I am not free. I am compelled to live in Switzerland."

Maria-Gabriella found me lying on the pillows with my eyes full of tears. As she reached for the tray, I wanted to say, "Knock that fish off the table before you go, will you?" but it would have shocked her, and puzzled the boys had they come to learn of it. Maria-Gabriella paused, in fact, to admire the fish, and said, "They must have saved their pocket money for weeks." It occurred to me then that *poisson d'avril* means a joke, it means playing an April-fool joke on someone. No, the fish is not a joke. First of all, none of them has that much imagination, the fish was too expensive, and, finally, they wouldn't dare. To tell the truth, I don't really want them. I don't even want the Freud letter. I wanted the little Vietnam girl. Yes, what I really want is a girl with beautiful manners, I have wanted her all my life, but no one will ever give me one. ◆

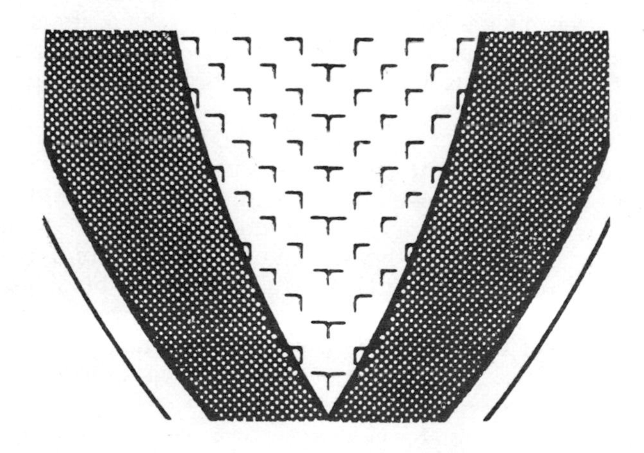

# Nadine Gordimer

# MY FIRST TWO WOMEN

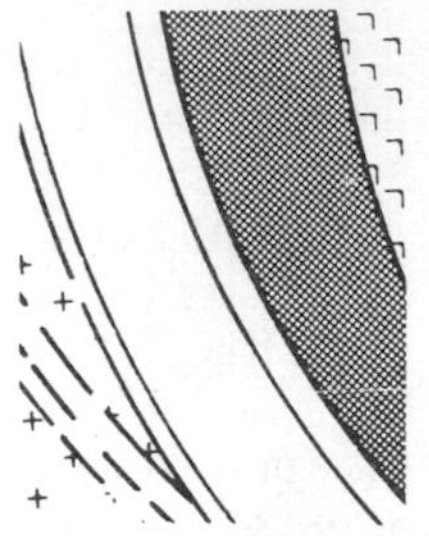

I HAVE BEEN TRYING TO REMEMBER when and where I saw my father's second wife for the first time. I must have seen her frequently, without singling her out or being aware of her, at many of those houses, full of friends, where my father and I were guests in the summer of 1928. My father had many friends, and it seems to me (I was not more than four years old at the time) that, at weekends at least, we were made much of at a whole roster of houses, from tiny shacks, which young couples had "fixed up" for themselves, to semi-mansions, where we had two guest rooms and a bathroom all to ourselves. Whether we sat under a peach tree on painted homemade chairs at a shack, or around the swimming pool on cane chaises longues at a mansion, the atmosphere of those Saturdays and Sundays was the same: the glasses of warm beer, full of sun, into which I sometimes stuck a finger; the light and color of a Johannesburg[1] summer, with thousands of midges, grasshoppers, and other weightless leaping atoms exploding softly over your face as you lay down on the grass; the laughter and voices of the men and women, as comforting and pleasant as the drunken buzz of the great bluebottles that fell sated from rotting fruit, or bees that hung a moment over your head, on their way to and fro between elaborate flowering rockeries. She must have been there

---

"My First Two Women" by Nadine Gordimer from collection of short stories in SIX FEET OF THE COUNTRY published by Simon and Schuster 1956 © by Nadine Gordimer. Reprinted by permission of the Shirley Collier Agency.

1. *Johannesburg,* chief commercial city of the Union of South Africa.

often—one of the women who would help me into the spotted rubber Loch Ness monster that kept me afloat, or bring me a lemonade with a colored straw to drink it through—so often that I ceased to see her.

During the months of that summer, I lived at one or another of those friends' houses, along with the children of the house; sometimes my father stayed there with me, and sometimes he did not. But even if he was not actually living in the same place with me, he was in and out every day, and the whole period has in my mind the blurring change and excitement of a prolonged holiday—children to play with, a series of affectionate women who arranged treats, settled fights, and gave me presents. The whereabouts of my mother were vague to me and not particularly troubling. It seems to me that I believed her not to be back yet from her visit to my grandmother in Kenya,[2] and yet I have the recollection of once speaking to her on the telephone, as if she were in Johannesburg after all. I remember saying, "When are you coming back?" and then not waiting for her to answer but going on, "Guess what I've got in my hand?" (It was a frog, which had just been discovered to have completed its metamorphosis from a tadpole in a tin basin full of stones and water.)

The previous winter, when my mother had gone to Kenya, my father and I had lived in our house, my parents' own house, alone. This was not unusual; I am aware that I had been alone with him, in the care of servants, time and again before that. In fact, any conception I have in my mind of my mother and father and me living together as a family includes her rather as a presence—rooms that were hers, books and trinkets belonging to her, the mute testimony of her grand piano—rather than a flesh-and-blood actuality. Even if she *was* there she did little or nothing of an intimate nature for me; I do not connect her with meal or bath times. So it came about, I suppose, that I scarcely

---

2. *Kenya,* an East African republic, formerly a British colony.

understood, that summer, that there was a real upheaval and change over my head. My father and I were never to go back to that house together. In fact, we both had left it for good; even though I, before the decision was to be made final for me, was to return for a few weeks, it was not to the *same house*, in any but the brick-and-mortar sense, and my position in it and the regrouping of its attention in relation to me were so overwhelmingly changed that they wiped out, in a blaze of self-importance and glory, the dim near babyhood that had gone before.

For, suddenly, in a beautiful autumn month (it must have been March) I found myself back in our house with my mother. The willows around the lawn were fountains spouting pale yellow leaves on the grass that was kept green all year round. I slept with my mother, in her bed. Surely I had not done so before. When I said to her, "Mummy, didn't I used to sleep in the nursery before you went to Kenya?" she said, "Darling, I really have no idea where your Daddy put you to sleep while I was away."

She had short, shiny black hair cut across her forehead in a fringe. She took me to the barber and had my hair, my black hair, cut in a fringe. (Daddy used to brush my hair back, first dipping the brush in water. "Water dries out the hair," she said.) We would get out of her car together, at the houses of friends, and she would walk with me slowly up the path toward them, hand in hand. We looked exactly alike, they all said, exactly alike; it was incredible that a small boy could look so much the image of his mother.

My mother would put me up on the long stool beside her while she played the piano; I had never been so close to a piano while it was being played, and sometimes the loud parts of the music swelled through my head frighteningly, like the feeling once when I slipped through my Loch Ness monster and went under in a swimming pool. Then I got used to the sensation and found it exciting, and I would say to her, "Play loudly, Mummy. Make it boom." Sometimes she would stop playing suddenly and whirl around and hold me tight, looking out over my head at the guests who had been listening. I would hear the last reverberation die away in the great rosewood shape behind us while silence held in the room.

My mother walked up and down a room when she talked, and she talked a great deal, to people who seemed to have no chance to answer her, but were there to listen. Once, in the bathroom, I threw a wet toy and it hit my African nanny on the mouth, and when she smacked my behind and I yelled, my mother rushed in and raged at her, yelling as loudly as I did. My mother was beautiful when she was angry, for she was one of those women who cry with anger, and her eyes glistened and her natural pallor was stained bright with rising blood.

She took me to a circus. She took me to a native mine-workers' "war" dance. She came home from town with a pile of educational toys and sat over me, watching, while I hesitated, caught her long, black, urging eye, brilliant as the eye of an animal that can see in the dark, and then, with a kind of hypnotized instinct born of the desire to please, fitted the right shape on the right peg.

There were still a few leaves, like droplets not yet shaken off, on the twigs of the willows when my clothes and toys were packed up again and my father came to fetch me away.

This time I went to the sea, with the family of three little boys and their mother, with whom I had stayed before. I had a wonderful time, and when I came back, it was to a new house that I had never seen. In it were my father and his second wife.

I was not surprised to see this woman, and, as I have said, she was not a stranger to me. I liked her, and, made gregarious by the life of the past year, asked, "How much days can Deb stay with us?"

"For always," said my father.

"Doesn't she ever have to go home?"

"This is her home, and yours, and Daddy's."

"Why?"

"Because she is married to me now, Nick. She is my wife, and husbands and wives love each other and live together in the same house."

There was a pause, and when I spoke again, what I said must have been very different from what they expected. They did not know that while I was on holiday at the sea I had been taken, one rainy afternoon, along with the older children, to the cinema. There I had seen, in all the rose and crystalline blur of Technicolor, a man and woman dance out beneath the chandeliers of a ballroom. When I had asked what they were doing, I was told that this was a wedding—the man and the woman had just been married.

"Do you mean like this?" I asked my father and my stepmother, taking my father's hand, bending my knees, and shaping out my arms in a jiglike posture. I hopped around solemnly, dragging him with me.

"Dancing?" guessed my father, mystified and affectionate, appealing to his wife.

"Oh, that's wonderful!" she cried in sudden delight. "Bless his formal heart! A real wedding!"

There followed a confusion of hugging, all around. I was aware only that in some way I had pleased them.

I was now nearly five years old and due to begin going to school. My stepmother took me to town with her, and together we bought the supplies for my birthday party, and my school uniform, and a satchel with a fancy lock—soon to be stained as greasy as an old fish-and-chip wrapping with the print of successive school lunches—and the elaborate equipment of pencil sharpeners, erasers, and rulers indispensable to the child who has not yet learned to write. Deb understood what a birthday party for a five-year-old boy should be like. She had ideas of her own, and could sway a wavering torment of indecision between candleholders in the guise of soldiers or elephants, imparting to the waverer a comforting sense of the rightness of the final choice, but she also knew when to efface her own preferences entirely and let me enjoy my own choice for my own unexplained reasons. In fact, she was so good at the calm management of the practical details of my small life that I suppose I quickly assumed this stability as my right, and took it altogether for granted, as children, in their fierce unconscious instinct for personal salvation, take all those rights which, if withheld from them, they cannot consciously remark, but whose lack they exhibit and revenge with equal unconscious ferocity. Of course Deb bought neat and comfortable clothes for me, found the books I would best like to hear her read from, took me with her on visits that would be interesting to me, but left me at home to play when she was going where there would be nothing to amuse me; she always had, hadn't she, right from the first day?

The children at school wanted to know why I called my mother "Deb." When I said that she was not my mother, they insisted that she must be. "Are you my mother now, Deb?" I asked her.

"No," she said. "You know that you have your own mother."

"They say you must be, because you live with Daddy and me."

"I'm your second mother," she said, looking to see if that would do.

"Like my godmother?"

"That's right."

I dashed off to play; it was perfectly satisfactory.

There came a stage when school, the preparation for which had been so enjoyable, palled. I suppose there must have been some incident there, some small failure which embarrassed or shamed me. I do not remember. But I know that, suddenly, I didn't want to go to school. Deb was gentle but insistent. I remember my own long, sullen silence one day, after a wrangle of "Why's" from me and firm explanations from her. At last I said, "When I'm at my mother's I stay home all the time."

My stepmother was squatting on her heels in front of a low cupboard, and her eyes opened up toward me like the eyes of those sleeping dolls which girl children alternately lower and raise by inclining the doll's body, but her voice was the same as usual. "If you lived with your mother now, you would go to school just as you do here," she said.

I stood right in front of her. She looked up at me again, and I said, "No, I wouldn't." I waited. Then I said, "She lets me do what I like." I waited again. "I can even play her piano. She's got a big piano. As big as this room."

My stepmother went on slowly putting back into the cupboard the gramophone records she had been sorting and cleaning. Standing over her, I could see the top of her head, an unfamiliar aspect of a grownup. It was then, I think, that I began to see her for the first time, not as one of the succession of pretty ladies who petted and cared for me, but as Deb, as someone connected in wordless depths with my father and me, as my father and I and, yes, my mother were connected. Someone who had entered, irrevocably, the atavistic tension of that cunning battle for love and supremacy that exists between children and parents sometimes even beyond the grave, when one protagonist is dead and mourned, and lives on in the fierce dissatisfaction of the other's memory.

She was a fair woman, this Deb, this woman beloved of my father; on all faces there is some feature, some plane that catches the light in characteristic prominence of that face, and on her face, at that moment and always, it was her long golden eyebrows, shining. They were bleached from much swimming, but her dull, curly hair, always protected from sun and water by a cap, hung colorless and nowhere smooth enough to shine. The face was broad and brown across strong cheekbones, and she had a big, orange-painted mouth, the beautiful underlip of which supported the upper as calmly as a carved pediment. Her eyes, moving from record to cupboard, lowered under my presence, were green or blue, depending upon what color she wore. She was the sort of fair woman who would never be called a blonde.

Deb. I knew what it smelled like in that pink freckled neck. I knew the stiff and ugly ears that she kept hidden under that hair, and that sometimes, when she was hot and lifted her hair off her neck a moment for coolness, were suddenly discovered.

I shall never forget the feeling I had as I stood there over her. If I search my adult experience as a man to approximate it, I can only say that now it seems to me that physically it was rather like the effect of the first drink you take after a long wet day of some strenuous exercise—rowing or hunting. It was a feeling of power that came like an inflow of physical strength. I was only five years old but power is something of which I am convinced there is no innocence this side of the womb, and I knew what it was, all right; I understood, without a name for it, what I had. And with it came all the weapons—that bright, clinical set that I didn't need to have explained to me, as my father had had to explain to me the uses of the set of carpenter's tools I had been given for my birthday. My hand would go out unfalteringly for these drills and probes, and the unremembered pain of where they had been used on me would guide me to their application.

"Deb," I said, "why didn't Daddy marry my mother?"

"He did," she said. "Once he was married to her. But they were not happy with each other. Not like Daddy and me—and you. Not happy together like us." She did not ask me if I remembered this, but her voice suggested the question, in spite of her.

Daddy. My mother. My mother was simply a word I was using at that moment. I could not see her in my head. She was a mouth moving, singing; for a second she sat at the piano, smiled at me, one of her swift, startling smiles that was like someone jumping out of concealment and saying "Boo!" Inside me, it gave me a fright. If my dog had been there, I would have pulled back his ears, hard, to hear him yelp. There was Deb, squatting in front of me. I said, "My mother's got a piano as big as this house. I want to go and stay with her."

Deb got up from the floor. "Soon," she said. "You'll go on a visit soon, I'm sure. Let's see if tea's ready." We did not take each other's hand, but walked out onto the porch side by side, with a space between us.

It was after that day that I began to be conscious of the relationship between my father and Deb. This was not the way he and those others—the pretty, helpful friends who were the mothers of my friends—had behaved toward each other. I watched with unbiased interest as I would have watched a bird bringing his mate tidbits where she balanced on our paling fence, when my father ate an apple bite-and-bite-about with this woman, or, passing her chair at breakfast, after he had kissed me good-by in the morning, paused to press his cheek silently, and with closed eyes, against hers. Sometimes, in the evenings, both she and I sat on his lap at once.

There were no images in my memory to which to match these. They were married, Deb and my father. This behavior was marriage. Deb herself had told me that marriage once had existed between my father and my mother. One day I came home from a visit to my mother and remarked, conversationally, in the bedroom Deb and my father shared, "My mother's got a bed just like yours, Deb, and that's where Daddy and she used to sleep when he lived there, didn't you, Daddy?"

It was Sunday, and my father still lay in bed, reading the paper, though Deb's place was empty and she was gathering her clothes together before she went off to the bathroom. He said, "No, son. Don't you remember? Mine was the room with the little balcony."

"Oh, yes," I said. "Of course, I know." All at once I remembered the smell of that rather dark, high room, a smell of shirts fresh from the iron, of the two leather golf bags in the corner, and some chemical with which the carpet had been cleaned. All this—the smell of my father—had disappeared under the warmer, relaxing, and polleny scents of the room he now shared with a woman, where peach-colored dust from her powder settled along his hairbrushes, and the stockings she peeled off retained the limp, collapsed semblance of her legs, like the newly shed skin of a snake I had come upon in the bush when I was on holiday at the sea.

I think there must have been something strongly attractive to me in the ease of this feminine intimacy to which my father and I found ourselves admitted with such naturalness. Yet because it was unfamiliar, the very seductiveness of its comfort seemed, against the confusion of my short life, a kind of disloyalty, to which I was party and of which I was guilty. Disloyalty—to what? Guilty—of what?

I was too young for motives; I could only let them bubble up, manifest in queer little words and actions. I know that that Sunday morning I said stoutly, as if I were explaining some special system of living, "There we each had our *own* rooms. Everybody slept in their own room."

Before the end of the first year of the marriage that power that had come to me like a set of magical weapons, the day when my stepmother knelt before me at the record cupboard, became absolute. It crushed upon my little-boy's head the vainglory and triumph of the tyrant, crown or thorn. I was to wear it as my own for the rest of my childhood.

I was cuddling Deb, secure in her arms one day, when I said, out of some gentle honey of warmth that I felt peacefully within me, "I'm going to call you Mummy because I love you best." I am sure that she knew that the statement was not quite so stunning and meaningful as it sounds now, out of the context of childhood. Quite often, she had heard me say of an animal or a new friend, "You know whom I love. I love only Eddie." (Or "Sam," or "Chris.") Sometimes the vehement preference was expressed not out of real feeling for the friend or animal in question, but out of pique toward some other child or animal. At other times it was merely an unreasonable welling up of well-being that had to find an object. But I had never before said this particular thing to her. She shook back her hair fumblingly and held her face away from mine to look at me; she was awkward with joy. I looked up into the stare of her eyes—grown-up eyes that fell before mine—and in me, like milk soured by a flash of lightning, the sweet secretion of affection became insipid in the fearful, amazed thrill of victim turned victor.

That was our story, really, for many years. My father and Deb were deeply in love and theirs was a serene marriage. The three of us lived together in amity; it was a place of warmth for a child to grow in. I visited my mother at regular, if widely spaced, intervals. I went to her for short periods at Christmas, birthdays, and during holidays. Thus along with her, with that elegant black head and those hard wrists volatile with all the wonderful bracelets she had picked up all over the world, went excitement and occasion, treats and parties, people who exclaimed over me, and the abolishment of that guillotine of joys, bedtime. Sometimes the tide of grown-up activities would pass on over my head and leave me stranded and abandoned on a corner of somebody's sofa, rubbing my eyes against the glare of forgotten lights. It did not matter; the next day, or the day after that, I was sure to be delivered back to Deb and my father and the comfort of my child's pace.

Thus it was, too, that along with home and Deb and my father went everyday life, the greater part of life, with time for boredom, for transgressions and punishments. When I visited my mother for a weekend or a day, I was on my best behavior, befitting a treat or an occasion; I was never with her long enough to need chastisement. So when, at home, I was naughty and my father or Deb had to punish me, I would inflame myself against them with the firm belief that my mother would never punish me. At these times of resentment and injury, I would see her clearly and positively, flaming in the light of a Christmas tree or the fiery ring of candles on a birthday cake, my champion against a world that would not bend entirely to my own will. In the same way, for the first few days after my return from a visit to her, everything about the way she lived and the things about her were lit up by the occasion with which my visit had coincided; her flat (when I was seven or eight she moved into a luxurious penthouse in a block overlooking a country club) was like the glowing cardboard interior of the king's castle, carried away in my mind from a pantomime matinee. "There's a swimming pool right on top of the building, on the roof garden," I would tell Deb. "I swim there every morning. Once I swam at night. My mother lets me. The lift doesn't go up to the top—you have to walk the last flight of stairs from the twelfth floor." "My mother's got a car with an overhead drive. Do you know what that is, Deb? It means you don't have to change the gears with your hands." "I wish we had a swimming pool here. I don't like this old house without even a swimming pool."

Deb always answered me quietly and evenly. Never, even when I was very young, did she try to point out rival attractions at home. But in time, when I grew older and was perhaps eleven or twelve, I struggled against something that went more than quiet—went dead—in her during these one-sided conversations. I felt not that she was not listening, but that she was listless, without interest in what I said. And then I did not know at whom the resentment I suddenly felt was directed, whether at my mother—that glossy-haired kingfisher flashing in and out of my life—for having a roof-garden swimming pool and a car without gears, or at Deb, for her lack of attention and negative reaction to my relation of these wonders. This reaction of hers was all the more irking, and in some vague, apprehensive way dismaying, when one remembered the way she watched and listened to me sometimes, with that look in her eyes that wanted something from me, wondered, hesitated, hopeful—that look I had known how to conjure up ever since the first day when I suggested I would call her my mother, and that, in perverse, irresistible use of the same power, I had also known how never to allow to come to articulacy, to emotional fulfillment, between us. The business of my calling her mother, for instance; it had come up several times again, while I was small. But she, in the silence that followed, had never managed anything more than, once, an almost unintelligibly murmured "If you like." And I, once the impulsive, casually pronounced sentence had exploded and left its peculiar after-silence, had dropped my avowal as I left a toy, here or there, for someone else to pick up in house or garden. I never did call her mother; in time, I think I should have been surprised to hear that there had ever been any question that she should be anything else but "Deb."

I was strongly attached to her, and when, at twelve or thirteen, I entered adolescence and boarding school at the same time, there was in fact a calm friendship between us, unusual between a woman and a boy walking the knife edge dividing small-boy scorn of the feminine from awakening sex interest. I suppose, if she had been truly in the position of a mother, this relationship would not have been possible. Her position must have been curiously like that of the woman who, failing to secure as a lover the man with whom she has fallen in love, is offered instead his respect and his confidences.

I was fifteen when I asked the question that had taken a thousand different forms—doubts, anxieties, and revenges—all through my life but had never formulated itself directly. The truth was, I had never known what that question *was*—only felt it, in all my blood and bones, fumbled toward it under the kisses of people who loved me, asked it with my seeking of my father's hands, the warmth of Deb's lap, the approval of my form master's eye, the smiles of my friends. Now it came to me matter-of-factly, in words.

I was home from school for the weekend, and there had been guests at lunch. They had discussed the divorce of a common friend and the wrangle over the custody of the children of the marriage. One of the guests was a lawyer, and he had gone into the legal niceties in some detail. After the guests had gone, my father went off for his nap and Deb and I dragged our favorite canvas chairs out onto the lawn. As I settled mine at a comfortable angle, I asked her, curiously, "Deb, how was it that my mother didn't get me? The custody of me, I mean."

She thought for a moment, and I thought she must be trying how best to present some legal technicality in a way that both she and I would understand.

"I mean, their divorce was an arranged thing, wasn't it—one of those things arranged to look like desertion that Derrick spoke about? Why didn't my mother get me?" The lawyer had explained that where parents contested the custody, unless there was some strong factor to suggest that the mother was unsuitable to rear a child, a young child was usually awarded to her care.

Then quite suddenly Deb spoke. Her face was red and she looked strange, and she spoke so fast that what she said was almost blurted. "She gave you up."

Her face and tone so astonished me that the impact of what she had said missed its mark. I stared at her, questioning.

She met my gaze stiffly, with a kind of jerky bravado, intense, looking through me.

"How do you mean?"

"Voluntarily. She gave you over to your father."

The pressure in her face died slowly down; her hands moved, as if released, on the chair arms. "I should never have told you," she said flatly. "I'd promised myself I never should."

"You mean she didn't want me?"

"We don't know what her reasons were, Nick. We can't know them."

"Didn't try to get me?"

There was a long silence. "We made up our minds. We decided it was best. We decided we would try and make your relationship with her as normal as possible. Never say anything against her. I promised myself I wouldn't try—for myself. I often wanted to tell you—oh, lots of things. I wanted to punish you for what I withheld for your sake. I wanted to hurt you; I suppose I forgot you were a child. . . . Well, what does it matter anyway? It's all worked itself out, long ago. Only I shouldn't have told you now. It's pointless." She smiled at me, as at a friend who can be counted on to understand a confession. "It didn't even give me any pleasure."

My stepmother talked about this whole situation in which we had all lived as if it were something remembered from the past, instead of a living situation out of the continuity of which I was then, at that moment, beginning my life as a man. All worked itself out, long ago. Perhaps it had. Yes, she was right. All worked itself out, without me. Above and about me, over my head, saving me the risk and the opportunity of my own volition.

My mother? That black-haired, handsome woman become rather fleshy, who, I discovered while I sat, an awkward visitor among her admiring friends (I had inherited her love of music), sang off-key.

But it was not toward her that I felt anger, regret, and a terrible, mournful anguish of loss, which brought up from somewhere in my tall, coarse, half-man's, half-child's body what I was alarmed to recognize as the racking turmoil that precedes tears.

"We're really good friends, aren't we?" said my stepmother lovingly, with quiet conviction.

It was true: that was what we were—all we were.

I have never forgiven her for it. ◆

# James Joyce

## COUNTERPARTS

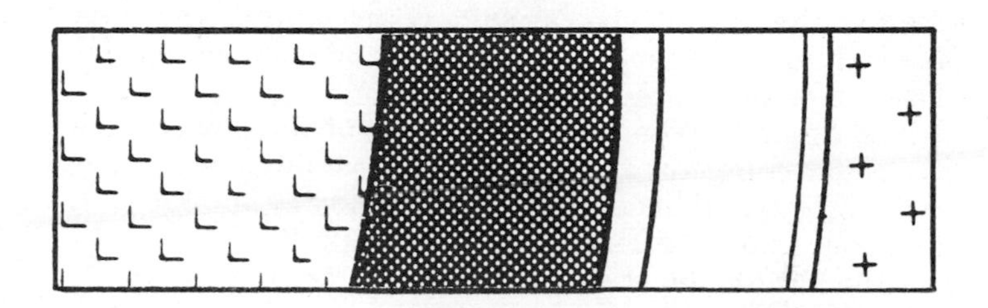

THE BELL RANG FURIOUSLY and, when Miss Parker went to the tube, a furious voice called out in a piercing North of Ireland accent:

"Send Farrington here!"

Miss Parker returned to her machine, saying to a man who was writing at a desk:

"Mr. Alleyne wants you upstairs."

The man muttered "*Blast* him!" under his breath and pushed back his chair to stand up. When he stood up he was tall and of great bulk. He had a hanging face, dark wine-coloured, with fair eyebrows and moustache: his eyes bulged forward slightly and the whites of them were dirty. He lifted up the counter and, passing by the clients, went out of the office with a heavy step.

He went heavily upstairs until he came to the second landing, where a door bore a brass plate with the inscrip-

---

"Counterparts" by James Joyce from THE PORTABLE JAMES JOYCE. Copyright 1946, 1947 by The Viking Press, Inc. All rights reserved. Reprinted by permission of The Viking Press, Inc., Jonathan Cape Ltd. and the executors of the James Joyce Estate.

tion *Mr. Alleyne.* Here he halted, puffing with labour and vexation, and knocked. The shrill voice cried:

"Come in!"

The man entered Mr. Alleyne's room. Simultaneously Mr. Alleyne, a little man wearing gold-rimmed glasses on a clean-shaven face, shot his head up over a pile of documents. The head itself was so pink and hairless it seemed like a large egg reposing on the papers. Mr. Alleyne did not lose a moment:

"Farrington? What is the meaning of this? Why have I always to complain of you? May I ask you why you haven't made a copy of that contract between Bodley and Kirwan? I told you it must be ready by four o'clock."

"But Mr. Shelley said, sir——"

"*Mr. Shelley said, sir.* . . . Kindly attend to what I say and not to what *Mr. Shelley says, sir.* You have always some excuse or another for shirking work. Let me tell you that if the contract is not copied before this evening I'll lay the matter before Mr. Crosbie. . . . Do you hear me now?"

"Yes, sir."

"Do you hear me now? . . . Ay and another little matter! I might as well be talking to the wall as talking to you. Understand once for all that you get a half an hour for your lunch and not an hour and a half. How many courses do you want, I'd like to know. . . . Do you mind me now?"

"Yes, sir."

Mr. Alleyne bent his head again upon his pile of papers. The man stared fixedly at the polished skull which directed the affairs of Crosbie & Alleyne, gauging its fragility. A spasm of rage gripped his throat for a few moments and then passed, leaving after it a sharp sensation of thirst. The man recognised the sensation and felt that he must have a good night's drinking. The middle of the month was passed and, if he could get the copy done in time, Mr. Alleyne might give him an order on the cashier. He stood still, gazing fixedly at the head upon the pile of papers. Suddenly Mr. Alleyne began to upset all the papers, searching for something. Then, as if he had been unaware of the man's presence till that moment, he shot up his head again, saying:

"Eh? Are you going to stand there all day? Upon my word, Farrington, you take things easy!"

"I was waiting to see . . . "

"Very good, you needn't wait to see. Go downstairs and do your work."

The man walked heavily towards the door and, as he went out of the room, he heard Mr. Alleyne cry after him that if the contract was not copied by evening Mr. Crosbie would hear of the matter.

He returned to his desk in the lower office and counted the sheets which remained to be copied. He took up his pen and dipped it in the ink but he continued to stare stupidly at the last words he had written: *In no case shall the said Bernard Bodley be . . .* The evening was falling and in a few minutes they would be lighting the gas: then he could write. He felt that he must slake the thirst in his throat. He stood up from his desk and, lifting the counter as before, passed out of the office. As he was passing out the chief clerk looked at him inquiringly.

"It's all right, Mr. Shelley," said the man, pointing with his finger to indicate the objective of his journey.

The chief clerk glanced at the hatrack, but, seeing the row complete, offered no remark. As soon as he was on the landing the man pulled a shepherd's plaid cap out of his pocket, put it on his head and ran quickly down the rickety stairs. From the street door he walked on furtively on the inner side of the path towards the corner and all at once dived into a doorway. He was now safe in the dark snug[1] of O'Neill's shop, and, filling up the little window that looked into the bar with his inflamed face, the colour of dark wine or dark meat, he called out:

"Here, Pat, give us a g.p., like a good fellow."

---

1. *snug*, a small private room in a tavern.

The curate brought him a glass of plain porter. The man drank it at a gulp and asked for a caraway seed. He put his penny on the counter and, leaving the curate to grope for it in the gloom, retreated out of the snug as furtively as he had entered it.

Darkness, accompanied by a thick fog, was gaining upon the dusk of February and the lamps in Eustace Street had been lit. The man went up by the houses until he reached the door of the office, wondering whether he could finish his copy in time. On the stairs a moist pungent odour of perfumes saluted his nose: evidently Miss Delacour had come while he was out in O'Neill's. He crammed his cap back again into his pocket and reentered the office, assuming an air of absent-mindedness.

"Mr. Alleyne has been calling for you," said the chief clerk severely. "Where were you?"

The man glanced at the two clients who were standing at the counter as if to intimate that their presence prevented him from answering. As the clients were both male the chief clerk allowed himself a laugh.

"I know that game," he said. "Five times in one day is a little bit . . . Well, you better look sharp and get a copy of our correspondence in the Delacour case for Mr. Alleyne."

This address in the presence of the public, his run upstairs and the porter he had gulped down so hastily confused the man and, as he sat down at his desk to get what was required, he realised how hopeless was the task of finishing his copy of the contract before half-past five. The dark damp night was coming and he longed to spend it in the bars, drinking with his friends amid the glare of gas and the clatter of glasses. He got out the Delacour correspondence and passed out of the office. He hoped Mr. Alleyne would not discover that the last two letters were missing.

The moist pungent perfume lay all the way up to Mr. Alleyne's room. Miss Delacour was a middle-aged woman of Jewish appearance. Mr. Alleyne was said to be sweet on her or on her money. She came to the office often and stayed a long time when she came. She was sitting beside his desk now in an aroma of perfumes, smoothing the handle of her umbrella and nodding the great black feather in her hat. Mr. Alleyne had swivelled his chair round to face her and thrown his right foot jauntily upon his left knee. The man put the correspondence on the desk and bowed respectfully but neither Mr. Alleyne nor Miss Delacour took any notice of his bow. Mr. Alleyne tapped a finger on the correspondence and then flicked it towards him as if to say: *"That's all right: you can go."*

The man returned to the lower office and sat down again at his desk. He stared intently at the incomplete phrase: *In no case shall the said Bernard Bodley be . . .* and thought how strange it was that the last three words began with the same letter. The chief clerk began to hurry Miss Parker, saying she would never have the letters typed in time for post. The man listened to the clicking of the machine for a few minutes and then set to work to finish his copy. But his head was not clear and his mind wandered away to the glare and rattle of the public house. It was a night for hot punches. He struggled on with his copy, but when the clock struck five he had still fourteen pages to write. Blast it! He couldn't finish it in time. He longed to execrate aloud, to bring his fist down on something violently. He was so enraged that he wrote *Bernard Bernard* instead of *Bernard Bodley* and had to begin again on a clean sheet.

He felt strong enough to clear out the whole office single-handed. His body ached to do something, to rush out and revel in violence. All the indignities of his life enraged him. . . . Could he ask the cashier privately for an advance? No, the cashier was no good, no damn good: he wouldn't give an advance. . . . He knew where he would meet the boys: Leonard and O'Halloran and Nosey Flynn. The barometer of his emotional nature was set for a spell of riot.

His imagination had so abstracted him that his name

was called twice before he answered. Mr. Alleyne and Miss Delacour were standing outside the counter and all the clerks had turned round in anticipation of something. The man got up from his desk. Mr. Alleyne began a tirade of abuse, saying that two letters were missing. The man answered that he knew nothing about them, that he had made a faithful copy. The tirade continued: it was so bitter and violent that the man could hardly restrain his fist from descending upon the head of the manikin before him:

"I know nothing about any other two letters," he said stupidly.

*"You—know—nothing.* Of course you know nothing," said Mr. Alleyne. "Tell me," he added, glancing first for approval to the lady beside him, "do you take me for a fool? Do you think me an utter fool?"

The man glanced from the lady's face to the little egg-shaped head and back again; and, almost before he was aware of it, his tongue had found a felicitous moment:

"I don't think, sir," he said, "that that's a fair question to put to me."

There was a pause in the very breathing of the clerks. Everyone was astounded (the author of the witticism no less than his neighbours) and Miss Delacour, who was a stout amiable person, began to smile broadly. Mr. Alleyne flushed to the hue of a wild rose and his mouth twitched with a dwarf's passion. He shook his fist in the man's face till it seemed to vibrate like the knob of some electric machine:

"You impertinent ruffian! You impertinent ruffian! I'll make short work of you! Wait till you see! You'll apologise to me for your impertinence or you'll quit the office instanter! You'll quit this, I'm telling you, or you'll apologise to me!"

He stood in a doorway opposite the office watching to see if the cashier would come out alone. All the clerks passed out and finally the cashier came out with the chief clerk. It was no use trying to say a word to him when he was with the chief clerk. The man felt that his position was bad enough. He had been obliged to offer an abject apology to Mr. Alleyne for his impertinence but he knew what a hornet's nest the office would be for him. He could remember the way in which Mr. Alleyne had hounded little Peake out of the office in order to make room for his own nephew. He felt savage and thirsty and revengeful, annoyed with himself and with everyone else. Mr. Alleyne would never give him an hour's rest; his life would be a hell to him. He had made a proper fool of himself this time. Could he not keep his tongue in his cheek? But they had never pulled together from the first, he and Mr. Alleyne, ever since the day Mr. Alleyne had overheard him mimicking his North of Ireland accent to amuse Higgins and Miss Parker: that had been the beginning of it. He might have tried Higgins for the money, but sure Higgins never had anything for himself. A man with two establishments to keep up, of course he couldn't. . . .

He felt his great body again aching for the comfort of the public house. The fog had begun to chill him and he wondered could he touch Pat in O'Neill's. He could not touch him for more than a bob[2]—and a bob was no use. Yet he must get money somewhere or other: he had spent his last penny for the g.p. and soon it would be too late for getting money anywhere. Suddenly, as he was fingering his watch chain, he thought of Terry Kelly's pawn office in Fleet Street. That was the dart! Why didn't he think of it sooner?

He went through the narrow alley of Temple Bar quickly, muttering to himself that they could all go to hell because he was going to have a good night of it. The clerk in Terry Kelly's said *A crown!* but the consignor held out for six shillings; and in the end the six shillings was allowed him literally. He came out of the pawn office joyfully, making a

---

2. *bob*, a shilling. (See "English Money," page 298.)

little cylinder of the coins between his thumb and fingers. In Westmoreland Street the footpaths were crowded with young men and women returning from business and ragged urchins ran here and there yelling out the names of the evening editions. The man passed through the crowd, looking on the spectacle generally with proud satisfaction and staring masterfully at the office girls. His head was full of the noises of tram gongs and swishing trolleys and his nose already sniffed the curling fumes of punch. As he walked on he preconsidered the terms in which he would narrate the incident to the boys:

"So, I just looked at him—coldly, you know, and looked at her. Then I looked back at him again—taking my time, you know. 'I don't think that that's a fair question to put to me,' says I."

Nosey Flynn was sitting up in his usual corner of Davy Byrne's and, when he heard the story, he stood Farrington a half-one, saying it was as smart a thing as ever he heard. Farrington stood a drink in his turn. After a while O'Halloran and Paddy Leonard came in and the story was repeated to them. O'Halloran stood tailors of malt, hot, all round and told the story of the retort he had made to the chief clerk when he was in Callan's of Fownes's Street; but, as the retort was after the manner of the liberal shepherds in the eclogues,[3] he had to admit that it was not as clever as Farrington's retort. At this Farrington told the boys to polish off that and have another.

Just as they were naming their poisons who should come in but Higgins! Of course he had to join in with the others. The men asked him to give his version of it, and he did so with great vivacity for the sight of five small hot whiskies was very exhilarating. Everyone roared laughing when he showed the way in which Mr. Alleyne shook his fist in

---

3. *after the manner . . . the eclogues.* An eclogue is a short poem, usually a pastoral. The word *liberal* is being used here to mean licentious, or obscene.

Farrington's face. Then he imitated Farrington, saying *"And here was my nabs, as cool as you please,"* while Farrington looked at the company out of his heavy dirty eyes, smiling and at times drawing forth stray drops of liquor from his moustache with the aid of his lower lip.

When that round was over there was a pause. O'Halloran had money but neither of the other two seemed to have any; so the whole party left the shop somewhat regretfully. At the corner of Duke Street, Higgins and Nosey Flynn bevelled off to the left while the other three turned back towards the city. Rain was drizzling down on the cold streets and, when they reached the Ballast Office, Farrington suggested the Scotch House. The bar was full of men and loud with the noise of tongues and glasses. The three men pushed past the whining match sellers at the door and formed a little party at the corner of the counter. They began to exchange stories. Leonard introduced them to a young fellow named Weathers who was performing at the Tivoli as an acrobat and knockabout *artiste.* Farrington stood a drink all round. Weathers said he would take a small Irish and Apollinaris. Farrington, who had definite notions of what was what, asked the boys would they have an Apollinaris too; but the boys told Tim to make theirs hot. The talk became theatrical. O'Halloran stood a round and then Farrington stood another round, Weathers protesting that the hospitality was too Irish. He promised to get them in behind the scenes and introduce them to some nice girls. O'Halloran said that he and Leonard would go, but that Farrington wouldn't go because he was a married man; and Farrington's heavy dirty eyes leered at the company in token that he understood he was being chaffed. Weathers made them all have just one little tincture at his expense and promised to meet them later on at Mulligan's in Poolbeg Street.

When the Scotch House closed they went round to Mulligan's. They went into the parlour at the back and O'Halloran ordered small hot specials all round. They were all beginning to feel mellow. Farrington was just standing another round when Weathers came back. Much to Farrington's relief he drank a glass of bitter this time. Funds were getting low but they had enough to keep them going. Presently two young women with big hats and a young man in a check suit came in and sat at a table close by. Weathers saluted them and told the company that they were out of the Tivoli. Farrington's eyes wandered at every moment in the direction of one of the young women. There was something striking in her appearance. An immense scarf of peacock-blue muslin was wound round her hat and knotted in a great bow under her chin; and she wore bright yellow gloves, reaching to the elbow. Farrington gazed admiringly at the plump arm which she moved very often and with much grace; and when, after a little time, she answered his gaze he admired still more her large dark brown eyes. The oblique staring expression in them fascinated him. She glanced at him once or twice and, when the party was leaving the room, she brushed against his chair and said *"O, pardon!"* in a London accent. He watched her leave the room in the hope that she would look back at him, but he was disappointed. He cursed his want of money and cursed all the rounds he had stood, particularly all the whiskies and Apollinaris which he had stood to Weathers. If there was one thing that he hated it was a sponge. He was so angry that he lost count of the conversation of his friends.

When Paddy Leonard called him he found that they were talking about feats of strength. Weathers was showing his biceps muscle to the company and boasting so much that the other two had called on Farrington to uphold the national honour. Farrington pulled up his sleeve accordingly and showed his biceps muscle to the company. The two arms were examined and compared and finally it was agreed to have a trial of strength. The table was cleared and the two men rested their elbows on it, clasping hands. When Paddy Leonard said *"Go!"* each was to try to bring down the other's hand on to the table. Farrington looked very serious and determined.

The trial began. After about thirty seconds Weathers brought his opponent's hand slowly down on to the table. Farrington's dark wine-coloured face flushed darker still with anger and humiliation at having been defeated by such a stripling.

"You're not to put the weight of your body behind it. Play fair," he said.

"Who's not playing fair?" said the other.

"Come on again. The two best out of three."

The trial began again. The veins stood out on Farrington's forehead, and the pallor of Weathers' complexion changed to peony. Their hands and arms trembled under the stress. After a long struggle Weathers again brought his opponent's hand slowly on to the table. There was a murmur of applause from the spectators. The curate, who was standing beside the table, nodded his red head towards the victor and said with stupid familiarity:

"Ah! that's the knack!"

"What the hell do you know about it?" said Farrington fiercely, turning on the man. "What do you put in your gab for?"

"Sh, sh!" said O'Halloran, observing the violent expression of Farrington's face. "Pony up,[4] boys. We'll have just one little smahan[5] more and then we'll be off."

A very sullen-faced man stood at the corner of O'Connell Bridge waiting for the little Sandymount tram to take him home. He was full of smouldering anger and revengefulness. He felt humiliated and discontented; he did not even feel drunk; and he had only twopence in his pocket. He cursed everything. He had done for himself in the office, pawned his watch, spent all his money; and he had not even got drunk. He began to feel thirsty again and he longed to be back again in the hot reeking public house. He

---

4. *pony up,* pay up. 5. *smahan,* a small drink.

had lost his reputation as a strong man, having been defeated twice by a mere boy. His heart swelled with fury and, when he thought of the woman in the big hat who had brushed against him and said *Pardon!* his fury nearly choked him.

His tram let him down at Shelbourne Road and he steered his great body along in the shadow of the wall of the barracks. He loathed returning to his home. When he went in by the side door he found the kitchen empty and the kitchen fire nearly out. He bawled upstairs:

"Ada! Ada!"

His wife was a little sharp-faced woman who bullied her husband when he was sober and was bullied by him when he was drunk. They had five children. A little boy came running down the stairs.

"Who is that?" said the man, peering through the darkness.

"Me, pa."

"Who are you? Charlie?"

"No, pa. Tom."

"Where's your mother?"

"She's out at the chapel."

"That's right. . . . Did she think of leaving any dinner for me?"

"Yes, pa, I——"

"Light the lamp. What do you mean by having the place in darkness? Are the other children in bed?"

The man sat down heavily on one of the chairs while the little boy lit the lamp. He began to mimic his son's flat accent, saying half to himself: *"At the chapel. At the chapel, if you please!"* When the lamp was lit he banged his fist on the table and shouted:

"What's for my dinner?"

"I'm going . . . to cook it, pa," said the little boy.

The man jumped up furiously and pointed to the fire.

"On that fire! You let the fire out! By God, I'll teach you to do that again!"

He took a step to the door and seized the walking stick which was standing behind it.

"I'll teach you to let the fire out!" he said, rolling up his sleeve in order to give his arm free play.

The little boy cried *"O, pa!"* and ran whimpering round the table, but the man followed him and caught him by the coat. The little boy looked about him wildly but, seeing no way of escape, fell upon his knees.

"Now, you'll let the fire out the next time!" said the man, striking at him vigorously with the stick. "Take that, you little whelp!"

The boy uttered a squeal of pain as the stick cut his thigh. He clasped his hands together in the air and his voice shook with fright.

"O, pa!" he cried. "Don't beat me, pa! And I'll . . . I'll say a *Hail Mary* for you. . . . I'll say a *Hail Mary* for you, pa, if you don't beat me. . . . I'll say a *Hail Mary*. . . . " ◆

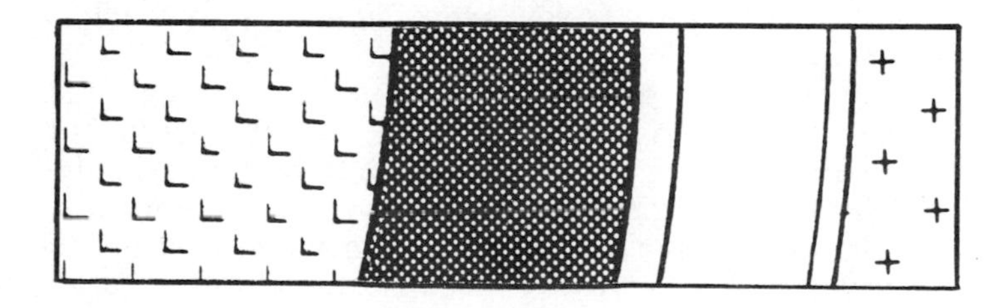

# Mary Lavin

## STORY OF THE WIDOW'S SON

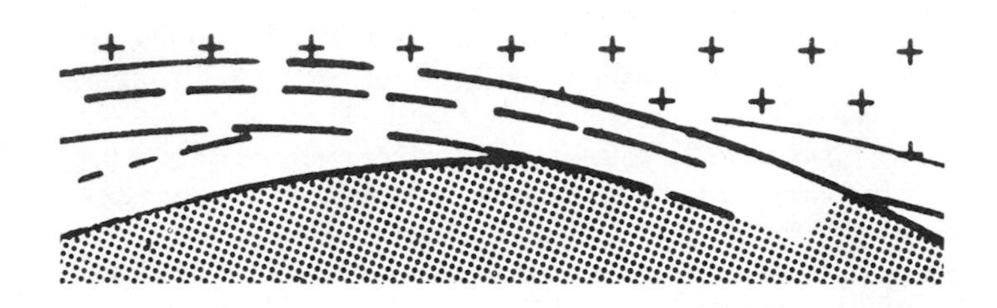

THIS IS THE STORY of a widow's son, but it is a story that has two endings.

There was once a widow, living in a small neglected village at the foot of a steep hill. She had only one son, but he was the meaning of her life. She lived for his sake. She wore herself out working for him. Every day she made a hundred sacrifices in order to keep him at a good school in the town, four miles away, because there was a better teacher there than the village dullard that had taught herself.

She made great plans for Packy, but she did not tell him about her plans. Instead she threatened him, day and night, that if he didn't turn out well, she would put him to work on the roads, or in the quarry under the hill.

But as the years went by, everyone in the village, and even Packy himself, could tell by the way she watched him

---

"Story of the Widow's Son" by Mary Lavin from IRISH HARVEST. Reprinted by permission of the author.

out of sight in the morning, and watched to see him come into sight in the evening, that he was the beat of her heart, and that her gruff words were only a cover for her pride and her joy in him.

It was for Packy's sake that she walked for hours along the road, letting her cow graze the long acre of the wayside grass, in order to spare the few poor blades that pushed up through the stones in her own field. It was for his sake she walked back and forth to the town to sell a few cabbages as soon as ever they were fit. It was for his sake that she got up in the cold dawning hours to gather mushrooms that would take the place of foods that had to be bought with money. She bent her back daily to make every penny she could, and as often happens, she made more by industry, out of her few bald acres, than many of the farmers around her made out of their great bearded meadows. Out of the money she made by selling eggs alone, she paid for Packy's clothes and for the greater number of his books.

When Packy was fourteen, he was in the last class in the school, and the master had great hopes of his winning a scholarship to a big college in the city. He was getting to be a tall lad, and his features were beginning to take a strong cast. His character was strengthening too, under his mother's sharp tongue. The people of the village were beginning to give him the same respect they gave to the sons of the farmers who came from their fine colleges in the summer, with blue suits and bright ties. And whenever they spoke to the widow they praised him up to the skies.

One day in June, when the air was so heavy the scent that rose up from the grass was imprisoned under the low clouds and hung in the air, the widow was waiting at the gate for Packy. There had been no rain for some days and the hens and chickens were pecking irritably at the dry ground and wandering up and down the road in bewilderment.

A neighbor passed.

"Waiting for Packy?" said the neighbor, pleasantly, and

he stood for a minute to take off his hat and wipe the sweat of the day from his face. He was an old man.

"It's a hot day!" he said. "It will be a hard push for Packy on that battered old bike of his. I wouldn't like to have to face into four miles on a day like this!"

"Packy would travel three times that distance if there was a book at the other end of the road!" said the widow, with the pride of those who cannot read more than a line or two without wearying.

The minutes went by slowly. The widow kept looking up at the sun.

"I suppose the heat is better than the rain!" she said, at last.

"The heat can do a lot of harm, too, though," said the neighbor, absent-mindedly, as he pulled a long blade of grass from between the stones of the wall and began to chew the end of it. "You could get sunstroke on a day like this!" He looked up at the sun. "The sun is a terror," he said. "It could cause you to drop down dead like a stone!"

The widow strained out further over the gate. She looked up the hill in the direction of the town.

"He will have a good cool breeze on his face coming down the hill, at any rate," she said.

The man looked up the hill. "That's true. On the hottest day of the year you would get a cool breeze coming down that hill on a bicycle. You would feel the air streaming past your cheeks like silk. And in the winter it's like two knives flashing to either side of you, and peeling off your skin like you'd peel the bark off a sally-rod!"[1] He chewed the grass meditatively. "That must be one of the steepest hills in Ireland," he said. "That hill is a hill worthy of the name of a hill." He took the grass out of his mouth. "It's my belief," he said, earnestly looking at the widow—"it's my belief that that hill is to be found marked with a name in the Ordnance Survey map!"

---

1. *sally-rod,* a willow branch.

"If that's the case," said the widow, "Packy will be able to tell you all about it. When it isn't a book he has in his hand it's a map."

"Is that so?" said the man. "That's interesting. A map is a great thing. A map is not an ordinary thing. It isn't everyone can make out a map."

The widow wasn't listening.

"I think I see Packy!" she said, and she opened the wooden gate and stepped out into the roadway.

At the top of the hill there was glitter of spokes as a bicycle came into sight. Then there was a flash of blue jersey as Packy came flying downward, gripping the handlebars of the bike, with his bright hair blown back from his forehead. The hill was so steep, and he came down so fast, that it seemed to the man and woman at the bottom of the hill that he was not moving at all, but that it was the bright trees and bushes, the bright ditches and wayside grasses that were streaming away to either side of him.

The hens and chickens clucked and squawked and ran along the road looking for a safe place in the ditches. They ran to either side with femininc fuss and chatter. Packy waved to his mother. He came nearer and nearer. They could see the freckles on his face.

"Shoo!" cried Packy, at the squawking hens that had not yet left the roadway. They ran with their long necks straining forward.

"Shoo!" said Packy's mother, lifting her apron and flapping it in the air to frighten them out of his way.

It was only afterwards, when the harm was done, that the widow began to think that it might, perhaps, have been the flapping of her own apron that frightened the old clucking hen, and sent her flying out over the garden wall into the middle of the road.

The old hen appeared suddenly on top of the grassy ditch and looked with a distraught eye at the hens and chickens as they ran to right and left. Her own feathers began to stand out from her. She craned her neck forward and gave a distracted squawk, and fluttered down into the middle of the hot dusty road.

Packy jammed on the brakes. The widow screamed. There was a flurry of white feathers and a spurt of blood. The bicycle swerved and fell. Packy was thrown over the handlebars.

It was such a simple accident that, although the widow screamed, and although the old man looked around to see if there was help near, neither of them thought that Packy was very badly hurt, but when they ran over and lifted his head, and saw that he could not speak, they wiped the blood from his face and looked around, desperately, to measure the distance they would have to carry him.

It was only a few yards to the door of the cottage, but Packy was dead before they got him across the threshold.

"He's only in a weakness!" screamed the widow, and she urged the crowd that had gathered outside the door to do something for him. "Get a doctor!" she cried, pushing a young laborer towards the door. "Hurry! Hurry! The doctor will bring him around."

But the neighbors that kept coming in the door, quickly, from all sides, were crossing themselves, one after another, and falling on their knees, as soon as they laid eyes on the boy, stretched out flat on the bed, with the dust and dirt and the sweat marks of life on his dead face.

When at last the widow was convinced that her son was dead, the other women had to hold her down. She waved her arms and cried out aloud, and wrestled to get free. She wanted to wring the neck of every hen in the yard.

"I'll kill every one of them. What good are they to me, now? All the hens in the world aren't worth one drop of human blood. That old clucking hen wasn't worth more than six shillings, at the very most. What is six shillings? Is it worth poor Packy's life?"

But after a time she stopped raving, and looked from one face to another.

"Why didn't he ride over the old hen?" she asked. "Why

did he try to save an old hen that wasn't worth more than six shillings? Didn't he know he was worth more to his mother than an old hen that would be going into the pot one of these days? Why did he do it? Why did he put on the brakes going down one of the worst hills in the country? Why? Why?"

The neighbors patted her arm.

"There now!" they said. "There now!" and that was all they could think of saying, and they said it over and over again. "There now! There now!"

And years afterwards, whenever the widow spoke of her son Packy to the neighbors who dropped in to keep her company for an hour or two, she always had the same question to ask—the same tireless question.

"Why did he put the price of an old clucking hen above the price of his own life?"

And the people always gave the same answer.

"There now!" they said, "There now!" And they sat as silently as the widow herself, looking into the fire.

But surely some of those neighbors must have been stirred to wonder what would have happened had Packy not yielded to his impulse of fear, and had, instead, ridden boldly over the old clucking hen? And surely some of them must have stared into the flames and pictured the scene of the accident again, altering a detail here and there as they did so, and giving the story a different end. For these people knew the widow, and they knew Packy, and when you know people well it is as easy to guess what they would say and do in certain circumstances as it is to remember what they actually did say and do in other circumstances. In fact it is sometimes easier to invent than to remember accurately, and were this not so two great branches of creative art would wither in an hour: the art of the storyteller and the art of the gossip. So, perhaps, if I try to tell you what I myself think might have happened had Packy killed that cackling old hen, you will not accuse me of abusing my privileges as a writer. After all, what I am about to tell you is no more of a fiction than what I have already told, and I lean no heavier now upon your credulity than, with your full consent, I did in the first instance.

And moreover, in many respects the new story is the same as the old.

It begins in the same way too. There is the widow grazing her cow by the wayside, and walking the long roads to the town, weighted down with sacks of cabbages that will pay for Packy's schooling. There she is, fussing over Packy in the mornings in case he would be late for school. There she is in the evening watching the battered clock on the dresser for the hour when he will appear on the top of the hill at his return. And there too, on a hot day in June, is the old laboring man coming up the road, and pausing to talk to her, as she stood at the door. There he is dragging a blade of grass from between the stones of the wall, and putting it between his teeth to chew, before he opens his mouth.

And when he opens his mouth at last it is to utter the same remark.

"Waiting for Packy?" said the old man, and then he took off his hat and wiped the sweat from his forehead. It will be remembered that he was an old man. "It's a hot day," he said.

"It's very hot," said the widow, looking anxiously up the hill. "It's a hot day to push a bicycle four miles along a bad road with the dust rising to choke you, and sun striking spikes off the handlebars!"

"The heat is better than the rain, all the same," said the old man.

"I suppose it is," said the widow. "All the same, there were days when Packy came home with the rain dried into his clothes so bad they stood up stiff like boards when he took them off. They stood up stiff like boards against the wall, for all the world as if he was still standing in them!"

"Is that so?" said the old man. "You may be sure he got a

good petting on those days. There is no son like a widow's son. A ewe lamb!"

"Is it Packy?" said the widow, in disgust. "Packy never got a day's petting since the day he was born. I made up my mind from the first that I'd never make a soft one out of him."

The widow looked up the hill again, and set herself to raking the gravel outside the gate as if she were in the road for no other purpose. Then she gave another look up the hill.

"Here he is now!" she said, and she raised such a cloud of dust with the rake that they could hardly see the glitter of the bicycle spokes, and the flash of blue jersey as Packy came down the hill at a breakneck speed.

Nearer and nearer he came, faster and faster, waving his hand to the widow, shouting at the hens to leave the way!

The hens ran for the ditches, stretching their necks in gawky terror. And then, as the last hen squawked into the ditch, the way was clear for a moment before the whirling silver spokes.

Then, unexpectedly, up from nowhere it seemed, came an old clucking hen and, clucking despairingly, it stood for a moment on the top of the wall and then rose into the air with the clumsy flight of a ground fowl.

Packy stopped whistling. The widow screamed. Packy yelled and the widow flapped her apron. Then Packy swerved the bicycle, and a cloud of dust rose from the braked wheel.

For a minute it could not be seen what exactly had happened, but Packy put his foot down and dragged it along the ground in the dust till he brought the bicycle to a sharp stop. He threw the bicycle down with a clatter on the hard road and ran back. The widow could not bear to look. She threw her apron over her head.

"He's killed the clucking hen!" she said. "He's killed her! He's killed her!" and then she let the apron fall back into place, and began to run up the hill herself. The old man spat out the blade of grass that he had been chewing and ran after the woman.

"Did you kill it?" screamed the widow, and as she got near enough to see the blood and feathers she raised her arm over her head, and her fist was clenched till the knuckles shone white. Packy cowered down over the carcass of the fowl and hunched up his shoulders as if to shield himself from a blow. His legs were spattered with blood, and the brown and white feathers of the dead hen were stuck to his hands, and stuck to his clothes, and they were strewn all over the road. Some of the short white inner feathers were still swirling with the dust in the air.

"I couldn't help it, Mother. I couldn't help it. I didn't see her till it was too late!"

The widow caught up the hen and examined it all over, holding it by the bone of the breast, and letting the long neck dangle. Then, catching it by the leg, she raised it suddenly above her head, and brought down the bleeding body on the boy's back, in blow after blow, spattering the blood all over his face and his hands, over his clothes and over the white dust of the road around him.

"How dare you lie to me!" she screamed, gaspingly, between the blows. "You saw the hen. I know you saw it. You stopped whistling! You called out! We were watching you. We saw." She turned upon the old man. "Isn't that right?" she demanded. "He saw the hen, didn't he? He saw it?"

"It looked that way," said the old man, uncertainly, his eye on the dangling fowl in the widow's hand.

"There you are!" said the widow. She threw the hen down on the road. "You saw the hen in front of you on the road, as plain as you see it now," she accused, "but you wouldn't stop to save it because you were in too big a hurry home to fill your belly! Isn't that so?"

"No, Mother. No! I saw her all right but it was too late to do anything."

"He admits now that he saw it," said the widow, turning

and nodding triumphantly at the onlookers who had gathered at the sound of the shouting.

"I never denied seeing it!" said the boy, appealing to the onlookers as to his judges.

"He doesn't deny it!" screamed the widow. "He stands there as brazen as you like, and admits for all the world to hear that he saw the hen as plain as the nose on his face, and he rode over it without a thought!"

"But what else could I do?" said the boy, throwing out his hand; appealing to the crowd now, and now appealing to the widow. "If I'd put on the brakes going down the hill at such a speed I would have been put over the handlebars!"

"And what harm would that have done you?" screamed the widow. "I often saw you taking a toss when you were wrestling with Jimmy Mack and I heard no complaints afterwards, although your elbows and knees would be running blood, and your face scraped like a gridiron!" She turned to the crowd. "That's as true as God. I often saw him come in with his nose spouting blood like a pump, and one eye closed as tight as the eye of a corpse. My hand was often stiff for a week from sopping out wet cloths to put poultices on him and try to bring his face back to rights again." She swung back to Packy again. "You're not afraid of a fall when you go climbing trees, are you? You're not afraid to go up on the roof after a cat, are you? Oh, there's more in this than you want me to know. I can see that. You killed that hen on purpose—that's what I believe! You're tired of going to school. You want to get out of going away to college. That's it! You think if you kill the few poor hens we have there will be no money in the box when the time comes to pay for books and classes. That's it!" Packy began to redden.

"It's late in the day for me to be thinking of things like that," he said. "It's long ago I should have started those tricks if that was the way I felt. But it's not true. I want to go to college. The reason I was coming down the hill so fast was to tell you that I got the scholarship. The teacher told me as I was leaving the schoolhouse. That's why I was pedaling so hard. That's why I was whistling. That's why I was waving my hand. Didn't you see me waving my hand from once I came in sight of the top of the hill?"

The widow's hands fell to her side. The wind of words died down within her and left her flat and limp. She didn't know what to say. She could feel the neighbors staring at her. She wished that they were gone away about their business. She wanted to throw out her arms to the boy, to drag him against her heart and hug him like a small child. But she thought of how the crowd would look at each other and nod and snigger. A ewe lamb! She didn't want to satisfy them. If she gave in to her feelings now they would know how much she had been counting on his getting the scholarship. She wouldn't please them! She wouldn't satisfy them!

She looked at Packy, and when she saw him standing there before her, spattered with the furious feathers and the crude blood of the dead hen, she felt a fierce disappointment for the boy's own disappointment, and a fierce resentment against him for killing the hen on this day of all days, and spoiling the great news of his success.

Her mind was in confusion. She started at the blood on his face, and all at once it seemed as if the blood was a bad omen of the future that was for him. Disappointment, fear, resentment, and above all defiance, raised themselves within her like screeching animals. She looked from Packy to the onlookers.

"Scholarship! Scholarship!" she sneered, putting as much derision as she could into her voice and expression.

"I suppose you think you are a great fellow now? I suppose you think you are independent now? I suppose you think you can go off with yourself now, and look down on your poor slave of a mother who scraped and sweated for you with her cabbages and her hens? I suppose you think to yourself that it doesn't matter now whether the hens are alive or dead? Is that the way? Well, let me tell you this!

You're not as independent as you think. The scholarship may pay for your books and your teacher's fees but who will pay for your clothes? Ah ha, you forgot that, didn't you?" She put her hands on her hips. Packy hung his head. He no longer appealed to the gawking neighbors. They might have been able to save him from blows but he knew enough about life to know that no one could save him from shame.

The widow's heart burned at sight of his shamed face, as her heart burned with grief, but her temper too burned fiercer and fiercer, and she came to a point at which nothing could quell the blaze till it had burned itself out. "Who'll buy your suits?" she yelled. "Who'll buy your boots?" She paused to think of more humiliating accusations. "Who'll buy your breeches?" She paused again and her teeth bit against each other. What would wound deepest? What shame could she drag upon him? "Who'll buy your nightshirts or will you sleep in your skin?"

The neighbors laughed at that, and the tension was broken. The widow herself laughed. She held her sides and laughed, and as she laughed everything seemed to take on a newer and simpler significance. Things were not as bad as they seemed a moment before. She wanted Packy to laugh too. She looked at him. But as she looked at Packy her heart turned cold with a strange new fear.

"Get into the house!" she said, giving him a push ahead of her. She wanted him safe under her own roof. She wanted to get him away from the gaping neighbors. She hated them, man, woman and child. She felt that if they had not been there things would have been different. And she wanted to get away from the sight of the blood on the road. She wanted to mash a few potatoes and make a bit of potato cake for Packy. That would comfort him. He loved that.

Packy hardly touched the food. And even after he had washed and scrubbed himself there were stains of blood turning up in the most unexpected places: behind his ears, under his fingernails, inside the cuff of his sleeve.

"Put on your good clothes," said the widow, making a great effort to be gentle, but her manners had become as twisted and as hard as the branches of the trees across the road from her, and even the kindly offers she made sounded harsh. The boy sat on the chair in a slumped position that kept her nerves on edge and set up a further conflict of irritation and love in her heart. She hated to see him slumping there in the chair, not asking to go outside the door, but still she was uneasy whenever he as much as looked in the direction of the door. She felt safe while he was under the roof; inside the lintel under her eyes.

Next day she went in to wake him for school, but his room was empty; his bed had not been slept in, and when she ran out into the yard and called him everywhere there was no answer. She ran up and down. She called at the houses of the neighbors but he was not in any house. And she thought she could hear sniggering behind her in each house that she left, as she ran to another one. He wasn't in the village. He wasn't in the town. The master of the school said that she should let the police have a description of him. He said he never met a boy as sensitive as Packy. A boy like that took strange notions into his head from time to time.

The police did their best but there was no news of Packy that night. A few days later there was a letter saying that he was well. He asked his mother to notify the master that he would not be coming back, so that some other boy could claim the scholarship. He said that he would send the price of the hen as soon as he made some money.

Another letter in a few weeks said that he had got a job on a trawler, and that he would not be able to write very often but that he would put aside some of his pay every week and send it to his mother whenever he got into port. He said that he wanted to pay her back for all she had done for him. He gave no address. He kept his promise about the money but he never gave any address when he wrote. . . . And so the people may have let their thoughts run on, as they sat by the fire with the widow, many a night, listening to her complaining voice saying the same thing over and over. "Why did he put the price of an old hen above the price of his own life?" And it is possible that their version of the story has a certain element of truth about it too. Perhaps all our actions have this double quality about them; this possibility of alternative, and that it is only by careful watching and absolute sincerity, that we follow the path that is destined for us, and, no matter how tragic that may be, it is better than the tragedy we bring upon ourselves. ◆

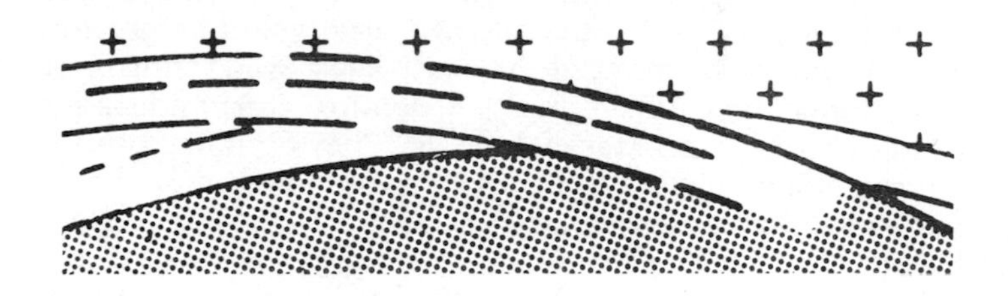

# D. H. Lawrence

## THINGS

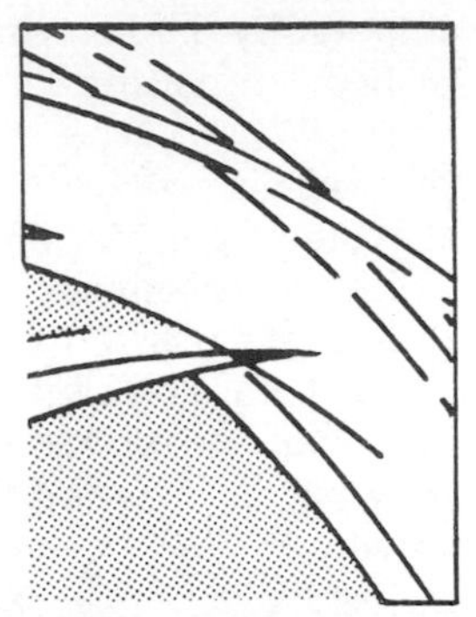

THEY WERE TRUE IDEALISTS from New England. But that is some time ago: before the war. Several years before the war, they met and married; he a tall, keen-eyed young man from Connecticut, she a smallish, demure, Puritan-looking young woman from Massachusetts. They both had a little money. Not much, however. Even added together, it didn't make three thousand dollars a year. Still—they were free. Free!

Ah! Freedom! To be free to live one's own life! To be twenty-five and twenty-seven, a pair of true idealists with a mutual love of beauty, and an inclination towards "Indian thought"—meaning, alas, Mrs. Besant[1]—and an income a little under three thousand dollars a year! But what is money? All one wishes to do is to live a full and beautiful life. In Europe, of course, right at the fountainhead of tradition. It might possibly be done in America: in New England, for example. But at a forfeiture of a certain

---

"Things" from THE COMPLETE SHORT STORIES OF D. H. LAWRENCE, Volume III. Copyright 1934 by Frieda Lawrence, renewal copyright © 1962 by Angelo Ravagli and C. Montague Weekley, Executors of the Estate of Frieda Lawrence Ravagli. All rights reserved. Reprinted by permission of The Viking Press, Inc., Laurence Pollinger Ltd. and the Estate of the late Mrs. Frieda Lawrence.

1. *"Indian thought" . . . Mrs. Besant.* Annie Besant (1847–1933) was a popularizer of Indian religious thought.

amount of "beauty." True beauty takes a long time to mature. The baroque is only half-beautiful, half-matured. No, the real silver bloom, the real golden-sweet bouquet of beauty had its roots in the Renaissance,[2] not in any later or shallower period.

Therefore the two idealists, who were married in New Haven, sailed at once to Paris: Paris of the old days. They had a studio apartment on the Boulevard Montparnasse, and they became real Parisians, in the old, delightful sense, not in the modern, vulgar. It was the shimmer of the pure impressionists, Monet[3] and his followers, the world seen in terms of pure light, light broken and unbroken. How lovely! How lovely the nights, the river, the mornings in the old streets and by the flower stalls and the bookstalls, the afternoons up on Montmartre or in the Tuileries,[4] the evenings on the boulevards!

They both painted, but not desperately. Art had not taken them by the throat, and they did not take Art by the throat. They painted: that's all. They knew people—nice people, if possible, though one had to take them mixed. And they were happy.

Yet it seems as if human beings must set their claws in *something*. To be "free," to be "living a full and beautiful life," you must, alas, be attached to something. A "full and beautiful life" means a tight attachment to *something*—at least, it is so for all idealists—or else a certain boredom supervenes; there is a certain waving of loose ends upon the air, like the waving, yearning tendrils of the vine that spread and rotate, seeking something to clutch, something

---

**2.** *Renaissance,* the period in European history from the fourteenth through the sixteenth century, marked by great artistic activity. **3.** *impressionists, Monet.* Claude Monet (1840–1926), a French landscape painter, was one of the originators of impressionism, a school of art which attempted to portray the effect of light on objects by the use of broken color. **4.** *Montmartre . . . the Tuileries.* Montmartre is a district in Paris popular with artists and celebrated for its night-life. The Tuileries are formal gardens which formerly surrounded a royal palace. The palace was destroyed by fire in 1871.

up which to climb towards the necessary sun. Finding nothing, the vine can only trail, half-fulfilled, upon the ground. Such is freedom!—a clutching of the right pole. And human beings are all vines. But especially the idealist. He is a vine, and he needs to clutch and climb. And he despises the man who is a mere *potato,* or turnip, or lump of wood.

Our idealists were frightfully happy, but they were all the time reaching out for something to cotton on to. At first, Paris was enough. They explored Paris *thoroughly.* And they learned French till they almost felt like French people, they could speak it so glibly.

Still, you know, you never talk French with your *soul.* It can't be done. And though it's very thrilling, at first, talking in French to clever Frenchmen—they seem *so* much cleverer than oneself—still, in the long run, it is not satisfying. The endlessly clever *materialism* of the French leaves you cold, in the end, gives a sense of barrenness and incompatibility with true New England depth. So our two idealists felt.

They turned away from France—but ever so gently. France had disappointed them. "We've loved it, and we've got a great deal out of it. But after a while, after a considerable while, several years, in fact, Paris leaves one feeling disappointed. It hasn't quite got what one wants."

"But Paris isn't France."

"No, perhaps not. France is quite different from Paris. And France is lovely—quite lovely. But to *us,* though we love it, it doesn't say a great deal."

So, when the war came, the idealists moved to Italy. And they loved Italy. They found it beautiful, and more poignant than France. It seemed much nearer to the New England conception of beauty: something pure, and full of sympathy, without the *materialism* and the *cynicism* of the French. The two idealists seemed to breathe their own true air in Italy.

And in Italy, much more than in Paris, they felt they

could thrill to the teachings of the Buddha.[5] They entered the swelling stream of modern Buddhistic emotion, and they read the books, and they practised meditation, and they deliberately set themselves to eliminate from their own souls greed, pain, and sorrow. They did not realise—yet—that Buddha's very eagerness to free himself from pain and sorrow is in itself a sort of greed. No, they dreamed of a perfect world, from which all greed, and nearly all pain, and a great deal of sorrow, were eliminated.

But America entered the war, so the two idealists had to help. They did hospital work. And though their experience made them realise more than ever that greed, pain, and sorrow *should* be eliminated from the world, nevertheless the Buddhism, or the theosophy,[6] didn't emerge very triumphant from the long crisis. Somehow, somewhere, in some part of themselves, they felt that greed, pain, and sorrow would never be eliminated, because most people don't care about eliminating them, and never will care. Our idealists were far too Western to think of abandoning all the world to damnation, while they saved their two selves. They were far too unselfish to sit tight under a bho tree and reach Nirvana[7] in a mere couple.

It was more than that, though. They simply hadn't enough *Sitzfleisch*[8] to squat under a bho tree and get to Nirvana by contemplating anything, least of all their own navel. If the whole wide world was not going to be saved, they, personally, were not so very keen on being saved just by themselves. No, it would be so lonesome. They were

---

5. *Buddha,* "the Enlightened One," the title given to Prince Gautama Sakyamuni (c. 563–483 B.C.), the founder of Buddhism. 6. *theosophy,* a general heading under which many mystical traditions can be placed. The Theosophical Society of America, with which theosophy is now generally associated, was founded in 1875 by Mme. Helena Blavatsky. 7. *bho tree . . . Nirvana.* It was while sitting in meditation beneath a bho tree that the Buddha achieved enlightenment and entered *Nirvana,* a Sanskrit word which means "a blowing out," as of a candle, and describes a state of selfless release from the endless cycle of rebirths which all beings are otherwise compelled to undergo. 8. *Sitzfleisch,* buttocks. [*German*]

New Englanders, so it must be all or nothing. Greed, pain, and sorrow must either be eliminated from *all the world,* or else, what was the use of eliminating them from oneself? No use at all! One was just a victim.

And so, although they still *loved* "Indian thought," and felt very tender about it: well, to go back to our metaphor, the pole up which the green and anxious vines had clambered so far now proved dry-rotten. It snapped, and the vines came slowly subsiding to earth again. There was no crack and crash. The vines held themselves up by their own foliage, for a while. But they subsided. The beanstalk of "Indian thought" had given way before Jack and Jill had climbed off the tip of it to a further world.

They subsided with a slow rustle back to earth again. But they made no outcry. They were again "disappointed." But they never admitted it. "Indian thought" had let them down. But they never complained. Even to one another, they never said a word. They were disappointed, faintly but deeply disillusioned, and they both knew it. But the knowledge was tacit.

And they still had so much in their lives. They still had Italy—dear Italy. And they still had freedom, the priceless treasure. And they still had so much "beauty." About the fullness of their lives they were not quite so sure. They had one little boy, whom they loved as parents should love their children, but whom they wisely refrained from fastening upon, to build their lives on him. No, no, they must live their own lives! They still had strength of mind to know that.

But they were now no longer very young. Twenty-five and twenty-seven had become thirty-five and thirty-seven. And though they had had a very wonderful time in Europe, and though they still loved Italy—dear Italy!—yet: they were disappointed. They had got a lot out of it: oh, a very great deal indeed! Still, it hadn't given them quite, not *quite,* what they had expected. Europe was lovely, but it was dead. Living in Europe, you were living on the past. And

Europeans, with all their superficial charm, were not *really* charming. They were materialistic, they had no *real* soul. They just did not understand the inner urge of the spirit, because the inner urge was dead in them, they were all survivals. There, that was the truth about Europeans: they were survivals, with no more getting ahead in them.

It was another beanpole, another vine support crumbled under the green life of the vine. And very bitter it was, this time. For up the old tree trunk of Europe the green vine had been clambering silently for more than ten years, ten hugely important years, the years of real living. The two idealists had *lived* in Europe, lived on Europe and on European life and European things as vines in an everlasting vineyard.

They had made their home here: a home such as you could never make in America. Their watchword had been "beauty." They had rented, the last four years, the second floor of an old palazzo on the Arno,[9] and here they had all their "things." And they derived a profound, profound satisfaction from their apartment: the lofty, silent, ancient rooms with windows on the river, with glistening, dark-red floors, and the beautiful furniture that the idealists had "picked up."

Yes, unknown to themselves, the lives of the idealists had been running with a fierce swiftness horizontally, all the time. They had become tense, fierce, hunters of "things" for their home. While their souls were climbing up to the sun of old European culture or old Indian thought, their passions were running horizontally, clutching at "things." Of course they did not buy the things for the things' sakes, but for the sake of "beauty." They looked upon their home as a place entirely furnished by loveliness, not by "things" at all. Valerie had some very lovely curtains at the windows of the long *salotto,*[10] looking on the river:

---

**9.** *Arno,* a river of west central Italy which flows through Florence. **10.** *salotto,* living room. [*Italian*] curtains of queer ancient material that looked like finely-knitted silk, most beautifully faded down from vermilion and orange, and gold, and black, down to a sheer soft glow. Valerie hardly ever came into the *salotto* without mentally falling on her knees before the curtains. "Chartres!"[11] she said. "To me they are Chartres!" And Melville never turned and looked at his sixteenth-century Venetian bookcase, with its two or three dozen of choice books, without feeling his marrow stir in his bones. The holy of holies!

The child silently, almost sinisterly, avoided any rude contact with these ancient monuments of furniture, as if they had been nests of sleeping cobras, or that "thing" most perilous to the touch, the Ark of the Covenant.[12] His childish awe was silent and cold, but final.

Still, a couple of New England idealists cannot live merely on the by-gone glory of their furniture. At least, one couple could not. They got used to the marvellous Bologna cupboard, they got used to the wonderful Venetian bookcase, and the books, and the Siena curtains and bronzes, and the lovely sofas and side tables and chairs they had "picked up" in Paris. Oh, they had been picking things up since the first day they landed in Europe. And they were still at it. It is the last interest Europe can offer to an outsider: or to an insider either.

When people came, and were thrilled by the Melville interior, then Valerie and Erasmus felt they had not lived in vain: that they still were living. But in the long mornings, when Erasmus was desultorily working at Renaissance Florentine literature, and Valerie was attending to the apartment: and in the long hours after lunch; and in the long, usually very cold and oppressive evenings in the ancient palazzo: then the halo died from around the furni-

---

**11.** *Chartres,* a medieval French cathedral which is famous for its stained glass. **12.** *the Ark of the Covenant,* the chest containing various sacred objects which the Jews carried with them on their wanderings in the desert. It was later placed in the Temple at Jerusalem.

ture, and the things became things, lumps of matter that just stood there or hung there, *ad infinitum,* and said nothing; and Valerie and Erasmus almost hated them. The glow of beauty, like every other glow, dies down unless it is fed. The idealists still dearly loved their things. But they had got them. And the sad fact is, things that glow vividly while you're getting them, go almost quite cold after a year or two. Unless, of course, people envy them very much, and the museums are pining for them. And the Melvilles' "things," though very good, were not quite so good as that.

So, the glow gradually went out of everything, out of Europe, out of Italy—"the Italians are *dears*"—even out of that marvellous apartment on the Arno. "Why, if I had this apartment, I'd never, never even want to go out of doors! It's too lovely and perfect." That was something, of course—to hear that.

And yet Valerie and Erasmus went out of doors: they even went out to get away from its ancient, cold-floored, stone-heavy silence and dead dignity. "We're living on the past, you know, Dick," said Valerie to her husband. She called him Dick.

They were grimly hanging on. They did not like to give in. They did not like to own up that they were through. For twelve years, now, they had been "free" people living a "full and beautiful life." And America for twelve years had been their anathema, the Sodom and Gomorrah[13] of industrial materialism.

It wasn't easy to own that you were "through." They hated to admit that they wanted to go back. But at last, reluctantly, they decided to go, "for the boy's sake."—"We can't *bear* to leave Europe. But Peter is an American, so he had better look at America while he's young." The Melvilles had an entirely English accent and manner; almost; a little Italian and French here and there.

---

**13.** *Sodom and Gomorrah,* two wicked cities which God destroyed by a rain of fire. (Genesis 18, 19)

They left Europe behind, but they took as much of it along with them as possible. Several van loads, as a matter-of-fact. All those adorable and irreplaceable "things." And all arrived in New York, idealists, child, and the huge bulk of Europe they had lugged along.

Valerie had dreamed of a pleasant apartment, perhaps on Riverside Drive, where it was not so expensive as east of Fifth Avenue, and where all their wonderful things would look marvellous. She and Erasmus house-hunted. But alas! their income was quite under three thousand dollars a year. They found—well, everybody knows what they found. Two small rooms and a kitchenette, and don't let us unpack a *thing!*

The chunk of Europe which they had bitten off went into a warehouse, at fifty dollars a month. And they sat in two small rooms and a kitchenette, and wondered why they'd done it.

Erasmus, of course, ought to get a job. This was what was written on the wall, and what they both pretended not to see. But it had been the strange, vague threat that the Statue of Liberty had always held over them: "Thou shalt get a job!" Erasmus had the tickets, as they say. A scholastic career was still possible for him. He had taken his exams brilliantly at Yale, and had kept up his "researches" all the time he had been in Europe.

But both he and Valerie shuddered. A scholastic career! The scholastic world! The *American* scholastic world! Shudder upon shudder! Give up their freedom, their full and beautiful life? Never! Never! Erasmus would be forty next birthday.

The "things" remained in warehouse. Valerie went to look at them. It cost her a dollar an hour, and horrid pangs. The "things," poor things, looked a bit shabby and wretched, in that warehouse.

However, New York was not all America. There was the great clean West. So the Melvilles went West, with Peter, but without the things. They tried living the simple life, in the mountains. But doing their own chores became almost a nightmare. "Things" are all very well to look at, but it's awful handling them, even when they're beautiful. To be the slave of hideous things, to keep a stove going, cook meals, wash dishes, carry water and clean floors: pure horror of sordid anti-life!

In the cabin on the mountains, Valerie dreamed of Florence, the lost apartment; and her Bologna cupboard and Louis Quinze chairs, above all, her "Chartres" curtains, stood in New York and costing fifty dollars a month.

A millionaire friend came to the rescue, offering them a cottage on the Californian coast—California! Where the new soul is to be born in man. With joy the idealists moved a little farther west, catching at new vine props of hope.

And finding them straws! The millionaire cottage was perfectly equipped. It was perhaps as labour-savingly perfect as is possible: electric heating and cooking, a white-and-pearl-enamelled kitchen, nothing to make dirt except the human being himself. In an hour or so the idealists had got through their chores. They were "free"—free to hear the great Pacific pounding the coast, and to feel a new soul filling their bodies.

Alas! the Pacific pounded the coast with hideous brutality, brute force itself! And the new soul, instead of sweetly stealing into their bodies, seemed only meanly to gnaw the old soul out of their bodies. To feel you are under the fist of the most blind and crunching brute force: to feel that your cherished idealist's soul is being gnawed out of you, and only irritation left in place of it: well, it isn't good enough.

After about nine months, the idealists departed from the Californian West. It had been a great experience, they were glad to have had it. But, in the long run, the West was not the place for them, and they knew it. No, the people who wanted new souls had better get them. They, Valerie and Erasmus Melville, would like to develop the old soul a little further. Anyway, they had not felt any influx of new soul on the Californian coast. On the contrary.

So, with a slight hole in their material capital, they returned to Massachusetts and paid a visit to Valerie's parents, taking the boy along. The grandparents welcomed the child—poor expatriated boy—and were rather cold to Valerie, but really cold to Erasmus. Valerie's mother definitely said to Valerie, one day, that Erasmus ought to take a job, so that Valerie could live decently. Valerie haughtily reminded her mother of the beautiful apartment on the Arno, and the "wonderful" things in store in New York, and of the "marvellous and satisfying life" she and Erasmus had led. Valerie's mother said that she didn't think her daughter's life looked so very marvellous at present: homeless, with a husband idle at the age of forty, a child to educate, and a dwindling capital: looked the reverse of marvellous to *her*. Let Erasmus take some post in one of the universities.

"What post? What university?" interrupted Valerie.

"That could be found, considering your father's connections and Erasmus's qualifications," replied Valerie's mother. "And you could get all your valuable things out of store, and have a really lovely home, which everybody in America would be proud to visit. As it is, your furniture is eating up your income, and you are living like rats in a hole, with nowhere to go to."

This was very true. Valerie was beginning to pine for a home, with her "things." Of course, she could have sold her furniture for a substantial sum. But nothing would have induced her to. Whatever else passed away, religions, cultures, continents, and hopes, Valerie would *never* part from the "things" which she and Erasmus had collected with such passion. To these she was nailed.

But she and Erasmus still would not give up that freedom, that full and beautiful life they had so believed in. Erasmus cursed America. He did not *want* to earn a living. He panted for Europe.

Leaving the boy in charge of Valerie's parents, the two idealists once more set off for Europe. In New York they paid two dollars and looked for a brief, bitter hour at their "things." They sailed "student class"—that is, third. Their income now was less than two thousand dollars instead of three. And they made straight for Paris—cheap Paris.

They found Europe, this time, a complete failure. "We have returned like dogs to our vomit," said Erasmus, "but the vomit has staled in the meantime." He found he couldn't stand Europe. It irritated every nerve in his body. He hated America too. But America at least was a darn sight better than this miserable, dirt-eating continent; which was by no means cheap any more, either.

Valerie, with her heart on her things—she had really burned to get them out of that warehouse, where they had stood now for three years, eating up two thousand dollars—wrote to her mother she thought Erasmus would come back if he could get some suitable work in America. Erasmus, in a state of frustration bordering on rage and insanity, just went round Italy in a poverty-stricken fashion, his coat cuffs frayed, hating everything with intensity. And when a post was found for him in Cleveland University, to teach French, Italian, and Spanish literature, his eyes grew more beady, and his long, queer face grew sharper and more ratlike with utter baffled fury. He was forty, and the job was upon him.

"I think you'd better accept, dear. You don't care for Europe any longer. As you say, it's dead and finished. They offer us a house on the college lot, and mother says there's room in it for all our things. I think we'd better cable 'Accept.'"

He glowered at her like a cornered rat. One almost expected to see rat's whiskers twitching at the sides of the sharp nose.

"Shall I send the cablegram?" she asked.

"Send it!" he blurted.

And she went out and sent it.

He was a changed man, quieter, much less irritable. A load was off him. He was inside the cage.

But when he looked at the furnaces of Cleveland, vast and like the greatest of black forests, with red and white-hot cascades of gushing metal, and tiny gnomes of men, and terrific noises, gigantic, he said to Valerie:

"Say what you like, Valerie, this is the biggest thing the modern world has to show."

And when they were in their up-to-date little house on the college lot of Cleveland University, and that woebegone débris of Europe: Bologna cupboard, Venice bookshelves, Ravenna bishop's chair, Louis Quinze side tables, "Chartres" curtains, Siena bronze lamps, all were arrayed, and all looked perfectly out of keeping, and therefore very impressive; and when the idealists had had a bunch of gaping people in, and Erasmus had showed off in his best European manner, but still quite cordial and American; and Valerie had been most ladylike, but for all that, "we prefer America"; then Erasmus said, looking at her with queer, sharp eyes of a rat:

"Europe's the mayonnaise all right, but America supplies the good old lobster—what?"

"Every time!" she said, with satisfaction.

And he peered at her. He was in the cage: but it was safe inside. And she, evidently, was her real self at last. She had got the goods. Yet round his nose was a queer, evil scholastic look of pure scepticism. But he liked lobster. ◆

# Alwyn Lee

# THE CORVIDAE

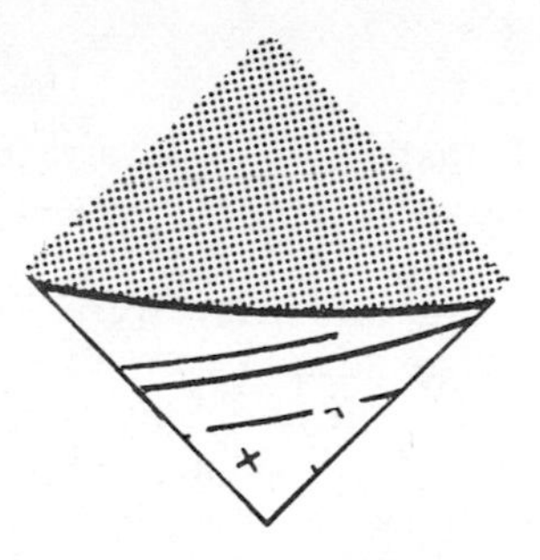

MOST AUSTRALIANS LIVE IN CITIES, but they are ashamed of this arrangement. Theoretically they are all sunburned horsemen in "the bush"—a term that is used for any part of the continent not actually covered by asphalt. At least, this was so when I was a small boy growing up in a limitless tract of Melbourne suburb. My mother and father had been born on Australian farms. When they spoke of Home, they meant the British Isles; when they spoke of "back home," they meant "upcountry." Thus, my parents conceived of it as both a kindness and a discipline that I should spend every school holiday—the two term holidays and the long Christmas summer holidays—with my country uncles. These were all on my mother's side, for my father's family seems to have survived only one generation of Australian farming, which is no picnic.

The choice of uncles was wide; there was a whole tribe or clan of them "on the land." They had place names, like a lot of barbarous feudal chieftains. There were the Kinnabulla McInstries, the Dimboola Leslies, the Wanboon Adamses (my mother was an Adams), not to speak of various related Gordons, Mahoods, Flockharts, and Glasgows, all with sound Ulster names (apart from their territorial designations) and all in sheep, though one aunt ("poor Aunt Bonnie") had married a man called Murphy, who drank and had a fruit farm—three equally disgraceful things.

---

"The Corvidae" by Alwyn Lee from THE NEW YORKER, (March 17, 1956). Reprinted by permission; copyright © 1956 The New Yorker Magazine, Inc.

If Australia was empty, it was not my uncles' fault. I had twenty-two first cousins—twenty of them on my mother's side. The tribe originated in County Antrim, round Ballymena, and they were everything an Irishman means when he says "Orangeman" or "Black Ulsterman."[1] I see now that they held my father in some contempt for his city job, his Methodism, and his lack of land, money, or Scots-Irish blood. It is not in a boy, mercifully, to hold his father to account, but, little snob that I was, I regarded these Ulster-Australian graziers as greater men. This was especially true of the Wanboon McInstries. They were the richest and, as they say at sheep shows, the most "typie." It was mostly to the Wanboon McInstries, in northwestern Victoria,[2] that I was sent. My mother had been named for my Great-Aunt Maggie McInstrie and had been a favorite niece, so it must have been out of regard for her that the Wanboon McInstries would give houseroom to a schoolboy, lest he sicken and die in malignant Melbourne air. For another thing, the family was comparatively small. The one son—my second cousin Rob—had grown up. He had become the Coongabbie McInstrie, with a place of his own "up" in New South Wales.[3] There were still five daughters, married and unmarried, about the place. The family—or, rather, the clan—spirit was strong, and I was made to feel at home, although I must have been a nuisance, like a sheepdog pup underfoot in the stables.

I was dispatched from Melbourne by train. It was slow—twelve hours to do about two hundred miles. It shed parts as it went along, and toward the end of the journey it dwindled to a single coach trailing a string of empty freight cars. The engine sounded mournful blasts on its whistle,

---

**1.** *County Antrim . . . "Black Ulsterman."* Ballymena is a town in Antrim, one of the six counties of Ulster, or Northern Ireland. An Orangeman or Black Ulsterman is an Irish Protestant. The Orangemen were originally so called because of their support of the Protestant king of England, William of Orange (1689–1702). **2.** *Victoria,* a state in southeastern Australia. **3.** *New South Wales,* a state in southeastern Australia, north of Victoria.

like a fogbound steamer, as it groaned its way from one inconclusive settlement to another. Dusk would come, and very bright stars, one by one, from the black edge of the plains, and then a more surprising thing—men standing beside the tracks crying, "Paper! Paper!" (This was before the wireless came to break the silence of the bush, and men marooned out there would go mad from the loneliness often enough for there to be a special word for them. "Hatters," these loony exiles were called. Bushmen who worked alone were the worst victims; they would ride for miles to the railway like scrub cattle blorting their way to a salt lick. It was the custom—as much honored as a swagman's[4] right to water—for the passengers to throw out their city newspapers and magazines on the cry of "Paper!") In the middle of nowhere, you would see faces and tethered horses suddenly in the glare of the windows, then nothing again. Arriving at Wanboon (population nil; it was just a siding surrounded by the land of various McInstries) was arriving at nowhere. There was a mile or so by buggy to the homestead; then, in the morning, I would wake in my cousin's old bed, to the sound of a million sheep and magpies.

The homestead, Gracelands, stood in the middle of I don't know how many thousand acres of sheep run. A sprawling jumble of buildings lay about it. Apart from the sheep, there were about thirty horses, a dozen dogs, a cow or two, and a vast proletariat of chickens. It was not at all like those streamlined American farms that look so neat photographed from the air, and I found it confusing, although there was no doubt in my mind who ruled the huge roost. The lord of man and brute was my Great-Uncle Hugh McInstrie, and I was very scared of him. He represented power and authority. He bellowed at his immigrant hands, housed them in huts papered with old newspapers, and made them heartily regret that they had left the intimate

---

4. *swagman,* a hobo.

and familiar misery of a London slum or a Durham mine village. I think now there was no deliberate harshness in this; it was simply a product of the profound conviction that those who do not own land cannot expect to be happy in this life. Bearded and mounted on one of his seventeen-hand hacks, Uncle Hugh was a patriarchal figure; at seventy he had a "back" like a trooper of the Victorian Mounted Police, whose black helmets, carbines, bandoleers, "concertina" boots with white whipcord tights, and gray horses contributed a somewhat menacing ceremony to civic processions. The association was fixed in my mind by a verse in "Waltzing Matilda," the national song, that recounts the fatal consequences of stealing sheep:

*Down came the squatter mounted on his thoroughbred,*
*Down came the troopers, One! Two! Three!*

On an aged, big-barrelled pony, a relic of my Cousin Rob's childhood, I tooled along behind this personage, chafed at my bare knees, bursting with chatter and not daring to open my little gob. One visit, when I was twelve, I remember in particular, because of an experience with some crows. It was a dry year in a dry land. The thin trees shed their bark like snakeskin; the grass was brown and did not fully cover the hard brown earth. The plain was the color of a mangy brindled greyhound, and over it the sheep moved like lice. From time to time, the vigilant old master shepherd would see something untoward; it was lambing time, and there had been frosts, mild but enough to cramp the peristaltic movements of birth, so that here and there the legs or the head of a half-born lamb protruded from the hinder parts of a distressed ewe. Deft yet perfunctory, Uncle Hugh went among the lambing mob, a mounted midwife. Now and then a ewe would flee in panic from her deliverer; it was my role to dismount and run down this recalcitrant mother—a disconcerting task, because sometimes the face of the unborn lamb stared back reproachfully, it seemed to me, as I sprinted in its wake. Uncle Hugh would say nothing except to bark at the ragtaggle of dogs, but every now and then a heroic belch, a detonation like a threepenny firecracker, would issue from the thickets of his beard. He was the victim of some corrosive kind of indigestion. As he rode, he swigged a solution of baking soda from a silver flask; as far as I could hear, it did nothing to dampen the fires within.

In addition to this, as a sort of base fuel dump, a big gazogene of soda water stood perpetually on the south side of the veranda at Gracelands. This engine, about the size and shape of an old-fashioned, wasp-waisted dressmaker's form, it was the business of my Cousin Ishbel—the practical one—to fill. This she did with some trepidation. The device generated its own gas—carbon dioxide, I suppose—from the action of chemicals, and it needed strong nerves and light fingers to get the top screwed on before pressure built up. Once or twice, she was too late; the metal top whistled past her averted face like the warhead of a rocket, to bury itself in the plasterboard ceiling of the kitchen. Whenever I helped myself to this bubbly water, I did so with the knowledge that if my Cousin Ishbel chanced by, I would be given a *look*. As a congenitally displaced person, I was then, as now, very afraid of *looks*.

Uncle Hugh's indigestion, I learned much later, was no casual affliction; it had deep roots in history and theology. He was one of, I think, six sons of Big Alec McInstrie, the first settler of this region—called the Mallee, from the hard-leaf, scrubby growth that covered the flat plains and gave shelter to the wallaby, the mallee hen, the emu, and the blackfellow.[5] The tables of consanguinity are all jumbled in my head now, but I seem to recall that there was some marriage of cousins—Adamses, Glasgows, or McInstries—in this generation that related me to both sides of the family. It is difficult to see how they could have avoided

---

5. *blackfellow,* an Australian aborigine.

this sort of marriage, short of the unthinkable expedients of marrying Catholics, English, or blackfellows. Rollers made of massive logs and towed by bullock teams demolished the scrubby growth of the Mallee, and Big Alec tore a huge "holding" out of this ill-favored wilderness. Here he held sway in a manner that was part patriarchal, part theocratic.[6] He must indeed have been like those least sympathetic of pioneers, the Boers of South Africa. Mercifully, there was one difference: the blackfellows, unlike the Zulus and Hottentots,[7] declined to become a race of slaves. When domesticated, they stole; they took off their pants to "go walkabout" (i.e., reverted to nomadism); conveniently and, it would seem, unanimously they decided to die, and flickered away into the dwindling bush to cough out their lungs amid the bones of sheep and kangaroo. They built no houses; their disappearance was total. Within sixty years of my ancestors' arrival on their unhappy hunting grounds, it was as if blackfellows had never been. There was no war and no Little Big Horn.[8] They died, for the most part, of children's ailments—whooping cough and measles. It must have been an old story to the big harsh Ulsterman; had not his family, a few generations before, shouldered the aboriginal Catholic Irish off their ancient lands? Sly and feckless Gael, sly and feckless aborigine. It must have confirmed the patriarch in his savageries against land and flesh, confirmed his pitiless Calvinism.[9]

So began a pastoral aristocracy, unique in that it had no serfs, though the God of John Knox would provide these in the fullness of time. Meanwhile, it fell to Big Alec's six sons

---

**6.** *theocratic.* Theocracy is government by a priestly elite as representatives of God. **7.** *Boers . . . Hottentots.* The Boers were Dutch who settled in South Africa in the middle of the seventeenth century. Zulus and Hottentots are native races of South Africa. **8.** *Little Big Horn,* a battle fought near the Little Big Horn River in southern Montana on June 25, 1876, in which the Sioux defeated and killed General George Armstrong Custer and his entire detachment. **9.** *Calvinism,* a Protestant sect established by John Calvin (1509–1564), which emphasized predestination. John Knox (1505?–1572), the founder of Scottish Presbyterianism, was a disciple of Calvin's.

to supply the omission. They were the arrows in his quiver, though the Biblical image is somewhat too delicate for the case; their work was brutal, continuous, backbreaking. Nasty, long, brutish, and hard. There is something fitting, I suppose, in the fact that the doctrine of Knox and Calvin should have returned at last, in its pure form, to the sort of terrain from which it had sprung—back to this near-desert, far from the winebibbers, tax gatherers, and bedizened women. Under the roof of bark or iron, the pioneer McInstrie presided—priest, taskmaster, and patriarch—in prayers to the just and jealous deity whom he resembled, or perhaps merely represented. At family meals—mutton, homemade bread, and tea—old McInstrie alone took a seat. He dispensed his blessing on this Spartan board, and the sons, huge, bearded, red-wristed, ate standing at their places. "Slow at meat, slow at work," said the patriarch. Across the years, my Great-Uncle Hugh's gastric juices sounded a protest against this scheme of things, though he never formulated his objections in words.

Needless to say, my character failed to meet the exacting standards of my great-uncle. I was a puny little fellow; I always had my nose in some book; I would never grow up to be an Ulsterman. What is more, I knew what an Ulsterman was. "A Scotchman," Uncle Hugh told me, "is an improved kind of man. An Ulsterman is an improved kind of Scotchman." It was probably meant as some kind of dim Scotch joke, but at that age I believed what I was told by men of seventy with beards. Of course, I was half an Adams, but then the name Lee cuts no ice in the real Deep South; it is merely English. Nor did I know the worst, though the McInstries must have known it. My father's mother's name was Guinney. She was the daughter of a Corkman, who was possibly a transportee,[10] certainly a Catholic, and the McInstries must have been watching me narrowly for the

---

**10.** *transportee*, a felon sent to one of the penal colonies.

moment this Papist taint should show itself. I think it must have been on my peculiar attitude toward birds that the family suspicion focussed.

In those dreary plains, the sky and the birds that inhabited it alone had beauty. It was a magical experience to see a "mob" of galahs rise screeching from the khaki-colored plains; they kept a strict flight pattern, showing now their dove-gray backs and now, in a flash, their rose-colored breasts. Budgerigars were common as sparrows, and we ate them in game pie, like quail. Always the air was filled with the lovely carolling of "magpies"—really a kind of shrike, with a voice range between tenor flute and oboe. The "robins" were red as tanagers, and there were "wrens" like blue enamel. There were mallee hens, who hatch their eggs in nesting mounds in the manner of turtles, and there was the bowerbird, which makes a display house of woven sticks decorated with bright pebbles, wildflowers, and bits of broken glass. One species even paints the sticks with the juice of crushed berries. It was my ambition to find such a bower; the bird was the only artist living in that vast region, and may still be, for all I know.

My relatives thought there was something not quite normal in all this interest in ornithology. I should have been out massacring rabbits instead of mooning over birds. Nor was this the worst. Somehow, it had come out that I had signed a pledge to protect native birds. There was some propaganda in the schools about birds being fostered, and I was probably its most devout believer. I had joined the Gould League of Bird Lovers (John Gould was the Audubon of Australia), and had been awarded books and a very light gold medal for some ornithological precocity. I thus took my covenant very solemnly, but it must have seemed not quite manly, and even impertinent, to my country relatives. They knew that practically all living things except sheep, horses, and dogs (cows they despised) were destructive or, at best, useless. Long ago they had slaughtered the last emus, and if other birds were tolerated, it was only because they did not kill themselves by getting tangled up in barbed-wire fences. Certainly my relatives were not going to be informed by me that the straw-necked ibis ate grasshoppers or that the wedge-tailed eagle preferred rabbit. These magnificent eagles were common. My uncle shot them and spread their eight-foot wings along the top of fences, presumably as a warning to the others; someday one of them might take a lamb. Scotch-Irish Presbyterians have a natural and doctrinal faculty for putting others in the wrong, and subtly I was made to feel that I was in league with the enemies of good animal husbandry.

Sunday was a dreadful day; after breakfast, I had to put on my best blue serge suit and drive with the family, in my uncle's car, for thirty miles to church. The hot leather car seat prickled all the way. The church was perched on poles capitaled with sheet tin to defeat the "white ants," or termites. It had a corrugated-iron roof to let the heat in and wooden sides to keep it there. For never less than forty-five minutes, a man with a Scottish accent preached to the beards and sensible hats below him. There were also hymns. My head nodded in the heat; it would have hatched an emu's egg. The service, I daresay, had come unchanged from the wet stone kirks[11] of Antrim or Perthshire; but, cold or hot, the discomfort, no doubt, was the main thing. I envied "the men"—Englishmen and slaves, and therefore not Presbyterians—lolling on their burlap bunks in the hut and reading three-month-old copies of *John O'London's Weekly*.

I was not supposed to do anything on Sunday. I could read, because reading was not doing anything—James Oliver Curwood and Zane Grey, or a fascinating veterinary encyclopedia called the Australian Stock and Station Doctor, or a coverless copy of Emile Zola's *Nana,* which I had found behind the dresser—or I could play with Cousin

---

11. *kirks,* churches. [*Scottish*]

Rob's model donkey engine. It was a beautiful little machine of brass and steel, activated by a lamp of methylated spirits. I had seen with wonder how its little piston and flywheel worked in just the same way as the great early Steam Age monster near the haystacks, which powered the chaffcutter.

After Sunday-night family prayers, it was Great-Aunt Maggie's gentle custom to read from a popular anthology of Australian verse entitled *Bush Ballads and Galloping Rhymes.* My favorite was "The Sick Stockrider," one stanza of which my great-aunt always read with a peculiar intonation.

*A steer ripped up McPherson at the Cooraminta yards*
*And Donavan was drowned at Sink-or-Swim;*
*Tim Burke who got in trouble in that business with the cards:*
*It matters little what became of him!*
*And Sullivan the rider at The Horsefall broke his neck;*
*Faith! The wonder was he saved his neck so long!*
*And Mostyn! Poor Frank Mostyn died at last a fearful wreck*
*In The Horrors at the Upper Wandinong.*

I did not know at the time that "The Horrors" was Australian for delirium tremens, or that my Cousin Rob had taken to drink; I was under the impression it was the name for some terrible stretch of quicksand. In the books I was reading at the time, half the villains perished in bogs, quagmires, or quicksands; why not Mostyn?

One Sunday afternoon after lunch, still in my blue serge suit, I dawdled out to the stables and quietly saddled the pony. She was an opinionated little brute, and contested my invasion of her retirement with every mule-headed quirk at her command. She liked to trot, but finally I forced her into a resentful canter. I was not a confident horseman; moreover, the comfortable rocking-horse gait went better with the galloping metre of "The Sick Stockrider," which was then buzzing through my head. I had not broken the Sabbath idly; I had an objective—the lambing paddock behind the cathedral-size woolshed. I had seen plovers there. Like a small wading bird to look at, the plover has more a lark's habits; it lays its speckled eggs in a shallow cup on the open ground. There was a fair-sized mob of ewes and lambs in the paddock, and even more crows than usual. There were always crows. I tethered the pony and walked to where I had last seen the plovers. I was lucky. After about two hundred yards or so afoot, a plover dropped at my feet, crying and trailing a wing, pretending that it was broken. This was what I had come to "observe"—the plover's "broken-wing" defense of its open nest. My prize books had put me on to the dodge; I backed away from the plover, knowing that I was getting closer to the nest. This distressed the plover, which repeated its tactics several times. It is a pretty thing to watch, and perhaps even then I was conscious of its realism, in that it is based on an appeal to cruelty rather than pity. I must have cut an odd figure, weaving and backing in the middle of a thirty-acre paddock, a small blue-clad form pursued by ghosts in the glare of a hot spring afternoon. In this way, I fell, literally, having backed into a ewe, and cracked the back of my head on the iron-hard ground. I started to laugh—at that age one always tried to laugh—although there was no one there, but stopped, for I saw that the ewe had had its eyes pecked out.

The crows that had done this circled in the air out of gunshot range. The plover forgotten, I looked at the ewe; blood ran from each empty eye socket in a thin red line and clotted its whiskered cheeks. I tried to get the ewe on its feet; it kicked convulsively. I straddled it and heaved at the valances of greasy wool round its shoulders. No use. A single sheep is no more tractable than a wild goat; nothing can be done with a single blind sheep. Panting and close to tears, I started for my pony, which stood flicking its tail at the flies in the shade of the thin mallee. I had got halfway there in a sobbing run when I was aware that the circling crows had dropped into an efficient circle round the ewe.

The Corvidae are good at observing people. I ran back, trying to roar like my uncle. The crows again circled in the air.

I don't know how long I stood looking at the ewe. The sermon that day had dealt with Abraham and Isaac[12]—Presbyterians are very fond of the Old Testament. During it I had opened and shut the blades of my clasp knife, trying to keep awake. It seemed now like an intimation of what I should do. I then discovered how hard it is to cut a sheep's throat with a small knife, and I was shaken and bloody by the time the ewe seemed to die. The pony shied at my bloody hands and shied again at an eagle spread on the woodshed fence. By the time I got back to the stables, I was pretty much of a nervous wreck. I washed my hands and the clasp knife before I took the bridle off the pony. I took my time; I was in no hurry to go into the house with my sensational confession.

They were all in the kitchen, eating scones and drinking tea round the long table, and talking about the *hubris*[13] some neighbor had displayed in his choice of a hotel when he went to Melbourne. Although only a sheep farmer like the McInstries themselves, who stayed at Scott's, or even at my father's modest house, this neighbor put up at Menzies', where the "breeders" went.

"Menzies' for His Lordship," said my cousin Ishbel. *"Menzies'."* My Cousin Marie and her husband, Craig Gordon, were visiting. He was a big man who had ridden with the Australian Light Horse, and he voiced his distaste for the neighbor, who had been seen to wear plus fours.[14]

---

12. *Abraham and Isaac.* Abraham, instructed by God to offer his son Isaac in sacrifice as a test of fidelity, was halted in this act at the last moment by an angel, who pointed out a ram caught in a nearby thicket as an acceptable substitute. (Genesis 22:1–14) 13. *hubris,* an arrogant and impious disregard of moral laws. 14. *plus fours,* a style of loose-fitting pants gathered at the knee, so called because they were four inches longer than the knickerbockers of which they were a type.

Even my Cousin Flo (the kind one) showed her disapproval. "They buy butter and even eggs. *Eggs!*" she said.

"Ride in silk, beg in frieze,"[15] said Uncle Hugh cryptically. I brooded with them for a while about the criminal folly of this man who stayed at *Menzies'*, bought eggs, and wore plus fours. At least he had not killed a sheep. I decided to count to a hundred and then break the news.

"I had to kill a sheep!" I blurted out.

Full of scone, their jaws gaped.

"You had to kill a sheep," they all said.

My Cousin Ishbel gave me one of her *looks.*

"What?" bellowed my uncle. "A ewe? Where? Why?"

Miserably, I began my narrative. I was soon made to understand its weak points; they all knew why the ewe was "down"—a hard lambing. Now, if I had ridden straight back to the house, there was a chance the lamb could have been saved.

"The crows," I went on explaining. "The crows kept coming back."

After a while, my uncle went out to tell one of the men to yoke up a gig and drive out and skin the ewe. I slunk out to the orchard with a book, and the family debate on my conduct got under way.

There were the usual prayers after Sunday-night tea. After we creaked to our feet (we had been crouching at our chairs), my Great-Aunt Maggie disposed herself to read. She chose a piece less lively than "The Sick Stockrider." As I recall, it presented in verse dialogue a debate on the virtues of bush life versus that of the city. It was very long, and my aunt read slowly; it was longer than my uncle's prayers, and a good deal more intelligible, since her accent was less Scottish and she did not have the acoustical hazard of a beard. While she read, I looked at the rug she had spread on her knees—for in that near-desert the nights were cold after the hottest day. It was of tartan wool on one

---

**15.** *frieze,* a kind of coarse woolen cloth.

side and patchwork on the other. The patchwork was fur, the skins of many domestic cats—black, tabby, tortoise-shell, gray, and one splendid ginger-colored pelt big as a doormat. One of the farm cats had been caught with the feathers of a new-hatched chicken on its jaws, so they were all exterminated; with Presbyterian thrift, their skins had been sent to the fellmonger's. My great-aunt had personally conducted this felicide, by a technique I need not describe.

My great-aunt's recitation came to its end. As might be expected, the protagonist of the pioneering virtues had the last word. She read this passage with the same peculiar intonation she used for the "Horrors" passage. As it concerned me, I got the point. The ballad ended:

*For the bush will never suit you*
*And you'll never suit the bush.*

I felt I had been preached at for the second time that day, and I was glad to escape to bed.

Over morning porridge and tea, I avoided all eyes. After breakfast, my uncle took up his stance at the soda-water gazogene. Between barks and rumblings, he bellowed at me, "Well, what do you think of your birds now?" I said nothing.

Next: "How would you like to make a crow trap?"

As far as his principles let him, my uncle was a kind man, and I saw that he was offering me a chance to redeem myself. But there was something more. What about the pledge? Crows were native birds, were they not? A wild thought came to me. Would I have to return my gold medal?

By this time, I was trotting at my uncle's heels toward what was called the machinery shed. Open-sided, thatched with wheat straw, pillared with bleached trunks of iron-bark trees, this structure did give shelter of a kind to a rank of large, crude horse-drawn implements. All of them—the gang plows, harrows, seed drills, harvesters, and so on—

were thickly gloved in a calcified blizzard of chicken dung. There were always a few crows about, hoping perhaps for eggs and grain, or more likely for the pickings to be had below the gallows rigged at one end to butcher the weekly sheep for the farm tables.

Here would be the place for a trap. My uncle's roars set one of his Englishmen scurrying about in the shed and the smithy for two-by-fours, spades, wire netting, and nails. I was issued a hammer and saw. While this went on, it occurred to me that my uncle knew more about crows than seemed possible for a non-member of the Gould League of Bird Lovers; in fact, he knew more about them than I did. His trap was based on the observation that crows, like buzzards and other carrion-feeding birds, need a short take-off run before they are airborne. Accordingly, from his instructions I set about making a net cage about ten feet long and six feet high with a crow-sized opening at the top. The crows would be lured into the trap by the carcass of a sheep and have no room to fly out the way they had come. No one knew better than I that a carcass was available, out there in the lambing paddock.

It took me all day to construct the trap. It was a pretty good job, although I had to get help with the netting from Walter, one of the Englishmen. He was rather surly about it. With his national instinct for social lines, Walter had shrewdly assessed my standing in the household, and he spoke freely. "Bleedin' abaht. Old baskit thinks 'e'll catch just one flamin' crow with this bleedin' contraption, 'e's got another think comin'." This while between us we hefted the carcass of my sheep into the middle of the trap.

Walter was bleedin' well wrong. Next morning, there were a dozen splendid black crows screeching like lost souls and flapping against the wire. I came back to the house to report my success, and traced my uncle by ear to the soda-water gazogene. "Twelve of them," I said with pride. He gave me a couple of stunning pats on the back and cocked an eye at me quizzically.

A disc plowshare hung on the veranda. My uncle beat a brisk tattoo on this with a short club—evidently the handle of a cricket bat—and two of his Englishmen came up to the gate. Then something else occurred to me about my uncle; he not only knew more about crows than I did, he was enjoying himself more than I was. He was a boyish patriarch. He walked jauntily out to the crow trap, twirling the broken piece of cricket bat like a shillelagh.

"Thirteen." He corrected my count with decision. "Thirteen black devils from hell. In you go," he added. The Englishmen gaped, and so did I. "Always kill what you trap," said my uncle. He handed me the club. "In you go," he repeated as he made an opening for me in the wire.

Recurrent nightmares bring the scene back to me to this day. I only ask of the reader that he should imagine himself required to club to death thirteen large black birds with a wingspread little short of his own outstretched arms.

One thought filled my mind as I received the congratulations of all. Would this killing of crows go on day after day?

The crows solved the problem for me; the Corvidae are the most intelligent of birds as well as the drabbest. Not a one came near my trap again.

As I left Wanboon, I received two gifts to take on the long trip home. One I had long coveted—my cousin's donkey engine, the only piece of machinery I have ever properly understood. The other was the cat-skin rug. It was felt that somehow one or the other would make a man of me in the end. ♦

# Alun Lewis

# THE RAID

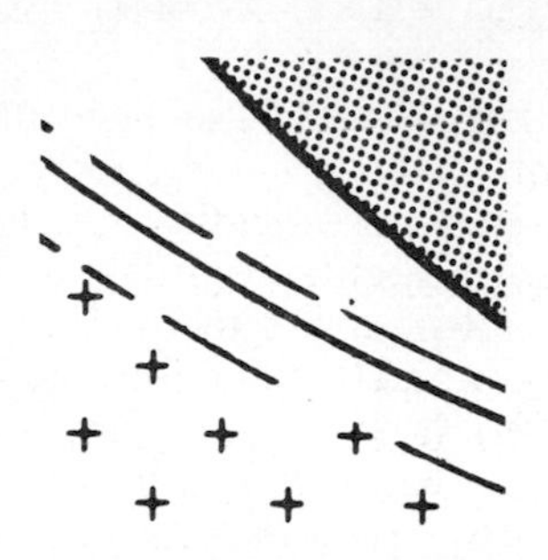

MY PLATOON AND I were on training that morning. We've been on training every morning for the last three years, for that matter. On this occasion it was Current Affairs, which always boils down to how long the war is going to last, and when the orderly told me the C. O. wanted me in his office I broke the lads off for a cup of tea from the charwallah[1] and nipped over to the orderly room, tidying myself as I went. I didn't expect anything unusual until I took a cautionary peep through the straw window of his matting shed and saw a strange officer in there. So I did a real dapper salute and braced myself. Self-defence is always the first instinct, self-suspicion the second. But I hadn't been drunk since I came to India and I hadn't written anything except love in my letters. As for politics, as far as they're concerned I don't exist, I'm never in. The other chap was a major and had a red armband.

"Come in, Selden," the colonel said. "This is the D. A. P. M. Head of military police. Got a job for you. Got your map case?"

"No sir. It's in company office."

"Hurry off and fetch it."

When I came back they were hard at it, bending over the

---

"The Raid" by Alun Lewis from IN THE GREEN TREE. Reprinted by permission of George Allen & Unwin Ltd.

1. *charwallah,* a servant.

inch map. The C. O. looked up. His face got very red when he bent.

"Here's your objective, Selden. This village here, Chaudanullah. Eighteen miles away. Route: track south of Morje, riverbed up to Pimpardi, turn south a mile before Pimpardi and strike across the watershed on a fixed bearing. Work it out with a protractor on the map and set your compass before you march off. Strike the secondary road below this group of huts here, 247568, cross the road and work up the canal to the village. Throw a cordon round the village with two sections of your platoon. Take the third yourself and search the houses methodically. Government has a paid agent in the village who will meet you at this canal bridge here—got it?—at 06.00 hours.[2] The agent reported that your man arrived there last night after dark and is lying up in one of the hovels."

"What man, sir?" I asked.

"Christ, didn't I tell you? Why the devil didn't you stop me? This fellow, what's-his-name—it's all on that paper there—he's wanted. Remember the bomb in the cinema last Tuesday, killed three British other ranks? He's wanted for that. Read the description before you go. Any questions so far? Right. Well, you'll avoid all houses, make a detour round villages, keep off the road all the way. Understand? News travels faster than infantry in India. He'll be away before you're within ten miles if you show yourself. Let's see. Twenty miles by night. Give you ten hours. Leave here at 19.30 hours. Arrive an hour before first light. Go in at dawn, keep your eyes skinned. M. T. will R. V.[3] outside the village at dawn. Drive the prisoner straight to jail. D. A. P. M. will be there."

"Very good, sir. Dress, sir?" I said.

"Dress? P.T. shoes, cloth caps, overalls, basic pouches,

---

2. *06.00 hours.* To avoid confusion between the hours before and after noon, military time is expressed on a twenty-four hour basis. Thus, 06.00 hours is 6 A.M. The time 6 P.M. would be expressed as 18.00 hours. 3. *M. T. will R. V.*, military transport will rendezvous.

rifles, fifty rounds of .303 per man, and grenades. Sixty-nine grenades if he won't come out, thirty-six grenades if he makes a fight of it. Anything else?"

"No, sir."

"Good. Remember to avoid the villages. Stalk him good and proper. Keep upwind of him. I'm picking you and your platoon because I think you're the best I've got. I want results, Selden."

"I'll give you a good show, sir."

"Bloody good shot with a point 22, Selden is," the C. O. said to the D. A. P. M. by way of light conversation. "Shot six mallard with me last Sunday."

"Of course we want the man alive, sir, if it's at all possible," the D. A. P. M. said, fiddling with his nervous pink moustache. "He's not proved guilty yet, you see, sir, and with public opinion in India what it is."

"Quite," said the colonel. "Quite. Make a note of that, Selden. Tell your men to shoot low."

"Very good, sir."

"Got the route marked on your talc?"

"Yes, sir." I'd marked the route in chinograph pencil and the Chaudanullah place in red as we do for enemy objectives. It was all thick.

"Rub it all off, then. Security. Read his description. Have you read it? What is it?"

"Dark eyes, sir. Scar on left knee. Prominent cheekbones. Left corner of mouth droops. Front incisor discoloured. Last seen wearing European suit, may be dressed in native dhoti, Mahratta style."

"And his ring?" said the C. O. He's as keen as mustard the old man is.

"Oh yes, sir. Plain gold wedding ring."

"Correct. Don't forget these details. Invaluable sometimes. Off with you."

I saluted and marched out.

"Damn good fellow, Selden," I heard the C. O. say. "Your man is in the bag."

I felt pretty pleased with that. Comes of shooting those six mallard.

The platoon was reassembling after their tea and I felt pretty important, going back with all that dope. After all, it was the first bit of action we'd seen in two and a half years. It would be good for morale. I knew they'd moan like hell, having to do a twenty-mile route march by night, but I could sell them that all right. So I fell them in in threes and called them to attention for disciplinary reasons and told them they'd been picked for a special job and this was it. . . .

They were very impressed by the time I'd finished.

"Any questions?" I said.

"Yes, sir," said Chalky White. He was an L. P. T. B. conductor and you won't find him forgetting a halfpenny. "Do we take haversack rations and will we be in time for breakfast?" He thinks the same way as Napoleon.[4]

"Yes," I said. "Anything else?"

"What's this fellow done, sir?" Bottomley asked, then. Bottomley always was a bit Bolshie, and he's had his knife into me for two and a half years because I was a bank clerk in Civvy Street and played golf on Sundays.

"Killed three troops, I think," I said. "Is that good enough?"

I felt I'd scored pretty heavy over his Red stuff this time.

"Right," I said. "Break off till 19.00 hours. Keep your mouths shut. White will draw rations at the cookhouse. No cigarettes or matches will be taken."

I did that for disciplinary purposes. They didn't say a word. Pretty good.

We crossed the start line dead on 19.30 hours and everybody looked at us with some interest. I felt mighty "hush-hush." My security was first class. Hadn't told a soul, except Ken More and Ted Paynter.

---

4. *He thinks . . . as Napoleon.* The observation that "an army marches on its stomach" has been attributed to Napoleon.

"Bring 'em back alive," a soldier jeered outside the cookhouse.

Somebody's let the cat out of the bag. Damn them all. Can't trust a soul in the ranks with the skin of a sausage.

Anyway, we got going bang away. I knew the first stretch past Morje and Pimpardi and we did about three miles an hour there. The night was breathless and stuffy; we put hankies round our foreheads to keep the sweat out of our eyes. And the perpetual buzzing of the crickets got on my nerves like a motor horn when the points jam and all the pedestrians laugh. I suppose I was a bit worked up. Every time a mosquito or midge touched me I let out a blow fit to knacker a bull. But I settled down after a while and began to enjoy the sense of freedom and deep still peace that informs the night out in the tropics. You've read all about tropical stars; well, it's quite true. They're marvellous; and we use some of them for direction-finding at night too. The Plough, for instance, and one called Cassiopeia that you bisect for the Pole Star.

Then there was the tricky bit over the mountain by compass. I just hoped for the best on that leg. Luckily the moon came up and put the lads in a good mood. I allowed them to talk in whispers for one hour and they had to keep silent for the next hour for disciplinary reasons. We halted for half an hour on the crest of the watershed and ate our bully beef sandwiches with relish, though bully tastes like a hot poultice out here. It was a damn fine view from that crest. A broad valley a thousand feet below with clusters of fires in the villages and round a hill temple on the other side. Either a festival or a funeral, obviously. I could hear the drums beating there, too; it was very clear and echoing, made my flesh creep. You feel so out of it in India somehow. You just slink around in the wilds and you feel very white and different. I don't know. . . . You know, I'd have said that valley *hated* us that night, on those rocky crests. Queer.

I didn't know which group of huts was which, but I could

see the canal glittering in the moonlight so I was near enough right, praise be. The jackals were howling too, and some creature came right up to us, it gave me a scare. I knew that bully had a pretty bad stench. Anyway we got on the move again, Chalky White saying next stop Hammersmiff Bridge, and we slithered down as quietly as we could, hanging on to each other's rifles on the steep bits. We made our way between the villages and the drums beat themselves into a frenzy that had something personal about it. Then we went up the canal for about four miles, keeping about a hundred yards off the path and pretty rough going it was. Then we came to what I felt must be our objective, a cluster of crumbled huts on the foothills, pretty poor show even for these parts, and the boys were blistered and beat so I scattered them under the bushes and told them to lie low. It was only 5.30A.M. and the agent fellow wasn't due until six. I had a nap myself, matter-of-fact, though it's a shootable offence. I woke up with a start and it was five past six, and I peered round my tree and there wasn't a sound. No drums, no jackals, no pie dogs.[5] It was singing in my ears, the silence, and I wished to God we'd got this job over. It could go wrong so easily. He might fight, or his pals might help him, or he might have got wind of us, or I might have come to the wrong place. I was like an old woman. I loaded my Colt and felt better. Then I went down the canal to look for the chowkey fellow.[6] I took a pretty poor view of a traitor, but I took a poorer view of him not turning up. He wasn't there and I walked up the path and just when I was getting really scared he appeared out of nowhere and I damn near shot him on the spot.

"Officer sahib huzzoor," he said. "Mai Sarkar ko dost hai," something. And he said the name of the man I was after, which was the password.

"Achiba," I said, meaning good show. "Tairo a minute

---

5. *pie dogs*, pariah dogs, half-wild animals that act as scavengers around Indian villages. 6. *chowkey fellow*, a lookout.

while I bolo my phaltan and then we'll jao jillo." He got the idea.

I nipped back and roused the lads quietly from under the trees and we moved up like ghosts on that village. I never want to see that village again. It was so still and fragile in the reluctant grey light. Even the pie dogs were asleep, and the bullocks lying on their sides. Once I travelled overnight from Dieppe to Paris and the countryside looked just as ghostly that morning. But this time it was dangerous. I had a feeling somebody was going to die and there'd be a hell of a shemozzle. And at the same time the houses looked so poor and harmless, almost timid somehow. And the chowkey bloke was like a ghost. It was seeing him so scared that put me steady again. He was afraid of being seen with us as far as I could make out, and said he'd show us where this fellow was lying up and then he'd disappear please. I said never mind about the peace, let's get the war over first, and I told Bottomley to watch the bloke in case he had anything up his sleeve.

We got to the ring of trees outside the village without a sound, and the two section leaders led their men round each side of the village in a pincer movement. All the boys were white and dirty and their eyes were like stones. I remember suddenly feeling very proud of them just then.

I gave them ten minutes to get into position and close the road at the rear of the village. And then a damned pie dog set up a yelp over on the right flank and another replied with a long shivering howl. I knew things would start going wrong if I didn't act quickly. We didn't want the village to find out until we'd gone if possible. For political reasons. And for reasons of health, I thought. So I gave the "follow-me" sign and closed in on the huddled houses. There were a couple of outlying houses with a little shrine, and then the village proper with a crooked street running down it. The chowkey seemed to know where to go. I pointed to the single buildings and he said, "Nay, sahib," and pointed to the street. So I posted a man to picket the shrine and led the rest through the bush behind our scruffy guide. He moved like a beaten dog, crouching and limping, barefoot. There was a dead ox in the bush and a pair of kites sleeping and gorged beside it. It stank like a bad death. Turned me. We hurried on. The bushes were in flower, sort of wisteria, the blossoms closed and drooping. We crept along under a tumbledown wall and paused, kneeling, at the street corner. I posted two men there, one on each side with fixed bayonets, to fire down the street if he bolted. The other two sections would be covering it from the other end. Then I nudged the chowkey man and signalled to my grenade man and rifleman to cover me in. I slipped round the corner and went gingerly down the street. Suddenly I felt quite cool and excited at the same time. The chowkey went about fifteen yards down the street and then slunk against the wall on his knees, pointing inwards to the house he was kneeling against. It was made of branches woven with straw and reed, a beggared place. He looked up at me and my revolver and he was sweating with fear. He had the pox all over his face, too. I took a breath to steady myself, took the first pressure on my trigger, kicked the door lattice aside and jumped in. Stand in the light in the doorway and you're a dead man.

I crouched in the dark corner. It was very dark in there still. There was a pile of straw on the floor and straw heaped in the corner. And some huge thing moved ponderously. I nearly yelped. Then I saw what it was. It was a cow. Honestly. A sleepy fawn cow with a soft mild face like somebody's dream woman.

"She never frew no bomb," Chalky said. He was my rifleman. Cool as ice. His voice must have broken the fellow's nerve. There was a huge rustle in the straw in the corner behind the cow and a man stood up, a man in a white dhoti, young, thin, sort of smiling. Discoloured teeth. Chalky lunged his bayonet. The chap still had plenty of nerve left. He just swayed a little.

"Please," he said. "Have you got a smoke upon you?"

"Watch him, White," I said. I searched him.

"Please," he said. "I have nothing." He was breathing quickly and smiling.

"Come on," I said. "Quietly."

"You know you are taking me to my death?" he said. "No doubt?"

"I'm taking you to Poona," I said. "You killed three of our men."

The smile sort of congealed on his face. Like a trick. His head nodded like an old doll. "Did I?" he said. "Three men died? Did I?"

"Come on," I said. "It's daylight."

"It's dreadful," he said. He looked sick. I felt sorry for him, nodding his head and sick, sallow. Looked like a student, I should say.

"Keep your hands up," Chalky said, prodding him in the back.

We went quietly down the street, no incident at all, and I signalled the two enveloping sections together and we got down the road out of sight. I was in a cold sweat and I wanted to laugh.

The trucks weren't there. God, I cursed them, waiting there. They might bitch the whole show. The villagers were going to the well quite close.

"What did you do it for, mate?" I heard Bottomley ask.

After a long silence the chap said very quietly, "For my country."

Chalky said, "Everybody says that. Beats me." Then we heard the trucks, and Chalky said, "We ought to be there in time for breakfast, boys." ◆

# Katherine Mansfield

## THE FLY

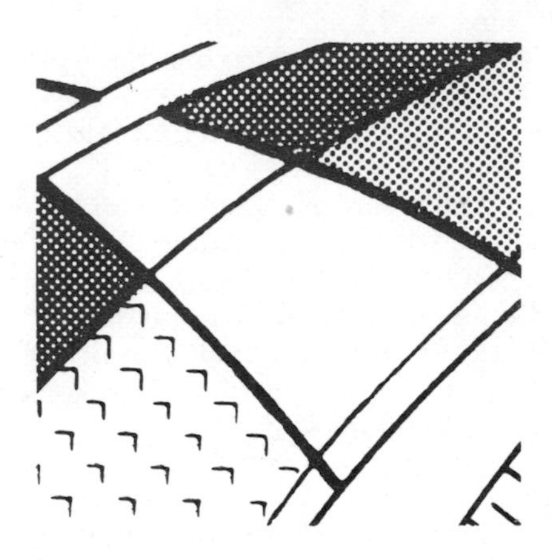

"Y'ARE VERY SNUG in here," piped old Mr. Woodifield, and he peered out of the great, green leather armchair by his friend the boss' desk as a baby peers out of its pram. His talk was over; it was time for him to be off. But he did not want to go. Since he had retired, since his . . . stroke, the wife and the girls kept him boxed up in the house every day of the week except Tuesday. On Tuesday he was dressed up and brushed and allowed to cut back to the City for the day. Though what he did there the wife and girls couldn't imagine. Made a nuisance of himself to his friends, they supposed. . . . Well, perhaps so. All the same, we cling to our last pleasures as the tree clings to its last leaves. So there sat old Woodifield, smoking a cigar and staring almost greedily at the boss, who rolled in his office chair,

---

"The Fly" from THE SHORT STORIES OF KATHERINE MANSFIELD. Copyright 1922 and renewed 1950 by J. Middleton Murry. Reprinted by permission of Alfred A. Knopf, Inc. and The Society of Authors as the literary representative of the Estate of Katherine Mansfield.

stout, rosy, five years older than he, and still going strong, still at the helm. It did one good to see him.

Wistfully, admiringly, the old voice added, "It's snug in here, upon my word!"

"Yes, it's comfortable enough," agreed the boss, and he flipped the *Financial Times* with a paper knife. As a matter-of-fact he was proud of his room; he liked to have it admired, especially by old Woodifield. It gave him a feeling of deep, solid satisfaction to be planted there in the midst of it in full view of that frail old figure in the muffler.

"I've had it done up lately," he explained, as he had explained for the past—how many?—weeks. "New carpet," and he pointed to the bright red carpet with a pattern of large white rings. "New furniture," and he nodded towards the massive bookcase and the table with legs like twisted treacle.[1] "Electric heating!" He waved almost exultantly towards the five transparent, pearly sausages glowing so softly in the tilted copper pan.

But he did not draw old Woodifield's attention to the photograph over the table of a grave-looking boy in uniform standing in one of those spectral photographers' parks with photographers' storm clouds behind him. It was not new. It had been there for over six years.

"There was something I wanted to tell you," said old Woodifield, and his eyes grew dim remembering. "Now what was it? I had it in my mind when I started out this morning." His hands began to tremble, and patches of red showed above his beard.

Poor old chap, he's on his last pins, thought the boss. And, feeling kindly, he winked at the old man, and said jokingly, "I tell you what. I've got a little drop of something here that'll do you good before you go out into the cold again. It's beautiful stuff. It wouldn't hurt a child." He took a key off his watch chain, unlocked a cupboard below his desk, and drew forth a dark, squat bottle. "That's the

---

1. *treacle*, molasses.

medicine," said he. "And the man from whom I got it told me on the strict Q. T. it came from the cellars at Windsor Cassel."[2]

Old Woodifield's mouth fell open at the sight. He couldn't have looked more surprised if the boss had produced a rabbit.

"It's whisky, ain't it?" he piped, feebly.

The boss turned the bottle and lovingly showed him the label. Whisky it was.

"D'you know," said he, peering up at the boss wonderingly, "they won't let me touch it at home." And he looked as though he was going to cry.

"Ah, that's where we know a bit more than the ladies," cried the boss, swooping across for two tumblers that stood on the table with the water bottle, and pouring a generous finger into each. "Drink it down. It'll do you good. And don't put any water with it. It's sacrilege to tamper with stuff like this. Ah!" He tossed off his, pulled out his handkerchief, hastily wiped his moustaches, and cocked an eye at old Woodifield, who was rolling his in his chaps.

The old man swallowed, was silent a moment, and then said faintly, "It's nutty!"

But it warmed him; it crept into his chill old brain—he remembered.

"That was it," he said, heaving himself out of his chair. "I thought you'd like to know. The girls were in Belgium last week having a look at poor Reggie's grave, and they happened to come across your boy's. They're quite near each other, it seems."

Old Woodifield paused, but the boss made no reply. Only a quiver in his eyelids showed that he heard.

"The girls were delighted with the way the place is kept," piped the old voice. "Beautifully looked after. Couldn't be better if they were at home. You've not been across, have yer?"

---

2. *Windsor Cassel,* a play on "Windsor Castle," a royal residence.

"No, no!" For various reasons the boss had not been across.

"There's miles of it," quavered old Woodifield, "and it's all as neat as a garden. Flowers growing on all the graves. Nice broad paths." It was plain from his voice how much he liked a nice broad path.

The pause came again. Then the old man brightened wonderfully.

"D'you know what the hotel made the girls pay for a pot of jam?" he piped. "Ten francs! Robbery, I call it. It was a little pot, so Gertrude says, no bigger than a half crown. And she hadn't taken more than a spoonful when they charged her ten francs. Gertrude brought the pot away with her to teach 'em a lesson. Quite right, too; it's trading on our feelings. They think because we're over there having a look around we're ready to pay anything. That's what it is." And he turned towards the door.

"Quite right, quite right!" cried the boss, though what was quite right he hadn't the least idea. He came round by his desk, followed the shuffling footsteps to the door, and saw the old fellow out. Woodifield was gone.

For a long moment the boss stayed, staring at nothing, while the grey-haired office messenger, watching him, dodged in and out of his cubbyhole like a dog that expects to be taken for a run. Then: "I'll see nobody for half an hour, Macey," said the boss. "Understand? Nobody at all."

"Very good, sir."

The door shut, the firm heavy steps recrossed the bright carpet, the fat body plumped down in the spring chair, and leaning forward, the boss covered his face with his hands. He wanted, he intended, he had arranged to weep. . . .

It had been a terrible shock to him when old Woodifield sprang that remark upon him about the boy's grave. It was exactly as though the earth had opened and he had seen the boy lying there with Woodifield's girls staring down at him. For it was strange. Although over six years had passed away, the boss never thought of the boy except as lying unchanged, unblemished in his uniform, asleep for ever. "My son!" groaned the boss. But no tears came yet. In the past, in the first months and even years after the boy's death, he had only to say those words to be overcome by such grief that nothing short of a violent fit of weeping could relieve him. Time, he had declared then, he had told everybody, could make no difference. Other men perhaps might recover, might live their loss down, but not he. How was it possible? His boy was an only son. Ever since his birth the boss had worked at building up this business for him; it had no other meaning if it was not for the boy. Life itself had come to have no other meaning. How on earth could he have slaved, denied himself, kept going all those years without the promise forever before him of the boy's stepping into his shoes and carrying on where he left off?

And that promise had been so near being fulfilled. The boy had been in the office learning the ropes for a year before the war. Every morning they had started off together; they had come back by the same train. And what congratulations he had received as the boy's father! No wonder; he had taken to it marvellously. As to his popularity with the staff, every man jack of them down to old Macey couldn't make enough of the boy. And he wasn't in the least spoilt. No, he was just his bright, natural self, with the right word for everybody, with that boyish look and his habit of saying, "Simply splendid!"

But all that was over and done with as though it never had been. The day had come when Macey had handed him the telegram that brought the whole place crashing about his head. "Deeply regret to inform you . . . " And he had left the office a broken man, with his life in ruins.

Six years ago, six years . . . How quickly time passed! It might have happened yesterday. The boss took his hands from his face; he was puzzled. Something seemed to be wrong with him. He wasn't feeling as he wanted to feel. He decided to get up and have a look at the boy's photograph. But it wasn't a favorite photograph of his; the expression was unnatural. It was cold, even stern looking. The boy had never looked like that.

At that moment the boss noticed that a fly had fallen into his broad inkpot, and was trying feebly but desperately to clamber out again. Help! help! said those struggling legs. But the sides of the inkpot were wet and slippery; it fell back again and began to swim. The boss took up a pen, picked the fly out of the ink, and shook it on to a piece of blotting paper. For a fraction of a second it lay still on the dark patch that oozed round it. Then the front legs waved, took hold, and, pulling its small sodden body up, it began the immense task of cleaning the ink from its wings. Over and under, over and under, went a leg along a wing, as the stone goes over and under the scythe. Then there was a pause, while the fly, seeming to stand on the tips of its toes, tried to expand first one wing and then the other. It succeeded at last, and, sitting down, it began, like a minute cat, to clean its face. Now one could imagine that the little front legs rubbed against each other lightly, joyfully. The horrible danger was over; it had escaped; it was ready for life again.

But just then the boss had an idea. He plunged his pen back into the ink, leaned his thick wrist on the blotting paper, and as the fly tried its wings down came a great heavy blot. What would it make of that? What indeed! The little beggar seemed absolutely cowed, stunned, and afraid to move because of what would happen next. But then, as if painfully, it dragged itself forward. The front legs waved, caught hold, and, more slowly this time, the task began from the beginning.

He's a plucky little devil, thought the boss, and he felt a real admiration for the fly's courage. That was the way to tackle things; that was the right spirit. Never say die: it was only a question of . . . But the fly had again finished its laborious task, and the boss had just time to refill his pen, to shake fair and square on the new-cleaned body yet another dark drop. What about it this time? A painful moment of suspense followed. But behold, the front legs were again waving; the boss felt a rush of relief. He leaned over the fly and said to it tenderly, "You artful little b . . . " And he actually had the brilliant notion of breathing on it to help the drying process. All the same, there was something timid and weak about its efforts now, and the boss decided that this time should be the last, as he dipped the pen into the inkpot.

It was. The last blot on the soaked blotting paper, and the draggled fly lay in it and did not stir. The back legs were stuck to the body; the front legs were not to be seen.

"Come on," said the boss. "Look sharp!" And he stirred it with his pen—in vain. Nothing happened or was likely to happen. The fly was dead.

The boss lifted the corpse on the end of the paper knife and flung it into the wastepaper basket. But such a grinding feeling of wretchedness seized him that he felt positively frightened. He started forward and pressed the bell for Macey.

"Bring me some fresh blotting paper," he said, sternly, "and look sharp about it." And while the old dog padded away he fell to wondering what it was he had been thinking about before. What was it? It was . . . He took out his handkerchief and passed it inside his collar. For the life of him he could not remember. ◆

# Joyce Marshall

## THE OLD WOMAN

He has changed, Molly thought, the instant she glimpsed her husband in the station at Montreal. He has changed. . . . The thought thudded hollowly through her mind, over and over during the long train ride into northern Quebec.

It was more than the absence of uniform. His face seemed so still, and there was something about his mouth—a sort of slackness. And at times she would turn and find him looking at her, his eyes absorbed and watchful.

"I *am* glad to see you," he kept saying. "I thought you would never make it, Moll."

"I know," she said. "But I had to wait till Mother was really well. . . . It *has* been a long three years, hasn't it?"

Apart from repeating his gladness at her arrival, he seemed to have little to say. He was just strange with her, she tried to soothe herself. They had known each other less than a year when they married in England during the war,

---

"The Old Woman" by Joyce Marshall from CANADIAN SHORT STORIES, edited by Robert Weaver. Reprinted by permission of the author.

and he had left for Canada so soon without her. He must have found it hard to hold a picture of her, just as she had found it hard to hold a picture of him. As soon as they got home—whatever home might be in this strange romantic north to which the train was drawing them—he would be more nearly the Toddy she had known.

It was grey dawn faintly disturbed with pink when they left the train, the only passengers for this little town of Missawani, at the tip of Lake St. John. The name on the greyed shingle reassured Molly a little. How often she had spelled out the strange syllables on letters to Toddy—the double *s,* the unexpected single *n.* Somewhere beyond this huddle of low wooden shacks, she knew, was the big Mason paper mill, and Toddy's powerhouse—one of several that supplied it with electricity—was more than thirty miles away. There was a road, Toddy had told her, but it was closed in winter.

A sullen youth waited behind the station with the dogs. Such beautiful dogs, black brindled with cream, their mouths spread wide in what seemed to Molly happy smiles of welcome. She put a hand towards the nose of the lead dog, but he lunged and Toddy drew her back.

"They're brutes," he told her. "All of them wolfish brutes."

It was a long strange journey over the snow, first through pink-streaked grey, then into a sun that first dazzled and then inflamed the eyes.

Snow that was flung up coarse and stinging from the feet of the dogs, black brittle fir trees, birches gleaming like white silk. No sound but the panting breath of the dogs, the dry leatherlike squeak of the snow under the sleigh's runners, and Toddy's rare French-spoken commands to the dogs.

At last he poked her back wordlessly and pointed a mittened hand over her shoulder. For an instant the picture seemed to hang suspended before Molly's eyes: the bare hill with the square red house at its top, the dam level with the top of the hill, the waterfall steaming down to a white swirl of rapids, the powerhouse like a squat grey cylinder at its foot.

"My old woman," Toddy shouted, and she saw that he was pointing, not up the hill towards the house where they would live, but to the powerhouse below.

In England his habit of personalizing an electric generating plant had charmed her, fitting her picturesque notions of the Canadian north. But now she felt uneasiness prod her. It was such a sinister-looking building, and the sound of falling water was so loud and engulfing.

The kitchen of the red house had what Molly thought of as a "poor" smell about it. Still, no one expected a man to be a good housewife. As soon as she could shut the door and get rid of the sound of that water, she told herself, it would be better. She looked quickly behind her, but Toddy had shut the door already. There must be a window open somewhere. It couldn't be possible that the waterfall was going to live with them in the house like this. It couldn't be possible.

"Cheerful sort of sound," said Toddy.

Molly looked at him vaguely, half-hearing. A window somewhere—there must be a window she could close.

He showed her quickly over the house, which was fairly well furnished and comfortably heated by electricity. Then he turned to her almost apologetically.

"I hope you won't mind if I go down right away," he said. "I'd like to see what kind of shape the old woman's got herself into while I've been away."

He looked elated and eager, and she smiled at him.

"Go ahead," she said, "I'll be all right."

After he had gone she unpacked her bags and went down to the living room. It had a broad window, overlooking the powerhouse, the rapids, and a long snow field disappearing into the black huddle of pine bush. Snow, she thought. I always thought snow was white, but it's blue. Blue and treacherous as steel. And fully for the first time she realized how cut off they were to be—cut off from town by thirty odd miles of snow and tangled bush and roadlessness.

She found a pail and mop and began to clean the kitchen. She would have it all fresh and nice by the time Toddy came back. She would have no time to look out into the almost instantly blinding glare of the snow. She might even be able to ignore the thundering of the water. She was going to have to spend a lot of time alone in this house. She would have to learn to keep busy.

Toddy did not come up till evening. The powerhouse was in very bad shape, he told her.

"Those French operators and assistants are a lazy bunch of bums. It's amazing how they can let things go to hell in just two days."

Molly had set dinner on a little table in the living room. Toddy had wolfed his meal, his face preoccupied.

He *was* different. She hadn't just been imagining it. She had thought he would seem closer to her here, but he was more withdrawn than ever. For an instant she had a curious sense that none of this was real to him—not the dinner, nothing but the turbines and generators in the plant below.

Well, so you married this man, she told herself briskly, because you were thirty-eight and he looked nice in his officer's uniform. You followed him here because you were entranced with the idea of a strange and different place. So it is strange and different. And you have to start imagining things, just because your husband is a busy man who seems scarcely to notice that you are here.

"I'm going to make this place ever so much cosier," she heard herself saying, in a voice so importunate she scarcely recognized it as her own.

"What—oh yes—yes, fine. Make any changes you like."

He finished eating and stood up.

"Well, I must be going back now."

"Back?" He wasn't even apologizing this time, she realized dully. "Won't your old woman give you an evening off—even when your wife has just come from the old country?"

"I've still things to do," he said. "You needn't be lonely. There's a radio—though I'm afraid the static's pretty bad on account of the plant. And I'll be only fifty feet away."

It was a week before he considered the powerhouse in suitable shape to show her. He showed her around it proudly—the squat gleaming turbines lying like fat sleepers along the floor, one of the four dismantled so that he could explain the power generator within, the gauges on the wall.

"It's very interesting, dear," she said, trying to understand his love for these inanimates, his glowing delight in the meshing parts.

"Perhaps now she looks so slick," she added, "you won't have to give her so much of your time."

"You'd be surprised how quickly she can go wrong," said Toddy.

He continued to spend all his hours there, from eight in the morning until late at night, with only brief spaces for meals.

Molly worked vigorously about the house and soon it was cleaned and sparkling from top to bottom. After that it was harder to keep busy. She read all the books she had brought, even the ancient magazines she found about the house. She could not go out. It was impossible to do more than keep a path cleared down to the powerhouse. There were no skis or snowshoes, and Toddy could not seem to find time to teach her to drive the dogs. There were no neighbours within miles, no telephone calls or visits from milkman or baker—only one of Toddy's sweepers coming in once a fortnight with supplies and mail from Missawani.

She looked forward almost wildly to these visits, for they meant a break as well as letters from home. The men all lived on the nearby concessions—"ranges" they were called here in northern Quebec—six or seven or eight miles away, driving back and forth to the powerhouse by dog team. She tried to get them to tell her about their lives and their families, but they were taciturn, just barely polite, and she felt that they simply did not like this house of which she was a part.

She tried constantly to build up some sort of closeness between herself and Toddy. But he seemed only to become less talkative—he had always had a lot of cheerful small talk in England—and more absorbed in the powerhouse. He seemed to accept her presence as a fact which pleased him, but he had no companionship to spare for her.

"I wish," she said to him one day, "that you could go out with me soon and teach me to drive the dogs."

"But where would you go?" he asked.

"Oh," she said, "around. Over the snow."

"But I'm so busy," he said. "I'm sorry—but this is my work, and I'm so busy."

As he spoke, she saw in his eyes again that look that had terrified her so the first day. Now she thought she recognized what it was. It was a watchful look, a powerful look, as if he were still in the presence of his machinery.

"But couldn't you take an afternoon? Those machines look as if they practically ran themselves. Couldn't you even take a Sunday, Toddy?"

"What if something went wrong while I was away?"

"Oh, Toddy, it can't need you every minute. I'm your wife and I need you too. You seemed so anxious for the time when I'd be able to come here. I can imagine how a person might get to hate being here alone, with that water always roaring and——"

Toddy's face became suddenly angry and wild.

"What do you mean?" he demanded.

"Just that you had three years here alone," she began.

"I have never been bushed," Toddy interrupted furiously. "How dare you suggest that such a thing could ever happen to me? My God, apart from the war, I've lived in this country for twenty years."

Bushed. The suggestion was his, and for a moment she

allowed herself to think about it. She was familiar with the term. Toddy used it constantly about others who had come up north to live. He knew the country, but he had been away. And then he had returned alone to this place, where for so long every year the winter buried you, snow blinded you, the wind screamed up the hill at night, and the water thundered. . . .

"Toddy," she said, afraid of the thought, putting it out of her mind, "when spring comes, couldn't we get a cow or two. I *do* know about cattle—I wasn't in the Land Army all through the war for nothing. I think it would give me an interest."

Toddy stared at her.

"Aren't you my wife?" he asked.

"Why yes—yes, of course."

"Then how can you speak about needing an interest? Isn't there interest enough for you in simply being my wife?"

"But I'm—I'm left so much alone. You have your work, but I have so little to do."

Toddy turned on his heel, preparing to go again to the powerhouse. At the door he glanced back over his shoulder, not speaking, merely watching her.

He doesn't want me to have an interest, thought Molly, her mind bruised with horror and fear. He looks at me watchfully, as if I were one of his machines. Perhaps that's what he wants me to be—a generator, quiet and docile, waiting for him here, moving only when he tells me to move.

And I am the sort of woman who must have work to do. If I don't, my mind will grow dim and misty. Already I can feel the long sweep of the snow trying to draw my thoughts out till they become diffused and vague. I can feel the sound of the water trying to crush and madden me.

After that, it seemed as if Toddy were trying to spend more time with her. Several times he sat and talked with her after dinner, telling her about the powerhouse and the catastrophes he had averted that day. But always his eyes would be turning to the window and the powerhouse showing grey and sullen against the snow.

"Oh, you can go down now, Toddy," Molly would say. "Obviously, that is where you wish to be."

And then one day she found the work she wanted.

She looked up from her dishes to see Louis-Paul, one of the powerhouse oilers, standing in the doorway, snow leaking from his great felt boots on to the floor.

"Madame——" he said.

"Oh Louis, hello," said Molly warmly, for she was friendlier with this slight fair youth than with any of Toddy's other workmen. They had long solemn conversations—she practising her French and he his English. "But don't tell the Curé,"[1] Louis would say. "He does not like it if we speak English."

"Did you come for my list?" Molly asked him. "Are you going to town?"

"No, madame, I have—how you say it?—I am today in big trouble. My Lucienne——"

"Oh, the baby—has your baby been born, Louis-Paul?"

"Yes, madame——"

With a hopeless gesture he relinquished his English. From his rapid, desperate French, Molly learned that there was something that prevented Lucienne from nursing her child, and none of the cows on any of the ranges were giving milk that winter.

"If you could come, madame, you might know—you might do something——"

His team of yellow dogs was tied at the kitchen stoop. Together Louis-Paul and Molly dashed across the snow to the house at the first range. Just a little bit of a house that Louis-Paul's father had built for him six years ago when he divided his thin-soiled farm and his timber lots among his sons. Its roof was the warm grey of weathered wood, almost as deeply curved as the roof of a Chinese pagoda.

1. *the Curé*, the parish priest.

In the kitchen Lucienne's mother and sisters and aunts in all their black wept noisily, one of them holding the crying child. And in the bedroom the girl Lucienne was sobbing, because she realized that the presence of her relatives in their best black meant that her child could not be saved.

Molly looked at her for a moment—the swarthy broad cheeks, the narrow eyes, that showed a tinge of Indian blood.

"Would you be shy with me, Lucienne?" she asked. "Too shy to take off your nightgown while I am here?"

"I would never be shy with you, madame," said Lucienne.

Something hot came into Molly's throat as she eased the nightgown from the girl's shoulders and went into the kitchen for hot and cold water and a quantity of cloths.

Tenderly she bathed the heavy breasts with alternate hot and cold water, explaining that the nipples were inverted and that this should bring them into place. And before she left, Lucienne was holding the baby's dark head against her breast, weeping silently, the wailing in the kitchen had ceased, and Louis-Paul was fixing stiff portions of whisky blanc and homemade wine, passing the one wineglass around and around the assembly.

Not until she was back at the red house, actually stamping the snow from her boots on the kitchen stoop, did Molly realize that it was long past the early dinner that Toddy liked. She went in quickly.

Toddy was standing in the middle of the room, his hands dangling with a peculiar slackness at his sides. He looked at her, and there was a great empty bewilderment on his face.

"You have been out?" he asked.

"Yes," she said, elated still from her afternoon. "I went over to Louis-Paul's with him. His wife's had her baby and——"

"He asked you?" said Toddy.

"Yes," she said. "He was desperate, poor lad, so I just had to offer to do what I could."

He's afraid I'll go away, she thought. He must have come up here and found the stove cold and thought I had gone forever. The thought alternately reassured and chilled her. It was simple and ordinary for him to be anxious, but his expression was neither simple nor ordinary. Now that she had explained, he should not be staring at her still, his gaze thinned by surprise and fear.

"I'm sorry about dinner," she said, "but I'll hurry and fix something easy. You have a smoke and I'll tell you all about it."

She told him, but he would not join in her enthusiasm.

"Another French-Canadian brat," he said. "Molly, you're a fool."

A few weeks later she realized she now had a place even in this barren land. Louis-Paul appeared again in the kitchen, less shy, for now she was his friend. His sister-in-law was having a baby and something was wrong. They would have taken her to Missawani, but there was every sign of a blizzard blowing up. Madame had been so good with Lucienne. Perhaps she could do something for Marie-Claire as well.

"I don't see how I could," said Molly. "I've helped bring little calves and pigs into the world, but never a baby——"

"She may die," said Louis. "They say the baby is placed wrong. They have given her blood of a new-born calf to drink, but still——"

"All right," said Molly, "I'll go."

She set a cold meal for Toddy and propped a note against his plate. The thought of him nudged her mind guiltily during the dash over the snow to the little house. But that was absurd. She would be away only a few hours. Toddy would have to learn to accept an occasional absence. He was a little—well, selfish about her. He would have to learn.

With some help from an ancient grandmother, Molly delivered a child on the kitchen table of the little house. An old Cornish farmhand had showed her once how to turn a calf that was breached. Much the same thing was involved now—deftness, daring, a strong hand timed to the bitter contractions of the girl on the table.

When she returned home late in the evening, she had not thought of Toddy for hours.

This time he was angry, mumblingly, shakingly angry.

"Molly," he shouted, "you must put an end to this nonsensical——"

"But it's not nonsensical," she said, serene still from the miracle of new life she had held across her hands. "I brought a nice little boy into the world. He might never have been born except for me."

"These women have been popping kids for years without you."

"I know," said Molly, "but sometimes they lose them. And they're so—superstitious. I can help them, Toddy, I can."

She paused, then spoke more gently.

"What is it, Toddy? Why don't you want me to go?"

The question caught him somehow, and his face, his whole expression became loosed, as if suddenly he did not understand his own rage.

"You're my wife," he said. "I want you here."

"Well, cheer up," she said, speaking lightly because his look had chilled her so. "I am, usually."

After that, no woman in any of the ranges ever had a baby without her husband's dogs whisking over the fields to the red house.

Molly now was famed for miles. She was good luck at a birth, and when something unexpected happened she could act with speed and ingenuity. She liked the people and felt that they liked her. Even the Curé, who hated the powerhouse and all it represented, bowed and passed the time of day when he and Molly met in a farmhouse kitchen.

She sent away for government pamphlets and a handful of texts. Though it was true, as Toddy said, that these women had had babies without her, it pleased her that she was cutting down the percentage of early deaths.

Each of her errands meant a scene with Toddy. There was a struggle here, she felt, between her own need for life and work and what she tried to persuade herself was merely selfishness in him. In her new strength and happiness she felt that she ought to be able to draw Toddy into taking an interest in something beyond the powerhouse. But he would not be drawn.

Surely when the snows broke it would be possible. She would persuade him to take the old car in the barn and drive with her about the countryside. He was only a trifle bushed from the long winter. Though she had been shocked at first by the suggestion that he might be bushed, she found the hope edging into her mind more and more often now that it was nothing more.

And then one day it was Joe Blanchard's turn to come to get her. His wife was expecting her tenth child.

All day Molly was restless, going to the window to strain her eyes into the glare for a sight of Joe's sleigh and his tough yellow dogs winding out of the bush. Sunset came and she prepared dinner, and still he had not come.

Once she looked up from her plate and saw Toddy staring at her, his lips trembling in an odd small way.

"Is anything wrong?" she asked.

"No," he said, "nothing."

His lips still trembled.

"Toddy," she said, gently, and under her gentleness afraid. "I'll probably be going out tonight. I promised Joe Blanchard I'd help Mariette."

Toddy looked at her, and his face blazed.

"No," he shouted, "by God—you will stay where you belong."

"Why?" she asked, as she had before. "Why don't you want me to go?"

He seemed to search through his mind for words.

"Because I won't have you going out at night with that ruffian—because, damn it, it's too dangerous."

"Then you come too," she said. "You come with us."

"Don't be a fool," he said. "How could I leave?"

"Well, stay home tonight," she said. "Stay here and—and rest. We'll decide what to do when Joe comes."

"Rest—what do you mean?"

"I think you're—tired," she said. "I think you should stay home just one evening."

Toddy scraped back his chair.

"Don't be a fool, Molly. Of course I can't stay. I can't."

He walked to the door, then turned back to her.

"I shall find you here," he said, "when I return."

The evening dragged between the two anxieties—between wondering when Joe would come and watching for Toddy's return.

Midnight came, and still neither Toddy nor Joe had come. Her anxiety grew. Toddy had never stayed this late before. It had been ten-thirty first, then eleven.

The sound of the back door opening sent her flying to the kitchen. Joe stood in the doorway, his broad face beaming.

"You ready, madame?"

Molly began to put on her heavy clothes, her snow boots. Anxiety licked still in her mind. Past twelve o'clock and Toddy had not returned.

"Joe," she said, "you'll wait just a minute while I go down and tell my husband?"

Her feet slipped several times on the icy steps Toddy kept cut in the hillside. She felt a sudden terrible urgency. She must reassure herself of something. She didn't quite know what.

She pulled open the door of the powerhouse and was struck, as she had been before, by the way the thunder of the waterfall was suddenly replaced by a low even whine.

For an instant she did not see Toddy. Louis-Paul was propped in a straight chair dozing, across the room. Then she saw Toddy, his back, leaning towards one of the turbines. As she looked, he moved, with a curious scuttling speed, to one of the indicators on the wall. She saw the side of his face then, its expression totally absorbed, gloating.

"Toddy!" she called.

He turned, and for a long moment she felt that he did not know who she was. He did not speak.

"I didn't want you to worry," she said. "I'm going with Joe. If I shouldn't be back for breakfast——"

She stopped, for he did not seem to be listening.

"I probably *will* be back for breakfast," she said.

He glared at her. He moved his lips as if to speak. Then his gaze broke and slid back to the bright indicator on the wall.

At that moment she understood. The struggle she had sensed without being able to give it a name had been between herself and the powerhouse. In an indistinct way Toddy had realized it when he said, "I want you here."

"Toddy!" she shouted.

He turned his back to her in a vague automatic way, and she saw that his face was quite empty except for a strange glitter that spread from his eyes over his face. He did not answer her.

For a moment she forgot that she was not alone with him, until a sound reminded her of Louis-Paul, awake now and standing by the door. And from the expression of sick shaking terror on his face she knew what the fear had been that she had never allowed herself to name.

"Oh Louis," she said.

"Come madame," he said. "We can do nothing here. In the morning I will take you to Missawani. I will bring the doctor back."

"But is he safe?" she asked. "Will he—damage the machines perhaps?"

"Oh no. He would never hurt these machines. For years I watch him fall in love with her. Now she has him for herself." ◆

# W. Somerset Maugham

## MACKINTOSH

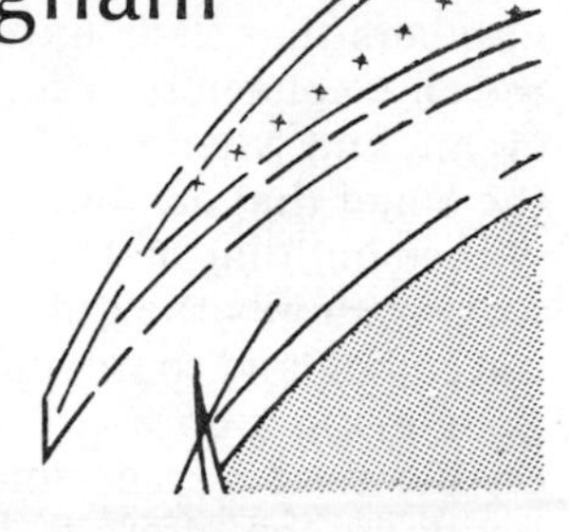

HE SPLASHED ABOUT for a few minutes in the sea; it was too shallow to swim in and for fear of sharks he could not go out of his depth; then he got out and went into the bath-house for a shower. The coldness of the fresh water was grateful after the heavy stickiness of the salt Pacific, so warm, though it was only just after seven, that to bathe in it did not brace you but rather increased your languor; and when he had dried himself, slipping into a bath-gown, he called out to the Chinese cook that he would be ready for breakfast in five minutes. He walked barefoot across the patch of coarse grass which Walker, the administrator, proudly thought was a lawn, to his own quarters and dressed. This did not take long, for he put on nothing but a shirt and a pair of duck trousers and then went over to his chief's house on the other side of the compound. The two men had their meals together, but the Chinese cook told him that Walker had set out on horseback at five and would not be back for another hour.

Mackintosh had slept badly and he looked with distaste at the paw-paw and the eggs and bacon which were set before him. The mosquitoes had been maddening that

"Mackintosh" copyright 1920 by International Magazine Co. from EAST AND WEST by W. Somerset Maugham. Reprinted by permission of Doubleday & Company, Inc., The Literary Executor of W. Somerset Maugham and William Heinemann Ltd.

night; they flew about the net under which he slept in such numbers that their humming, pitiless and menacing, had the effect of a note, infinitely drawn out, played on a distant organ, and whenever he dozed off he awoke with a start in the belief that one had found its way inside his curtains. It was so hot that he lay naked. He turned from side to side. And gradually the dull roar of the breakers on the reef, so unceasing and so regular that generally you did not hear it, grew distinct on his consciousness, its rhythm hammered on his tired nerves and he held himself with clenched hands in the effort to bear it. The thought that nothing could stop that sound, for it would continue to all eternity, was almost impossible to bear, and, as though his strength were a match for the ruthless forces of nature, he had an insane impulse to do some violent thing. He felt he must cling to his self-control or he would go mad. And now, looking out of the window at the lagoon and the strip of foam which marked the reef, he shuddered with hatred of the brilliant scene. The cloudless sky was like an inverted bowl that hemmed it in. He lit his pipe and turned over the pile of Auckland papers that had come over from Apia[1] a few days before. The newest of them was three weeks old. They gave an impression of incredible dullness.

Then he went into the office. It was a large, bare room with two desks in it and a bench along one side. A number of natives were seated on this, and a couple of women. They gossiped while they waited for the administrator, and when Mackintosh came in they greeted him.

*"Talofa li."*

He returned their greeting and sat down at his desk. He began to write, working on a report which the governor of Samoa had been clamouring for and which Walker, with his usual dilatoriness, had neglected to prepare. Mack-

---

1. *Auckland papers . . . Apia.* Auckland is the capital of New Zealand. Apia is the capital of the Territory of Western Samoa, a group of islands in the South Pacific northeast of New Zealand.

intosh as he made his notes reflected vindictively that Walker was late with his report because he was so illiterate that he had an invincible distaste for anything to do with pens and paper; and now when it was at last ready, concise and neatly official, he would accept his subordinate's work without a word of appreciation, with a sneer rather or a gibe, and send it on to his own superior as though it were his own composition. He could not have written a word of it. Mackintosh thought with rage that if his chief pencilled in some insertion it would be childish in expression and faulty in language. If he remonstrated or sought to put his meaning into an intelligible phrase, Walker would fly into a passion and cry:

"What the hell do I care about grammar? That's what I want to say and that's how I want to say it."

At last Walker came in. The natives surrounded him as he entered, trying to get his immediate attention, but he turned on them roughly and told them to sit down and hold their tongues. He threatened that if they were not quiet he would have them all turned out and see none of them that day. He nodded to Mackintosh.

"Hulloa, Mac; up at last? I don't know how you can waste the best part of the day in bed. You ought to have been up before dawn like me. Lazy beggar."

He threw himself heavily into his chair and wiped his face with a large bandana.

"By heaven, I've got a thirst."

He turned to the policeman who stood at the door, a picturesque figure in his white jacket and *lava-lava,* the loin cloth of the Samoan, and told him to bring *kava.*[2] The *kava* bowl stood on the floor in the corner of the room, and the policeman filled a half coconut shell and brought it to Walker. He poured a few drops on the ground, murmured the customary words to the company, and drank with

---

2. *kava,* an intoxicating drink made from the crushed root of several species of pepper plant.

relish. Then he told the policeman to serve the waiting natives, and the shell was handed to each one in order of birth or importance and emptied with the same ceremonies.

Then he set about the day's work. He was a little man, considerably less than of middle height, and enormously stout; he had a large, fleshy face, clean-shaven, with the cheeks hanging on each side in great dewlaps, and three vast chins; his small features were all dissolved in fat; and, but for a crescent of white hair at the back of his head, he was completely bald. He reminded you of Mr. Pickwick.[3] He was grotesque, a figure of fun, and yet, strangely enough, not without dignity. His blue eyes, behind large gold-rimmed spectacles, were shrewd and vivacious, and there was a great deal of determination in his face. He was sixty, but his native vitality triumphed over advancing years. Notwithstanding his corpulence his movements were quick, and he walked with a heavy, resolute tread as though he sought to impress his weight upon the earth. He spoke in a loud, gruff voice.

It was two years now since Mackintosh had been appointed Walker's assistant. Walker, who had been for a quarter of a century administrator of Talua, one of the larger islands in the Samoan group, was a man known in person or by report through the length and breadth of the South Seas; and it was with lively curiosity that Mackintosh looked forward to his first meeting with him. For one reason or another he stayed a couple of weeks at Apia before he took up his post and both at Chaplin's hotel and at the English club he heard innumerable stories about the administrator. He thought now with irony of his interest in them. Since then he had heard them a hundred times from Walker himself. Walker knew that he was a character, and proud of his reputation, deliberately acted up to it. He was

---

3. *Mr. Pickwick,* the obese hero of Charles Dickens' novel *The Pickwick Papers.*

jealous of his "legend" and anxious that you should know the exact details of any of the celebrated stories that were told of him. He was ludicrously angry with anyone who had told them to the stranger incorrectly.

There was a rough cordiality about Walker which Mackintosh at first found not unattractive, and Walker, glad to have a listener to whom all he said was fresh, gave of his best. He was good-humoured, hearty, and considerate. To Mackintosh, who had lived the sheltered life of a government official in London till at the age of thirty-four an attack of pneumonia, leaving him with the threat of tuberculosis, had forced him to seek a post in the Pacific, Walker's existence seemed extraordinarily romantic. The adventure with which he started on his conquest of circumstance was typical of the man. He ran away to sea when he was fifteen and for over a year was employed in shovelling coal on a collier. He was an undersized boy and both men and mates were kind to him, but the captain for some reason conceived a savage dislike of him. He used the lad cruelly so that, beaten and kicked, he often could not sleep for the pain that racked his limbs. He loathed the captain with all his soul. Then he was given a tip for some race and managed to borrow twenty-five pounds from a friend he had picked up in Belfast. He put it on the horse, an outsider, at long odds. He had no means of repaying the money if he lost, but it never occurred to him that he could lose. He felt himself in luck. The horse won and he found himself with something over a thousand pounds in hard cash. Now his chance had come. He found out who was the best solicitor in the town—the collier lay then somewhere on the Irish coast—went to him, and, telling him that he heard the ship was for sale, asked him to arrange the purchase for him. The solicitor was amused at his small client, he was only sixteen and did not look so old, and, moved perhaps by sympathy, promised not only to arrange the matter for him but to see that he made a good bargain. After a little while Walker found himself the owner of the ship. He went back to her and had what he described as the most glorious moment of his life when he gave the skipper notice and told him that he must get off *his* ship in half an hour. He made the mate captain and sailed on the collier for another nine months, at the end of which he sold her at a profit.

He came out to the islands at the age of twenty-six as a planter. He was one of the few white men settled in Talua at the time of the German occupation[4] and had then already some influence with the natives. The Germans made him administrator, a position which he occupied for twenty years, and when the island was seized by the British he was confirmed in his post. He ruled the island despotically, but with complete success. The prestige of this success was another reason for the interest that Mackintosh took in him.

But the two men were not made to get on. Mackintosh was an ugly man, with ungainly gestures, a tall thin fellow, with a narrow chest and bowed shoulders. He had sallow, sunken cheeks, and his eyes were large and sombre. He was a great reader, and when his books arrived and were unpacked Walker came over to his quarters and looked at them. Then he turned to Mackintosh with a coarse laugh.

"What in hell have you brought all this muck for?" he asked.

Mackintosh flushed darkly.

"I'm sorry you think it muck. I brought my books because I want to read them."

"When you said you'd got a lot of books coming I thought there'd be something for me to read. Haven't you got any detective stories?"

"Detective stories don't interest me."

"You're a damned fool then."

"I'm content that you should think so."

---

4. *German occupation.* The Territory of Western Samoa was a German possession from 1899 to 1914. Seized by the British early in the First World War, it was placed under mandate to New Zealand in 1920.

Every mail brought Walker a mass of periodical literature, papers from New Zealand and magazines from America, and it exasperated him that Mackintosh showed his contempt for these ephemeral publications. He had no patience with the books that absorbed Mackintosh's leisure and thought it only a pose that he read Gibbon's *Decline and Fall* or Burton's *Anatomy of Melancholy.* And since he had never learned to put any restraint on his tongue, he expressed his opinion of his assistant freely. Mackintosh began to see the real man, and under the boisterous good-humour he discerned a vulgar cunning which was hateful; he was vain and domineering, and it was strange that he had notwithstanding a shyness which made him dislike people who were not quite of his kidney. He judged others, naïvely, by their language, and if it was free from the oaths and the obscenity which made up the greater part of his own conversation, he looked upon them with suspicion. In the evening the two men played piquet. He played badly but vaingloriously, crowing over his opponent when he won and losing his temper when he lost. On rare occasions a couple of planters or traders would drive over to play bridge, and then Walker showed himself in what Mackintosh considered a characteristic light. He played regardless of his partner, calling up in his desire to play the hand, and argued interminably, beating down opposition by the loudness of his voice. He constantly revoked, and when he did so said with an ingratiating whine: "Oh, you wouldn't count it against an old man who can hardly see." Did he know that his opponents thought it as well to keep on the right side of him and hesitated to insist on the rigour of the game? Mackintosh watched him with an icy contempt. When the game was over, while they smoked their pipes and drank whisky, they would begin telling stories. Walker told with gusto the story of his marriage. He had got so drunk at the wedding feast that the bride had fled and he had never seen her since. He had had numberless adventures, commonplace and sordid, with the women of the island and he described them with a pride in his own prowess which was an offence to Mackintosh's fastidious ears. He was a gross, sensual old man. He thought Mackintosh a poor fellow because he would not share his promiscuous amours and remained sober when the company was drunk.

He despised him also for the orderliness with which he did his official work. Mackintosh liked to do everything just so. His desk was always tidy, his papers were always neatly docketed, he could put his hand on any document that was needed, and he had at his fingers' ends all the regulations that were required for the business of their administration.

"Fudge, fudge," said Walker. "I've run this island for twenty years without red tape, and I don't want it now."

"Does it make it any easier for you that when you want a letter you have to hunt half an hour for it?" answered Mackintosh.

"You're nothing but a damned official. But you're not a bad fellow; when you've been out here a year or two you'll be all right. What's wrong about you is that you won't drink. You wouldn't be a bad sort if you got soused once a week."

The curious thing was that Walker remained perfectly unconscious of the dislike for him which every month increased in the breast of his subordinate. Although he laughed at him, as he grew accustomed to him, he began almost to like him. He had a certain tolerance for the peculiarities of others, and he accepted Mackintosh as a queer fish. Perhaps he liked him, unconsciously, because he could chaff him. His humour consisted of coarse banter and he wanted a butt. Mackintosh's exactness, his morality, his sobriety, were all fruitful subjects; his Scot's name gave an opportunity for the usual jokes about Scotland; he enjoyed himself thoroughly when two or three men were there and he could make them all laugh at the expense of Mackintosh. He would say ridiculous things about him to the natives, and Mackintosh, his knowledge of Samoan still imperfect, would see their unrestrained mirth when

Walker had made an obscene reference to him. He smiled good-humouredly.

"I'll say this for you, Mac," Walker would say in his gruff loud voice, "you can take a joke."

"Was it a joke?" smiled Mackintosh. "I didn't know."

"Scots wha hae!" shouted Walker, with a bellow of laughter. "There's only one way to make a Scotchman see a joke and that's by a surgical operation."

Walker little knew that there was nothing Mackintosh could stand less than chaff. He would wake in the night, the breathless night of the rainy season, and brood sullenly over the gibe that Walker had uttered carelessly days before. It rankled. His heart swelled with rage, and he pictured to himself ways in which he might get even with the bully. He had tried answering him, but Walker had a gift of repartee, coarse and obvious, which gave him an advantage. The dullness of his intellect made him impervious to a delicate shaft. His self-satisfaction made it impossible to wound him. His loud voice, his bellow of laughter, were weapons against which Mackintosh had nothing to counter, and he learned that the wisest thing was never to betray his irritation. He learned to control himself. But his hatred grew till it was a monomania. He watched Walker with an insane vigilance. He fed his own self esteem by every instance of meanness on Walker's part, by every exhibition of childish vanity, of cunning and of vulgarity. Walker ate greedily, noisily, filthily, and Mackintosh watched him with satisfaction. He took note of the foolish things he said and of his mistakes in grammar. He knew that Walker held him in small esteem, and he found a bitter satisfaction in his chief's opinion of him; it increased his own contempt for the narrow, complacent old man. And it gave him a singular pleasure to know that Walker was entirely unconscious of the hatred he felt for him. He was a fool who liked popularity, and he blandly fancied that everyone admired him. Once Mackintosh had overheard Walker speaking of him.

"He'll be all right when I've licked him into shape," he said. "He's a good dog and he loves his master."

Mackintosh silently, without a movement of his long, sallow face, laughed long and heartily.

But his hatred was not blind; on the contrary, it was peculiarly clear-sighted, and he judged Walker's capabilities with precision. He ruled his small kingdom with efficiency. He was just and honest. With opportunities to make money he was a poorer man than when he was first appointed to his post, and his only support for his old age was the pension which he expected when at last he retired from official life. His pride was that with an assistant and a half-caste clerk he was able to administer the island more competently than Upolu, the island of which Apia is the chief town, was administered with its army of functionaries. He had a few native policemen to sustain his authority, but he made no use of them. He governed by bluff and his Irish humour.

"They insisted on building a jail for me," he said. "What the devil do I want a jail for? I'm not going to put the natives in prison. If they do wrong I know how to deal with them."

One of his quarrels with the higher authorities at Apia was that he claimed entire jurisdiction over the natives of his island. Whatever their crimes he would not give them up to courts competent to deal with them, and several times an angry correspondence had passed between him and the governor at Upolu. For he looked upon the natives as his children. And that was the amazing thing about this coarse, vulgar, selfish man; he loved the island on which he had lived so long with passion, and he had for the natives a strange rough tenderness which was quite wonderful.

He loved to ride about the island on his old grey mare and he was never tired of its beauty. Sauntering along the grassy roads among the coconut trees he would stop every now and then to admire the loveliness of the scene. Now and then he would come upon a native village and stop while the head man brought him a bowl of *kava.* He would look at the little group of bell-shaped huts with their high thatched roofs, like beehives, and a smile would spread over his fat face. His eyes rested happily on the spreading green of the breadfruit trees.

"By George, it's like the garden of Eden."

Sometimes his rides took him along the coast and through the trees he had a glimpse of the wide sea, empty, with never a sail to disturb the loneliness; sometimes he climbed a hill so that a great stretch of country, with little villages nestling among the tall trees, was spread out before him like the kingdom of the world, and he would sit there for an hour in an ecstasy of delight. But he had no words to express his feelings and to relieve them would utter an obscene jest; it was as though his emotion was so violent that he needed vulgarity to break the tension.

Mackintosh observed this sentiment with an icy disdain. Walker had always been a heavy drinker, he was proud of his capacity to see men half his age under the table when he spent a night in Apia, and he had the sentimentality of the toper. He could cry over the stories he read in his magazines and yet would refuse a loan to some trader in difficulties whom he had known for twenty years. He was close with his money. Once Mackintosh said to him:

"No one could accuse you of giving money away."

He took it as a compliment. His enthusiasm for nature was but the drivelling sensibility of the drunkard. Nor had Mackintosh any sympathy for his chief's feelings towards the natives. He loved them because they were in his power, as a selfish man loves his dog, and his mentality was on a level with theirs. Their humour was obscene and he was never at a loss for the lewd remark. He understood them and they understood him. He was proud of his influence over them. He looked upon them as his children and he mixed himself in all their affairs. But he was very jealous of his authority; if he ruled them with a rod of iron, brooking no contradiction, he would not suffer any of the white men on the island to take advantage of them. He watched the missionaries suspiciously and, if they did anything of which he disapproved, was able to make life so unendurable to them that if he could not get them removed they were glad to go of their own accord. His power over the natives was so great that on his word they would refuse labour and food to their pastor. On the other hand he showed the traders no favour. He took care that they should not cheat the natives; he saw that they got a fair reward for their work and their copra and that the traders made no extravagant profit on the wares they sold them. He was merciless to a bargain that he thought unfair. Sometimes the traders would complain at Apia that they did not get fair opportunities. They suffered for it. Walker then hesitated at no calumny, at no outrageous lie, to get even with them, and they found that if they wanted not only to live at peace, but to exist at all, they had to accept the situation on his own terms. More than once the store of a trader obnoxious to him had been burned down, and there was only the appositeness of the event to show that the administrator had instigated it. Once a Swedish half-caste, ruined by the burning, had gone to him and roundly accused him of arson. Walker laughed in his face.

"You dirty dog. Your mother was a native and you try to cheat the natives. If your rotten old store is burned down it's a judgment of Providence; that's what it is, a judgment of Providence. Get out."

And as the man was hustled out by two native policemen the dministrator laughed fatly.

"A judgment of Providence."

And now Mackintosh watched him enter upon the day's work. He began with the sick, for Walker added doctoring to his other activities, and he had a small room behind the office full of drugs. An elderly man came forward, a man with a crop of curly grey hair, in a blue *lava-lava,* elaborately tattooed, with the skin of his body wrinkled like a wineskin.

"What have you come for?" Walker asked him abruptly.

In a whining voice the man said that he could not eat without vomiting and that he had pains here and pains there.

"Go to the missionaries," said Walker. "You know that I only cure children."

"I have been to the missionaries and they do me no good."

"Then go home and prepare yourself to die. Have you lived so long and still want to go on living? You're a fool."

The man broke into querulous expostulation, but Walker, pointing to a woman with a sick child in her arms, told her to bring it to his desk. He asked her questions and looked at the child.

"I will give you medicine," he said. He turned to the half-caste clerk. "Go into the dispensary and bring me some calomel pills."

He made the child swallow one there and then and gave another to the mother.

"Take the child away and keep it warm. Tomorrow it will be dead or better."

He leaned back in his chair and lit his pipe.

"Wonderful stuff, calomel. I've saved more lives with it than all the hospital doctors at Apia put together."

Walker was very proud of his skill, and with the dogmatism of ignorance had no patience with the members of the medical profession.

"The sort of case I like," he said, "is the one that all the doctors have given up as hopeless. When the doctors have said they can't cure you, I say to them, 'come to me.' Did I ever tell you about the fellow who had a cancer?"

"Frequently," said Mackintosh.

"I got him right in three months."

"You've never told me about the people you haven't cured."

He finished this part of the work and went on to the rest. It was a queer medley. There was a woman who could not get on with her husband and a man who complained that his wife had run away from him.

"Lucky dog," said Walker. "Most men wish their wives would too."

There was a long complicated quarrel about the ownership of a few yards of land. There was a dispute about the sharing out of a catch of fish. There was a complaint against a white trader because he had given short measure. Walker listened attentively to every case, made up his mind quickly, and gave his decision. Then he would listen to nothing more; if the complainant went on he was hustled out of the office by a policeman. Mackintosh listened to it all with sullen irritation. On the whole, perhaps, it might be admitted that rough justice was done, but it exasperated the assistant that his chief trusted his instinct rather than the evidence. He would not listen to reason. He browbeat the witnesses and, when they did not see what he wished them to, called them thieves and liars.

He left to the last a group of men who were sitting in the corner of the room. He had deliberately ignored them. The party consisted of an old chief, a tall, dignified man with short, white hair, in a new *lava-lava,* bearing a huge fly wisp as a badge of office, his son, and half a dozen of the important men of the village. Walker had had a feud with them and had beaten them. As was characteristic of him he meant now to rub in his victory, and because he had them down, to profit by their helplessness. The facts were peculiar. Walker had a passion for building roads. When he had come to Talua there were but a few tracks here and there, but in course of time he had cut roads through the country, joining the villages together, and it was to this that a great part of the island's prosperity was due. Whereas in the old days it had been impossible to get the produce of the land, copra chiefly, down to the coast where it could be put on schooners or motor launches and so taken to Apia, now transport was easy and simple. His ambition was to make a road right round the island and a great part of it was already built.

"In two years I shall have done it, and then I can die or they can fire me, I don't care."

His roads were the joy of his heart and he made excursions constantly to see that they were kept in order. They were simple enough, wide tracks, grass covered, cut through the scrub or through the plantations; but trees had to be rooted out, rocks dug up or blasted, and here and there levelling had been necessary. He was proud that he had surmounted by his own skill such difficulties as they presented. He rejoiced in his disposition of them so that they were not only convenient, but showed off the beauties of the island which his soul loved. When he spoke of his roads he was almost a poet. They meandered through those lovely scenes, and Walker had taken care that here and there they should run in a straight line, giving you a green vista through the tall trees, and here and there should turn and curve so that the heart was rested by the diversity. It was amazing that this coarse and sensual man should exercise so subtle an ingenuity to get the effects which his fancy suggested to him. He had used in making his roads all the fantastic skill of a Japanese gardener. He received a grant from headquarters for the work but took a curious pride in using but a small part of it, and the year before had spent only a hundred pounds of the thousand assigned to him.

"What do they want money for?" he boomed. "They'll only spend it on all kinds of muck they don't want; what the missionaries leave them, that is to say."

For no particular reason, except perhaps pride in the economy of his administration and the desire to contrast his efficiency with the wasteful methods of the authorities at Apia, he got the natives to do the work he wanted for wages that were almost nominal. It was owing to this that he had lately had difficulty with the village whose chief men now were come to see him. The chief's son had been in Upolu for a year and on coming back had told his people of the large sums that were paid at Apia for the public works. In long, idle talks he had inflamed their hearts with the desire for gain. He held out to them visions of vast wealth and they thought of the whisky they could buy—it was dear, since there was a law that it must not be sold to natives, and so it cost them double what the white man had to pay for it—they thought of the great sandalwood boxes in which they kept their treasures, and the scented soap and potted salmon, the luxuries for which the Kanaka will sell his soul; so that when the administrator sent for them and told them he wanted a road made from their village to a certain point along the coast and offered them twenty pounds, they asked him a hundred. The chief's son was called Manuma. He was a tall, handsome fellow, copper-coloured, with his fuzzy hair dyed red with lime, a wreath of red berries round his neck, and behind his ear a flower like a scarlet flame against his brown face. The upper part of his body was naked, but to show that he was no longer a savage, since he had lived in Apia, he wore a pair of dungarees instead of a *lava-lava.* He told them that if they held together the administrator would be obliged to accept their terms. His heart was set on building the road and when he found they would not work for less he would give them what they asked. But they must not move; whatever he said they must not abate their claim; they had asked a hundred and that they must keep to. When they mentioned the figure, Walker burst into a shout of his long, deep-voiced laughter. He told them not to make fools of themselves, but to set about the work at once. Because he was in a good humour that day he promised to give them a feast when the road was finished. But when he found that no attempt was made to start work, he went to the village and asked the men what silly game they were playing. Manuma had coached them well. They were quite calm, they did not attempt to argue—and argument is a passion with the Kanaka—they merely shrugged their shoulders: they would do it for a hundred pounds, and if he would not give them that they would do no work. He could please himself. They did not care. Then Walker flew into a passion. He was ugly then. His short fat neck swelled ominously, his red face grew purple, he foamed at the mouth. He set upon the natives with invective. He knew well how to wound and how to humiliate. He was terrifying. The older men grew pale and uneasy. They hesitated. If it had not been for Manuma, with his knowledge of the great world, and their dread of his ridicule, they would have yielded. It was Manuma who answered Walker.

"Pay us a hundred pounds and we will work."

Walker, shaking his fist at him, called him every name he could think of. He riddled him with scorn. Manuma sat still and smiled. There may have been more bravado than confidence in his smile, but he had to make a good show before the others. He repeated his words.

"Pay us a hundred pounds and we will work."

They thought that Walker would spring on him. It would not have been the first time that he had thrashed a native with his own hands; they knew his strength, and though Walker was three times the age of the young man and six inches shorter they did not doubt that he was more than a match for Manuma. No one had ever thought of resisting the savage onslaught of the administrator. But Walker said nothing. He chuckled.

"I am not going to waste my time with a pack of fools," he said. "Talk it over again. You know what I have offered. If you do not start in a week, take care."

He turned round and walked out of the chief's hut. He untied his old mare and it was typical of the relations between him and the natives that one of the elder men hung on to the off stirrup while Walker from a convenient boulder hoisted himself heavily into the saddle.

That same night when Walker according to his habit was

strolling along the road that ran past his house, he heard something whizz past him and with a thud strike a tree. Something had been thrown at him. He ducked instinctively. With a shout, "Who's that?" he ran towards the place from which the missile had come and he heard the sound of a man escaping through the bush. He knew it was hopeless to pursue in the darkness, and besides he was soon out of breath, so he stopped and made his way back to the road. He looked about for what had been thrown, but could find nothing. It was quite dark. He went quickly back to the house and called Mackintosh and the Chinese boy.

"One of those devils has thrown something at me. Come along and let's find out what it was."

He told the boy to bring a lantern and the three of them made their way back to the place. They hunted about the ground, but could not find what they sought. Suddenly the boy gave a guttural cry. They turned to look. He held up the lantern, and there, sinister in the light that cut the surrounding darkness, was a long knife sticking into the trunk of a coconut tree. It had been thrown with such force that it required quite an effort to pull it out.

"By George, if he hadn't missed me I'd have been in a nice state."

Walker handled the knife. It was one of those knives, made in imitation of the sailor knives brought to the islands a hundred years before by the first white men, used to divide the coconuts in two so that the copra might be dried. It was a murderous weapon, and the blade, twelve inches long, was very sharp. Walker chuckled softly.

"The devil, the impudent devil."

He had no doubt it was Manuma who had flung the knife. He had escaped death by three inches. He was not angry. On the contrary, he was in high spirits; the adventure exhilarated him, and when they got back to the house, calling for drinks, he rubbed his hands gleefully.

"I'll make them pay for this!"

His little eyes twinkled. He blew himself out like a turkey

cock, and for the second time within half an hour insisted on telling Mackintosh every detail of the affair. Then he asked him to play piquet, and while they played he boasted of his intentions. Mackintosh listened with tightened lips.

"But why should you grind them down like this?" he asked. "Twenty pounds is precious little for the work you want them to do."

"They ought to be precious thankful I give them anything."

"Hang it all, it's not your own money. The government allots you a reasonable sum. They won't complain if you spend it."

"They're a bunch of fools at Apia."

Mackintosh saw that Walker's motive was merely vanity. He shrugged his shoulders.

"It won't do you much good to score off the fellows at Apia at the cost of your life."

"Bless you, they wouldn't hurt me, these people. They couldn't do without me. They worship me. Manuma is a fool. He only threw that knife to frighten me."

The next day Walker rode over again to the village. It was called Matautu. He did not get off his horse. When he reached the chief's house he saw that the men were sitting round the floor in a circle, talking, and he guessed they were discussing again the question of the road. The Samoan huts are formed in this way: Trunks of slender trees are placed in a circle at intervals of perhaps five or six feet; a tall tree is set in the middle and from this downwards slopes the thatched roof. Venetian blinds of coconut leaves can be pulled down at night or when it is raining. Ordinarily the hut is open all round so that the breeze can blow through freely. Walker rode to the edge of the hut and called out to the chief.

"Oh, there, Tangatu, your son left his knife in a tree last night. I have brought it back to you."

He flung it down on the ground in the midst of the circle, and with a low burst of laughter ambled off.

On Monday he went out to see if they had started work. There was no sign of it. He rode through the village. The inhabitants were about their ordinary avocations. Some were weaving mats of the pandanus leaf, one old man was busy with a *kava* bowl, the children were playing, the women went about their household chores. Walker, a smile on his lips, came to the chief's house.

*"Talofa li,"* said the chief.

*"Talofa,"* answered Walker.

Manuma was making a net. He sat with a cigarette between his lips and looked up at Walker with a smile of triumph.

"You have decided that you will not make the road?"

The chief answered.

"Not unless you pay us one hundred pounds."

"You will regret it." He turned to Manuma. "And you, my lad, I shouldn't wonder if your back was very sore before you're much older."

He rode away chuckling. He left the natives vaguely uneasy. They feared the fat sinful old man, and neither the missionaries' abuse of him nor the scorn which Manuma had learnt in Apia made them forget that he had a devilish cunning and that no man had ever braved him without in the long run suffering for it. They found out within twenty-four hours what scheme he had devised. It was characteristic. For next morning a great band of men, women, and children came into the village and the chief men said that they had made a bargain with Walker to build the road. He had offered them twenty pounds and they had accepted. Now the cunning lay in this, that the Polynesians have rules of hospitality which have all the force of laws; an etiquette of absolute rigidity made it necessary for the people of the village not only to give lodging to the strangers, but to provide them with food and drink as long as they wished to stay. The inhabitants of Matautu were outwitted. Every morning the workers went out in a joyous band, cut down trees, blasted rocks, levelled here and there and then in the evening tramped back again, and ate and drank, ate heartily, danced, sang hymns, and enjoyed life. For them it was a picnic. But soon their hosts began to wear long faces; the strangers had enormous appetites, and the plantains and the breadfruit vanished before their rapacity; the alligator-pear trees, whose fruit sent to Apia might sell for good money, were stripped bare. Ruin stared them in the face. And then they found that the strangers were working very slowly. Had they received a hint from Walker that they might take their time? At this rate by the time the road was finished there would not be a scrap of food in the village. And worse than this, they were a laughing-stock; when one or other of them went to some distant hamlet on an errand he found that the story had got there before him, and he was met with derisive laughter. There is nothing the Kanaka can endure less than ridicule. It was not long before much angry talk passed among the sufferers. Manuma was no longer a hero; he had to put up with a good deal of plain speaking, and one day what Walker had suggested came to pass: a heated argument turned into a quarrel and half a dozen of the young men set upon the chief's son and gave him such a beating that for a week he lay bruised and sore on the pandanus mats. He turned from side to side and could find no ease. Every day or two the administrator rode over on his old mare and watched the progress of the road. He was not a man to resist the temptation of taunting the fallen foe, and he missed no opportunity to rub into the shamed inhabitants of Matautu the bitterness of their humiliation. He broke their spirit. And one morning, putting their pride in their pockets, a figure of speech, since pockets they had not, they all set out with the strangers and started working on the road. It was urgent to get it done quickly if they wanted to save any food at all, and the whole village joined in. But they worked silently, with rage and mortification in their hearts, and even the children toiled in silence. The women wept as they carried away bundles of brushwood. When Walker saw them he laughed so much that he almost rolled out of his saddle. The news spread quickly and tickled the people of the island to death. This was the greatest joke of all, the crowning triumph of that cunning old white man whom no Kanaka had ever been able to circumvent; and they came from distant villages, with their wives and children, to look at the foolish folk who had refused twenty pounds to make the road and now were forced to work for nothing. But the harder they worked the more easily went the guests. Why should they hurry, when they were getting good food for nothing and the longer they took about the job the better the joke became? At last the wretched villagers could stand it no longer, and they were come this morning to beg the administrator to send the strangers back to their own homes. If he would do this they promised to finish the road themselves for nothing. For him it was a victory complete and unqualified. They were humbled. A look of arrogant complacence spread over his large, naked face, and he seemed to swell in his chair like a great bullfrog. There was something sinister in his appearance, so that Mackintosh shivered with disgust. Then in his booming tones he began to speak.

"Is it for my good that I make the road? What benefit do you think I get out of it? It is for you, so that you can walk in comfort and carry your copra in comfort. I offered to pay you for your work, though it was for your own sake the work was done. I offered to pay you generously. Now *you* must pay. I will send the people of Manua back to their homes if you will finish the road and pay the twenty pounds that I have to pay them."

There was an outcry. They sought to reason with him. They told him they had not the money. But to everything they said he replied with brutal gibes. Then the clock struck.

"Dinner time," he said. "Turn them all out."

He raised himself heavily from his chair and walked out of the room. When Mackintosh followed him he found him already seated at table, a napkin tied round his neck, holding his knife and fork in readiness for the meal the Chinese cook was about to bring. He was in high spirits.

"I did 'em down fine," he said, as Mackintosh sat down. "I shan't have much trouble with the roads after this."

"I suppose you were joking," said Mackintosh icily.

"What do you mean by that?"

"You're not really going to make them pay twenty pounds?"

"You bet your life I am."

"I'm not sure you've got any right to."

"Ain't you? I guess I've got the right to do any damned thing I like on this island."

"I think you've bullied them quite enough."

Walker laughed fatly. He did not care what Mackintosh thought.

"When I want your opinion I'll ask for it."

Mackintosh grew very white. He knew by bitter experience that he could do nothing but keep silence, and the violent effort at self-control made him sick and faint. He could not eat the food that was before him and with disgust he watched Walker shovel meat into his vast mouth. He was a dirty feeder, and to sit at table with him needed a strong stomach. Mackintosh shuddered. A tremendous desire seized him to humiliate that gross and cruel man; he would give anything in the world to see him in the dust, suffering as much as he had made others suffer. He had never loathed the bully with such loathing as now.

The day wore on. Mackintosh tried to sleep after dinner, but the passion in his heart prevented him; he tried to read, but the letters swam before his eyes. The sun beat down pitilessly, and he longed for rain; but he knew that rain would bring no coolness; it would only make it hotter and more steamy. He was a native of Aberdeen and his heart yearned suddenly for the icy winds that whistled through the granite streets of that city. Here he was a prisoner, imprisoned not only by that placid sea, but by his hatred for that horrible old man. He pressed his hands to his aching head. He would like to kill him. But he pulled himself together. He must do something to distract his mind, and since he could not read he thought he would set his private papers in order. It was a job which he had long meant to do and which he had constantly put off. He unlocked the drawer of his desk and took out a handful of letters. He caught sight of his revolver. An impulse, no sooner realized than set aside, to put a bullet through his head and so escape from the intolerable bondage of life flashed through his mind. He noticed that in the damp air the revolver was slightly rusted, and he got an oil rag and began to clean it. It was while he was thus occupied that he grew aware of someone slinking round the door. He looked up and called:

"Who is there?"

There was a moment's pause, then Manuma showed himself.

"What do you want?"

The chief's son stood for a moment, sullen and silent, and when he spoke it was with a strangled voice.

"We can't pay twenty pounds. We haven't the money."

"What am I to do?" said Mackintosh. "You heard what Mr. Walker said."

Manuma began to plead, half in Samoan and half in English. It was a sing-song whine, with the quavering intonations of a beggar, and it filled Mackintosh with disgust. It outraged him that the man should let himself be so crushed. He was a pitiful object.

"I can do nothing," said Mackintosh irritably. "You know that Mr. Walker is master here."

Manuma was silent again. He still stood in the doorway.

"I am sick," he said at last. "Give me some medicine."

"What is the matter with you?"

"I do not know. I am sick. I have pains in my body."

"Don't stand there," said Mackintosh sharply. "Come in and let me look at you."

Manuma entered the little room and stood before the desk.

"I have pains here and here."

He put his hands to his loins and his face assumed an expression of pain. Suddenly Mackintosh grew conscious that the boy's eyes were resting on the revolver which he had laid on the desk when Manuma appeared in the doorway. There was a silence between the two which to Mackintosh was endless. He seemed to read the thoughts which were in the Kanaka's mind. His heart beat violently. And then he felt as though something possessed him so that he acted under the compulsion of a foreign will. Himself did not make the movements of his body, but a power that was strange to him. His throat was suddenly dry, and he put his hand to it mechanically in order to help his speech. He was impelled to avoid Manuma's eyes.

"Just wait here," he said, his voice sounding as though someone had seized him by the windpipe, "and I'll fetch you something from the dispensary."

He got up. Was it his fancy that he staggered a little? Manuma stood silently, and though he kept his eyes averted, Mackintosh knew that he was looking dully out of the door. It was this other person that possessed him, that drove him out of the room, but it was himself that took a handful of muddled papers and threw them on the revolver in order to hide it from view. He went to the dispensary. He got a pill and poured out some blue draught into a small bottle, and then came out into the compound. He did not want to go back into his own bungalow, so he called to Manuma.

"Come here."

He gave him the drugs and instructions how to take them. He did not know what it was that made it impossible for him to look at the Kanaka. While he was speaking to him he kept his eyes on his shoulder. Manuma took the medicine and slunk out of the gate.

Mackintosh went into the dining room and turned over once more the old newspapers. But he could not read them. The house was very still. Walker was upstairs in his room asleep, the Chinese cook was busy in the kitchen, the two policemen were out fishing. The silence that seemed to brood over the house was unearthly, and there hammered in Mackintosh's head the question whether the revolver still lay where he had placed it. He could not bring himself to look. The uncertainty was horrible, but the certainty would be more horrible still. He sweated. At last he could stand the silence no longer, and he made up his mind to go down the road to the trader's, a man named Jervis, who had a store about a mile away. He was a half-caste, but even that amount of white blood made him possible to talk to. He wanted to get away from his bungalow, with the desk littered with untidy papers, and underneath them something, or nothing. He walked along the road. As he passed the fine hut of a chief a greeting was called out to him. Then he came to the store. Behind the counter sat the trader's daughter, a swarthy broad-featured girl in a pink blouse and a white drill skirt. Jervis hoped he would marry her. He had money, and he had told Mackintosh that his daughter's husband would be well-to-do. She flushed a little when she saw Mackintosh.

"Father's just unpacking some cases that have come in this morning. I'll tell him you're here."

He sat down and the girl went out behind the shop. In a moment her mother waddled in, a huge old woman, a chiefess, who owned much land in her own right, and gave him her hand. Her monstrous obesity was an offence, but she managed to convey an impression of dignity. She was cordial without obsequiousness; affable, but conscious of her station.

"You're quite a stranger, Mr. Mackintosh. Teresa was saying only this morning: 'Why, we never see Mr. Mackintosh now.' "

He shuddered a little as he thought of himself as that old native's son-in-law. It was notorious that she ruled her husband, notwithstanding his white blood, with a firm hand. Hers was the authority and hers the business head.

She might be no more than Mrs. Jervis to the white people, but her father had been a chief of the blood royal, and his father and his father's father had ruled as kings. The trader came in, small beside his imposing wife, a dark man with a black beard going grey, in ducks, with handsome eyes and flashing teeth. He was very British, and his conversation was slangy, but you felt he spoke English as a foreign tongue; with his family he used the language of his native mother. He was a servile man, cringing and obsequious.

"Ah, Mr. Mackintosh, this is a joyful surprise. Get the whisky, Teresa; Mr. Mackintosh will have a gargle with us."

He gave all the latest news of Apia, watching his guest's eyes the while, so that he might know the welcome thing to say.

"And how is Walker? We've not seen him just lately. Mrs. Jervis is going to send him a sucking-pig one day this week."

"I saw him riding home this morning," said Teresa.

"Here's how," said Jervis, holding up his whisky.

Mackintosh drank. The two women sat and looked at him, Mrs. Jervis in her black Mother Hubbard,[5] placid and haughty, and Teresa, anxious to smile whenever she caught his eye, while the trader gossiped insufferably.

"They were saying in Apia it was about time Walker retired. He ain't so young as he was. Things have changed since he first come to the islands and he ain't changed with them."

"He'll go too far," said the old chiefess. "The natives aren't satisfied."

"That was a good joke about the road," laughed the trader. "When I told them about it in Apia they fair split their sides with laughing. Good old Walker."

Mackintosh looked at him savagely. What did he mean by talking of him in that fashion? To a half-caste trader he

---

**5.** *Mother Hubbard,* a type of loose gown.

was Mr. Walker. It was on his tongue to utter a harsh rebuke for the impertinence. He did not know what held him back.

"When he goes I hope you'll take his place, Mr. Mackintosh," said Jervis. "We all like you on the island. You understand the natives. They're educated now, they must be treated differently to the old days. It wants an educated man to be administrator now. Walker was only a trader same as I am."

Teresa's eyes glistened.

"When the time comes if there's anything anyone can do here, you bet your bottom dollar we'll do it. I'd get all the chiefs to go over to Apia and make a petition."

Mackintosh felt horribly sick. It had not struck him that if anything happened to Walker it might be he who would succeed him. It was true that no one in his official position knew the island so well. He got up suddenly and scarcely taking his leave walked back to the compound. And now he went straight to his room. He took a quick look at his desk. He rummaged among the papers.

The revolver was not there.

His heart thumped violently against his ribs. He looked for the revolver everywhere. He hunted in the chairs and in the drawers. He looked desperately, and all the time he knew he would not find it. Suddenly he heard Walker's gruff, hearty voice.

"What the devil are you up to, Mac?"

He started. Walker was standing in the doorway and instinctively he turned round to hide what lay upon his desk.

"Tidying up?" quizzed Walker. "I've told 'em to put the grey in the trap. I'm going down to Tafoni to bathe. You'd better come along."

"All right," said Mackintosh.

So long as he was with Walker nothing could happen. The place they were bound for was about three miles away, and there was a fresh-water pool, separated by a thin barrier of rock from the sea, which the administrator had blasted out for the natives to bathe in. He had done this at spots round the island, wherever there was a spring; and the fresh water, compared with the sticky warmth of the sea, was cool and invigorating. They drove along the silent grassy road, splashing now and then through fords, where the sea had forced its way in, past a couple of native villages, the bell-shaped huts spaced out roomily and the white chapel in the middle, and at the third village they got out of the trap, tied up the horse, and walked down to the pool. They were accompanied by four or five girls and a dozen children. Soon they were all splashing about, shouting and laughing, while Walker, in a *lava-lava,* swam to and fro like an unwieldy porpoise. He made lewd jokes with the girls, and they amused themselves by diving under him and wriggling away when he tried to catch them. When he was tired he lay down on a rock, while the girls and children surrounded him; it was a happy family; and the old man, huge, with his crescent of white hair and his shining bald crown, looked like some old sea god. Once Mackintosh caught a queer soft look in his eyes.

"They're dear children," he said. "They look upon me as their father."

And then without a pause he turned to one of the girls and made an obscene remark which sent them all into fits of laughter. Mackintosh started to dress. With his thin legs and thin arms he made a grotesque figure, a sinister Don Quixote, and Walker began to make coarse jokes about him. They were acknowledged with little smothered laughs. Mackintosh struggled with his shirt. He knew he looked absurd, but he hated being laughed at. He stood silent and glowering.

"If you want to get back in time for dinner you ought to come soon."

"You're not a bad fellow, Mac. Only you're a fool. When you're doing one thing you always want to do another. That's not the way to live."

But all the same he raised himself slowly to his feet and began to put on his clothes. They sauntered back to the village, drank a bowl of *kava* with the chief, and then, after a joyful farewell from all the lazy villagers, drove home.

After dinner, according to his habit, Walker, lighting his cigar, prepared to go for a stroll. Mackintosh was suddenly seized with fear.

"Don't you think it's rather unwise to go out at night by yourself just now?"

Walker stared at him with his round blue eyes.

"What the devil do you mean?"

"Remember the knife the other night. You've got those fellows' backs up."

"Pooh! They wouldn't dare."

"Someone dared before."

"That was only a bluff. They wouldn't hurt me. They look upon me as a father. They know that whatever I do is for their own good."

Mackintosh watched him with contempt in his heart. The man's self-complacency outraged him, and yet something, he knew not what, made him insist.

"Remember what happened this morning. It wouldn't hurt you to stay at home just tonight. I'll play piquet with you."

"I'll play piquet with you when I come back. The Kanaka isn't born yet who can make me alter my plans."

"You'd better let me come with you."

"You stay where you are."

Mackintosh shrugged his shoulders. He had given the man full warning. If he did not heed it that was his own lookout. Walker put on his hat and went out. Mackintosh began to read; but then he thought of something; perhaps it would be as well to have his own whereabouts quite clear. He crossed over to the kitchen and, inventing some pretext, talked for a few minutes with the cook. Then he got out the gramophone and put a record on it, but while it ground out its melancholy tune, some comic song of a London music hall, his ear was strained for a sound away there in the night. At his elbow the record reeled out its loudness, the words were raucous, but notwithstanding he seemed to be surrounded by an unearthly silence. He heard the dull roar of the breakers against the reef. He heard the breeze sigh, far up, in the leaves of the coconut trees. How long would it be? It was awful.

He heard a hoarse laugh.

"Wonders will never cease. It's not often you play yourself a tune, Mac."

Walker stood at the window, red-faced, bluff and jovial.

"Well, you see I'm alive and kicking. What were you playing for?"

Walker came in.

"Nerves a bit dicky, eh? Playing a tune to keep your pecker up?"

"I was playing your requiem."

"What the devil's that?"

"'Alf o' bitter an' a pint of stout."

"A rattling good song too. I don't mind how often I hear it. Now I'm ready to take your money off you at piquet."

They played and Walker bullied his way to victory, bluffing his opponent, chaffing him, jeering at his mistakes, up to every dodge, browbeating him, exulting. Presently Mackintosh recovered his coolness, and standing outside himself, as it were, he was able to take a detached pleasure in watching the overbearing old man and in his own cold reserve. Somewhere Manuma sat quietly and awaited his opportunity.

Walker won game after game and pocketed his winnings at the end of the evening in high good humour.

"You'll have to grow a little bit older before you stand much chance against me, Mac. The fact is I have a natural gift for cards."

"I don't know that there's much gift about it when I happen to deal you fourteen aces."

"Good cards come to good players," retorted Walker. "I'd have won if I'd had your hands."

He went on to tell long stories of the various occasions on which he had played cards with notorious sharpers and to their consternation had taken all their money from them. He boasted. He praised himself. And Mackintosh listened with absorption. He wanted now to feed his hatred; and everything Walker said, every gesture, made him more detestable. At last Walker got up.

"Well, I'm going to turn in," he said with a loud yawn. "I've got a long day tomorrow."

"What are you going to do?"

"I'm driving over to the other side of the island. I'll start at five, but I don't expect I shall get back to dinner till late."

They generally dined at seven.

"We'd better make it half-past seven then."

"I guess it would be as well."

Mackintosh watched him knock the ashes out of his pipe. His vitality was rude and exuberant. It was strange to think that death hung over him. A faint smile flickered in Mackintosh's cold, gloomy eyes.

"Would you like me to come with you?"

"What in God's name should I want that for? I'm using the mare and she'll have enough to do to carry me; she don't want to drag you over thirty miles of road."

"Perhaps you don't quite realize what the feeling is at Matautu. I think it would be safer if I came with you."

Walker burst into contemptuous laughter.

"You'd be a fine lot of use in a scrap. I'm not a great hand at getting the wind up."

Now the smile passed from Mackintosh's eyes to his lips. It distorted them painfully.

"*Quem deus vult perdere prius dementat.*"[6]

"What the hell is that?" said Walker.

---

6. *"Quem deus vult perdere prius dementat,"* "He whom God wishes to destroy he first makes mad." [*Latin*]

"Latin," answered Mackintosh as he went out.

And now he chuckled. His mood had changed. He had done all he could and the matter was in the hands of fate. He slept more soundly than he had done for weeks. When he awoke next morning he went out. After a good night he found a pleasant exhilaration in the freshness of the early air. The sea was a more vivid blue, the sky more brilliant, than on most days, the trade wind was fresh, and there was a ripple on the lagoon as the breeze brushed over it like velvet brushed the wrong way. He felt himself stronger and younger. He entered upon the day's work with zest. After luncheon he slept again, and as evening drew on he had the bay saddled and sauntered through the bush. He seemed to see it all with new eyes. He felt more normal. The extraordinary thing was that he was able to put Walker out of his mind altogether. So far as he was concerned he might never have existed.

He returned late, hot after his ride, and bathed again. Then he sat on the verandah, smoking his pipe, and looked at the day declining over the lagoon. In the sunset the lagoon, rosy and purple and green, was very beautiful. He felt at peace with the world and with himself. When the cook came out to say that dinner was ready and to ask whether he should wait, Mackintosh smiled at him with friendly eyes. He looked at his watch.

"It's half-past seven. Better not wait. One can't tell when the boss'll be back."

The boy nodded, and in a moment Mackintosh saw him carry across the yard a bowl of steaming soup. He got up lazily, went into the dining room, and ate his dinner. Had it happened? The uncertainty was amusing and Mackintosh chuckled in the silence. The food did not seem so monotonous as usual, and even though there was hamburger steak, the cook's invariable dish when his poor invention failed him, it tasted by some miracle succulent and spiced. After dinner he strolled over lazily to his bungalow to get a book. He liked the intense stillness, and now that the night had fallen the stars were blazing in the sky. He shouted for a lamp and in a moment the boy pattered over on his bare feet, piercing the darkness with a ray of light. He put the lamp on the desk and noiselessly slipped out of the room. Mackintosh stood rooted to the floor, for there, half hidden by untidy papers, was his revolver. His heart throbbed painfully, and he broke into a sweat. It was done then.

He took up the revolver with a shaking hand. Four of the chambers were empty. He paused a moment and looked suspiciously out into the night, but there was no one there. He quickly slipped four cartridges into the empty chambers and locked the revolver in his drawer.

He sat down to wait.

An hour passed, a second hour passed. There was nothing. He sat at his desk as though he were writing, but he neither wrote nor read. He merely listened. He strained his ears for a sound travelling from a far distance. At last he heard hesitating footsteps and knew it was the Chinese cook.

"Ah-Sung," he called.

The boy came to the door.

"Boss velly late," he said. "Dinner no good."

Mackintosh stared at him, wondering whether he knew what had happened, and whether, when he knew, he would realize on what terms he and Walker had been. He went about his work, sleek, silent, and smiling, and who could tell his thoughts?

"I expect he's had dinner on the way, but you must keep the soup hot at all events."

The words were hardly out of his mouth when the silence was suddenly broken into by a confusion, cries, and a rapid patter of naked feet. A number of natives ran into the compound, men and women and children; they crowded round Mackintosh and they all talked at once. They were unintelligible. They were excited and frightened and some of them were crying. Mackintosh pushed his way through them and went to the gateway. Though he had scarcely understood what they said he knew quite well what had happened. And as he reached the gate the dogcart arrived. The old mare was being led by a tall Kanaka, and in the dogcart crouched two men, trying to hold Walker up. A little crowd of natives surrounded it.

The mare was led into the yard and the natives surged in after it. Mackintosh shouted to them to stand back and the two policemen, sprang suddenly from God knows where, pushed them violently aside. By now he had managed to understand that some lads who had been fishing, on their way back to their village had come across the cart on the home side of the ford. The mare was nuzzling about the herbage and in the darkness they could just see the great white bulk of the old man sunk between the seat and the dashboard. At first they thought he was drunk and they peered in, grinning, but then they heard him groan, and guessed that something was amiss. They ran to the village and called for help. It was when they returned, accompanied by half a hundred people, that they discovered Walker had been shot.

With a sudden thrill of horror Mackintosh asked himself whether he was already dead. The first thing at all events was to get him out of the cart, and that, owing to Walker's corpulence, was a difficult job. It took four strong men to lift him. They jolted him and he uttered a dull groan. He was still alive. At last they carried him into the house, up the stairs, and placed him on his bed. Then Mackintosh was able to see him, for in the yard, lit only by half a dozen hurricane lamps, everything had been obscured. Walker's white ducks were stained with blood, and the men who had carried him wiped their hands, red and sticky, on their *lava-lavas.* Mackintosh held up the lamp. He had not expected the old man to be so pale. His eyes were closed. He was breathing still, his pulse could be just felt, but it was obvious that he was dying. Mackintosh had not bargained for the shock of horror that convulsed him. He saw that the native clerk was there, and in a voice hoarse with fear told him to go into the dispensary and get what was necessary for a hypodermic injection. One of the policemen had brought up the whisky, and Mackintosh forced a little into the old man's mouth. The room was crowded with natives. They sat about the floor, speechless now and terrified, and every now and then one wailed aloud. It was very hot, but Mackintosh felt cold, his hands and his feet were like ice, and he had to make a violent effort not to tremble in all his limbs. He did not know what to do. He did not know if Walker was bleeding still, and if he was, how he could stop the bleeding.

The clerk brought the hypodermic needle.

"You give it to him," said Mackintosh. "You're more used to that sort of thing than I am."

His head ached horribly. It felt as though all sorts of little savage things were beating inside it, trying to get out. They watched for the effect of the injection. Presently Walker opened his eyes slowly. He did not seem to know where he was.

"Keep quiet," said Mackintosh. "You're at home. You're quite safe."

Walker's lips outlined a shadowy smile.

"They've got me," he whispered.

"I'll get Jervis to send his motorboat to Apia at once. We'll get a doctor out by tomorrow afternoon."

There was a long pause before the old man answered,

"I shall be dead by then."

A ghastly expression passed over Mackintosh's pale face. He forced himself to laugh.

"What rot! You keep quiet and you'll be as right as rain."

"Give me a drink," said Walker. "A stiff one."

With shaking hand Mackintosh poured out whisky and water, half and half, and held the glass while Walker drank greedily. It seemed to restore him. He gave a long sigh and a little colour came into his great fleshy face. Mackintosh felt extraordinarily helpless. He stood and stared at the old man.

"If you'll tell me what to do I'll do it," he said.

"There's nothing to do. Just leave me alone. I'm done for."

He looked dreadfully pitiful as he lay on the great bed, a huge, bloated, old man; but so wan, so weak, it was heart-rending. As he rested, his mind seemed to grow clearer.

"You were right, Mac," he said presently. "You warned me."

"I wish to God I'd come with you."

"You're a good chap, Mac, only you don't drink."

There was another long silence, and it was clear that Walker was sinking. There was an internal hemorrhage and even Mackintosh in his ignorance could not fail to see that his chief had but an hour or two to live. He stood by the side of the bed stock-still. For half an hour perhaps Walker lay with his eyes closed, then he opened them.

"They'll give you my job," he said, slowly. "Last time I was in Apia I told them you were all right. Finish my road. I want to think that'll be done. All round the island."

"I don't want your job. You'll get all right."

Walker shook his head wearily.

"I've had my day. Treat them fairly, that's the great thing. They're children. You must always remember that. You must be firm with them, but you must be kind. And you must be just. I've never made a bob out of them. I haven't saved a hundred pounds in twenty years. The road's the great thing. Get the road finished."

Something very like a sob was wrung from Mackintosh.

"You're a good fellow, Mac. I always liked you."

He closed his eyes, and Mackintosh thought that he would never open them again. His mouth was so dry that he had to get himself something to drink. The Chinese cook silently put a chair for him. He sat down by the side of the bed and waited. He did not know how long a time passed. The night was endless. Suddenly one of the men sitting there broke into uncontrollable sobbing, loudly, like a child, and Mackintosh grew aware that the room was crowded by this time with natives. They sat all over the floor on their haunches, men and women, staring at the bed.

"What are all these people doing here?" said Mackintosh. "They've got no right. Turn them out, turn them out, all of them."

His words seemed to rouse Walker, for he opened his eyes once more, and now they were all misty. He wanted to speak, but he was so weak that Mackintosh had to strain his ears to catch what he said.

"Let them stay. They're my children. They ought to be here."

Mackintosh turned to the natives.

"Stay where you are. He wants you. But be silent."

A faint smile came over the old man's white face.

"Come nearer," he said.

Mackintosh bent over him. His eyes were closed and the words he said were like a wind sighing through the fronds of the coconut trees.

"Give me another drink. I've got something to say."

This time Mackintosh gave him his whisky neat. Walker collected his strength in a final effort of will.

"Don't make a fuss about this. In 'ninety-five when there were troubles white men were killed, and the fleet came and shelled the villages. A lot of people were killed who'd had nothing to do with it. They're damned fools at Apia. If they make a fuss they'll only punish the wrong people. I don't want anyone punished."

He paused for a while to rest.

"You must say it was an accident. No one's to blame. Promise me that."

"I'll do anything you like," whispered Mackintosh.

"Good chap. One of the best. They're children. I'm their father. A father don't let his children get into trouble if he can help it."

A ghost of a chuckle came out of his throat. It was astonishingly weird and ghastly.

"You're a religious chap, Mac. What's that about forgiving them? You know."

For a while Mackintosh did not answer. His lips trembled.

"Forgive them, for they know not what they do?"[7]

"That's right. Forgive them. I've loved them, you know, always loved them."

He sighed. His lips faintly moved, and now Mackintosh had to put his ears quite close to them in order to hear.

"Hold my hand," he said.

Mackintosh gave a gasp. His heart seemed wrenched. He took the old man's hand, so cold and weak, a coarse, rough hand, and held it in his own. And thus he sat until he nearly started out of his seat, for the silence was suddenly broken by a long rattle. It was terrible and unearthly. Walker was dead. Then the natives broke out with loud cries. The tears ran down their faces, and they beat their breasts.

Mackintosh disengaged his hand from the dead man's, and staggering like one drunk with sleep he went out of the room. He went to the locked drawer in his writing desk and took out the revolver. He walked down to the sea and walked into the lagoon; he waded out cautiously, so that he should not trip against a coral rock, till the water came to his armpits. Then he put a bullet through his head.

An hour later half a dozen slim brown sharks were splashing and struggling at the spot where he fell. ◆

---

7. *"Forgive them, for they know not what they do,"* words spoken by Christ on the Cross. (Luke 23:34)

# Frank O'Connor

## JUDAS

I'LL FORGET A LOT OF THINGS before I forget that night. As I was going out the mother said: "Sure, you won't be late, Jerry?" and I only laughed at her and said: "Am I ever late?" As I went down the road I was thinking it was months since I had taken her to the pictures. You might think that funny, Michael John, but after the father's death we were thrown together a lot. And I knew she hated being alone in the house after dark.

At the same time I had troubles of my own. You see, Michael John, being an only child, I never knocked round with girls the way others did. All the chaps in the office went with girls, or at any rate they let on they did. They said: "Who was the old doll I saw you with last night, Jerry? Aha, Jerry, you'd better mind yourself, boy, or you'll be

---

Copyright 1948 by Frank O'Connor. Reprinted from MORE STORIES BY FRANK O'CONNOR by permission of Alfred A. Knopf, Inc. and A. D. Peters and Company.

getting into trouble!" Paddy Kinnane, for instance, talked like that, and he never saw how it upset me. I think he thought it was a great compliment. It wasn't until years after that I began to suspect that Paddy's acquaintance with dolls was about of one kind with my own.

Then I met Kitty Doherty. Kitty was a hospital nurse, and all the chaps in the office said a fellow should never go with hospital nurses—they knew too much. I knew when I met Kitty that that was a lie. She was a well-educated, superior girl; she lived up the river in a posh locality, and her mother was on all sorts of councils and committees. She was small and wiry; a good-looking girl, always in good humor, and when she talked, she hopped from one thing to another like a robin on a frosty morning.

Anyway, she had me dazzled. I used to meet her in the evenings up the river road, as if I was walking there by accident and very surprised to see her. "Fancy meeting you!" I'd say, or "Well, well, isn't this a great surprise?" Then we'd stand talking for half an hour and I'd see her home. Several times she asked me in, but I was too nervous. I knew I'd lose my head, break the china, use some dirty word, and then go home and cut my throat. Of course, I never asked her to come to the pictures or anything like that. I knew she was above that. My only hope was that if I waited long enough I might be able to save her from drowning, the white slave traffic, or something of the sort. That would show in a modest, dignified way how I felt about her. Of course, I knew at the same time I ought to stay at home more with the mother, but the very thought that I might be missing an opportunity like that would be enough to spoil a whole evening on me.

This night in particular I was nearly distracted. It was three weeks since I'd seen Kitty. You know what three weeks are at that age. I was sure that at the very least the girl was dying and asking for me and that no one knew my address. A week before, I'd felt I simply couldn't bear it any longer, so I made an excuse and went down to the post office. I rang up the hospital and asked for her. I fully expected them to say that she was dead, and I got a shock when the girl at the other end asked my name. "I'm afraid," I said, "I'm a stranger to Miss Doherty, but I have an important message for her." Then I got completely panic-stricken. What could a girl like Kitty make of a damned deliberate lie like that? What else was it but a trap laid by an old and cunning hand. I held the receiver out and looked at it. "Moynihan," I said to it, "you're mad. An asylum, Moynihan, is the only place for a fellow like you." Then I heard her voice, not in my ear at all, but in the telephone booth as if she were standing before me, and I nearly dropped the receiver with terror. I put it to my ear and asked in a disguised voice: "Who is that speaking, please?" "This is Kitty Doherty," she said rather impatiently. "Who are you?" "I am Monsieur Bertrand," said I, speaking in what I hoped was a French accent. "I am afraid I have de wrong number." Then I put down the receiver carefully and thought how nice it would be if only I had a penknife handy to cut my throat with. It's funny, but from the moment I met Kitty I was always coveting sharp things like razors and penknives.

After that an awful idea dawned on my mind. Of course, I should have thought of it before, but, as you've probably guessed, I wasn't exactly knowledgeable. I began to see that I wasn't meeting Kitty for the very good reason that Kitty didn't want to meet me. That filled me with terror. I examined my conscience to find out what I might have said to her. You know what conscience is at that age. I remembered every remark I'd made and they were all brutal, indecent or disgusting. I had talked of Paddy Kinnane as a fellow who "went with dolls." What could a pure-minded girl think of a chap who naturally used such a phrase except—what, unfortunately, was true—that he had a mind like a cesspit.

It was a lovely summer evening, with views of hillsides and fields between the gaps in the houses, and that raised my spirits a bit. Maybe I was wrong, maybe she hadn't found out the sort I was and wasn't avoiding me, maybe we might meet and walk home together. I walked the full length of the river road and back, and then started off to walk it again. The crowds were thinning out as fellows and girls slipped off up the lanes or down to the river. As the streets went out like lamps about me I grew desperate. I saw clearly that she was avoiding me; that she knew I wasn't the quiet, good-natured chap I let on to be but a volcano of brutality and lust. "Lust, lust, lust!" I hissed to myself, clenching my fists.

Then I glanced up and saw her on a tram. I forgot instantly about the lust and smiled and waved my cap at her, but she was looking ahead and didn't see me. I ran after the car, intending to jump on it, to sit on one of the back seats on top and then say as she was getting off: "Fancy meeting you here!" (Trams were always a bit of a problem. If you sat beside a girl and paid for her, it might be considered forward; if you didn't, it looked mean. I never quite knew.) But as if the driver knew what was in my mind, he put on speed and away went the tram, tossing and screeching down the straight, and I stood panting in the middle of the road, smiling as if missing a tram was the best joke in the world and wishing all the time I had the penknife and the courage to use it. My position was hopeless. Then I must have gone a bit mad, for I started to race the tram. There were still lots of people out walking, and they stared after me, so I lifted my fists to my chest in the attitude of a professional runner and dropped into a comfortable stride which I hoped vaguely would delude them into the belief that I was in training for a big race.

Between the running and the halts I just managed to keep the tram in view all the way through town and out at the other side. When I saw Kitty get off and go up a hilly street I collapsed and was just able to drag myself after her. When she went into a house on a terrace I sat on the curb with my head between my knees till the panting stopped. At any rate I felt safe. I could now walk up and down before the house till she came out, and accost her with an innocent smile and say: "Fancy meeting you!"

But my luck was dead out that night. As I was walking up and down out of range of the house I saw a tall chap come strolling up at the opposite side and my heart sank. It was Paddy Kinnane.

"Hullo, Jerry," he chuckled with that knowing grin he put on whenever he wanted to compliment you on being discovered in a compromising situation, "what are you doing here?"

"Ah, just waiting for a chap I had a date with, Paddy," I said, trying to sound casual.

"Begor," said Paddy, "you look to me more like a man that was waiting for an old doll. Still waters run deep. . . . What time are you supposed to be meeting him?"

"Half-eight," I said at random.

"Half-eight?" said Paddy in surprise. " 'Tis nearly nine now."

"I know," said I, "but as I waited so long I may as well give him another few minutes."

"Ah, I'll wait along with you," said Paddy, leaning against the wall and taking out a packet of fags. "You might find yourself stuck by the end of the evening. There's people in this town and they have no consideration for anyone."

That was Paddy all out; no trouble too much for him if he could do you a good turn.

"As he kept me so long," I said hastily, "I don't think I'll bother with him. It only struck me this very minute that there's a chap up the Asragh road that I have to see on urgent business. You'll excuse me, Paddy. I'll tell you about it another time."

And away I went hell for leather to the tram. When I reached the tram stop below Kitty's house I sat on the river wall in the dusk. The moon was rising, and every quarter of an hour the trams came grunting and squeaking over the old bridge and then went black out while the conductors switched the trolleys. I stood on the curb in the moonlight searching for Kitty. Then a bobby came along, and as he seemed to be watching me, I slunk slowly off up the hill and stood against a wall in the shadow. There was a high wall at the other side too, and behind it the roofs of a house shining in the moon. Every now and then a tram would come in and people would pass in the moonlight, and the snatches of conversation I caught were like the warmth from an open door to the heart of a homeless man. It was quite clear now that my position was hopeless. The last tram came and went, and still there was no Kitty and still I hung on.

Then I heard a woman's step. I couldn't even pretend to myself that it might be Kitty till she shuffled past me with that hasty little walk of hers. I started and called out her name; she glanced over her shoulder and, seeing a man emerging from the shadow, took fright and ran. I ran too, but she put on speed and began to outdistance me. At that I despaired. I stood on the pavement and shouted after her at the top of my voice.

"Kitty!" I cried. "Kitty, for God's sake, wait for me!"

She ran a few steps further and then halted, turned, and came back slowly down the path.

"Jerry Moynihan!" she whispered, lifting her two arms to her breasts as if I had found her with nothing on. "What in God's name are you doing here?"

I was summoning up strength to tell her that I just happened to be taking a stroll in that direction and was astonished to see her when I realized the improbability of it and began to cry instead. Then I laughed. I suppose it was nerves. But Kitty had had a bad fright and now that she was getting over it she was as cross as two sticks.

"What's wrong with you, I say," she snapped. "Are you out of your senses or what?"

"Well, you see," I stammered awkwardly, half in dread I was going to cry again, "I didn't see you in town."

"No," she replied with a shrug, "I know you didn't. I wasn't out. What about it?"

"I thought it might be something I said to you," I said desperately.

"No," said Kitty candidly, "it wasn't anything to do with you. It's Mother."

"Why?" I asked almost joyously. "Is there something wrong with her?"

"I don't mean that," said Kitty impatiently. "It's just that she made such a fuss, I felt it wasn't worth it."

"But what did she make a fuss about?" I asked.

"About you, of course," said Kitty in exasperation. "What did you think?"

"But what did I do?" I asked, clutching my head. This was worse than anything I'd ever imagined. This was terrible.

"You didn't do anything," said Kitty, "but people were talking about us. And you wouldn't come in and be introduced to her like anyone else. I know she's a bit of a fool, and her head is stuffed with old nonsense about her family. I could never see that they were different to anyone else, and anyway, she married a commercial[1] herself, so she has nothing much to boast about. Still, you needn't be so superior. There's no obligation to buy, you know."

I didn't. There were cold shivers running through me. I had thought of Kitty as a secret between God, herself, and me and that she only knew the half of it. Now it seemed I didn't even know the half. People were talking about us! I was superior! What next?

"But what has she against me?" I asked despairingly.

"She thinks we're doing a tangle, of course," snapped Kitty as if she was astonished at my stupidity, "and I suppose she imagines you're not grand enough for a great-great-grandniece of Daniel O'Connell.[2] I told her you were

---

1. *a commercial*, a commercial traveler, a salesman. 2. *Daniel O'Connell* (1775–1847), great Irish nationalist.

a different sort of fellow entirely and above all that sort of thing, but she wouldn't believe me. She said I was a deep, callous, crafty little intriguer and that I hadn't a drop of Daniel O'Connell's blood in my veins." Kitty began to giggle at the thought of herself as an intriguer.

"That's all she knows," I said bitterly.

"I know," said Kitty with a shrug. "The woman has no sense. And anyway she has no reason to think I'm telling lies. Cissy and I always had fellows, and we spooned with them all over the shop under her very nose, so why should she think I'm lying to her now?"

At that I began to laugh like an idiot. This was worse than appalling. This was a nightmare. Kitty, whom I had thought so angelic, talking in cold blood about "spooning" with fellows all over the house. Even the bad women in the books I'd read didn't talk about love in that cold-blooded way. Madame Bovary[3] herself had at least the decency to pretend that she didn't like it. It was like another door opening on the outside world, but Kitty thought I was laughing at her and started to apologize.

"Of course I had no sense," she said. "You're the first fellow I ever met that treated me properly. The others only wanted to fool around with me, and now because I don't like it, Mother thinks I'm getting stuck-up. I told her I liked you better than any fellow I knew, but that I'd grown out of all that sort of thing."

"And what did she say to that?" I asked fiercely. It was—how can I describe it?—like a man who'd lived all his life in a dungeon getting into the sunlight for the first time and afraid of every shadow.

"Ah, I told you the woman was silly," said Kitty, getting embarrassed.

"Go on!" I shouted. "I want to know everything. I insist on knowing everything."

---

3. *Madame Bovary,* heroine of the novel of the same name by Gustave Flaubert (1857).

"Well," said Kitty with a demure little grin, "she said you were a deep, designing guttersnipe who knew exactly how to get round feather-pated little idiots like me. . . . You see," she added with another shrug, "it's quite hopeless. The woman is common. She doesn't understand."

"But I tell you she does understand," I shouted frantically. "She understands better than you do. I only wish to God I was deep and designing so that I'd have some chance with you."

"Do you really?" asked Kitty, opening her eyes wide. "To tell you the truth," she added after a moment, "I thought you were a bit keen the first time, but then I didn't know. When you didn't kiss me or anything, I mean."

"God," I said bitterly, "when I think of what I've been through in the past couple of weeks!"

"I know," said Kitty, biting her lip. "I was the same." And then we said nothing for a few moments.

"You're sure you're serious?" she asked suspiciously.

"I tell you, girl," I shouted, "I was on the point of committing suicide."

"What good would that be?" she asked with another shrug, and then she looked at me and laughed outright—the little jade!

It is all as clear in my mind as if it had happened last night. I told Kitty about my prospects. She didn't care, but I insisted on telling her. It was as if a stone had been lifted off my heart, and I went home in the moonlight singing. Then I heard the clock strike, and the singing stopped. I remembered the mother at home, waiting, and began to run again. This was desperation too, but a different sort.

The door was ajar and the kitchen in darkness. I saw her sitting before the fire by herself, and just as I was going to throw my arms about her, I smelt Kitty's perfume round me and was afraid to go near her. God help us, as if it would have told her anything!

"Hallo, Mum," I said with a laugh, rubbing my hands, "you're all in darkness."

"You'll have a cup of tea?" she said.

"I might as well," said I.

"What time is it?" she said, lighting the gas. "You're very late."

"Ah, I met a fellow from the office," I said, but at the same time I was stung by the complaint in her tone.

"You frightened me," she said with a little whimper. "I didn't know what happened to you. What kept you at all?"

"Oh, what do you think?" I said, goaded into retorting. "Drinking and blackguarding as usual."

I could have bitten my tongue off when I'd said it; it sounded so cruel, as if some stranger had said it instead of me. She turned to me for a moment with a frightened stare as if she was seeing the stranger too, and somehow I couldn't bear it.

"God Almighty," I said, "a fellow can have no life in his own house," and away with me upstairs.

I lit the candle, undressed and got into bed. I was wild. A chap could be a drunkard and blackguard and not be made to suffer more reproach than I was for being late one single night. That, I felt, was what you got for being a good son.

"Jerry," she called from the foot of the stairs, "will I bring you up your cup?"

"I don't want it now, thanks," I said.

I heard her give a heavy sigh and turn away. Then she locked the two doors front and back. She didn't wash up, and I knew my cup of tea was standing there on the table with a saucer on top in case I changed my mind. She came slowly up the stairs, and she walked like an old woman. I blew out the candle before she reached the landing in case she came in to ask me if I wanted anything else, and the moonlight came in the attic window and brought me memories of Kitty. But every time I tried to imagine her face while she grinned up at me, waiting for me to kiss her, it was the mother's face that came up with that look like a child's when you strike him the first time—as if he suddenly saw the stranger in you. I remembered all our life together from the night the father—God rest him!—died; our early Mass on Sunday; our visits to the pictures; our plans for the future, and Christ, Michael John, it was as if I was inside her mind and she sitting by the fire, waiting for the blow to fall! And now it had fallen, and I was a stranger to her, and nothing I ever did could make us the same to each other again. There was something like a cannon ball stuck in my chest, and I lay awake till the cocks started crowing. Then I couldn't bear it any longer. I went out on to the landing and listened.

"Are you awake, Mother?" I asked in a whisper.

"What is it, Jerry?" she said in alarm, and I knew she hadn't slept any more than I had.

"I only came to say I was sorry," I said, opening the room door, and then as I saw her sitting up in bed under the Sacred Heart lamp, the cannon ball burst inside me and I began to bawl like a kid.

"Oh, child, child," she cried out, "what are you crying for at all, my little boy?" and she spread out her arms to me. I went to her and she hugged me and rocked me just as she did when I was only a nipper. "Oh, oh, oh," she was saying to herself in a whisper, "my storeen bawn,[4] my little man!"—all the names she hadn't called me since I was a kid. That was all we said. I couldn't bring myself to tell her what I'd done, and she wouldn't confess to me that she was jealous; all she could do was to try and comfort me for the way I'd hurt her, to make up to me for the nature she'd given me. "My storeen bawn," she said. "My little man!" ◆

---

4. *storeen bawn,* little fair-haired treasure. [*Irish*]

# Saki (H. H. Munro)

## THE LUMBER ROOM

THE CHILDREN WERE TO BE DRIVEN, as a special treat, to the sands at Jagborough. Nicholas was not to be of the party; he was in disgrace. Only that morning he had refused to eat his wholesome bread-and-milk on the seemingly frivolous ground that there was a frog in it. Older and wiser and better people had told him that there could not possibly be a frog in his bread-and-milk and that he was not to talk nonsense; he continued, nevertheless, to talk what seemed the veriest nonsense, and described with much detail the coloration and markings of the alleged frog. The dramatic part of the incident was that there really was a frog in Nicholas' basin of bread-and-milk; he had put it there himself, so he felt entitled to know something about it. The sin of taking a frog from the garden and putting it into a bowl of wholesome bread-and-milk was enlarged on at great length, but the fact that stood out clearest in the whole affair, as it presented itself to the mind of Nicholas, was that the older, wiser, and better people had been proved to be profoundly in error in matters about which they had expressed the utmost assurance.

"You said there couldn't possibly be a frog in my bread-

---

"The Lumber Room" from THE COMPLETE SHORT STORIES OF SAKI, (British title: THE BODLEY HEAD SAKI) by H. H. Munro. Copyright 1930, copyright renewed 1958 by The Viking Press, Inc. All rights reserved. Reprinted by permission of The Viking Press, Inc.

and-milk; there *was* a frog in my bread-and-milk," he repeated, with the insistence of a skilled tactician who does not intend to shift from favourable ground.

So his boy-cousin and girl-cousin and his quite uninteresting younger brother were to be taken to Jagborough sands that afternoon and he was to stay at home. His cousins' aunt, who insisted, by an unwarranted stretch of imagination, in styling herself his aunt also, had hastily invented the Jagborough expedition in order to impress on Nicholas the delights that he had justly forfeited by his disgraceful conduct at the breakfast table. It was her habit, whenever one of the children fell from grace, to improvise something of a festival nature from which the offender would be rigorously debarred; if all the children sinned collectively they were suddenly informed of a circus in a neighbouring town, a circus of unrivalled merit and uncounted elephants, to which, but for their depravity, they would have been taken that very day.

A few decent tears were looked for on the part of Nicholas when the moment for the departure of the expedition arrived. As a matter-of-fact, however, all the crying was done by his girl-cousin, who scraped her knee rather painfully against the step of the carriage as she was scrambling in.

"How she did howl," said Nicholas cheerfully, as the party drove off without any of the elation of high spirits that should have characterized it.

"She'll soon get over that," said the *soi-disant*[1] aunt; "it will be a glorious afternoon for racing about over those beautiful sands. How they will enjoy themselves!"

"Bobby won't enjoy himself much, and he won't race much either," said Nicholas with a grim chuckle; "his boots are hurting him. They're too tight."

"Why didn't he tell me they were hurting?" asked the aunt with some asperity.

---

1. *soi-disant,* so-called, self-styled. [*French*]

"He told you twice, but you weren't listening. You often don't listen when we tell you important things."

"You are not to go into the gooseberry garden," said the aunt, changing the subject.

"Why not?" demanded Nicholas.

"Because you are in disgrace," said the aunt loftily.

Nicholas did not admit the flawlessness of the reasoning; he felt perfectly capable of being in disgrace and in a gooseberry garden at the same moment. His face took on an expression of considerable obstinacy. It was clear to his aunt that he was determined to get into the gooseberry garden, "only," as she remarked to herself, "because I have told him he is not to."

Now the gooseberry garden had two doors by which it might be entered, and once a small person like Nicholas could slip in there he could effectually disappear from view amid the masking growth of artichokes, raspberry canes, and fruit bushes. The aunt had many other things to do that afternoon, but she spent an hour or two in trivial gardening operations among flower beds and shrubberies, whence she could keep a watchful eye on the two doors that led to the forbidden paradise. She was a woman of few ideas, with immense powers of concentration.

Nicholas made one or two sorties into the front garden, wriggling his way with obvious stealth of purpose towards one or other of the doors, but never able for a moment to evade the aunt's watchful eye. As a matter-of-fact, he had no intention of trying to get into the gooseberry garden, but it was extremely convenient for him that his aunt should believe that he had; it was a belief that would keep her on self-imposed sentry duty for the greater part of the afternoon. Having thoroughly confirmed and fortified her suspicions, Nicholas slipped back into the house and rapidly put into execution a plan of action that had long germinated in his brain. By standing on a chair in the library one could reach a shelf on which reposed a fat, important-looking key. The key was as important as it looked; it was the instrument which kept the mysteries of the lumber room[2] secure from unauthorized intrusion, which opened a way only for aunts and suchlike privileged persons. Nicholas had not had much experience of the art of fitting keys into keyholes and turning locks, but for some days past he had practised with the key of the schoolroom door; he did not believe in trusting too much to luck and accident. The key turned stiffly in the lock, but it turned. The door opened, and Nicholas was in an unknown land, compared with which the gooseberry garden was a stale delight, a mere material pleasure.

Often and often Nicholas had pictured to himself what the lumber room might be like, that region that was so carefully sealed from youthful eyes and concerning which no questions were ever answered. It came up to his expectations. In the first place it was large and dimly lit, one high window opening on to the forbidden garden being its only source of illumination. In the second place it was a storehouse of unimagined treasures. The aunt-by-assertion was one of those people who think that things spoil by use and consign them to dust and damp by way of preserving them. Such parts of the house as Nicholas knew best were rather bare and cheerless, but here there were wonderful things for the eye to feast on. First and foremost there was a piece of framed tapestry that was evidently meant to be a fire screen. To Nicholas it was a living, breathing story; he sat down on a roll of Indian hangings, glowing in wonderful colours beneath a layer of dust, and took in all the details of the tapestry picture. A man, dressed in the hunting costume of some remote period, had just transfixed a stag with an arrow; it could not have been a difficult shot because the stag was only one or two paces away from him; in the thickly growing vegetation that the picture suggested it would not have been difficult to creep up to a feeding stag, and the two spotted dogs that were springing

---

2. *lumber room*, a storeroom.

forward to join in the chase had evidently been trained to keep to heel till the arrow was discharged. That part of the picture was simple, if interesting, but did the huntsman see, what Nicholas saw, that four galloping wolves were coming in his direction through the wood? There might be more than four of them hidden behind the trees, and in any case would the man and his dogs be able to cope with the four wolves if they made an attack? The man had only two arrows left in his quiver, and he might miss with one or both of them; all one knew about his skill in shooting was that he could hit a large stag at a ridiculously short range. Nicholas sat for many golden minutes revolving the possibilities of the scene; he was inclined to think that there were more than four wolves and that the man and his dogs were in a tight corner.

But there were other objects of delight and interest claiming his instant attention: there were quaint twisted candlesticks in the shape of snakes, and a teapot fashioned like a china duck, out of whose open beak the tea was supposed to come. How dull and shapeless the nursery teapot seemed in comparison! And there was a carved sandalwood box packed tight with aromatic cotton wool, and between the layers of cotton wool were little brass figures, hump-necked bulls, and peacocks and goblins, delightful to see and to handle. Less promising in appearance was a large square book with plain black covers; Nicholas peeped into it, and, behold, it was full of coloured pictures of birds. And such birds! In the garden, and in the lanes when he went for a walk, Nicholas came across a few birds, of which the largest were an occasional magpie or wood pigeon; here were herons and bustards, kites, toucans, tiger bitterns, brush turkeys, ibises, golden pheasants, a whole portrait gallery of undreamed-of creatures. And as he was admiring the colouring of the mandarin duck and assigning a life history to it, the voice of his aunt in shrill vociferation of his name came from the gooseberry garden without. She had grown suspicious at his long disappearance, and had leapt to the conclusion that he had climbed over the wall behind the sheltering screen of the lilac bushes; she was now engaged in energetic and rather hopeless search for him among the artichokes and raspberry canes.

"Nicholas, Nicholas!" she screamed, "you are to come out of this at once. It's no use trying to hide there; I can see you all the time."

It was probably the first time for twenty years that any one had smiled in that lumber room.

Presently the angry repetitions of Nicholas' name gave way to a shriek, and a cry for somebody to come quickly. Nicholas shut the book, restored it carefully to its place in a corner, and shook some dust from a neighbouring pile of newspapers over it. Then he crept from the room, locked the door, and replaced the key exactly where he had found it. His aunt was still calling his name when he sauntered into the front garden.

"Who's calling?" he asked.

"Me," came the answer from the other side of the wall; "didn't you hear me? I've been looking for you in the gooseberry garden, and I've slipped into the rain-water tank. Luckily there's no water in it, but the sides are slippery and I can't get out. Fetch the little ladder from under the cherry tree——"

"I was told I wasn't to go into the gooseberry garden," said Nicholas promptly.

"I told you not to, and now I tell you that you may," came the voice from the rain-water tank, rather impatiently.

"Your voice doesn't sound like aunt's," objected Nicholas; "you may be the Evil One tempting me to be disobedient. Aunt often tells me that the Evil One tempts me and that I always yield. This time I'm not going to yield."

"Don't talk nonsense," said the prisoner in the tank; "go and fetch the ladder."

"Will there be strawberry jam for tea?" asked Nicholas innocently.

"Certainly there will be," said the aunt, privately resolving that Nicholas should have none of it.

"Now I know that you are the Evil One and not aunt," shouted Nicholas gleefully; "when we asked for strawberry jam yesterday she said there wasn't any. I know there are four jars of it in the store cupboard, because I looked, and of course you know it's there, but *she* doesn't, because she said there wasn't any. Oh, Devil, you *have* sold yourself!"

There was an unusual sense of luxury in being able to talk to an aunt as though one was talking to the Evil One, but Nicholas knew, with childish discernment, that such luxuries were not to be overindulged in. He walked noisily away, and it was a kitchenmaid, in search of parsley, who eventually rescued the aunt from the rain-water tank.

Tea that evening was partaken of in a fearsome silence. The tide had been at its highest when the children had arrived at Jagborough Cove, so there had been no sands to play on—a circumstance that the aunt had overlooked in the haste of organizing her punitive expedition. The tightness of Bobby's boots had had disastrous effect on his temper the whole of the afternoon, and altogether the children could not have been said to have enjoyed themselves. The aunt maintained the frozen muteness of one who has suffered undignified and unmerited detention in a rain-water tank for thirty-five minutes. As for Nicholas, he, too, was silent, in the absorption of one who has much to think about; it was just possible, he considered, that the huntsman would escape with his hounds while the wolves feasted on the stricken stag. ◆

# Muriel Spark

# THE PARTY THROUGH THE WALL

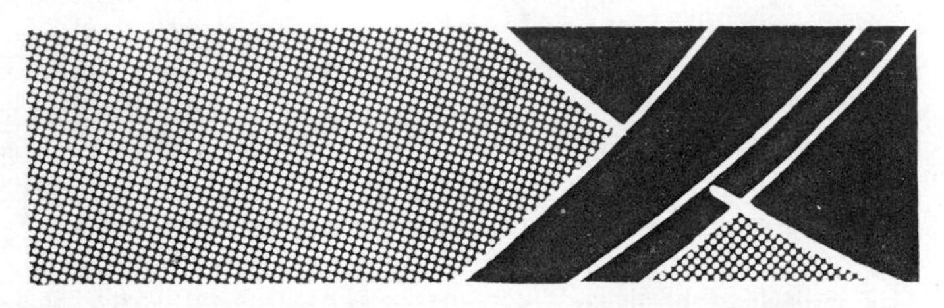

*Narrator (Dr. Fell).*[1] Most of the houses in Romney Terrace are bomb damage, they lie open to the Kensington weather like the decayed hollow teeth of some prone—or do I mean supine?—monster. Two of the houses at the end of the Terrace have been repaired and made over into flats. Some months ago, Miss Ethel Carson came to live in the last but one, number ten, on the third floor. I myself live next door in number eleven.

You will wonder how it is that I, with my secluded habits, came to know so much about Miss Carson. But, as you will see, I had unique opportunities to study this lady, even before she told me all about herself.

One of the first things Miss Carson asked the house-

---

"The Party Through the Wall" from the book VOICES AT PLAY by Muriel Spark. Copyright © 1961 by Muriel Spark. Reprinted by permission of J. B. Lippincott Company and Harold Ober Associates, Inc.

1. *Dr. Fell,* the person addressed in a nursery rhyme in which the speaker expresses inexplicable dislike:

> I do not like thee, Dr. Fell,
> The reason why I cannot tell;
> But this I know, and know full well,
> I do not like thee, Dr. Fell.

keeper when she came to look over the flat was a question which she always asked in these circumstances.
*Miss Carson.* Is it quiet?
*Housekeeper.* Too quiet, miss. Too quiet.
*Miss Carson.* It can't be too quiet for me. No wirelesses? No babies? I sleep badly. I suffer from my nerves. No late parties in the house?
*Housekeeper.* No, no parties, miss.
*Miss Carson.* It looks rather small. Is it damp?
*Housekeeper.* No, miss, no damp. See for yourself, miss.
*Miss Carson.* Don't call me miss, it gets on my nerves. My name is Miss Carson, Ethel Carson—you won't have heard of me but I am known in certain circles. Where's the bedroom? Is it facing the back? It has to face the back of the house. I can't stand traffic. I suffer from sleeplessness.
*Housekeeper.* In here. It looks out on the back.
*Miss Carson.* It's rather small. Who lives on the other side of the wall?
*Housekeeper.* That's number eleven. All made over into flats.
*Miss Carson.* The wall is very thin. Are they noisy at number eleven? Shall I hear them at night having parties or quarrelling and screaming? Do they have the wireless on late at night? The wall is rather thin.
*Housekeeper.* It's a quiet place. Ideal for anyone that's getting on in life.
*Miss Carson.* It must be ideal for *you.* Tell me, do you think it odd that I am wearing these clothes at my age? Where's the kitchen? Does it smell?
*Housekeeper.* Do you want the flat? There's another party after it.
*Miss Carson.* Oh, must I make up my mind right away? How disturbing.
*Housekeeper.* There's another party wants it that's out all day.
*Narrator.* Miss Carson took the flat and moved in the following week. I believe she was generally satisfied,

though, in the first month of her stay, I understand there was some trouble about mice.

*Miss Carson.* Mice in my kitchen. I am a vegetarian, which attracts mice. I mean the cheese, I use a lot of cheese. I cannot have mice.

*Housekeeper.* I'll set a trap, miss.

*Miss Carson.* No, no. I should be unable to sleep at night because of the squeaking of mice in the trap. And don't call me miss, it gets on my nerves.

*Housekeeper.* I'll put a cat in the kitchen at night, then.

*Miss Carson.* Oh, I call that very cruel. I couldn't bear it. How disturbing.

*Narrator.* Eventually the mice were eliminated by means of a powdered preparation which killed them silently and without evidence.

For at least three months I watched Miss Carson's comings and goings, and noted her special times and habits. Really I conceived an interest in her. Of course, it was a detached interest, as becomes my position in life.

I observed that, for a woman in her fifties, she looked, I will not say young, but neat and unusual. She must have been a little unusual from the time of her youth.

*Miss Carson.* I have been an unusual person from the time of my youth. My earliest memories——

*Housekeeper.* I can see that, miss.

*Narrator.* And as a rule, when Miss Carson emerged from the front door of number ten she was wearing a snow-white duffle coat over pink velvet corduroy jeans. She kept her hair a pale yellow, drawn straight back so that its thinness was concealed. Her rimless glasses added to the pastel effect. She was most quaint. I could see she was an exceptional, a very exceptional case.

One day, at last, when no one was about, I spoke to her. Ever since my retirement I have tried to keep in the background, and to some extent I avoid company. But as we were alone in the street, about three in the afternoon, I spoke. "Good afternoon, madam," I said. "Nice day."

*Miss Carson.* I beg your pardon?
*Narrator.* I said, beautiful day.
*Miss Carson.* Oh, I suppose it is.
*Narrator.* Allow me to introduce myself. I am your next door neighbour, as it were. I believe you have not been here long?
*Miss Carson.* No, I suppose I haven't.
*Narrator.* I am the proprietor of number eleven. My name is Fell.
*Miss Carson.* Good afternoon, Mr. Fell. I am in rather a hurry, if you don't mind.
*Narrator. Doctor* Fell, madam. A man of medicine.
*Miss Carson.* Indeed, that is interesting. Do you practise?
*Narrator.* If you are in a hurry, madam, perhaps another time.
*Miss Carson.* Do you practise here, Dr. Fell? I'm in no great hurry.
*Narrator.* Rarely, madam, in these days. Unless I find an exceptionally interesting case. I am a specialist, and an exceptional case is a very great temptation, very great, madam.
*Miss Carson.* You keep calling me madam; I must tell you it jars on my nerves. My name is Ethel Carson. You won't have heard of me, but I am known in certain circles. What do you specialise in, Dr. Fell?
*Narrator.* Nerves, madam. I specialise in nerves. But only exceptional cases—they are irresistible.
*Miss Carson.* Now that *is* fascinating. We must have some talks together, Dr. Fell.
*Narrator.* For some months Miss Carson was satisfied with the quietness of Romney Terrace. A street which is nearly all bomb damage is always quiet. We have no traffic. Not many rough children play here by day, not many stray cats come here at night. Numbers ten and eleven are occupied by people of silent habits—Miss Carson, how about the housekeeper?
*Miss Carson.* Oh, she's quiet enough. Of course, she is sly.

But she is quiet. I should explain that I lead a sequestered though busy life. I am devoted to art and to all spiritual matters: I should rather say, dedicated.

*Narrator.* The dedicated life takes up an enormous amount of Miss Carson's time. And also, she has to look after her investments which take up an enormous amount of time. As Miss Carson says, she can't leave these matters to others.

In the mornings she has her bath, does her deep breathing, and meditates. On Monday afternoons she goes to the hairdresser, and from there to her physiotherapist who is also a masseuse.

*Miss Carson.* Dr. Fell, do you believe in the occult?

*Narrator.* One thing at a time, madam, if you please . . . To continue with Miss Carson's daily round. Sometimes she meets her young friends while she is out and about. Most of her friends are young. She doesn't care for old fogies. That's why I, who am getting on, am favoured in having cultivated Miss Carson's acquaintance.

*Miss Carson.* I wish you would call me Ethel, Dr. Fell. Miss Carson gets dreadfully on my nerves. All my friends call me Ethel. All my friends are young, except you, and sensitive to the spiritual life, like you.

*Narrator.* Thank you, Ethel.

On Tuesdays, Miss Carson attends to her business affairs, and in that way she has come across a number of interesting speculators.

*Miss Carson.* You would be surprised how sensitive some City men are to spiritual matters. . . .

*Narrator.* To continue with Miss Carson's daily round. Tuesday evening is her night for the Kensington Cabbalah Study Group of which she is an active member. Wednesdays, if her nerves permit, she spends on her automatic writing.

*Miss Carson.* Oh, Dr. Fell, have you ever experimented with automatic writing? Of course, in this rationalistic age it has gone out of fashion, but it will come back, like all those things. The great thing in life is to keep an open mind. By the way, Dr. Fell, have you ever had that extraordinary feeling that everything has happened before?

*Narrator.* Ethel, I must ask you to exercise patience. How can I tell the story when you keep interrupting?

*Miss Carson.* Rightee-o.

*Narrator.* I must request you, Ethel, not to say "rightee-o." It gets on my nerves.

*Miss Carson.* I don't think a professional man should use an expression like "gets on my nerves." It is rather low, in my opinion.

*Narrator (over above).* On Wednesdays her young friend David, who is a ballet dancer, comes to spend a few hours with Miss Carson.

*Miss Carson.* He is very sensitive and according to his horoscope his future is assured. He is . . .

*Narrator.* Miss Carson has explained what she does on Mondays, Tuesdays and Wednesdays. Well, Thursdays, Fridays, Saturdays and Sundays are much the same. She has her Dream Prognostication Circle and her Astral-Radiation Trance Club. She meditates much. And a great deal of her time is taken up in preparing her vegetarian meals.

*Miss Carson.* So many people neglect the roots and fruits of the earth; how they survive I can't think. And then, of course, I frequently spend a little time chatting to Dr. Fell, who, I must admit, is sensitive to the life of the spirit.

*Narrator.* Thank you, Ethel. I would invite you to tea, but I am prevented from entertaining because of my poor sister.

*Miss Carson.* I didn't know you had a sister. Is she ill? Is she bedridden? I can't stand illness, it gets on my . . . it does dreadful things to my nerves.

*Narrator.* She is confined to her room. She is as quiet as the grave.

*Miss Carson.* I sympathise with you, Dr. Fell. Invalids are a great trial.

*Narrator.* That was six weeks ago. Miss Carson has now

left Romney Terrace, isn't that so, Ethel? . . . You see, no answer. She's gone. Now I shall tell you why she left Romney Terrace.

Some days before she departed I saw Miss Carson coming out of number ten a little earlier than usual. She looked very put out that morning, and instead of turning up the street she stood out in the middle of the road and stared up at the windows of number eleven. I thought I had better put in an appearance. I said, "Good morning, Ethel. Is anything the matter?"

*Miss Carson.* I should think there is, Dr. Fell. I couldn't sleep a wink last night, on account of the dreadful noise.

*Narrator.* Noise, did you say? In Romney Terrace?

*Miss Carson.* The noise came from your house, Dr. Fell. It was a party.

*Narrator.* A party at number eleven? But we never have parties, on account of my poor sister.

*Miss Carson.* I insist that someone in your house held a party late last night. It was in the room next to my bedroom, on the third floor.

*Narrator.* That is my poor sister's room, Ethel. She is quiet as the grave.

*Miss Carson.* She must have been giving a party. It was frightful. It lasted till four in the morning. I was just coming to call on you to complain in the strongest terms.

*Narrator.* I was convinced that poor Miss Carson was suffering from her nerves. You see, she acted like a magnet upon me. You see, she called out the compulsive instinct of the specialist in me. I could not leave her alone, she was an extraordinary case. Indeed, she would not leave me alone, she was determined to complain of the noise.

*Miss Carson.* There was a great hubbub, Dr. Fell. Music and chatter. I had gone to bed about eleven o'clock, having just said good-bye to my young friend, David, the ballet dancer. I was rather worried about David because *he* was worried, and this was because one of his companions at the ballet school and that was because . . . *(Fade.)*

*Narrator.* Yes, yes . . . She took her phenobarbitone as usual. But she could not sleep. She lay awake worrying. . . .

*Miss Carson.* I lay awake till it must have been close on three in the morning.

*Narrator.* Observe that up to this point not even a clock ticked. Miss Carson has an electric clock to avoid the tick. Her bed is placed with the head against the wall which separates her flat from my sister's in number eleven.

*Miss Carson.* I had never before experienced trouble from number eleven, not a sound. But now, as I lay worrying, awake, I suddenly thought I heard a noise. Was it my imagination, or could that be the playing of a piano in the room through the wall? It wasn't my imagination, Dr. Fell.

(*Piano playing and party chatter.*)

*Voice 1 (over).* How beautifully you play, Countess. What are you playing? It is difficult to follow through this hullabaloo.

*Countess (young—in her twenties).* Liszt[2]—I was present at a party in London when he played, not long before his death. Do you think I should stop? Everyone is so noisy and occupied. They don't want music.

*Voice 1.* Don't stop, Countess, it's heavenly. How I do wish I were a widow!

(*Piano stops.*)

*Countess.* A widow! How comical you are, and you're not even married yet.

*Voice 1.* I wish to be a widow, rather. I would cultivate musicians, I would . . .

(*Noise as of banging on wall with a shoe. Chatter down.*)

*Miss Carson.* Stop that noise! I can't sleep.

(*More banging on wall with shoe. Chatter.*)

---

2. *Liszt.* Franz Liszt (1811-1886) was a Hungarian pianist and composer.

*Voice 3.* Good-bye then, Countess. A delightful evening . . .
*Voice 2.* You played beautifully. What was that last piece? Weber?
*Voice 3.* Meyerbeer . . . [3]
*Voice 2.* Oh, Meyerbeer, of course, of course . . .
*Voice 3.* Ta-ta, Countess, as they say . . .
*Voice 4.* Margaret dear, stand out of that draught; your kidneys . . .
*Voice 5.* . . . brought home a polar bear; of course it died . . . Countess, lovely party . . .

(*More banging on wall with shoe.*)

*Miss Carson.* Stop that noise! I can't sleep.

(*Party chatter continues under above.*)

*Voice 6.* Such a relief for you, Countess, now that your brother is away, I'm sure.
*Countess.* He isn't away, you know.
*Voice 6.* Not away, Countess? I heard to the contrary.
*Countess.* He is here, but out of sight.
*Voice 6.* Surely, my dear, he is not in this house?
*Countess.* Dear friend, can you keep a secret? My brother is in the attic.
*Voice 6.* The attic! Is he safe?
*Countess.* Altogether safe. We have made it very comfortable.
*Voice 6.* I mean is it safe for you? Has he a keeper?
*Countess.* He has an attendant.
*Voice 1.* Good-bye then, Countess. Charming party.
*Countess.* Good-bye, good night.
*Voice 2.* Tomorrow at five, Countess?
*Countess.* Tomorrow? Oh, that depends . . .
*Voice 3.* Ta-ta . . .
*Servant.* The carriages are waiting, sir.
*Countess.* Take care, it's turning cold. Good night.
*Voice 4.* The carriages. What a night!

---

3. *Weber . . . Meyerbeer.* Carl von Weber (1786–1826) was a German composer. Giacomo Meyerbeer (1791–1864) was a German operatic composer.

*Miss Carson (shouting from window).* Oh, go away home and stop that hell of a row. I want to sleep.
*Narrator.* Ethel, I think, if I may say so, you are suffering from nerves.
*Miss Carson. I* should say I am suffering from my nerves after a night like that. You must give your tenant notice to quit, Dr. Fell. I shall see my lawyer. It is an offence.
*Narrator.* Now, consider. You say that the guests were taken home in carriages. Is that likely? Is it reasonable? We are in the second half of the twentieth century, and you talk of carriages.
*Miss Carson.* I *saw* the carriages, Dr. Fell. A fancy-dress stunt, I daresay. Who occupies the room next to mine? Who is your tenant?
*Narrator.* My poor sister occupies that room. She is very feeble and quite incapable of parties.
*Miss Carson.* Her name?
*Narrator.* Oh, one calls her the Countess.
*Miss Carson.* I insist on seeing your sister. I want to get to the bottom of this.
*Narrator.* Cases like Miss Carson always want to get to the bottom of things, and when they get there, they don't like it. Follow me, Ethel, and I shall take you to my sister, so old and quiet, confined to her room.

(*Their footsteps.*)

*Miss Carson.* Oh, the passage is very dark. I can't see my way, Dr. Fell.
*Narrator.* We ought to have a light, but the bulb has gone. The ground floor tenant should see to it, but he is seldom at home. Follow me closely; my sister is on the third floor.
*Miss Carson.* In the room adjacent to my bedroom?
*Narrator.* Exactly adjacent, Ethel.
*Miss Carson.* I would rather you did not call me Ethel. I must get to the bottom of this, you realise.
*Narrator.* When I had introduced Miss Carson to the Countess, I made myself scarce, so to speak. My sister does not always care for my presence.

*Countess (aged).* Is my brother in the room? My eyes are weak. I do not at all care for his presence.
*Miss Carson.* No, Countess, Dr. Fell is not here.
*Countess.* Dr. Fell my eye.
*Miss Carson.* I beg your pardon?
*Countess.* I said, Dr. Fell my eye. My brother is a madman. What is your business? State your business.
*Miss Carson.* I live next door in number ten. My flat is on the third floor, on the other side of that wall which you are facing.
*Countess.* Return to it.
*Miss Carson.* What?
*Countess.* Your flat. Kindly return to it.
*Miss Carson.* I have come to complain. I was kept awake all last night by your guests. They were making a frightful noise. If it occurs again I shall see my solicitor and call the police.
*Countess.* Madam, I have not entertained for fifty years. Observe the dust.
*Miss Carson.* Dust everywhere, and such a lot of furniture. It is most peculiar.
*Countess.* So are you.
*Miss Carson.* What?
*Countess.* Most peculiar. This is a lumber room and I am part of the lumber.
*Miss Carson.* There was a Countess playing the piano and she had locked her brother in the attic. I won't have it. My nerves are not strong.
*Countess.* Madam, if I unwind myself from these shawls and rugs you will see my face, and your nerves will be less strong. Look at my hands, like claws. They have not touched a piano for half a century. Come, take my hand and feel it.
*Miss Carson.* Oh no, I'd rather not. I must go, I must.
*Countess.* Will you come again?
*Miss Carson.* I shall speak to Dr. Fell.
*Countess.* Because, if you come again, I shall see

my lawyer and call the police. Your attire is most peculiar.

*Miss Carson.* I shall speak to Dr. Fell.

*Countess.* Dr. Fell my eye.

*Narrator.* You see, Ethel, the trouble is that your nerves are very bad. You are a most interesting case. I specialise in nerves, and a particular type of nerves. I have diagnosed your case. You are quite my type of case. I have formed a theory.

*Miss Carson.* I shall get to the bottom of this, Dr. Fell.

*Narrator.* I shall help you to get to the bottom of it. My consulting room is upstairs. Follow me. You are an irresistible case, Ethel.

*Miss Carson.* I am aware that I am an interesting case. My friends at the Dream Prognostication Circle and the members of the Astral-Radiation Trance Club all tell me so, Dr. Fell.

*Narrator.* This way, Ethel. I live at the very top of the house.

*Miss Carson.* Oh, this is the attic! I wish to leave the house. Where's the front door?

*Narrator.* I thought you wanted to get to the bottom of things. Sit down and calm yourself. What did you think of my sister?

*Miss Carson.* Most objectionable. Quite unnatural, sitting alone amongst all that lumber. I shall definitely see my lawyer.

*Narrator.* That room was once the drawing room in this house. My sister preferred it to those on the lower floor, it gave so much more light. She used to entertain on a magnificent scale. Those times are past. But my sister broods a great deal. I daresay you observed that she is a little, shall we say, odd, weak in the head?

*Miss Carson.* I did. I was not told of it when I took my flat. I shall complain to my housekeeper. I can't be kept awake at nights by a disorderly neighbour who is wrong in the head. I call this a most unpleasant situation.

*Narrator.* While Miss Carson was talking I could see she was looking round my attic taking in everything like a greedy busybody. I suppose she thought the pictures on the wall very odd. They are very strange. Poor Miss Carson, after her sleepless night and her encounter with my sister, was in a rather jumpy state.
*Miss Carson.* I am in a rather jumpy state. Can't you do something about it, as you're a specialist in nerves?
*Narrator.* That's the very idea, Ethel. I can assist you with your nerves. This brings me to my theory. I specialise, Ethel, in a particular type of mentality which is exactly your type.
*Miss Carson.* Oh, what type is that?
*Narrator.* One which we might call ***haunted.*** Ethel, in common parlance you are being haunted. I specialise in hauntings. You must let me treat you. Place your confidence in me. I have the experience. I am sensitive to the spiritual life around us.
*Miss Carson.* Do you mean that I imagined the noise last night? Because if that's what you mean . . .
*Narrator. Imagined!* Let us not be crude, I don't speak of imagination, but of a rare acuteness of the senses, an extreme sensitivity to the life of the invisible world. Ethel, you are an exciting case.
*Miss Carson.* You are very perceptive, Dr. Fell. What is your theory?
*Narrator.* My theory is this. There, on the third floor, my old sister, the Countess, sits brooding on the past before she lost her fortune and her wits. She relives the past, returning fifty years to the time when she was a young woman, talented and beautiful, with a distinguished reputation. Now, by means of telepathy—
*Miss Carson.* Telepathy!
*Narrator.* —my sister's mind has been conveyed to yours, so that what you heard last night was an emanation, Ethel, from my poor sister. I need not remind you, Ethel, that you are a unique case, in that you are particularly alive

to the invisible forces around us. So am I. However, the fact remains that you have been haunted by the living thoughts of my sister. It is quite simple. I shall give you a course of analytic treatment and you will be haunted no more.

*Miss Carson.* I shall find another flat. I cannot continue to live in the next flat to that woman. I refuse to be haunted.

*Narrator.* You may be equally haunted elsewhere, Ethel.

*Miss Carson.* Don't call me Ethel. It all sounds a lot of rot to me.

*Narrator.* That is no way for a leading member of the Astral-Radiation Trance Club to talk, Ethel. Place your confidence in me. Now, I shall expect you to call on me at eleven tomorrow morning to report any unusual event which may have occurred during the night. I shall make no charge. I don't pretend to be disinterested, I am profoundly drawn towards a case of your kind.

*Miss Carson.* Oh, my nerves will never stand it! I am exhausted already.

*Narrator.* Leave your nerves to me, Ethel. Leave them to me.

*Miss Carson.* I went to bed that night at half-past ten. My nerves were so exhausted, I fell asleep immediately.

(*Piano.*)

About three in the morning I was awakened by a piano playing. It sounded perfectly clear, and I was quite sure that it came from the room of that frightful Countess. I sat up in bed and switched on the light, trying to keep myself as collected as possible.

*Narrator (slightly hoarse).* My sister, where's my sister? Ah, there you are. Why have you stopped playing?

*Countess.* What are you doing out of bed? Where is your attendant—what is he thinking of? Oh, don't glare at me in that terrible way. Keep calm. Follow me. Come upstairs with me.

*Narrator.* Why have you stopped playing? Do I frighten you?

*Countess.* Let me out of this room! Come away from that door and let me go! Where is your attendant?
*Narrator.* My keeper is upstairs in my attic. In my bed. With his throat cut.
*Countess (screams).*
*Narrator.* Stop screaming, my dear, stop screaming. Stop, stop, stop. That's better. Now you've stopped screaming, haven't you? (*Laughing.*)
*Miss Carson.* I took a couple of phenobarbitones at dawn, and slept late into the morning. Then I rose and dressed and went downstairs to speak to the housekeeper.
*Housekeeper.* Did you call me, miss?
*Miss Carson.* I shall have to leave this house.
*Housekeeper.* I should, miss.
*Miss Carson.* I have to complain about a frightful noise.
*Housekeeper.* I did hear you, miss. You give a scream. I suppose it was nightmares, miss.
*Miss Carson.* Don't call me miss, it shatters my nerves. I have to complain about the house next door. It is disorderly. The people are irresponsible. I shall see my lawyer and inform the police.
*Housekeeper.* Number eleven, miss? They are all very quiet and respectable people there. Too quiet. No gramophones, no wirelesses, no babies. It belongs to a private company that won't have anyone in the house except old retired parties.
*Miss Carson.* You are misinformed. It belongs to a Dr. Fell. He has been deliberately causing a disturbance these past two nights. I shall give him in charge.[4]
*Housekeeper.* I shouldn't do anything to provoke anyone, miss.
*Narrator.* My scientific curiosity mounted as Miss Carson came up the front door steps of our house at eleven o'clock that morning.

(*Bell.*)

---

4. *give him in charge,* have him arrested.

She seemed very incensed—didn't you, Ethel?

(*Bell.*)

Why did you ring the bell in that frantic fashion?

(*Door opens.*)

*Miss Carson.* Oh, who opened the door?

*Narrator.* You see, Miss Carson was surprised—weren't you, Ethel?—when the door opened apparently by itself.

*Miss Carson.* Dr. Fell, come downstairs at once! I have had enough of your irresponsible tricks; I wish to speak to you.

*Narrator.* I am downstairs. I am standing beside you. I'm glad to see you have come promptly for your treatment.

*Miss Carson.* I can't see you. Where are you? I hear your voice, Dr. Fell, but I can't see you. It is disgraceful, a nerve specialist upsetting a woman's nerves. You will be sued for heavy damages. You will be struck off the medical register. Come out of hiding and face me!

*Narrator.* Well, I didn't care to face her on that occasion. Why should I? The treatment was free. And, as I explained to Miss Carson, I have nothing to lose. I'm dead. So is my sister. I strangled her, as a matter-of-fact. (Didn't I, Ethel? You heard the screams last night. That was a good fifty years ago.)

Now, won't you come up to my attic, Ethel, and we shall get to the bottom of this. Come to the attic and we shall continue with your nerve treatment. Don't mind my being invisible.

*Miss Carson.* I'm being haunted! I shall see my solicitor! I shall call the police! I am haunted!

*Narrator.* Precisely my diagnosis, you must admit. I specialise in hauntings, I am sensitive to the life of the spirit around us. (*Pause.*)

Miss Carson has left number ten. Just as well, she was getting frightfully on my nerves, she gave me the creeps. Didn't you, Ethel? Didn't you give me the creeps? Didn't you get on my nerves? ◆

# Elizabeth Taylor

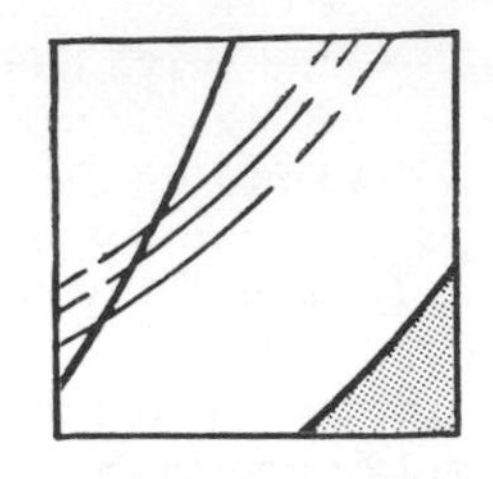

## A SAD GARDEN

THE WALL RUNNING ROUND THE SMALL GARDEN was pitted with hundreds of holes, and rusty nails flying little rags were to be seen in the spaces between the espaliers—the branches like candelabra, the glossy leaves, the long rough brown pears, the thin-skinned yellow ones and the mottled ones which lay against the bricks.

"There is no one to eat the fruit," said Sybil. "Take what you want." She handed her sister-in-law a small ripe William and sauntered away down the garden.

"Well, I certainly will," said Kathy, following eagerly after. "I could do with some for bottling."

"Take them, then. Take them." Sybil sat down on a stone seat at the end of the path. The day was nearly gone, but the brick wall still gave out its warmth. "Mind the wasps, Audrey," she said. "They're getting sleepy." (Audrey! she thought, watching her little niece coming carefully up the path. What a stupid name!)

The garden was filled with the smell of rotting fruit. Pears lay about on the paths, and wasps tunnelled into their ripeness. Audrey stepped timidly over them. She was all white and clean—face, serge coat, and socks. Her mother held the William pear in her gloved hand. "You shall have it when we get home," she promised. "Not in that coat, dear."

Sybil sighed sharply.

---

"A Sad Garden" from HESTER LILLY AND 12 SHORT STORIES by Elizabeth Taylor. Copyright 1947 by Elizabeth Taylor. All rights reserved. Reprinted by permission of The Viking Press, Inc., Elizabeth Taylor and Chatto & Windus.

"Well, if you really mean it, I could slip back home for the big garden basket," Kathy went on. She was doubtful always and nervous with her sister-in-law.

The others had long ago given up calling on Sybil. "She's had trouble," they admitted. "We can grant her that. But she makes no effort."

Kathy was the only one who was too kindhearted to give in. Every week she called. "You see, she's all on her own," she would tell the others. "We've got one another, but she's lost everything—husband and son. I try to think what that would mean to me." (Not that she had a son; but she had Audrey.)

"She was like it before," they reminded her. "Before ever Ralph died. Or Adam. Always queer, always moody and lazy and rude. She thinks she's too clever for us. After all, it's safer to be ordinary."

Kathy would try to explain, excuse, forgive, and they would never listen to her, for it was instinct that guided them, not reason. "She led Ralph the hell of a dance, anyway," they would always conclude.

Kathy glanced at Sybil now, sitting there on the stone seat, leaning back against the wall, with her eyes half-closed and a suggestion about her of power ill-concealed, of sarcasm, of immunity from human contact. Kathy—the others said she was deficient in instinct—saw nothing she could dislike—merely a tired woman who was lonely. There was nothing against her except that she had once been brave when she should have been overcome, and had spoken of her only child with too much indifference—and as for leading Ralph a dance, she had merely laughed at him sometimes and admired him, it seemed, somewhat less than they had always done at home.

"Well, fetch your basket," she was saying.

Kathy hesitated. "Coming, Audrey?"

"Oh, she can stay," said Sybil.

"Well, mind your socks; then they'll be clean for school tomorrow. I'll be back in a minute or two. Be a good girl."

Audrey had no idea of being anything else. She sat down timidly on the edge of the seat and watched her mother disappear round the side of the house.

Sybil looked at her without enthusiasm. "Do you like school?" she asked suddenly, harshly.

"Yes, thank you, Auntie."

Sybil's fingers wandered over the seat as if from habit until the tops of them lay at last in the rough grooves of some carved initials—the letters A. K. R. She had smacked him for that, for always cutting his name into other people's property, had taken away his chisel. When she did that he had stared at her in hatred—wild, beautiful, a stain on his mouth from the blackberries or some purple fruit, and a stain of anger on his cheeks. Her fingers gripped the seat.

"So you like school and never play truant?"

"Oh, no, Auntie"—a little shocked giggle. The child swung her feet, looking down placidly at her clean socks.

Thank God I never had a daughter, thought Sybil. "Would you like some fruit?"

"Mummy said not to in this coat."

"What *would* you like?" Sybil asked in exasperation, thrusting her hair back with a gesture of impatience.

The child looked puzzled.

"A swing? Would you like a swing?"

Audrey's mouth shaped a "No," but, seeing her aunt's look, she changed her mind and smiled and nodded, feigning delight.

She sat down on the swing and put her shiny shoes primly together. Even the seat of the swing was carved with initials. She knew that they were her cousin's and that he was dead, that it had been his swing; she remembered him refusing to allow her to sit on it. She did so now with pleasurable guilt, looking primly round at the clumps of Michaelmas daisies as if she half expected him to come bursting from them in anger. She allowed herself to rock gently to and fro.

Aunt Sybil stopped on her way to the house. "Can't you go higher than that?" she said, and she took the seat in two hands, drew it back to her, and then thrust it far away so that Audrey went high up into the leaves and fruit. Birds rose off the top of the tree in a panic.

"That's how Adam used to go," Sybil shouted as Audrey flew down again. "Right up into the leaves. He used to kick the pears down with his feet."

"I don't—I don't—" cried Audrey.

As she flew down, Sybil put her hands in the small of the child's back and thrust her away again. "Higher, higher," Adam used to shout. He was full of wickedness and devilry. She went on pushing, without thinking of Audrey. The garden was darkening. A question mark of white smoke rose from the quenched bonfire beside the rubbish heap.

"There you go. There you go," she cried. And she thought: But what a boring little girl—"Yes, Mummy. No, thank you, Auntie." I'd never have Adam tied to my apron strings. I'd push him out into the world. Push him. She gave a vehemence to her thought, and Audrey, with her hair streaming among the branches, flew dizzily away. Frantically now her aunt pushed her, crying, "There you go. There you go."

The child, whiter than ever, was unable to speak, to cry out. She sensed something terribly wrong and yet something which was inevitable and not surprising. Each time she dropped to earth a wave of darkness hit her face, and then she would fly up again in a wild agony. A strand of hair caught in some twigs and was torn from her head.

Sybil stood squarely on the grass. As the swing came down she put up her hands and, with the tips of her fingers and yet with all her strength, she pushed. She had lost consciousness and control and cried out each time exultingly, "There you go. There you go"—until all her body was trembling.

Kathy came screaming up the path. ◆

# Mary Walker

# MRS. CONFEDRINGTON

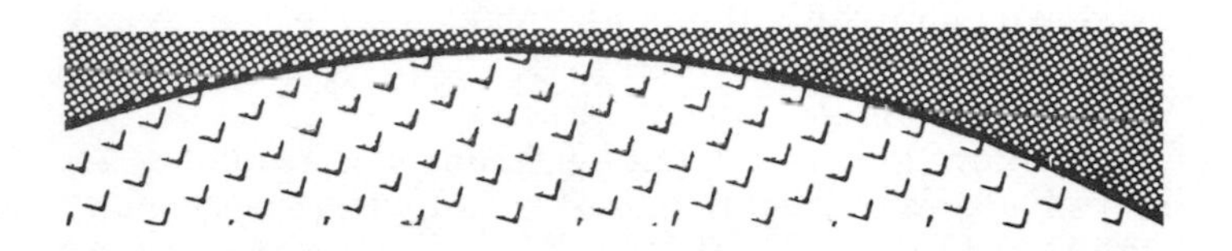

IN THE NARROW STREET behind the church was a café with lace curtains and glass-topped tables where Mrs. Confedrington drank coffee on market days between her shopping.

It was Friday morning and she stood at the counter waiting for the girl to finish her row of knitting and take the fourpence. An impressive row of bottled fruits filled the shelf high on the wall behind the counter. The jars were arranged in careful order, the tallest at the ends and the shortest in the middle, like a platoon drawn up for inspection. Mrs. Confedrington inspected them. The last loop of wool slipped over the points and joined the other stitches, leaving one long green needle bare.

"Yes?" said the girl. She had curly blond hair (The Bleach That Hollywood Prefers) and wide eyes and a soft little mouth for draping round chocolates and popular songs about love.

Mrs. Confedrington caught a refreshing glimpse of her own face in the mirror under the gooseberry jars.

"Ha!" she said. "One coffee, miss." She swept four pennies across the counter with a thin, rather dirty hand, and noted with further refreshment the interesting length of her nicotine-soaked fingers.

---

"Mrs. Confedrington" by Mary Walker from MADEMOISELLE. Reprinted by permission of Ann Elmo Agency, Inc.

The vicar overtook her at the door. "Your umbrella, Mrs. Confedrington."

It was an old, a sensible umbrella, with a yellow handle like a rigid banana. But there was no longer an old, sensible vicar: only this young man with his heavy horn-rimmed glasses and a smell of incense about him. Not that it mattered a toss to Mrs. Confedrington.

"Thank you." She saw his eyes lingering over her and wondered what were his conclusions.

She strode into the street, though it was not her custom to stride, for she thought it the duty of women to be beautiful.

"What a hat!" said the young vicar cautiously, under his breath, as he returned to his coffee, and, pianissimo, "What a face!"

As she turned the corner into the main street a child tugging on her mother's hand paused in mid-blow at her celluloid windmill. "Mummy!" said her awed, clear voice. "Look!"

Mrs. Confedrington passed superbly on to the butcher's.

"'Ere comes 'Elen of Troy,"[1] said the young assistant to Mr. Flaxman. Flaxman grunted, moving his hands, themselves like lumps of frozen meat, among the bloody carvings on the slab.

Protective coloration, Mrs. Confedrington thought, remembering botany lessons of thirty years ago. Not so protective, though. Suppose he should suddenly hack one of them off in mistake for a chop?

If he had sold it to her she would certainly have cooked it and she and Leopold would have eaten it unaware. It was no great matter what dish appeared at that table where Leopold sat hunched over the composition of his daily crossword puzzle with a dictionary of quotations at his elbow and his spectacles pushed up on his forehead, while

---

1. *'Elen of Troy,* a working-class pronunciation of Helen of Troy, the beautiful woman who was the cause of the war between the Greeks and the Trojans described by the poet Homer in the *Iliad.*

his wife, lost to the world, tipped her chair forward and peered at the *Collected Poems of T. S. Eliot* propped on the vinegar-and-mustard half of an old-fashioned cruet.

Four glass cherries and a lone marguerite flourished on her black straw hat.

"'Ighly unsuitable," said Mr. Flaxman, shaking his head between two hanging strings of sausage, as he watched her approach. No need to make people look when she had a nose that size to start with and a mouth going all ways at once and eyes like a fish that has been dead a long time.

"Well, mum, what will it be?"

She knew what he was thinking and it still amused her, after all the years he had been thinking it. Poor Flaxman! Year in, year out at his grisly trade, what would he know of beauty?

Her turn for liver. He wrapped it roughly and finished the parcel with an outer sheet of newspaper.

She remembered Leopold, peevish at the breakfast table. "I do like a paper with some guts in it," he'd said. She gave a shout of laughter, and the cherries battered on the daisy petals.

"Is she cracked as well, Mr. Flaxman?" asked the assistant in a hushed voice when she had left the shop.

"Absolutely dotty, 'Erbert."

"I wouldn't like to be 'er old man," said Herbert, sniggering.

Mr. Flaxman took up a long knife and wiped the blade across his white apron.

"Don't matter to 'im. 'E's as cracked as she is."

Swinging her basket, Mrs. Confedrington passed serenely down High Street. Serenely conscious she was of the impact of her surrealist[2] beauty that withered the passersby.

---

2. *surrealist,* typical of the art of the Surrealist movement, which attempted to portray the fantasies of the subconscious mind; thus, unusual, exotic, dreamlike, bizarre.

They're not ready for me, she told herself. Any more than they were ready for the great artists—the nearsighted, conventional minds. She likened herself to a picture by Picasso,[3] a masterpiece that had beauty only for the initiated few. And then, of course, she began to think of Leopold.

At that moment Leopold was on his way to the spare room to look at his silkworms. He had finished his puzzle early and was prowling about the house disconsolately in his black velvet smoking jacket, waiting for Mrs. Confedrington to come home.

The silkworms were in a large shoe box with a pattern of holes pierced in the lid. "Black Gents Shoes, Size 9," the label said. He chuckled as he raised the lid. "Odd. I don't know any black gents." He let a little extra light into the box and peered under the raised lid at the soft yellow cocoons inside. "Nearly had your sleep out now," he told them. "You'll be glad to wake up—'catching your heart up at the feel of June,'" he added. Leopold's solvers were literary types who thrived on quotation and allusion, so that he could hardly open his mouth any more without someone else's words coming out of it. "They'll have caught their hearts up long before June, anyway," he muttered irritably, and closed the lid and wandered into the front bedroom. He stared out of the window, wishing for her to come.

Suddenly she was there, inside the gate, under the monkey-puzzle tree. He waved and she brandished her basket at him.

"'She walks in beauty, like the night,'"[4] he whispered as he ran downstairs to meet her. "I missed you," he said.

"That was nice of you. Let's sit down for a minute."

They sat side by side on the stairs and stretched their legs out comfortably.

---

3. *Picasso.* Pablo Picasso (1881-     ), a Spanish painter and sculptor, was one of the originators of Cubism, a school of art in which the forms of objects were broken into angular solids and rearranged. 4. *"She walks in beauty, like the night,"* the title and first line of a poem by Lord Byron (1788–1824).

She pointed to the parcel of liver. "A paper with some guts in it," she said, and he laughed delightfully.

"Do you know my silkworms are in a box that says, 'Black gents shoes'? And the joke of it is I don't know a single Negro."

She gave her habitual shout of appreciation. "Leopold," she said a moment later, "there is no one else like us in the world; we are the same one. I walk in your sleep and you talk in my dreams. Leopold, do you think we have invented each other?"

"If we have, you are most talented—and I am a genius."

"I can't remember any life before you."

"'I wonder, by my troth, what thou and I did till we loved?' "[5] Leopold mused, trying to think far back, then he looked up at her quickly. "That's a fine hat. A completely esoteric hat. Other women never wear hats like that."

"No," she said, "no." And she took off the hat and held it on her lap, cuddling the glass fruit with her interesting fingers.

Leopold sprang up briskly. "Beans on toast and coffee for lunch. I'll make it."

When he had gone she rose slowly and went up the stairs, smiling, queening it, a collector's piece. The collector, meanwhile, hacked away in the kitchen, opening a tin of beans.

Mrs. Confedrington took the esoteric hat into her bedroom and laid it carefully on the bed. She went to the mirror and began to comb her hair. Out of the tail of her eye she saw the window cleaner outside on his ladder, polishing the panes with a wash leather. It was best to ignore him. She went on calmly with her combing.

With the single exception of Leopold, Mrs. Confedrington had always avoided the chance encounter. There was, alas,

---

5. *"I wonder, by my troth, what thou and I did till we loved?,"* the first line of "The Good Morrow" by John Donne (1573–1631).

so little appreciation in the world. But sometimes she misjudged. As in the case of Sammy Cohen out there on the ladder, for instance.

Sammy gave up all pretense of polishing when he saw her and leaned one elbow on the top rung and gazed in, watching the vigorous movement of the comb through her thick hair.

Lunch with Leopold, Mrs. Confedrington was saying to herself. He was burning the toast, she realized, but what did it matter? What mattered was the oneness, the aloneness, the savoring of beauty that was only for the two of them.

But Leopold, stirring the coffee, had a sudden glimpse of catastrophe and rushed to the bottom of the stairs. Supposing their alone-togetherness should end, supposing people should begin to know better and popular taste should crowd him out? "Rachel! Rachel!" he cried.

She smiled a little at the panic in his voice. What should he fear? None but he would ever have an eye for her secrets.

And yet the encroaching waves were already lapping around their walls. Sammy Cohen, outside on the ladder, was nobody's fool. He went to W.E.A. classes and could read novels in Esperanto.[6]

As Mrs. Confedrington ran out of the room and down the stairs to the unique Leopold, "Ah!" said Sammy Cohen. "What a beautiful woman!" ◆

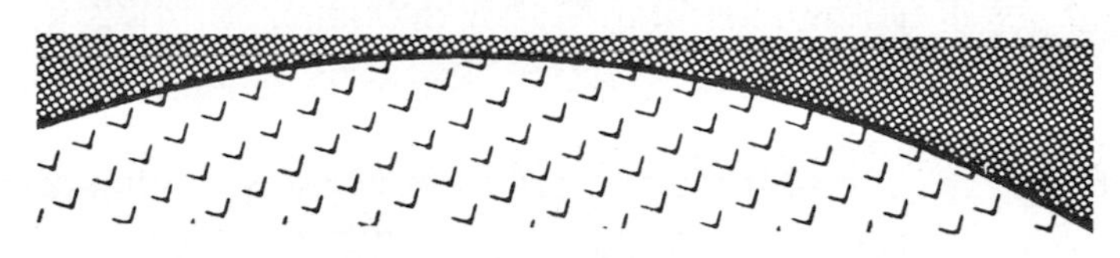

---

6. *W.E.A. classes . . . Esperanto.* The Workers' Educational Association was founded in 1903 as an institution for adult education. Esperanto is an artificial language introduced in 1887 by Ludovic Zamenhof in an attempt to create an international language.

# Sylvia Townsend Warner

## THE INSIDE-OUT

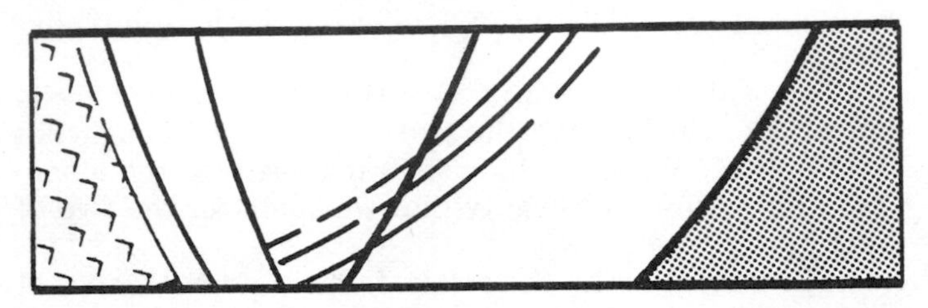

It was a lightless afternoon in February, not cold but with a stale cold in the air. The removal van stood outside Ullapool.[1] Furniture was being unloaded and carried in. It was furniture the two children had known all their lives, but it looked quite different out-of-doors: gaunt, and sorry for itself. It was abashing to find that the backs of familiar wardrobes and chests of drawers were just unpainted deal. Ullapool was built of greyish brick; it was a semidetached house and the other half of it was called Sorrento. Each half had a small garage attached to it. Other greyish brick houses of the same height extended on either side. All but one had garages. That one had a gravel path and a side gate of wood trellis, and behind the gate was a holly.

A strong smell of straw, sweat, and burlap came from the van. It was an interesting smell, and Clive and Stella snuffed it as they stood on the pavement, keeping out of the way. Inside the house Mother was running to and fro, telling the removal men where to put things; Father fol-

---

"The Inside-Out" by Sylvia Townsend Warner from THE NEW YORKER, (April 5, 1972). Reprinted by permission; © 1972 The New Yorker Magazine, Inc.

1. *Ullapool,* houses are often given names in England. In this instance the name is that of a town in northwestern Scotland.

lowed her silently, as if he might be found useful; from time to time he made a suggestion and Mother's voice became patient as she explained why it wouldn't do. So they had taken themselves off to the pavement, and watched the furniture being carried into Ullapool—more and more of it; and, after the furniture, crates, some nailed down, others without lids, holding things like frying pans and baking dishes swaddled in crumpled newspaper. And their feet began to grow cold, and the smell from the van made them thirsty, and they thought poorly of Ullapool, though when they arrived and ran about its emptiness they had rather liked it.

"I think it's a beastly house," said Stella—so loudly and clearly that one of the removal men said she would feel quite different when they were properly in and the beds made up, Missie. He was a local man and felt a concern for these strangers coming into the house where the mad old lady had ended her solitary days. He went on with a crate which was so heavy it made him grunt, and was halfway upstairs with it when Mother called out, "Kitchen, man, kitchen!"

It was then she noticed them standing on the pavement, and said something to Father, who came out and said, "Why don't you explore the garden? It's got a summerhouse. The back door's open."

In the garden it seemed much nearer nightfall. It was choked with weeds and grasses of last summer, full of straggling thickets of privet and laurel, overhung by conifers. Everything was matted, entangled, overgrown, and intensely still. Some plumes of pampas grass wagged slowly in the light breeze. They seemed to be the only living thing there. As though it were part of its territory, the garden enclosed a different texture of sound: the thump of distant machinery, soft snortings of ejected steam, the clank of a freight train, whistles, the drifting cry of hooters from river tugs—noises which had been screened from the children by passing traffic when they were in the street.

When they turned back and looked at the house, it already seemed quite a long way off. A light went on in an upper window.

"I don't think it's such a particularly beastly house," said Clive.

"It's pretty beastly."

He went ahead, partly because he was the elder and in double figures,[2] partly because he was enjoying himself. It was the first time they had been in a garden other than the public garden at Worple. When Mother said, "Now that your father has been moved to the bank at Burheaton, we'll have a house with a garden," they had imagined a bowling green, swings, a Jubilee Clock, lawns, and a motor mower, just as when they were babies, at the mention of their father's bank, they imagined him rolling down it.

The garden seemed endless; endless and directionless, because at every tenth step he had to turn aside to skirt a bush, to avoid a bramble patch. Stooping under a branch, he almost fell into the bathtub. Its white paint had mostly scaled off; what remained had a fish-belly shine. It had sifted up and was half full of a soup of dead leaves. They stirred the soup with their fingers, and tried vainly to turn the rusty taps.

"Hush, Clive! I believe I heard something. Don't breathe so hard. I believe it's hens."

"Wild hens, like in India," he said.

"Oh, goody goody!"

But hearing the noise again and listening more attentively, it seemed to him that the hens were in Sorrento.

Dense laurel hedges secluded them from the gardens on either side. A slimy network of bindweed hung on the Sorrento hedge like lace curtains, and strands of barbed wire ran inside it. Spiked iron railings backed the other hedge. Considering his reaction to this, Clive summed it up as an inside-out feeling. You couldn't get out; nobody could

---

2. *in double figures*, over ten.

get in; and you wore the feeling not quite sure whether you liked it or didn't like it. Inside-out. It depended which way you put it on. He turned to consult Stella—she was sometimes quite intelligent—and she wasn't there. The inside-out feeling tightened on him. But she was close by, hidden behind a bush. With an entranced countenance she was pulling strands of ivy off the trunk of a yew tree. "Come and pull, Clivey! It's a wonderful feeling." He pulled for a little, and it was a wonderful feeling; but the smell of ivy was oppressive.

"All those little feet holding on. . . . There!" Another length of ivy fell on the ground.

"Oh, come on, Stella! We'll never get it all off, and it's everywhere. Come on and explore for something else."

Glancing back at the yew, she saw that the bark they had stripped was a dull red, like a graze.

"I hope we haven't hurt it. Miss Harper, who took us in Botany last term, said ivy kills trees."

Clive agreed that it had rather a killing smell.

The endless garden ended in a brick wall, too high to be seen over. Beyond it, puffs of white smoke rose into the untrammelled sky, keeping time with the soft snortings.

"But we haven't found the summerhouse," said Stella. "We must find the summerhouse."

"It's there. At least, it *was* there."

An iron frame projected from the wall. A cloak of sedge lay below. When they tried to pick it up, it fell to pieces in their hands.

They did not dwell on the disappointment; by now they were wholly in love with their garden. "We haven't seen half of it yet," said Stella. "I'm sure I saw some flowerpots near the bathtub. We could plant roses in them and make a bower round it. And grow water lilies in the bathtub like the water garden at Worple."

"I know something else, too," said Clive. "There was a scraggy place in the hedge, just after the bath. We could have a squint at Sorrento through it."

Lights had gone on in most of the houses, and curtains been drawn. "Everyone's having tea," mused Stella. "I wonder if the Burheaton baker has barley scones, like at home."

Clive said firmly he didn't suppose so. For the bathtub glimmered before them, and the scraggy place in the hedge was at hand.

"Don't tear your clothes, for goodness' sake. Remember, it's your good suit."

He squirmed into the laurels. The barbed wire had been pulled aside. He got his head and shoulders through.

"Stap my vitals!" The school had done *Scenes from Sheridan*[3] last term, and this phrase had caught his fancy.

"Stap my vitals! They must *live* on them. Stella, come and look."

The whole of Sorrento's garden could be seen at a glance. At the near corner was a wire-netting enclosure, very neat, with some saddened hens in it. At the farther corner was a glittering glass house. The garden hadn't a weed in it, hadn't a tree in it, hadn't an inequality. And across it ran rows and rows of Brussels sprouts, exactly aligned, all of the same height, orderly as a regiment on the parade ground.

"I call it perfectly revolting," said Stella, and broke into laughter.

They squirmed back, and stood upright in their own garden, and its comfortable dusk closed round them. But now there was a compacter darkness overhead. Looking up, they saw a boy lying along the bough of a tree which rose out of the hedge. He looked as reposefully dangerous as a panther, and as watchful. He was some years older than they. His expression had a maturity of balefulness.

"Hullo," said Clive.

The boy said nothing.

---

3. *Scenes from Sheridan.* Richard Brinsley Sheridan (1751–1816), an English dramatist, was famous for his comedies of manners.

"Hullo," said Clive again, and Stella said, "Good evening." Still the boy said nothing.

Ostentatiously addressing his sister, Clive remarked, "Spying."

"Trespassing," she replied; and because she was the more frightened of the two, she added scathingly, "Sorrento!"

The boy gathered himself together as if he were going to leap on them. It was his voice which leaped. "I loathe you!"

They walked away, careful not to hurry, trying not to stumble over the brambles. A voice from Ullapool cried "Tea" on a falling third. They ran. A door closed.

The boy stared down into the lost paradise, the succoring shelter from which he was driven out. The bough began to quiver with the vehemence of his dry sobbing. Tomorrow he would buy a slingshot. ◆

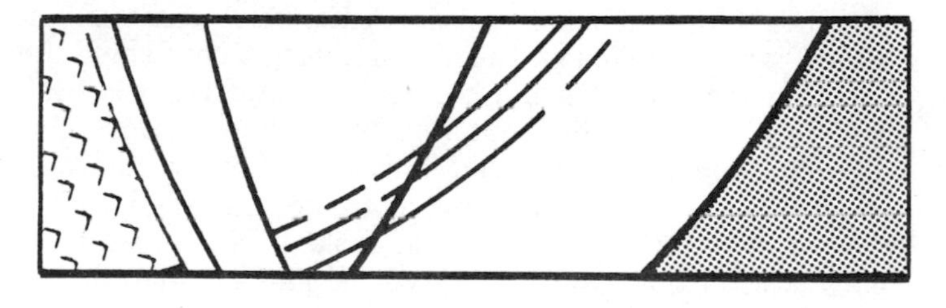

# Virginia Woolf

## THE NEW DRESS

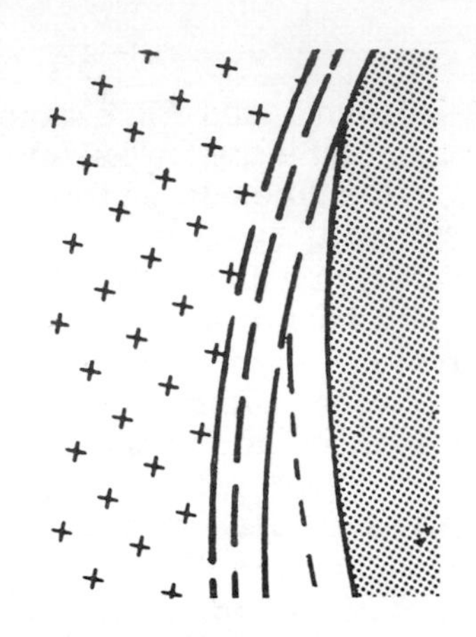

MABEL HAD HER FIRST SERIOUS SUSPICION that something was wrong as she took her cloak off and Mrs. Barnet, while handing her the mirror and touching the brushes and thus drawing her attention, perhaps rather markedly, to all the appliances for tidying and improving hair, complexion, clothes, which existed on the dressing table, confirmed the suspicion—that it was not right, not quite right, which growing stronger as she went upstairs and springing at her, with conviction as she greeted Clarissa Dalloway, she went straight to the far end of the room, to a shaded corner where a looking glass hung and looked. No! It was not *right*. And at once the misery which she always tried to hide, the profound dissatisfaction—the sense she had had, ever since she was a child, of being inferior to other people—set upon her, relentlessly, remorselessly, with an intensity which she could not beat off, as she would when she woke at night at home, by reading Borrow or Scott[1]; for oh these men, oh these women, all were thinking—"What's

---

From A HAUNTED HOUSE AND OTHER STORIES by Virginia Woolf, copyright, 1944, renewed, 1972, by Harcourt Brace Jovanovich, Inc. Reprinted by permission of Harcourt Brace Jovanovich, Inc., The Hogarth Press, and the Author's Literary Estate.

1. *Borrow . . . Scott.* George Borrow (1803–1881) was an English writer and traveler. Sir Walter Scott (1771–1832) was an English novelist and poet.

Mabel wearing? What a fright she looks! What a hideous new dress!"—their eyelids flickering as they came up and then their lids shutting rather tight. It was her own appalling inadequacy; her cowardice; her mean, water-sprinkled blood that depressed her. And at once the whole of the room where, for ever so many hours, she had planned with the little dressmaker how it was to go, seemed sordid, repulsive; and her own drawing room so shabby, and herself, going out, puffed up with vanity as she touched the letters on the hall table and said: "How dull!" to show off—all this now seemed unutterably silly, paltry, and provincial. All this had been absolutely destroyed, shown up, exploded, the moment she came into Mrs. Dalloway's drawing room.

What she had thought that evening when, sitting over the teacups, Mrs. Dalloway's invitation came, was that, of course, she could not be fashionable. It was absurd to pretend it even—fashion meant cut, meant style, meant thirty guineas at least—but why not be original? Why not be herself, anyhow? And, getting up, she had taken that old fashion book of her mother's, a Paris fashion book of the time of the Empire,[2] and had thought how much prettier, more dignified, and more womanly they were then, and so set herself—oh, it was foolish—trying to be like them, pluming herself in fact, upon being modest and old-fashioned and very charming, giving herself up, no doubt about it, to an orgy of self-love, which deserved to be chastised, and so rigged herself out like this.

But she dared not look in the glass. She could not face the whole horror—the pale yellow, idiotically old-fashioned silk dress with its long skirt and its high sleeves and its waist and all the things that looked so charming in the fashion book, but not on her, not among all these ordinary people. She felt like a dressmaker's dummy standing there, for young people to stick pins into.

"But, my dear, it's perfectly charming!" Rose Shaw said,

---

2. *the time of the Empire,* the period of Napoleon I (1804–1815).

looking her up and down with that little satirical pucker of the lips which she expected—Rose herself being dressed in the height of the fashion, precisely like everybody else, always.

"We are all like flies trying to crawl over the edge of the saucer," Mabel thought, and repeated the phrase as if she were crossing herself, as if she were trying to find some spell to annul this pain, to make this agony endurable. Tags of Shakespeare, lines from books she had read ages ago, suddenly came to her when she was in agony, and she repeated them over and over again. "Flies trying to crawl," she repeated. If she could say that over often enough and make herself see the flies, she would become numb, chill, frozen, dumb. Now she could see flies crawling slowly out of a saucer of milk with their wings stuck together; and she strained and strained (standing in front of the looking glass, listening to Rose Shaw) to make herself see Rose Shaw and all the other people there as flies, trying to hoist themselves out of something, or into something, meagre, insignificant, toiling flies. But she could not see them like that, not other people. She saw herself like that—she was a fly, but the others were dragonflies, butterflies, beautiful insects, dancing, fluttering, skimming, while she alone dragged herself up out of the saucer. (Envy and spite, the most detestable of the vices, were her chief faults.)

"I feel like some dowdy, decrepit, horribly dingy old fly," she said, making Robert Haydon stop just to hear her say that, just to reassure herself by furbishing up a poor weak-kneed phrase and so showing how detached she was, how witty, that she did not feel in the least out of anything. And, of course, Robert Haydon answered something quite polite, quite insincere, which she saw through instantly, and said to herself, directly he went (again from some book), "Lies, lies, lies!" For a party makes things either much more real, or much less real, she thought; she saw in a flash to the bottom of Robert Haydon's heart; she saw through everything. She saw the truth. *This* was true, this drawing room, this self, and the other false. Miss Milan's little workroom was really terribly hot, stuffy, sordid. It smelt of clothes and cabbage cooking; and yet, when Miss Milan put the glass in her hand, and she looked at herself with the dress on, finished, an extraordinary bliss shot through her heart. Suffused with light, she sprang into existence. Rid of cares and wrinkles, what she had dreamed of herself was there—a beautiful woman. Just for a second (she had not dared look longer, Miss Milan wanted to know about the length of the skirt), there looked at her, framed in the scrolloping mahogany, a grey-white, mysteriously smiling, charming girl, the core of herself, the soul of herself; and it was not vanity only, not only self-love that made her think it good, tender, and true. Miss Milan said that the skirt could not well be longer; if anything the skirt, said Miss Milan, puckering her forehead, considering with all her wits about her, must be shorter; and she felt, suddenly, honestly, full of love for Miss Milan, much, much fonder of Miss Milan than of anyone in the whole world, and could have cried for pity that she should be crawling on the floor with her mouth full of pins, and her face red and her eyes bulging—that one human being should be doing this for another, and she saw them all as human beings merely, and herself going off to her party, and Miss Milan pulling the cover over the canary's cage, or letting him pick a hempseed from between her lips, and the thought of it, of this side of human nature and its patience and its endurance and its being content with such miserable, scanty, sordid, little pleasures filled her eyes with tears.

And now the whole thing had vanished. The dress, the room, the love, the pity, the scrolloping looking glass, and the canary's cage—all had vanished, and here she was in a corner of Mrs. Dalloway's drawing room, suffering tortures, woken wide awake to reality.

But it was all so paltry, weak-blooded, and petty-minded to care so much at her age with two children, to be still so utterly dependent on people's opinions and not have principles or convictions, not to be able to say as other people did, "There's Shakespeare! There's death! We're all weevils in a captain's biscuit"—or whatever it was that people did say.

She faced herself straight in the glass; she pecked at her left shoulder; she issued out into the room, as if spears were thrown at her yellow dress from all sides. But instead of looking fierce or tragic, as Rose Shaw would have done—Rose would have looked like Boadicea[3]—she looked foolish and self-conscious, and simpered like a schoolgirl and slouched across the room, positively slinking, as if she were a beaten mongrel, and looked at a picture, an engraving. As if one went to a party to look at a picture! Everybody knew why she did it—it was from shame, from humiliation.

"Now the fly's in the saucer," she said to herself, "right in the middle, and can't get out, and the milk," she thought, rigidly staring at the picture, "is sticking its wings together."

"It's so old-fashioned," she said to Charles Burt, making him stop (which by itself he hated) on his way to talk to someone else.

She meant, or she tried to make herself think that she meant, that it was the picture and not her dress, that was old-fashioned. And one word of praise, one word of affection from Charles would have made all the difference to her at the moment. If he had only said, "Mabel, you're looking charming tonight!" it would have changed her life. But then she ought to have been truthful and direct. Charles said nothing of the kind, of course. He was malice itself. He always saw through one, especially if one were feeling particularly mean, paltry, or feeble-minded.

"Mabel's got a new dress!" he said, and the poor fly was absolutely shoved into the middle of the saucer. Really, he

---

3. *Boadicea* (d. 62 A.D.), a British queen who led an unsuccessful revolt against Roman rule. Following defeat by a Roman army, she committed suicide.

would like her to drown, she believed. He had no heart, no fundamental kindness, only a veneer of friendliness. Miss Milan was much more real, much kinder. If only one could feel that and stick to it, always. "Why," she asked herself —replying to Charles much too pertly, letting him see that she was out of temper, or "ruffled" as he called it ("Rather ruffled?" he said and went on to laugh at her with some woman over there)—"Why," she asked herself, "can't I feel one thing always, feel quite sure that Miss Milan is right, and Charles wrong and stick to it, feel sure about the canary and pity and love and not be whipped all round in a second by coming into a room full of people?" It was her odious, weak, vacillating character again, always giving at the critical moment and not being seriously interested in conchology, etymology, botany, archeology, cutting up potatoes and watching them fructify like Mary Dennis, like Violet Searle.

Then Mrs. Holman, seeing her standing there, bore down upon her. Of course a thing like a dress was beneath Mrs. Holman's notice, with her family always tumbling downstairs or having the scarlet fever. Could Mabel tell her if Elmthorpe was ever let for August and September? Oh, it was a conversation that bored her unutterably!—it made her furious to be treated like a house agent or a messenger boy, to be made use of. Not to have value, that was it, she thought, trying to grasp something hard, something real, while she tried to answer sensibly about the bathroom and the south aspect and the hot water to the top of the house; and all the time she could see little bits of her yellow dress in the round looking glass which made them all the size of boot buttons or tadpoles; and it was amazing to think how much humiliation and agony and self-loathing and effort and passionate ups and downs of feeling were contained in a thing the size of a threepenny bit. And what was still odder, this thing, this Mabel Waring, was separate, quite disconnected; and though Mrs. Holman (the black button) was leaning forward and telling her how her eldest boy had strained his heart running, she could see her, too, quite detached in the looking glass, and it was impossible that the black dot, leaning forward, gesticulating, should make the yellow dot, sitting solitary, self-centred, feel what the black dot was feeling, yet they pretended.

"So impossible to keep boys quiet"—that was the kind of thing one said.

And Mrs. Holman, who could never get enough sympathy and snatched what little there was greedily, as if it were her right (but she deserved much more for there was her little girl who had come down this morning with a swollen knee joint), took this miserable offering and looked at it suspiciously, grudgingly, as if it were a halfpenny when it ought to have been a pound and put it away in her purse, must put up with it, mean and miserly though it was, times being hard, so very hard; and on she went, creaking, injured Mrs. Holman, about the girl with the swollen joints. Ah, it was tragic, this greed, this clamour of human beings, like a row of cormorants, barking and flapping their wings for sympathy—it was tragic, could one have felt it and not merely pretended to feel it!

But in her yellow dress tonight she could not wring out one drop more; she wanted it all, all for herself. She knew (she kept on looking into the glass, dipping into that dreadfully showing-up blue pool) that she was condemned, despised, left like this in a backwater, because of her being like this a feeble, vacillating creature; and it seemed to her that the yellow dress was a penance which she had deserved, and if she had been dressed like Rose Shaw, in lovely, clinging green with a ruffle of swansdown, she would have deserved that; and she thought that there was no escape for her—none whatever. But it was not her fault altogether, after all. It was being one of a family of ten; never having money enough, always skimping and paring; and her mother carrying great cans, and the linoleum worn on the stair edges, and one sordid little domestic tragedy after another—nothing catastrophic, the sheep farm failing, but not utterly; her eldest brother marrying beneath him but not very much—there was no romance, nothing extreme about them all. They petered out respectably in seaside resorts; every watering place had one of her aunts even now asleep in some lodging with the front windows not quite facing the sea. That was so like them—they had to squint at things always. And she had done the same—she was just like her aunts. For all her dreams of living in India, married to some hero like Sir Henry Lawrence,[4] some empire builder (still the sight of a native in a turban filled her with romance), she had failed utterly. She had married Hubert, with his safe, permanent underling's job in the Law Courts, and they managed tolerably in a smallish house, without proper maids, and hash when she was alone or just bread and butter, but now and then—Mrs. Holman was off, thinking her the most dried-up, unsympathetic twig she had ever met, absurdly dressed, too, and would tell everyone about Mabel's fantastic appearance—now and then, thought Mabel Waring, left alone on the blue sofa, punching the cushion in order to look occupied, for she would not join Charles Burt and Rose Shaw, chattering like magpies and perhaps laughing at her by the fireplace—now and then, there did come to her delicious moments, reading the other night in bed, for instance, or down by the sea on the sand in the sun, at Easter—let her recall it—a great tuft of pale sand grass standing all twisted like a shock of spears against the sky, which was blue like a smooth china egg, so firm, so hard, and then the melody of the waves—"Hush, hush," they said, and the children's shouts paddling—yes, it was a divine moment, and there she lay, she felt, in the hand of the Goddess who was the world; rather a hard-hearted, but very beautiful Goddess, a little lamb laid on the altar (one did think these silly things, and it didn't matter so long as

---

4. *Sir Henry Lawrence* (1806–1857), a British general and colonial administrator in India. Lawrence died heroically during the Sepoy Rebellion.

one never said them). And also with Hubert sometimes she had quite unexpectedly—carving the mutton for Sunday lunch, for no reason, opening a letter, coming into a room—divine moments, when she said to herself (for she would never say this to anybody else), "This is it. This has happened. This is it!" And the other way about it was equally surprising—that is, when everything was arranged—music, weather, holidays, every reason for happiness was there—then nothing happened at all. One wasn't happy. It was flat, just flat, that was all.

Her wretched self again, no doubt! She had always been a fretful, weak, unsatisfactory mother, a wobbly wife, lolling about in a kind of twilight existence with nothing very clear or very bold, or more one thing than another, like all her brothers and sisters, except perhaps Herbert—they were all the same poor water-veined creatures who did nothing. Then in the midst of this creeping, crawling life, suddenly she was on the crest of a wave. That wretched fly—where had she read the story that kept coming into her mind about the fly and the saucer?—struggled out. Yes, she had those moments. But now that she was forty, they might come more and more seldom. By degrees she would cease to struggle any more. But that was deplorable! That was not to be endured! That made her feel ashamed of herself!

She would go to the London Library tomorrow. She would find some wonderful, helpful, astonishing book, quite by chance, a book by a clergyman, by an American no one had ever heard of; or she would walk down the Strand and drop, accidentally, into a hall where a miner was telling about the life in the pit, and suddenly she would become a new person. She would be absolutely transformed. She would wear a uniform; she would be called Sister Somebody[5]; she would never give a thought to clothes again. And forever after she would be perfectly clear about Charles Burt and

---

5. *Sister Somebody.* English nurses are given the title *sister.*

Miss Milan and this room and that room; and it would be always, day after day, as if she were lying in the sun or carving the mutton. It would be it!

So she got up from the blue sofa, and the yellow button in the looking glass got up too, and she waved her hand to Charles and Rose to show them she did not depend on them one scrap, and the yellow button moved out of the looking glass, and all the spears were gathered into her breast as she walked towards Mrs. Dalloway and said, "Good night."

"But it's too early to go," said Mrs. Dalloway, who was always so charming.

"I'm afraid I must," said Mabel Waring. "But," she added in her weak, wobbly voice which only sounded ridiculous when she tried to strengthen it, "I have enjoyed myself enormously."

"I have enjoyed myself," she said to Mr. Dalloway, whom she met on the stairs.

"Lies, lies, lies!" she said to herself, going downstairs, and "Right in the saucer!" she said to herself as she thanked Mrs. Barnet for helping her and wrapped herself, round and round and round, in the Chinese cloak she had worn these twenty years. ◆

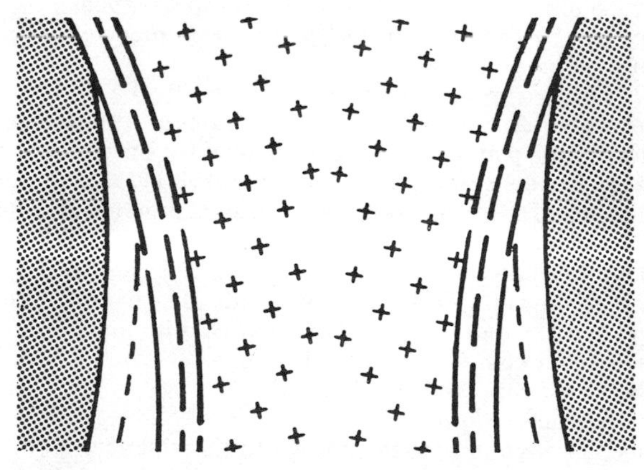

# ENGLISH MONEY

The monetary unit of the United Kingdom is the *pound sterling.* The exchange rate of the pound fluctuated at slightly under five dollars between 1900 and the Second World War. During the war the rate was set at $4.03. Since then the pound has been devalued twice, to $2.80 in 1949, and to $2.40 in 1967. Until February 15, 1971, when a decimalized system went into effect, the pound was worth twenty *shillings,* each worth twelve *pence.* The following is a list of the principal types of English currency and a few of the more common slang equivalents.

**bob**, a shilling. [*Slang*]
**crown**, a silver coin worth five shillings.
**fourpence**, a silver coin worth four pence, issued for special occasions, such as Lenten almsgiving. It is sometimes called a *groat.*
**florin**, a silver coin worth two shillings.
**guinea**, originally a gold coin worth twenty shillings, called a *guinea* because the first coins were supposedly struck from gold mined in Guinea. Fluctuation in the value of the silver shilling resulted in the revaluation of the guinea at twenty-one shillings, where it remained. The coin was discontinued in 1813, but the amount is still used to express professionals' fees, the prices of certain objects, etc.
**half crown**, a silver coin worth two shillings and sixpence.
**halfpenny**, *pl. halfpennies* or *halfpence,* a bronze coin worth one-half of a penny.
**penny**, *pl. pence,* a bronze coin worth one-twelfth of a shilling. Penny is abbreviated *d.,* from the initial of *denarius,* a Roman coin.
**pound sterling** or **pound**, the English monetary unit, worth twenty shillings of twelve pence each. Pound is abbreviated £., from the initial of *libra,* a Roman weight. It is issued in notes of denominations of one pound, five pounds, ten pounds, etc.
**quid**, a pound. [*Slang*]
**shilling**, a silver coin worth one-twentieth of a pound. Shilling is abbreviated *s.,* from the initial of *solidus,* a Roman coin.
**sixpence**, a silver coin worth six pence.
**sovereign**, a gold coin worth one pound.
**tanner**, a sixpence. [*Slang*]
**threepence**, an angular bronze coin worth three pence.
**twopence**, a silver coin worth two pence, issued for special occasions.

# DISCUSSION QUESTIONS

## Kingsley Amis:
### INTERESTING THINGS *(page 8)*

1. Gloria Davies and Mr. Huws-Evans see two movies together. What is the reaction of each to the first movie? to the second? What do you learn about Gloria and Mr. Huws-Evans from their reactions to the movies?
2. How does the incident of the crisps characterize Mr. Huws-Evans? What relationship does Gloria see between the string bag with crisps, the mackintosh hat, and the leather purse?
3. Gloria is wearing the "new liquid make-up everyone was talking about." At the restaurant she "remembered about poise" and "arranged herself at the table like one of the models who showed off jewellery on TV." How do these and other touches characterize Gloria?
4. Why doesn't Gloria let Mr. Huws-Evans kiss her?
5. Early in the story Gloria realizes "a girl would show herself up for a lump with no conversation and bad manners if she gave away to an older man the fact that uninteresting things didn't interest her" (page 11, paragraph 3). Discuss the truth of this statement.
6. At the party, Mr. Huws-Evans' brother takes Gloria aside and starts talking about "interesting things." What do you predict will be the nature of their relationship? Why is the story entitled "Interesting Things"?

## Elizabeth Bowen:
### THE CAT JUMPS *(page 20)*

1. Early in the story, the Harold Wrights are described: "They had light, bright, shadowless, thoroughly disinfected minds." How is this description borne out by the Wrights' behavior at the

beginning of the story? How have they changed from this description by the end of the story?

2. Muriel Barker, one of the weekend guests, "was not, as Jocelyn [Wright] realised later, the sort of girl to have asked at all." Why shouldn't she have been invited? How does she contribute to the developing sense of terror in the house?

3. Remember that the families who successively inhabit Rose Hill are the Harold Bentleys and the Harold Wrights; remember also that the "pearly bathroom" was the site of the murder. How do these two facts affect Harold Wright as he waits in the bathroom late in the weekend? Why does he feel that his wife "lay like a great cat, always, over the mouth of his life" (page 31, paragraph 1)? As Harold steps into the bedroom we read, "Harold was appalled. Jocelyn had fainted." Describe what has happened —what is fantasy or semifantasy and what is reality? Explain the title of the story.

4. Elizabeth Bowen could have given the full story of the Bentley murders at the very opening of the story. How do we learn about the murders? What is the effect of relating the murder story in this piecemeal fashion? How would the effect be changed by giving the full story at the beginning?

## Morley Callaghan:
### IT MUST BE DIFFERENT *(page 32)*

1. The behavior of Sylvia's parents angers Sylvia and Max. Discuss the nature of the behavior: is it calculated, innocent, hostile, normal, or abnormal?

2. Sylvia tells Max about her parents: "I don't think either one of them want to see me get married. Nothing ever happened the right way for them. I can remember ever since I was a kid." From the details revealed in the story, describe the kind of life Sylvia's parents have had.

3. At the end of the story, Sylvia, alone, discovers that her parents have gone to sleep. How does this discovery affect her? Explain her feeling at the story's conclusion—that her life had become "uncertain" and her happiness "terribly insecure."

## Roald Dahl:
### THE WAY UP TO HEAVEN *(page 39)*

1. The story opens with the sentence, "All her life Mrs. Foster had an almost pathological fear of missing a train, a plane, a boat, or even a theater curtain." A little later we read, "Mr. Foster may possibly have had a right to be irritated by this foolishness of his wife's, but he could have had no excuse for keeping her waiting unnecessarily. Mind you, it is by no means certain that this is what he did . . ." Do you believe he kept her waiting on purpose? Give details to support your answer.

2. What has been the relationship between Mr. and Mrs. Foster?

3. How does Mrs. Foster change after she finally departs on her trip to Paris?

4. Why does Mrs. Foster write regularly to her husband? Why does she send him a telegram informing him of her return to New York?

5. What is the meaning of the title, "The Way Up to Heaven"?

## Rhys Davies:
### THE DILEMMA OF CATHERINE FUCHSIAS *(page 54)*

1. In paragraph 6 we read: "A bad shock can work wonders with a person's sensibility. Buried talents can be whisked up into activity, a primitive cunning reign again in its shady empire of old instincts. Or such a shock can create—women especially being given to escape into this—a fantasy of bellicose truth, a performance of the imagination that has nothing to do with hypocrisy but is the terrified soul backing away from reality." Analyze the tone of the passage—is it serious or humorous? Discuss the truth of the generalizations. Show how the statement applies to what happens in the story.

2. When the minister, Mr. Davies, exclaims, "There must be no scandal in Banog!" Catherine Fuchsias "knew her battle was won." What is the battle Catherine has won? How was it won?

3. When Catherine Fuchsias replaces the coat on the dead Mr. Lewis, he "was heavily cumbersome as a big sack of turnips," and

the coat "fitted tight as the skin of a bladder of lard" (page 57, lines 6, 7, and 10, 11). How do these metaphors characterize Catherine and reveal something of the nature of life in Banog? Find other examples of descriptions or metaphors that reveal character or culture in the small Welsh town.

4. Throughout this story, generalizations are made about the nature of women, for example: "In every village there is a Jezebel or the makings of one, though sometimes these descend virtuous to their graves because of lack of opportunity or courage, fear of gossip or ostracism" (page 54, paragraph 2); and "As is well known, women hearken to words but rely more on the secret information obtained by the sense that has no language" (page 63, paragraph 5). Discuss the truth of these generalizations, the tone in which they are stated, and find others of similar nature in the story.

5. Near the end of the story Catherine receives a mysterious letter (page 68, paragraph 1). Why aren't we told immediately that it contains information about the legacy from Mr. Lewis? How does the author use Catherine's bicycle ride through Banog to characterize the village?

## E. M. Forster:
### THE CELESTIAL OMNIBUS *(page 73)*

1. What is the starting point of the omnibus? Where does it go? What is satiric about the announcement that service has been curtailed "owing to lack of patronage"?

2. According to Mr. Bons, the signpost, which had been in its place a long time, was the joke of a man named Shelley. How does the boy's mother act when Mr. Bons asks her whether "there is no Shelley in the house"? Cite incidents which illustrate the attitude of the boy's family toward poetry and the world of the imagination.

3. Who is the driver of the first omnibus? What was his original profession? Why did he become a writer?

4. Why does Mr. Bons finally agree to look for the omnibus? Why does he keep this fact secret from the boy's father and mother?

5. Why, when Mr. Bons discovers who the driver of the omnibus is, does his voice sound "as if he was in church"? Why, when the boy mentions Mrs. Gamp, is Mr. Bons irritated with him? What is significant about the fact that there is no reply when the boy

shouts to the dwellers in heaven that he is bringing Mr. Bons with him?

6. What happens to Mr. Bons? Why do you think this happens?

7. Does Mr. Bons' name spelled backward provide a clue to the meaning of the story? Explain.

## Mavis Gallant:
### APRIL FISH *(page 93)*

1. In the first paragraph of the story the narrator says, "I still have nightmares." She goes on to describe a "harrowing dream" in which one of her adopted children drowns. What do you think the meaning of the dream is? Consider the significance of the dress in which she sees herself, the loosened hair, and her statement, "I think I saved Igor; the memory is hazy. I seemed very competent and sure of my success." Does the narrator's interest in dreams tie in with any other element in the story?

2. When her adopted children present her with a glass fish as a birthday present, the narrator thinks, "The nightmare I ought to be having is a projection into the future . . ." What does she mean? What does the "projected nightmare" reveal about her attitude toward the adopted children?

3. In her telephone conversation with the solicitor, the narrator says, "Then I am not to have one of the burned children?" She continues, " . . . if it weren't for the income tax I'd pack up and leave" (page 96, paragraph 5). How do these statements reveal her character?

4. At the end of the story the narrator says that she has always wanted a "girl with beautiful manners." What would she consider "beautiful manners"? How would you describe her own manners?

## Nadine Gordimer:
### MY FIRST TWO WOMEN *(page 98)*

1. The narrator, Nick, remembers his earliest years with the "two women" only in the haziest kind of way. Discuss the nature of these early memories. (Try recalling your own earliest years and see if they are as hazy and indistinct as Nick's.)

2. At a particular moment, casual in itself, a new awareness

comes to Nick as he stands by his stepmother, Deb. He sees her suddenly as "someone who had entered, irrevocably, the atavistic tension of that cunning battle for love and supremacy that exists between children and parents sometimes even beyond the grave, when one protagonist is dead and mourned, and lives on in the fierce dissatisfaction of the other's memory." Explain this statement. Show how it applies to the story. Does it contain some element of truth which you can explore in your own experience or observation?

3. After this new awareness, Nick feels a strange kind of power—"It was a feeling of power that came like an inflow of physical strength" (page 105, paragraph 2). Explain this power. Does Nick use the power in any way? How?

4. Near the end of the story, Deb tells Nick that his own mother gave him up, voluntarily. Why does Nick ask the question that leads to this revelation? Why does Deb tell Nick at this point what she has refused to reveal before? What is the effect on Nick?

5. Nick concludes the story, referring to Deb's revelation: "I have never forgiven her for it"; yet he also concedes that he and Deb were "really good friends." Explain.

## James Joyce:
### COUNTERPARTS *(page 113)*

1. When Mr. Alleyne asks, "Do you think me an utter fool?" what causes Farrington to make his impertinent reply? What is the effect?

2. In the encounters between Farrington and Mr. Alleyne, there are several descriptions of Mr. Alleyne that seem to dehumanize him; for example, "The head itself was so pink and hairless it seemed like a large egg reposing on the papers." Find other such descriptions. Discuss their effect and their contribution to the movement of the story.

3. As Farrington heads for the pub after his exchange with Mr. Alleyne, we are told that he "preconsidered the terms in which he would narrate the incident to the boys." Why does he "preconsider" the terms of the narration? How does his version differ from the reality?

4. After what appears to be an evening of drink and merriment,

Farrington remains unhappy: "He was full of smouldering anger and revengefulness." Why?

5. At the end of the story, Farrington begins to beat his young son, ostensibly because he let the fire go out. What is the real reason? or reasons?

6. Before Farrington insults Mr. Alleyne, we are told that Farrington's "body ached to do something, to rush out and revel in violence. All the indignities of his life enraged him." Is this feeling peculiar to Farrington? Have you ever experienced something of the same kind of feeling? Where? Why? Have you ever observed someone apparently feeling similar emotions?

## Mary Lavin:
### STORY OF THE WIDOW'S SON *(page 126)*

1. In the first sentence of the story Mary Lavin writes, "This is the story of a widow's son, but it is a story that has two endings." What is the first ending? What is the second ending? What detail is altered to produce this second ending?

2. Mary Lavin uses the technique of the storyteller narrating an old tale. Cite passages in the story up to the first ending (page 131, paragraph 6) that are reminiscent of the folk tale. What idea does this part of the story give you about the relations between the widow and her son?

3. Reread the paragraph beginning "But surely some of those neighbors . . . " (page 131, paragraph 7). Why does the author here speak directly to the reader? What is the function of this paragraph?

4. In the paragraph noted in the preceding question, the author says some of the neighbors must have "pictured the scene of the accident again, altering a detail here and there as they did so." What significant changes in the conversation between the widow and the old laborer prepare for the second ending? What important change is there in the description of the coming of the "old clucking hen"? What happens to the value of the hen that the widow has earlier estimated as not "worth more than six shillings"?

5. What is the importance of the neighbors to the story itself?

6. Explain the meaning of the last two sentences in the story.

## D. H. Lawrence:
THINGS *(page 140)*

1. Examine the first three or four paragraphs of the story and analyze the tone. Does the narrator take his "idealists" seriously, or is he mocking them? What is the effect of such lines as: "But what is money? All one wishes to do is to live a full and beautiful life"?

2. In paragraph 5 the metaphor of the vine appears. Explain this metaphor, relating it to the attitude of the narrator and to the lives of Valerie and Erasmus. Later in the story the metaphor is reintroduced: " . . .well, to go back to our metaphor, the pole up which the green and anxious vines had clambered so far now proved dry-rotten . . . The beanstalk of 'Indian thought' had given way before Jack and Jill had climbed off the tip of it to a further world" (page 144, paragraph 1). Discuss the meaning and effect of this second development of the metaphor. The vine metaphor occurs a third time on page 145, paragraph 1: "It was another beanpole, another vine support crumbled under the green life of the vine." What "vine support" of the idealists has crumbled at this point in the story?

3. Near the end of the story, the rat metaphor is introduced, when Valerie's mother tells the two "idealists," "you are living like rats in a hole" (page 150, paragraph 3). Trace the development of the rat metaphor and discuss its meaning and effect. Explain the comment on Erasmus in the last paragraph: "He was in the cage: but it was safe inside."

4. Discuss the meaning of the title of the story.

## Alwyn Lee:
THE CORVIDAE *(page 153)*

1. In paragraph 4, the narrator describes the train trip from Melbourne to visit his relatives "upcountry." Analyze the details of this paragraph—for example, the "hatters," the men crying "Paper!"—and show how they contribute to the growing feeling of isolation and emptiness.

2. Much of the first part of the story is devoted to details that give background for understanding the kind of life lived in the Australian "bush." For example, we are told that the original inhabitants, the "blackfellows," have virtually disappeared. What has been their fate? What light does this information shed on the country and its present inhabitants? Find other details or descriptions that contribute to our understanding of the place and its people.

3. Great-Uncle Hugh McInstrie is one of the most vivid characters in the story. At one point, he is described: "At family meals—mutton, homemade bread, and tea—old McInstrie alone took a seat. He dispensed his blessing on this Spartan board, and the sons, huge, bearded, red-wristed, ate standing at their places." Find other details and descriptions that contribute to the characterization of Uncle Hugh. What kind of a man does he finally turn out to be?

4. The narrator describes himself: "I was a puny little fellow; I always had my nose in some book." And he says: "Somehow, it had come out that I had signed a pledge to protect native birds." Find other details that help to provide a vivid portrait of the narrator. How do these details contribute to an understanding of the central incident involving the blind sheep and the killing of the crows?

5. Explain the significance of the gifts (the donkey engine and cat-skin rug) the narrator is given at the end of his visit.

## Alun Lewis:
### THE RAID *(page 169)*

1. What impression do you gain of the narrator from his recounting of his interview with the C.O. and his instructions to his platoon? Why does he say, "As for politics, as far as they're concerned I don't exist, I'm never in" (page 169, paragraph 1)? As the story unfolds, do you think he might be considered as involved in politics?

2. During one of the rest stops on the long hike to capture the fugitive, the narrator muses: "You feel so out of it in India somehow. You just slink around in the wilds and you feel very

white and different" (page 173, paragraph 4). Show how this thought is substantiated by the action of the story. Relate this thought to the underlying theme or meaning of the story.

3. When the narrator makes his capture, the prisoner appears timid and friendly. What are the narrator's feelings toward his prisoner? What are your feelings and how do you explain them?

## Katherine Mansfield:
**THE FLY** *(page 178)*

1. At the beginning of the story, we see the boss through old Woodifield's envious eyes—and the boss appears in the pink of health and "still at the helm." How does our view of the boss change by the end of the story?

2. Woodifield's mention of the boss' dead son triggers a series of violent feelings in the boss. What feelings are mingled with his grief?

3. How are the boss' feelings about his son related to his playful cruelty with the fly? Explain.

4. At the end of the story the boss cannot remember what he had been thinking about before the incident with the fly. Explain.

## Joyce Marshall:
**THE OLD WOMAN** *(page 185)*

1. When Toddy comes to meet Molly in Montreal, he seems changed to her. What evidence is there that he has changed? What do all the clues suggest about the nature of his change?

2. Molly's first view of the "old woman," Toddy's powerhouse, comes as she arrives at his isolated house: " . . . the bare hill with the square red house at its top, the dam level with the top of the hill, the waterfall steaming down to a white swirl of rapids, the powerhouse like a squat grey cylinder at its foot." To her it may appear as only a "squat grey cylinder," but to her husband the "old woman" seems to have a life and personality of its own. Find the

passages in which the powerhouse is described as it appears to him, and show in what ways it is given almost human characteristics.

3. When Molly suggests that Toddy might spend less time with the "old lady" and more time with her, Toddy becomes terribly angry and shouts: "I have never been bushed." Explain the cause and nature of his anger. What does he mean by *bushed*? Does he become *bushed* at the end of the story? Explain.

4. As Molly becomes more and more active in the isolated community helping at childbirths and taking care of new babies, Toddy becomes more and more strange in his behavior. What is his attitude toward Molly? What is his attitude toward the French-speaking people she is helping? Is his behavior rational or irrational?

5. At the end of the story, Molly goes to the powerhouse to tell Toddy that she is leaving once again to help out at a childbirth. What does his behavior suggest has happened to him? What is Molly's attitude toward him? Hate? Pity? Fear?

## W. Somerset Maugham: MACKINTOSH *(page 199)*

1. Much of the story is given over to a characterization of Walker. What kind of man is he as observed by Mackintosh? When Walker presides as combination judge, doctor, and ruler, what kind of man does he seem to be? How would you characterize him in his dealings with the natives to get the road built? In the story as a whole, is there any evidence in Walker's actual behavior that suggests that Mackintosh may be partially wrong about him?

2. How would you describe Mackintosh? In making his harsh judgments of Walker, what does he reveal about his own character?

3. Describe and explain the attitude the natives of the rebellious village have toward Manuma. Trace the relationships between the following: *(a)* the throwing of the knife at Walker; *(b)* the beating of Manuma; *(c)* the theft of Mackintosh's revolver.

4. Discuss the ways in which Maugham maintains suspense

from the moment Mackintosh's revolver is taken. Note the various activities that are described and speculate on the reason for each in terms of the story itself.

5. During his dying hours Walker is revealed in a different light. Which is the real Walker? What is Mackintosh's attitude toward the old man during this period? Why does Mackintosh kill himself?

6. Given Mackintosh's character, do you think it realistic for Maugham to have him kill himself? Explain.

## Frank O'Connor:
### JUDAS *(page 238)*

1. The central tension in this story is summed up by the narrator near the end: "But every time I tried to imagine her [Kitty's] face while she grinned up at me, waiting for me to kiss her, it was the mother's face that came up with that look like a child's when you strike him the first time—as if he suddenly saw the stranger in you." Explain how this statement relates to the action of the story. Would you say the important things in the story happen outside or inside the narrator? Explain.

2. Why has O'Connor chosen to tell the story via a narrator talking to a friend, as a kind of confession?

3. Why is the story entitled "Judas"?

## Saki (H. H. Munro):
### THE LUMBER ROOM *(page 249)*

1. Nicholas shows himself to be a very clever boy in the course of this story. Discuss his cleverness in the episode in which he claims that there is a frog in his bread-and-milk; and in his replies to his aunt when she is trapped in the rain-water tank.

2. In the lumber room Nicholas is fascinated by the framed tapestry that he finds, showing a man shooting a stag, with four wolves approaching in the background. What are the "possibilities of the scene" that Nicholas finds in the tapestry? At the end of the

story, Nicholas recalls the tapestry and thinks that the hunter might have escaped while the "wolves feasted on the stricken stag." How might this escape be related to Nicholas' own adventures during the afternoon?

## Muriel Spark:
### THE PARTY THROUGH THE WALL *(page 256)*

1. Describe the setting of "The Party Through the Wall." In what ways is it particularly fitting to the story that unfolds?
2. Describe the interests and activities of Miss Ethel Carson. How do they prepare the listener for the strange events that follow?
3. The narrator, Dr. Fell, appears to be a kind of hovering presence, with an unusual knowledge of Ethel Carson. Who is Dr. Fell? Why is it appropriate that he serve as narrator?
4. The party, given by the young Countess, that Ethel hears through the wall seems to have a reality; her visit to the aged Countess also has a reality. What are the possible explanations for the mystery? What does Dr. Fell mean by calling the parties "emanations" (page 268, paragraph 11)?
5. How do you explain the mystery or the madness of the action?
6. Muriel Spark describes "The Party Through the Wall" as a "feature" rather than a "proper play." In such a feature, she writes, she assumes the freedom to deal with "characters and voices" as she pleases, without conforming to a specific literary form. What elements of drama and of short story do you find in this particular selection?

## Elizabeth Taylor:
### A SAD GARDEN *(page 272)*

1. Describe Sybil's character *(a)* as her relatives generally see her, *(b)* as Kathy sees her, *(c)* as Audrey sees her, and *(d)* as she really is as revealed in the story.
2. What must have been Sybil's behavior toward her now dead husband and son? How is this revealed in the story?

3. What is Sybil's attitude toward Audrey and Audrey's excessively obedient behavior? What causes her to lose control of herself as she pushes Audrey in the swing?

4. Explain the title of the story, "A Sad Garden."

## Mary Walker:
### MRS. CONFEDRINGTON *(page 276)*

1. In the first part of the story, we get the reactions to Mrs. Confedrington from the vicar, the child, Mr. Flaxman and his assistant, and others. Contrast their reactions to her with her concept of herself. Explain: "She likened herself to a picture by Picasso, a masterpiece that has beauty only for the initiated few."

2. Describe the interests that Mrs. Confedrington and her husband pursue and show how their interests characterize them. What does Mrs. Confedrington mean when she says: "Leopold, do you think we have invented each other?" (page 280, paragraph 3)?

3. Sammy Cohen, the window cleaner, has a different reaction to Mrs. Confedrington than the other outsiders do. What is this reaction, what is the reason for it, and why is it revealed only at the very end of the story? In what way has Leopold intuitively anticipated this reaction?

## Sylvia Townsend Warner:
### THE INSIDE-OUT *(page 282)*

1. What is the emotion of the children as they watch the furniture being unloaded from the van at their new home? Is there any significance in the detail that a "mad old lady had ended her solitary days" in Ullapool?

2. As the children explore their new garden, they discover that a hedge and barbed wire separate them from Sorrento, while spiked iron railings back the hedge on the other side. Seeing these barriers the boy has an "inside-out feeling." What does he mean? How is this meaning related to the title of the story?

3. The children see a boy watching them from a tree branch that

hangs over the garden. What is their attitude toward the boy? Why does the boy sob after the other children have gone into the house?

4. Do you think there is any particular reason the author speaks of the garden as "the lost paradise, the sheltering succor from which he [the boy] was driven out"?

## Virginia Woolf: THE NEW DRESS *(page 288)*

1. Throughout the story Mabel positions herself in such a way that she can watch herself from a distance in a mirror. What does this behavior tell us about her? Examine the passages in which she reflects on the "dots" in the mirror (page 293, paragraph 1, and page 297, paragraph 1). What is the effect of these passages?

2. Throughout the story we know what goes on in Mabel's mind but we never see into the minds of the people she encounters. At Clarissa Dalloway's party she speaks briefly with Rose Shaw, Robert Haydon, Charles Burt, and Mrs. Holman. Mabel guesses at what each is thinking. Is she right?

3. In the middle of her encounter with Robert Haydon, Mabel has a vivid memory of her dressmaker, Miss Milan, and *her* reaction to the dress. Why do you think this memory is introduced while Mabel is trying to make conversation with the party-goers?

4. Trace the image of the fly in the saucer through the story and comment on its effect—on Mabel and on the reader. Do you think "The Fly in the Saucer" would have been a good title for the story? Explain.

5. Near the end of the story Mabel remembers her life as made up of a few "divine moments" and the rest—nothing. She imagines what life would be like without those few moments, and fears that as she gets older such moments will become less frequent. What roles does she imagine for herself as a way of keeping these "delicious moments"? Are these realistic possibilities?

6. What is the cause for Mabel's extreme sensitivity? Her family's shortcomings? Her own genuine inadequacy? Her acute concern for herself? Does she seem to be a person doomed to a life of unhappiness?

7. If you met Mabel at a party in a new dress, what would you say to her?

# AUTHOR BIOGRAPHIES

## Kingsley Amis (1922- )

One of England's "Angry Young Men" of the 1950's (who are no longer very young or angry), Kingsley Amis grew up in the working-class area of London—where he was to find many of the characters and settings for his later fiction. His most famous novel is *Lucky Jim* (1954), a rollicking, irreverent story about college life that exposes the professors as much as it does the students. Amis continues to turn his satiric eye on various facets of modern English life, most of which displease, disturb, or amuse him. Some of his other works are the novels *That Uncertain Feeling* (1955), *I Like It Here* (1958), and *One Fat Englishman* (1964), and a collection of short stories *My Enemy's Enemy* (1963). He also takes a serious interest in science fiction and has edited several anthologies.

## Elizabeth Bowen (1899- )

Although she was born in Dublin, Elizabeth Bowen has spent most of her life in London. She has written a number of highly praised novels, among the best being *The House in Paris* (1936), in which she traces out the complex psychological relationships of her characters. In her concern for craft and technique, she has often been compared to the American psychological novelist, Henry James. In addition to her novels, she has written several volumes of short stories, including *A Day in the Dark* (1965).

## Morley Callaghan (1905- )

Morley Callaghan was born in Toronto and educated at the University of Toronto, and as a young man became associated with the American expatriates of the 1920's in Paris, particularly Ernest Hemingway and F. Scott Fitzgerald. He has published several novels and volumes of short stories, including *Strange Fugitive* (1928) and *They Shall Inherit the Earth* (1935). He is remembered particularly for an autobiographical volume, *That Summer in Paris: Memories of Tangled Friendships with Hemingway, Fitzgerald, and Some Others* (1963), in which he tells his side of a famous boxing match with Ernest Hemingway.

## Roald Dahl (1916-      )

Born in South Wales and educated in England, Roald Dahl went to work for Shell Oil in Tanganyika, and was in Africa at the start of World War II. He joined the Royal Air Force and served as a fighter pilot during that war. After the war, he discovered that he could write down the stories he was telling and publish them. He embarked on a writing career, and has become one of the best short-story writers of today. His stories usually deal with the strange and bizarre, and often evoke horror and a grim kind of laughter.

## Rhys Davies (1903-      )

Born in the coal-mining region of the Rhondda Valley in South Wales, the son of a shopkeeper, Davies as a writer has been "tied like Antaeus to his native valley for inspiration." He served in the War Office in London during World War II. He has published many volumes of stories, novels, and commentary, beginning with *The Withered Root* (1927), and including *The Black Venus* (1944) and *Girl Waiting in the Shade* (1960). His *Collected Stories* appeared in 1955.

## E. M. Forster (1879-1970)

One of the foremost English novelists of the twentieth century, E. M. Forster has built a large reputation on a relatively small body of work. He was born in London and educated at Cambridge, following which he traveled extensively. He published his first novel, *Where Angels Fear to Tread,* in 1905, and his fifth and last (during his lifetime), *Passage to India,* in 1924. In addition he published two volumes of short stories, which were collected in one volume in 1948. The work universally acknowledged as his masterpiece is *Passage to India.* Based on his experiences during a trip there in 1911, the novel describes in vivid detail the failures and stupidities of the British Empire and the complexities of India and its peoples and religions. In addition to his fiction, Forster published a number of books of essays, the most distinguished being *Aspects of the Novel* (1927), a discussion of the theory and technique of fiction.

## Mavis Gallant (1922-      )

Born in Canada and educated in "seventeen different schools, beginning with a convent at the age of four," Mavis Gallant first worked as a journalist in Montreal and then went to live in Paris. Her books of short stories include *My Heart Is Broken* (1964), *A Fairly Good Time* (1970), and *The Other Paris* (1970).

## Nadine Gordimer (1923-      )

Nadine Gordimer was born in South Africa, the daughter of a jeweler, and studied briefly at the University of Witwatersrand. She has published both novels and short stories and won a literary award for her collection of stories, *Friday's Footprint and Other Stories* (1960). Her novel, *World of Strangers* (1958), deals with the tragic consequences of apartheid (racial segregation) in South Africa. The theme of exile, alienation, and loneliness is basic to her work.

## James Joyce (1882-1941)

Probably the most gifted and brilliant novelist of the twentieth century, James Joyce was born in Dublin and attended Jesuit schools there. But at an early age he renounced his country and religion and went abroad to live in exile, turning up in Paris during the great period of the American expatriates of the 1920's. He spent a lifetime writing and shaping his fiction, and there are only four main titles. But what famous titles! *Dubliners* (1914) is a book of short stories that changed the nature of the modern short story. *A Portrait of the Artist as a Young Man* (1916) showed new ways of writing the "education novel" (the bildungsroman). *Ulysses* (1922) stunned the literary world with its amazing use of the stream-of-consciousness (flow of the mind) technique and the use of a mythical parallel for a modern story. In 1939, Joyce published *Finnegans Wake,* an enormously long work devoted to one night and the dreams of a pub owner, H. C. Earwicker (or Here Comes Everybody). Devotees of Joyce are still learning how to read this astonishingly brilliant work.

## Mary Lavin (1912-     )

Although born in Walpole, Massachusetts, Mary Lavin was taken to Ireland at the age of ten by her Irish parents. She was educated there, doing graduate work on Jane Austen at the National University of Ireland. Her first collection of stories, *Tales from Bective Bridge,* appeared in 1942. Although she has written novels, she is most widely known and admired for her short stories. Much of her writing is done at her farm home in County Meath, and many of the characters and settings of her stories are drawn from her experience of rural Ireland.

## D. H. Lawrence (1885-1930)

One of the most controversial novelists of modern literature, D. H. Lawrence was born in the coal-mining town of Eastwood in England, and attended Nottingham University. He turned briefly to teaching, but early began to try his hand at writing. The first novel to bring him wide attention was *Sons and Lovers* (1913), a highly autobiographical work vividly describing life in the English coal-mining country. He published an enormous amount during his relatively short life, including poetry, essays, plays, travel books, and novels. His generally acknowledged masterpiece is *Women in Love* (1920), concerned (as is most of his work) with the physical-spiritual relationship of men and women. He himself spent his life in search for the genuine in human relationships, living at various times in Italy, Australia, Mexico, and, finally, settling in Taos, New Mexico.

## Alwyn Lee (1912- )

Alwyn Lee was born and educated in Melbourne, where he worked as a journalist. He left Australia at the outbreak of World War II and came to the United States. Stopping in Mexico on the way, he became one of the few people to gain an interview with the exiled Communist leader Leon Trotsky. Lee joined the staff of *Time* magazine and has remained with them as a book reviewer.

## Alun Lewis (1915-1944)

Born in Aberdare, Wales, Alun Lewis grew up in Welsh mining country and was educated at Aberystwyth and Manchester universities. He taught briefly and was soon caught up in World War II, serving in India. He was killed in an accident in the service in 1944. He found the materials for his poetry and fiction in early Welsh experiences and his life in the British armed forces. His published work includes *Raider's Dawn* (1942), a volume of war poetry, and *The Last Inspection* (1942), a collection of short stories. *In the Green Tree* (1948), a collection of both letters and stories which draws mainly on his experiences in India, was published after his death.

## Katherine Mansfield (1888-1923)

Born in Wellington, New Zealand, and educated in a series of schools there, Katherine Mansfield first came to London in 1903, where she studied music. She returned to New Zealand in 1906, but rebelled against music and her father and returned to London in 1908. There she devoted herself to writing and published her first book of stories in 1911, attracting wide attention, including that of the essayist and critic John Middleton Murry, whom she later married. Almost singlehandedly, Katherine Mansfield changed the form of the modern short story, placing emphasis on the casual but highly illuminating moment which is subtly revealed as the turning point or the summing-up of a life. She died of tuberculosis at the age of thirty-four. Her volumes of short stories include *The Garden Party* (1922), *The Dove's Nest* (1923), and *Something Childish* (1924).

## Joyce Marshall (1913- )

Joyce Marshall was born in Montreal and educated at McGill University. In addition to writing she has worked as a sales clerk, a governess, a civil servant, a market researcher, and a manuscript reader. She has contributed to a number of Canadian periodicals. Her first novel, *Presently Tomorrow,* was published in 1946. She now lives in Toronto.

## W. Somerset Maugham (1874-1965)

One of the most prolific and popular writers of the twentieth century, W. Somerset Maugham spent the first ten years of his life in Paris (his father was with the British Embassy). He tried to fulfill the ambitions of his parents for him to become a doctor, studying in London for several years. It was this experience that he poured into his first highly successful novel, *Of Human Bondage,* still generally considered his best work. He wrote continuously, filling shelf after shelf with volumes of plays, short stories, travel books, essays, and novels. In 1938, he prematurely wrote his autobiography, *The Summing Up.* Like Joseph Conrad, he often used exotic settings for his stories, placing his characters in some remote Asian country or on a Pacific island. In some ways he was a latter-day Kipling, presenting glimpses of the remote corners of the British Empire at the time of its decline and decay.

## Frank O'Connor (1903-1966)

Born in a slum in Cork, Ireland, raised in poverty, and early involved in the Irish fight for independence from England, Frank O'Connor collected enough material for several writers during his early experience. He devoted himself to his native land, using his knowledge of Gaelic, the Irish language, to come to know the people who lived all over the island. He had an excellent ear for native speech, and an excellent eye for the common as well as the bizarre. His stories have appeared in a series of volumes, including *Bones of Contention* (1936) and *Crabapple Jelly* (1944). His book on the nature and theory of the short story, *The Lonely Voice* (1963), is one of the best short treatments available.

## Saki (H. H. Munro) (1870-1916)

H. H. Munro, one of the funniest writers of the modern period, worked under the pen name of "Saki," the cupbearer in *The Rubáiyát of Omar Khayyám,* a twelfth-century Persian celebration of the pleasures of wine, women, and song. Munro was born in Burma, where his father was an inspector-general of police. At his mother's death (when he was two), he was sent to England, where he was educated. He wrote for several newspapers, and gradually began to write short stories, publishing a volume, *Reginald,* in 1904. He devoted himself to writing short stories and novels until his death in World War I. His stories are memorable for their quirky and bizarre characters, true types of the British eccentric, and for their strange and wonderful wit.

## Muriel Spark (1918-      )

Born and educated in Edinburgh, Muriel Spark began her career as a critic and poet, but she soon became much better known as a novelist. An early novel, *Memento Mori* (1958), attracted considerable attention, as did *The Ballad of Peckham Rye* (1960). But it was with *The Prime of Miss Jean Brodie* (1961) that she won wide acknowledgment as a leading contemporary novelist. Her novels are characterized by a polished surface and brilliant dialogue. They are explorations of problems of conscience, the problem of the inherent duality of good and evil in man.

## Elizabeth Taylor (1912-      )

Elizabeth Coles was born and educated in Reading, England, and she married William Kendall Taylor in 1936. She has devoted her writing career primarily to fiction and has produced several volumes. Her books include *At Mrs. Lippincote's* (1945), *The Blush and Other Stories* (1959), and *A Dedicated Man* (1965). Her writing is concerned with describing the intricacies of human relations rather than with social conditions, and combines a mastery of atmospheric effects with a great economy of expression.

## Mary Walker (20th century)

Mary Walker was born in the industrial North of England. After finishing her education, she spent three years in the Auxiliary Territorial Service, the women's branch of the military, during World War II. After the war she began to write. Today she lives in the country near London with her husband and children.

## Sylvia Townsend Warner (1893- )

Sylvia Townsend Warner is an English novelist, poet, and short-story writer. Among her novels is *Lolly Willowes* (1926); her volumes of short stories include *The Museum of Cheats* (1947), *A Stranger with a Bag* (1966), and *The Innocent and the Guilty* (1971). Much of her writing concerns fantastic themes and characters, which she treats as if they were the ordinary.

## Virginia Woolf (1882-1941)

Born the daughter of the writer and critic, Sir Leslie Stephen, Virginia Stephen Woolf grew up in the family home in London in the midst of talk about literature by writers and artists. In 1912 she married Leonard Woolf and they founded the Hogarth Press. Their home in Bloomsbury district (London) became the meeting place for the "Bloomsbury Group," which included the economist John Maynard Keynes and the novelist E. M. Forster. Virginia devoted herself to writing, publishing her first novel, *The Voyage Out,* in 1915. Her best-known works are *Mrs. Dalloway* (1925) and *To the Lighthouse* (1927). She published many novels, volumes of short stories, essays, and biographies. Early in her life (in 1905) she showed signs of mental illness, and these signs recurred and became more intense. Her husband, Leonard Woolf, sustained her through many periods of instability, but her illness finally drove her to suicide in 1941. Her fiction, innovative like that of James Joyce, was the first to use in such ingenious ways the basic elements of poetry and the technique of the interior monologue.

# INDEX OF AUTHORS AND TITLES





1 2 3 4 5 6 7 8 9 10 11 12 13 14 15 16 17 18 19 20 21 22 23 24 25 80 79 78 77 76 75 74 73 72